INNOCENT
LIES

INNOCENT LIES

Colin Ward

Published by *In As Many Words*
www.inasmanywords.com
ISBN 978-1-9998089-5-2

Cover & book designed by Colin Ward

First printed November 2021

In loving memory,
and
finally fulfilling a promise.

Grandma tells us of the time
there was once,
before us, a boy
who like myself had friends.

And listening,
I saw with my eyes,
a brave struggle
for the fate of freedom.

Albanian children's song

Prologue

Ice-cold wind rocked the girl as she sat on the railing, clutching the lamppost with one hand.

Her other arm cradled the newborn.

Tears rolled down her face as misty rain drenched her from head to toe. She stared down at the tiny, wrinkled face wrapped safely in the makeshift sling.

Flickers of blue danced from each edge of Galton Bridge. Radios crackled and worried voices muttered. Everyone was keeping back.

Except one.

'I know it seems scary now, but you won't have to face this on your own.'

The girl didn't look up from the baby cradled in her arm. Her tears cut through the rain on her cheeks.

The officer crept closer. 'We just want you both safe.'

'There is no safe,' the girl replied, with a strong Albanian accent.

'Whatever you need me to do, I will do it. For you, and that little one.' The officer fought to keep her voice confident.

'Please, leave me. Let us go.'

The girl's sobbing grew stronger, rocking her more on the railing nearly one-hundred-and-fifty feet over the canal water.

Her grip on the post was unsteady.

The officer edged forward, speaking in softer, maternal tones. 'You've wrapped the little one up safe and warm. So beautiful.'

'You don't understand.'

'I want to.'

A radio crackled demands, and the girl shuddered.

The officer flung it behind her with a single whip of her arm. It clattered to the ground. A dark figure in the distance slammed a hand on a car roof.

Taking another cautious step, the officer lowered her voice.

'It's just me and you. I don't know what's happened, but I want to. Please, let me help you. Both of you. Beautiful baby, beautiful mummy.'

'I am beast.'

'Look at your beautiful baby.'

'I cannot live this more.'

'You can. Listen to your heart. You both have a whole life ahead of you, together.'

She looked into the officer's eyes. 'It too late. Everything is gone. Hope is gone.'

The officer moved another step, shifting to balance her weight as she took a deep breath to steady her voice. 'Let's talk? You and me. Your arm must be aching. We can hold baby. Keep her safe.'

The girl looked at the officer and something changed. Her whole body sagged, and a sigh deflated her entire being. Her long, dark hair framed a deathly white complexion in the moonlight. Her lips were almost blue from the icy wind.

She moved her shoulder, turning on the railing to point the tiny baby bundle towards the officer.

Taking the cue, and waving over to another to assist, the officer moved closer. 'Let's get baby into the warm.' The officer reached towards the girl and had to make a split-second decision. She wanted to lurch and pull them both back to safety but had to keep everything calm.

It was too wet for sudden movements.

There was no way she could take any risks with the baby in the girl's arms.

A uniformed officer approached and waited for the infant to be passed. She was keeping a close watch of the girl, whose grip on the lamppost was getting looser with every second. There was a glance between the two officers who shared the plan with just a nod.

The baby was passed between them like a porcelain doll.

The girl reached up to her neck and gripped a crudely made leather necklace. A tiny half-heart shape glistened in the flickering lights.

She kissed it.

The officer turned back with a smile. She reached out a hand. It was a mother's hand, held out to a child in danger. A child in pain.

The girl looked deep into the officer's eyes and reached out, speaking softly through her tears.

She dropped the necklace into the officer's hand as she let go of the lamppost with a gentle push.

And fell.

Chapter 1

'My Office. Now.'

DI Mike Stone swung his door open, letting it slam into the wall.

DS Bolton hammered the keys on her laptop before closing the screen and getting up from her desk. She walked into the office without making eye contact, so Stone threw his best glare across the incident room.

Everyone knew the look.

A second or two dragged like an eternity before the door clicked shut and everyone could breathe again. On any other day, there would have been a few snide remarks. But not that day. Not after the night before.

Stone closed the Venetian blinds in a rare act of privacy. Usually, it didn't harm those in the incident room to rubberneck an insubordinate officer's suffering. But he was weary over how difficult the conversation was going to get.

Bolton stared out the window of the tall West Midlands HQ building into a grey Saturday morning sky, willing it to break into a vicious thunderstorm. It would have been cathartic. Hundreds of people bustled around below in their hurried, urgent lives, not a clue about their insignificance. To see their nonchalance disrupted by an explosive crack of thunder would at least have felt like just a part of Nature's fury had been shared out.

If her weekend had to be ruined, why not everyone else'

She folded her arms tight into her chest, dragging down on the pale grey suit jacket. It matched the sky. The collar pulled against the back of her neck and sent a cold shiver down her spine. DS Bolton's long, dark hair was always tied in a non-descript bun at work. She could never be bothered with constant flicking and readjusting of her hair. The only drawback was it left her neck feeling exposed.

Her hands pulsated into fists clasped around her upper arms like she was trying to keep herself together.

Stone sat on the corner of his desk furthest from the window, giving her space.

'Well?' He kept his tone flat, neither admonishing nor patronising.

Bolton's head dropped as she closed her eyes to the world outside. And to him inside.

'I'm waiting.' He pressed. They could read each other like a book. That was how DS Sandra "Jedi" Bolton had gained her nickname and reputation. The only one able to tap inside his head. Not to mention the unnerving way she could unravel suspects in an interview room.

But that also meant he was able to do the same with her. And that was what she feared the most in those moments, wishing for the thunderclap, or a lightning strike to steal her away.

Stone knew far more caution was required when pointing a finger at his sergeant.

She shook her head. 'Don't do this. Not now.'

'I need a full report, Sands.' That small voice over his shoulder was telling him to push whichever buttons it needed. After all, he had to answer to those above him, too. He walked over and placed his hands on her shoulders, turning her to face him.

Their eyes met with an intensity not far from intimacy. But it was not romantic electricity that connected them. It was respect, friendship, and a relationship built on shared values tested by experiences most people never faced in their entire lives.

Tears filled Bolton's vision, struggling to defy gravity. She shook her head and tried to speak.

'Please, Mike, don't.' Her bottom lip curled like a terrified child as a frown aged her a generation the other way.

'This is me, Sands. No Sherlock, no shit. Whatever happened out there, I want a full report on you.'

DS Bolton closed her eyes, and her shoulders began to shudder. The tears rolled down her cheeks. Through a deep, growing sob, she pushed out her words.

'She was only a girl. Just a little girl.'

Her whole body shook as Stone took her weight, holding the back of her head as she buried her face into his shoulder.

Rank disregarded.

No matter how quiet she had tried to be, her sobbing could be heard through the thin walls of Stone's office, and for a moment the whole incident room froze. Typing paused. Phone calls held. Computer mice stopped clicking.

DS Bolton rightly commanded a lot of respect in the team. She was a symbol of strength and a role model. Everyone knew she wasn't too far from promotion to Detective Inspector, and deservedly so. To hear her break sent a chill through the room. Anything that knocked DS Sandra Bolton could crush a lesser officer out of the service.

A few tissues came out to rescue eyeliner. Masculine throats were cleared. Family photographs were touched.

After a moment passed, the room went back to its business a little more deflated than before.

DC Harinder Khan entered the incident room with an

order of tea and coffee. After handing them out, he left the tray with two extra mugs on the table just outside Stone's office. A few biscuits from the secret stash filled a small plate.

After a few minutes, Stone's office door opened and Khan pointed to the table.

'Thanks, Harry,' Stone nodded to a hand waving it off as nothing. 'Pete, how up to date is the file on yesterday?'

DS Pete Barry was another of Stone's central team. A rare officer who preferred the admin side of the job, and he was good at it. He was popular enough with colleagues but pushy enough to get things done.

'Still got reports coming in, guv, but most are ready. Minor pathology and coroner issue I need to discuss, but it's not urgent.'

Stone gave him a nod before returning to his office, tray in hand.

Bolton was sitting at his desk, one leg crossed over the other, suit pulled out of its crumples as if nothing had happened. Her professional mask was back on. Nearly.

Stone handed her the coffee and dropped a handful of sugar sachets from his drawer on his desk in front of her.

'I'm trying to avoid diabetes.' A dry wit was always her way of pacifying the worst parts of the job.

'Shock. Something about sweet drinks. I don't bloody know.' Stone shrugged, daring a partial smile.

Bolton laughed at the comment, but her eyes said "thank you."

Stone's nod said "no problem." He clicked at his computer and brought up her written statement. It was professional, detailed, but concise.

Several emergency calls had been taken reporting a girl on Galton Bridge holding a baby. The first stood out as it had come from a payphone close to the bridge.

Who the hell still uses payphones?

Officers responded within minutes and although a

specialist had been called to the scene, DS Bolton had been nearby and was one of the first in attendance.

The report explained how the girl handed the baby to DS Bolton, who'd passed it to a uniformed officer. When she turned back, the girl jumped.

'What did she say to you?' Stone asked, looking for any angle to find into how the whole situation would be dealt with. Regardless of the outcome, a death on scene would certainly result in an independent inquiry.

'It's in the report.'

He kept his eyes on the screen for a few more seconds before sitting back in his chair and looking at her. 'What did she say that you didn't put in the report, Sands?'

Bolton fixed her eyes on her coffee.

'I'm not the Complaints brigade,' he softened his tone. 'I want to know what happened for your sake.'

She let out a deep sigh. 'She said, "tell him I'm sorry".'

'Tell who?'

'I don't know.'

'Is the baby a boy?' Stone scanned the notes again. The baby was female. 'Or did she mean the father? Any idea who it is?'

She shook her head. 'There was no ID. I was only on-site until they retrieved the body from the canal and tried to revive her.'

Bolton stood and walked away from his desk, leaning up against the filing cabinet in the back corner next to the window. She looked out the window again before turning back to him.

'Why there? Why the Bridge? It was like there was something significant to her about the place.'

Galton Bridge is a well-known Birmingham landmark, spanning the canal in the Smethwick area of the city. One of Thomas Telford's constructions, it was the highest single-span bridge in the world when it was first built in the early eighteenth century.

Stone got up from his desk and joined her at the window. 'Let's chase the who and what first,' he said, without condescension.

Bolton's mind was already beginning to race. 'What if it wasn't suicide?'

'Any indication otherwise?'

'We hear too many stories these days. Young people mentally beaten, coerced until they can't see any other way out.'

'As this stage, that's conjecture.'

'I saw her look at that baby. There was a hopelessness in her eyes.' She walked back to the chair and leaned her weight into it, squeezing her thoughts through it. 'How many jumpers have you had?'

'Three.'

Her look asked the next question.

'I got two. The other one made his own way down.' Stone knew he could use gallows humour with her.

'I suppose two out of three ain't bad.'

'The two that came down didn't want to do it. They were caught up in the moment, blinkered by emotion. By the time they realised what was going on, they didn't know how to get down on their own.'

'Why did the third one go?'

Stone let out a deep sigh as he walked back round to his desk and dropped into his chair. He rubbed at his stubbled chin, his forefinger glancing over an old tracheostomy scar.

It was still the reminder of his own mortality.

'He was a paranoid schizophrenic consumed by a psychotic break. I doubt he could hear me any more than his own thoughts. He had no care for an audience. No idea about the impact of his death.' There was a flash of something dark in Stone's eyes. 'I've always wondered if he was killing the other voices, not himself.'

Bolton looked deep into his eyes.

'What?' Stone asked. 'I can hear you ticking away.'

'She wasn't having a psychotic break. She wasn't crying out from the depths of long-term depression.'

'You can't know that for sure.'

The previous evening had been a difficult one for him, too. The voice over his shoulder was trying to chastise him for not questioning the coincidence of two very serious cases breaking on the same night, and almost at the same time. If indeed a suicide was going to be treated as a case at all.

He placed his hands on the arms of his chair and pushed himself up.

'Right. I am going to make some calls, and ruffle some feathers. You are going home.' He raised a hand in advance of her indignation. 'Don't bother. You can consider this as an order.'

'You know I can't just go home and stew on this.'

'If anything goes belly-up today that you've had a hand in, even a bent paperclip, it could send some other case up shit-creek. Please, Sands. Let me earn some brownie points with HR. Go spend some extra time with your girls.'

Bolton growled her frustration at him, but couldn't help a slight smile escape.

'Thought you weren't a softy, DI Mike Stone.'

'I'm not. I might be a little bit squidgy at times. Occasionally a little bloated when Jack makes me eat strange fast food. But I am not a softy.'

She laughed. 'How is that poor boy of yours?'

'He's great, thanks. We're great.'

Stone's relationship with his son had been improving since he'd been making more effort to commit more time to him. The trigger for change was a shared traumatic experience that had occurred during a previous case.

Bolton smiled and nodded. They didn't need small talk. 'What happened with the shooting last night?'

Stone's face lost a little colour. 'That's a bloody mess. Paul Buchanan responded to a call-out on the old Baxter industrial estate, disrupted someone trying to dump a body, and ended up taking a bullet for it.'

'Bloody hell. How's he doing?'

'Lucky it was a through and through shoulder shot.'

'And it wasn't an armed call-out?'

'No, he called for armed back-up.' Stone put a hand on her shoulder. 'But that's not your concern right now.'

She opened her mouth to protest, but stopped and pushed out her bottom lip when she saw his look.

'I'm sorry I wasn't there for you last night. I was supposed to have Jack in the evening, and even that fell through when I got the call from DCI Palmers.'

'I'm a big girl, Mike,' she smiled.

'I wanted to come round, but it got late.'

'Will you stop it? Me and my girls had a movie night. That was my medicine. I needed it.'

Bolton knew he was right, but her curiosity wouldn't rest until she had several questions of her own answered. As far as she was concerned, when a fifteen-year-old girl who has just had a baby commits suicide, someone, somewhere was to blame.

But her conscience was burning a little more knowing that she still hadn't told DI Stone she'd recognised the girl on the bridge as soon as she'd seen her.

Chapter 2

'How is DS Bolton?' Chief Superintendent's tone was more dutiful than compassionate.

'Shaken, understandably. She's submitted her report. I think that is enough for now, so I've sent her home for the day.'

Carter's curt nod lacked sympathy and was little more than a politician's approval. It irritated DI Stone, but he knew better than to dive into insubordination on a Saturday morning and call her out for being cold-hearted.

'She saw a girl commit suicide last night.'

'There'll be an IOPC inquiry.'

'As there should.'

The Independent Office for Police Conduct investigates all serious cases where there is injury or death whilst there is Police involvement. A complaint doesn't have to be made to trigger an inquiry.

Carter raised her dark, finely plucked eyebrows at DI Stone. 'And you?'

'Me, what?'

'What's your view on it all?'

He took a deep breath and pulled at his jacket to sink better into the chair before replying. 'She did a damn good job. No one else has suggested otherwise. The whole team did a great job.'

Carter handed him a tablet PC. 'Take a look at notes

sent over from Missing Persons and Safeguarding.'

Stone held her gaze as he took the device. Her eyes had dulled and a few more wrinkles seemed to be trying to escape them at the corners. An almost imperceptible twitch of the outer edges conveyed a note of regret as if she was a magician revealing the secrets of an unpopular illusion.

He scrolled through the information that matched most of what he'd already seen.

But a name in the file notes leapt out, striking him in the chest. Stone felt his heart rate climb and breathing shallow.

'Why hasn't this been added to our file already?'

'More to the point, Mike, why didn't she tell you herself?'

'What makes you think she hasn't?'

Carter smiled with only one side of her mouth. 'You're not the only one who can read expressions, Inspector.'

DS Bolton hadn't told him that she'd met the girl before in connection with a sexual assault investigation.

Stone realised why Carter was trying to push his buttons. 'You're sure this girl, Amelja Halil, is the same girl?'

'We'll be able to confirm when DNA comes back.'

'Why was her DNA taken back in January?'

'She was a suspected rape victim.'

'Suspected rape nearly nine months ago, and she commits suicide just after giving birth?' Stone squeezed his eyes closed, pinching his temples. A few extra years of stress wrinkles joined his rugged complexion.

'Hell of a…'

'Don't even say that word,' he interrupted, raising a finger without opening his eyes.

Carter knew DI Stone hated coincidences.

Stone scratched at his stubble. 'You want to know if Bolton remembered the girl.'

'I want to know if anything is going to come back and bite us on the ass.'

You mean Bolton's ass.

Stone put the tablet down and sat back. A frown rippled his head. 'The baby was born underweight, probably a couple of weeks premature. That means it was conceived early January.'

Carter nodded, hoping he was going somewhere with the train of thought. 'We need to treat this as a lead in the rape case, which has been cold all this time.'

'Do we need a court order to get DNA from the baby?'

'That won't be hard, given the circumstances. The clothing they managed to take from the girl in January had a few DNA profiles mixed in with hers. She was homeless, which somewhat complicates forensic testing process and evidence viability, though.'

'How does a homeless girl bring a baby to term? Wouldn't that put a huge strain on the unborn baby?'

'The woman's body is an astonishing thing, Mr Stone. Some women go full term without even realising, having gone on living life as normal.'

It was his turn to raise an eyebrow with a wry smile. 'But trying to get enough to eat for one is hard enough if she was homeless all that time.'

'Clearly, she was resourceful enough to achieve it.'

Or she had help.

Carter sat back and rested her arms on the huge leather-clad wings of her executive chair. Stone wondered how much a chair like that cost, and how many meals could be bought for a homeless girl instead. Several cows had died in the making of it. And one more was sitting in…

Behave.

'One of the samples,' Carter continued, 'was sourced from semen. According to lab techs who analysed the clothes, it was the only DNA profile mixed into bloodstains.'

'Therefore, most likely connected to an attacker,' Stone completed the thought. 'If we match it to the baby, that might be a lead.'

'For the rape case, perhaps.'

DI Stone sat forward, conscious of how he was going to explain this to DS Bolton. 'You can't expect us to ignore this evidence, surely?'

'The girl's death isn't an investigation until we have the evidence to make it one. At the moment, it is little more than a coroner's inquest.'

Stone's eyes darkened and he stood with a suddenness that caught Carter off-guard. 'You're revving this bus up pretty damn quick.'

Carter stared at him.

'Is this the plan, then?' Stone's voice was rising. 'Either we brush a suicide under the carpet, or we follow it up, but throw Bolton under the bus as we do it.'

'You know that is not my plan.'

'But you do have a plan cooking up, though?'

Carter took a deep breath, intending Stone to hear it. 'Her involvement could easily be reflected badly if mainstream media get their claws into.'

'I know the political line. What's next for Sandra then? Two years on gardening leave as you dodge bullets with an inquiry and hold press conferences saying lessons must be learned?'

'She was only in the A&E by coincidence at the time and one of the nurses asked her opinion. She passed the case over to safeguarding.'

Stone didn't hide his cynicism. 'I think it's fair to say the situation has escalated somewhat.'

'We don't know that yet.'

'She deserves a bloody commendation. Let's not forget she saved the baby's life. And the very least you could do is afford us time to find out why that baby will never know its mother.'

Carter let out a frustrated sigh. 'I'm not funding a wild goose chase, Mike, and that's final.'

'Until the media get hold of that.' It wasn't a threat, but DI Stone knew what the media would do if it found out that a possible rape victim had committed suicide and the police weren't looking into it.

Carter grumbled and rubbed her eyes again. 'Paul Buchanan. The incident last night. Where are you on that?'

Stone looked at her. 'His surgery was simpler than it was first thought. He was bloody lucky. I need to go and see him and get a full statement. And I can find out how the boy's getting on while I'm there.'

'Keep me up to speed. We're behind on that, too. It's not going to be easy keeping a lid on details of a firearms incident. The ACC is coordinating the PR for the time being. Make sure nothing leaks from your team.'

Stone bit his lip to stop himself from telling her where she could shove her massive leather chair. 'I'm on my way now, and DCI Palmer is the lead on that. Last night was a busy one. A tough one. And we need to make sure the whole team feels supported.'

Carter raised her hands in submission. She knew what he was digging for. 'I'll give you forty-eight hours to see if there is anything to investigate on the suicide. But I want no talk of suspicious death until there is evidence to justify it.'

'Pathology? I have Reg?' There was no one else he wanted to work with other than Reg Walters.

She nodded. 'DCI Palmers is the senior officer on Buchanan's case. Tragic as it might be, suicide is not as dangerous as another gun on the streets.'

DI Stone shook his head. 'Most years we see no more than a handful of injuries or deaths from guns. Barely a scratch on the surface of hundreds of suicide attempts we even hear about.'

Carter sighed as she glanced out her office window. 'We

can only do what our resources allow.'

'Maybe the focus of meagre resources is the problem.' Stone made a point of looking around Carter's office. The expensive glass meeting table, large forty-inch monitor, leather casual sofa, and even the personal coffee machine probably added to a few thousand. He finally smiled at her as he nodded at the massive leather chair.

He walked over to her office door before turning back. 'Want to know two of the most dangerous things we fight every day in our job?'

Carter gave him a look that said "no, but you're going to anyway."

'The human mind and hypocrisy.' He shot her a wry smile. 'But at least you know to keep your enemies close, ma'am.'

As he left her office his mind was focused on one of his closest allies, and why she had kept an important piece of information from him.

Chapter 3

The energy drink was a cheap imitation of better-known brands, but the loose change Luke had left only stretched to one can and some crisps.

Leaning against the wall under the Priory Queensway bridge to shelter from the drizzle, he looked up the road to the city centre. He was just far enough from the fast-food outlets not to smell them. It had been nearly two days since he'd eaten a whole meal.

Years spent in foster care and children's homes had meant he'd had to learn to survive. Most carers gave up because he ran away repeatedly. He ran away because he knew that inevitably they would give up.

No one wanted the liability of being the one that should have done more. Luke was fine with that, but there was no way he'd also follow their rules.

Luke figured he'd probably end up dead somewhere. Maybe impaled on a spiked fence, or splattered and fried on a train track. The grotesque idea made him smile. Black humour was a way of holding onto his sanity. He'd never thought of himself as tough.

Smart, though.

Clenching his fists, he felt the bruised knuckles he'd

earned whilst collecting the package he was waiting to hand over.

He took another sip from the can. It was warm, flat, and unpleasant.

That's when she caught his eye from across the road. Her long, dark-brown hair was draped over a rough leather coat that looked too heavy for her shoulders. Her brown chinos dragged along the floor like wounded animals, and her hands were packed into small pockets. She paused at the bottom of the slope. Alone.

He knew the look too well.

She opted to walk under the bridge, clinging close to the wall as someone passed her.

Luke couldn't believe what he was seeing. Or feeling. He was drawn to her. Not just in the way a teenage boy would be, but by something in her spirit. Her aura.

She noticed him looking at her and appeared to lift her shoulders and quicken her pace.

Luke knew he must have come across as somewhat creepy. His heart thumped a little harder, compelling him to chase after her. Tell her he isn't like that.

Not a creep.

'Hey,' his voice trembled. He shocked himself, having not even noticed that his thought of chasing after her had become a reality thanks to his mouth acting entirely without permission.

She turned to look at him over her shoulder, and then sped up.

'Sorry. I didn't mean to…'

The girl turned to look at him. Her eyes reached across the ten yards between them, and Luke felt his breathing stop.

She reached up and pushed her hair back over her ear, revealing her face to him. Her skin was naturally smooth without the layers of make-up teenage girls often applied, desperate to approximate the photoshop look.

Her deep eyes fixed on Luke.

'Why you sorry?' she said, with an accent Luke couldn't quite place.

He shrugged his shoulders, with no idea how to speak to someone he found so beautiful. At least not without sounding like a moron.

'Dunno,' he stumbled. 'I wasn't, well, I didn't want you thinking I was. You know. Looking.'

'But you were.'

'Yes. But no.'

He saw the confusion written across her face.

'Not like that. I was just, well, I've not seen you around.'

The girl looked him up and down, assessing whether he was worth a conversation. She tilted her head with curiosity, the slightest smile shaping in her soft, pink lips.

'You around here a lot?' She said, not hiding her distaste for their surroundings.

'No. Hardly ever.'

'Maybe that why you don't see people much?' Her Eastern European accent was sounding stronger.

Luke kept digging. 'I see people. All the time. Just not like, um,' He stopped.

She knew what he hadn't said and walked a few paces closer to him. 'Not like what?' A frown squeezed her dark eyebrows closer together. Just a gentle touch of the fierce glare which she knew could turn an adolescent boy's legs to jelly.

And something else much less so.

Luke reached up to scratch at his head through rough, greasy hair as he glanced around hopelessly. He'd dived in the deep end without tightening his shorts, and exactly like the nightmare, lost them right at the end of the swimming lesson, just as the hottest teacher in the world had told him to get out of the pool.

'Well, anyway, I'm Luke.'

'Luke?'

'Yeh.' He was confused. Was it a weird name, now?

She smiled, taking a moment to look more closely at him. His face was tired, and the bags under his eyes stood out on skin was paler than it should have been. Besides the blushed cheeks. Thick black eyebrows gave him an inquisitive look, which was betrayed by a cherub chin and soft complexion that ran down his neck. Younger than he had appeared to the girl at first glance across the road.

'Nice to meet you, Luke,' she finally said. Then she turned to continue walking away from him.

'Hey, where are you going?' A little too much desperation crept into Luke's voice, which wavered in the early stages of breaking.

She'd turned away to hide the wide smile he had given her, not wanting to let him know that he'd successfully caught her eye.

That's when she noticed the other boy again. Much older. He wore a black coat over a dark blue hoody pulled up onto his head, but not far enough to hide his eyes. He had been walking up from the side of the building behind Luke. Something was familiar about him, but she couldn't place him. Had they met before?

Either way, her instincts hoped the nice Luke boy would follow her, but Luke had seen her face drop, and where her gaze had been. He crossed the road to speak to the older boy, and she knew it was time to pick up the pace and leave.

If only she could remember where she'd seen him before.

* * *

'Who's the meat?' the older male asked, wrapping his hand around Luke's shoulders as if they were old friends.

They weren't.

He slid his hand to give Luke a painful squeeze to the

cruck of the neck, helped by the six-inch height advantage. Nothing that anyone else would notice, but strong enough to make Luke wince.

At the other side of the flyover, he turned Luke so he was backed up to the wall. He placed his palms on either side of Luke's head and leaned.

'She got a name?' His breath stank and a small amount of spit landed on Luke's cheek, just below his eye. He rocked his head side to side, like a wild dog eyeing up its prey.

Luke shook his head.

'Bet you'd like to know her name, though, eh?'

He shook his head again, closing his eyes.

'I don't know about that, now.' He lowered one of his hands from the wall and gripped at Luke's crotch, squeezing just tight enough to make the boy freeze. 'Feels to me like there's a part of you what does. Anyways, y'need a name to grunt when you're fucking your right hand later, right?'

Luke held his breath, knowing there was nothing he could do but sink inside his mind. He knew he had the physical strength to escape, especially if he truly let go and lashed out. He'd tried it before. And it succeeded.

But only so far as to find himself introduced to the kinds of people the older boy was working for. And that was when he got reminded of his place in the pecking order. Once you were in, there was only one way out.

Finally, the grip was released, and Luke felt the rush of nausea hit his stomach. He had to bite down on his lip to hold back from vomiting.

'Now, my boy. Where's my royals?'

Luke took a brown envelope from his inside pocket and held it out.

'Christ, you fucking retard,' the older boy swiped at the envelope and glanced around to check no one was looking. 'What have I told you about discreet?' He slapped Luke on the side of his head, just over the ear. 'Come on. What I say?'

'Discreet rules the street.'

'Damn right, bruv.' He jabbed his middle finger into Luke's chest. 'Remember, you pay your debts in royals or I have other methods of collecting. Either way, your ass is mine.' He raised his eyebrows, demanding confirmation. Submission.

Luke nodded.

'Now, you gonna meet me soon for more jobs. In the meantime, I got an extra little some for you. That piece of pussy you don't know. You gonna meet her again. Get me her name.'

Luke stared into his eyes. 'I can't.'

'You can. You will. Don't want you tastin' that meat, right. You get me? She gonna purr her name without little Luke's help. We clear?'

Luke glanced up the road, glad to see that she'd already gone.

'I asked you a question. We clear?'

Luke nodded his head, once, fast. Reluctant, but resigned.

The older boy took a step back from Luke, reaching into his pocket for a phone. He answered with a single word as he held Luke's glare for a moment. Flicking his chin at Luke, he turned and swaggered away under the flyover.

Luke felt the churning sensation and swung around the corner just in time to double up and feel his body heave, throat burning from the acidic bile.

He closed his eyes and pictured her beautiful face and was torn between a longing to meet her again, and wishing she would stay as far away from him as possible.

Either that, or he had to find her and warn her to run.

Chapter 4

Reg Walters grimaced at his reflection. He was a mess. By his standards, at least. To others, he'd still look impeccably dressed in his three-piece suit and long wavey hair that few men could pull off well.

He concluded it was owing more to his mood that made his appearance look disturbed.

And DI Stone saw it, too.

'Mr Stone,' Walters said with a nod as he answered the door to his office.

'That's what my bank manager calls me.'

'I didn't know you spoke to him that often.'

'I try not to.' Stone looked Reg up and down.

'I tend to find one usually only ever speaks to one's bank manager out of necessity or desperation.'

Both men knew their small talk was delaying the inevitable.

'Why do you look like shit, Reg?'

The pathologist knew there was little point trying to deny it to Mike Stone. They had a long working relationship and a good friendship outside work. The Malcolm Glenn case the previous year brought them closer together.

'I take it you're here about the girl?' Walters asked.

'Carter said she could pull some strings for me.'

25

'On a suicide?'

Stone didn't answer but walked over to the chair across from Walters' desk. He took a deep breath and set the pathologist's Newton's cradle clicking away.

'Have you finished the PM yet?'

Walters joined him at the desk, tapping at his computer to open up screens. 'I've done the physical exam, yes.' Reg ran a hand through his hair and let a deep sigh escape.

A pause changed the atmosphere.

'I don't appreciate having my arm twisted even before I've had time to look at a body.'

Who the hell did that?

Walters read Stone's expression. 'Carter made a point to call me herself and ask me to get the PM done, and to put the case to bed as a suicide.'

'Ouch.'

'Chief Superintendent or not, I didn't take kindly to being told a coroner's verdict, let alone an official PM cause of death before I've even unzipped a body bag.'

'I hope you didn't say that to her.'

'I bloody did.'

Stone rolled his eyes. He knew that would come back to bite him at some point. 'Okay, well, that aside, did you find anything noteworthy?'

Walters raised his eyes and sat back in his chair. 'How's Sands, by the way.'

Ignoring the deflection. 'PM first, chit-chat second.'

'Okay. It's hard to pinpoint the exact cause of death without being facetious and just saying the impact from a one-hundred-and-fifty-foot fall.'

'Into water, though. Is that enough to kill someone outright? People dive from that height.'

Walters raised his eyebrows in surprise. 'Mike, even the best pros rarely dive from less than half that height. And she didn't dive. She fell and hit the water. Hitting water from just five metres is like hitting concrete.'

Stone let out a gasp. He made a mental note to do some research. Which meant watching amusing videos on YouTube and calling it research.

'She had multiple fractures. A break to the spine at the second and third vertebrates, severing the main spinal column. Fractures to the face and skull. Not to mention the internal trauma most organs, including the brain.'

'I get the point. She was reduced to a human ragdoll.'

Reg cleared his throat. 'There was canal water in her lungs, so her heart was still beating for a few seconds at least. She took her last breath underwater.' He paused again, unusually moved by delivering a summary. 'In the end, I'll record drowning leading to cardiac arrest as the final cause. The coroner will provide a more detailed account. It's all semantics, though.'

'It's a dead girl, Reg. It's never just semantics.'

He held up his hands, recognising the comment was a little too crass. 'I mean, from a physical point of view, the precise cause of death.'

Stone saw something in his eyes. An unspoken detail. 'What haven't you said yet?'

Walters brought his elbows up to the arms of his chair, clasped his hands, and rested his chin. He avoided Stone's glare for a moment, slowing his breathing.

But Stone could see more than a glint in his friend's eyes. Not quite tears, but not far off.

'Come on Reg. What am I not being told? First Carter is being cagey, and I find out Sands has kept something from me. And now you?'

'I am more concerned that Carter wanted this put to bed so quickly.' He looked at Stone. 'It is what I can surmise happened in this girl's life that makes me more concerned about the nature of her death. The wider context.'

'I thought the how was your job, and the why was mine,' Stone said, taking out his notepad.

'Not this time.' Reg swallowed deep enough to give

away his dry mouth. 'Firstly, according to files, there are questions about her having been raped. I can tell you there is scar tissue inconsistent with childbirth, but typical for sexual assault cases.'

'Any other injuries?'

'X-rays indicate old, healed fractures. You'd need a bone specialist for the best conclusions on those, but even I can say less than a year or so old.'

'Is she an abuse victim?'

He nodded, distracted by a different thought.

'Anything else?'

Reg continued, but quieter, more distant. 'Recent bruising which had enough time to start healing, so nothing to do with the fall.'

Stone stood and began pacing the office, tapping his bottom lip with the end of his pen.

Reg continued. 'Young people make bad choices. Especially when faced with inescapable suffering.'

Doing a post-mortem on a child was something Mike Stone couldn't get his head around. But Reg was unusually distracted. He watched as the pathologist got up from his chair and walked over to his coffee maker.

'Could she have been coerced?' Stone knew he was pressing a pathologist too hard towards speculation. But he also trusted Walters' opinion.

Reg fiddled with a capsule of expensive coffee product intended for his space-aged contraption, clearly being outsmarted by a small piece of foil.

That's when it happened. Stone had never seen it before in all the time he'd worked with Walters.

A single tear ran down his cheek.

Stone left the silence to hang for a moment.

'I know who she is, Mike.'

The weight of this fact sat heavily on the atmosphere. From a procedural perspective, he probably shouldn't have done the post-mortem. From a personal viewpoint,

Stone couldn't even begin to imagine the trauma. Most professions either had strict conduct rules or at least ethics of best practise to ensure an objective distance.

It also meant DI Stone had his closest DS and his best pathologists sideswiped by the same case. Both somehow connected to a girl who had taken her own life. Proof, should it ever be needed, of the wide impact suicide had.

And Stone dreaded to think what was coming next if he was to believe the old trope of bad things coming in threes.

'Which awkward question do you want me to ask you first, Reg?'

'I never met her. I had nothing to do with her death, or events leading up to her death.'

'And where were you on Friday evening?' Stone smiled in an attempt to try and lighten the mood. He knew it was an absurd question to ask, but due process meant it had to be. At some point. By someone.

Reg walked over to his desk and picked up a plastic evidence bag, handing it to Stone for closer inspection.

It was a homemade piece of metal shaped into half a heart, about the size of a thumb, hanging on a piece of leather lace. A single "L" was stamped into it.

'That was filed by DS Bolton,' Walters said so quietly it could have been to himself. He ran a hand through his long hair again, pushing it down the back of his neck.

'Is this significant?'

'Yes.' He sat heavily at his desk. 'I had my assistant prepare her body and check the file for pertinent details, as usual. But I felt like I knew her. I don't know how. It was like she looked vaguely like someone had described her to me. After the PM, as soon as I opened the file, I saw that necklace and read her name. Amelja.'

DI Stone looked at him, puzzled. He had no idea why she would be significant, not least to the pathologist.

'And with that girl on my slab right now, there's a

29

horrible chance we are going to be facing another body soon. A boy with the same necklace, but with an "A".'

No. Please do not be number three.

Stone's chest tightened as the thought swamped him. That voice screaming in his ear. Neither of the two victims in the case he had taken in the previous night had died yet.

But they were both critical.

Stone's phone rang and he took it out of his pocket. Waving an apology to Reg, he knew he had to take a call from DS Pete Barry.

'I'm with him now. Why?'

Reg Walters looked at Stone with a quizzical frown, picking up that the call was something to do with him.

Stone ended the call immediately and began tapping at the screen. His furrowed brow was enough to show he hadn't just been told to check out the latest hilarious kitten video.

'Anything I need to be worried about?' Walters quipped, but the slight tremor in his voice spoke more of his nerves. He watched Stone's face as he pinched and swiped on the screen.

'Oh, shit,' Stone whispered.

Walters held out his hands in submission, trying a half-smile, but his furrowed brow defied the expression.

Stone handed him his phone.

Reg took it, keeping his eyes fixed on the detective for a few more moments before glancing down at the screen. An image showing a crumpled business card in a clear plastic evidence bag filled the screen. It was zoomed in enough to show the card belonged to Dr Reginald Walters. Crumpled and marked with red smudges, which were clearly blood.

'Where the bloody hell has that come up?'

Stone took a deep breath. 'Last night, I was called out to a shooting incident. DC Paul Buchanan responded to a call on Baxter Industrial estate. A car abandonment. But he disturbed someone else there who turned a gun on him.

'Bloody hell.' Walters let out a laugh. 'Do I need another alibi?'

'The card was found in the pocket of the badly beaten boy found in the back of an abandoned car.' Stone waited, watching Reg's face drain to an unhealthy pallor. 'Scroll to the next image.'

Reg swiped the screen. He fell back into his chair, almost missing it.

The face was horrifically beaten, both eyes swollen, lips split, nose broken, and most of the skin was beginning to gather the purple glow of fresh bruising.

But the boy was still, just about recognisable.

'He's still alive, Reg. But critical.' Stone waited for a moment. 'I take it this is L?'

The pathologist nodded.

'How do you know him, Reg?'

'That's a long story,' he said, handing back the phone.

Stone walked over to the office door. 'You've got between here and the hospital to tell me.'

Chapter 5

January
Luke & Amelja

He'd run straight into the centre of town, his head spinning with a mix of fear and exhilaration. She had been too beautiful to let slip through his fingers. But now she was in danger, and that was his fault.

Luke knew he should just let her go, say he couldn't find her, and take the consequences.

But his heart told him otherwise.

He knew girls her age, and some that were years younger, getting mixed up with the wrong people. Not this girl. Her eyes and her gorgeous long hair swirled around in his memory.

He had to keep her safe. Hide her if he had to.

Luke made it to Bull Street, passing countless food outlets that screamed at his hunger. He continued up to the tram track and the thought hit him. Getting the girl out of the city to Wolverhampton on the tram would be easy. Not much better, but partly away from danger.

He jumped up onto a bench on Corporation Street, trying to see above the heads, hoping to spot that hair again.

The looks from people walking past were nothing new.

That's when he sensed a shadow cast over him. The

bright yellow of a PCSO with a disapproving look was glowering at him

'You here on your own?' she said.

Luke was adept at shrugging off and ducking police. 'I'm just looking for my mum.'

She smiled, thinking he looked a little old to be trying that line. 'Your mum?'

'Yeh, she brought me into town. Had to see a doctor and get a prescription.'

'For you or her?'

'Me. It's urgent, you see. Got problems down there,' he said, pointing at his crotch. He knew it was an effective way to end any further questions with most people.

'What's your name?'

'Richard. What's yours?'

'Which pharmacy did she go to?'

'I dunno. That's mum stuff. How many teenage boys do you know who can name a pharmacy?'

'You know there's a large Boots in New Street station, right?'

'I don't think she's gone to buy me shoes.' Luke smiled at his wit and looked in the direction of the station. 'I've just seen her actually, gotta go.'

'Hold on a second,' the PCSO shouted.

But Luke was already putting a good distance between them. He had to find the girl and knew the police were no help.

That's when his eye caught her.

She was walking down the slope leading to the station. Luke picked up the pace, dodging through lunchtime flock of coffee-carrying city workers. Certain she had turned left to double-back towards the Bullring, Luke gripped the wall threw himself around the corner.

She was gone.

'Following me?' the voice came from behind him.

Luke turned to see her leaning up against the window

of a small newsagent. She had a large, grin under her glistening eyes.

After a silence that seemed to last an eternity, they walked together to the front of the station, peering over to see the tracks. Several glances from each other bounced away fast in embarrassment as they both grinned.

'Aren't you going to ask for my name?' she finally spoke.

Luke was sure it had to be something pretty, soft, nice. He wanted it to match her hair, her bright green eyes and soft complexion. But a dark thought flashed through his mind. He'd been sent to learn her name, and now it was being offered, a part of him didn't want to know it.

He scratched at the back of his neck and shrugged his shoulders. 'I dunno, I kind of like the mystery.'

She laughed, relaxing in his company.

'Anyway, you're the one that ran off from me.'

She looked at him sternly. 'I do not like man with you.'

'I wasn't with him.'

'But you know him?'

'Only a bit.'

'He didn't look nice.'

'No, he's not.'

'A boy can only be as nice as boys he is with,' she said, philosophically. 'My Grandmother teach me this.'

Luke even loved her accent. 'Where are you from?' He tried to make the question casual, desperate not to offend her.

'Nowhere.' Her answer was abrupt.

'It's just, I can hear it in your voice'

'And this mean I must be from somewhere else?' Her tone was harsher, sounding resilient.

'I'm sorry,' Luke backtracked. 'I like it.'

'You like my voice?'

The only girls Luke had ever spent time around had been screwed up by their background. Most of them were aggressive or grossly promiscuous. They'd never been at all attractive to him.

'What do you like about my voice?' She smiled, laughing a little.

'It's nice.'

'Nice?'

Luke fumbled again, pointing awkwardly at her head. 'Like your hair.' He wanted the world to swallow him up. His mouth kept saying stupid things, and he couldn't stop it.

'You like my hair?' She held a handful of hair out to him and stroked it. 'My Grandmother used to say it was the prettiest hair of all princess in the world.'

Luke saw the pain in her expression. He didn't want to see her hurting.

She reached over and took his hand. Their eyes met, and she spoke softly.

'Amelja.'

Chapter 6

September

The journey to the hospital had been tense. But Reg Walters filled DI Stone in on his connection with the boy in the photograph.

Outside his Pathology work, Reg regularly supported local homelessness charities, soup kitchens, outreach projects and fundraising. He was an active member of the Salvation Army and Crisis on a national level and was particularly skilled in working with young people.

Luke had come to his attention almost a year before. He'd bounced between foster placements and homes but always ended up running away. He was a classic case of slipping through the net. Or, as Reg put it, cutting his way through a net that had done nothing but fail him.

Reg wasn't privy to Luke's whole background, but he'd developed a reasonable picture. Abuse of all forms, at the hands of too many.

'But he's not a stereotypical, angry teenager,' he'd said to DI Stone. 'He tried to maintain he was eighteen for a while. When he knew that wasn't working, he admitted to being younger, but never gave his actual age.'

Stone glanced at Reg with a little concern. It was risky business being involved with vulnerable young people, even though constantly calling Social Services usually just put them back onto another waiting list. But the potential for tragic outcomes was too great a risk.

And that weekend was looking like a horrible example.

Reg continued the explanation with an air of frustration and worry clipping every one of his well-pronounced words.

'There's something about him. He's so generous, kind, and compassionate. He has empathy I rarely see in adults. He can flare up at times, and he's a hormonal teenager, for sure. But he's a thoroughly likeable kid.' Reg looked quite pleadingly when he said it.

Stone asked about their relationship, careful not to offend his friend's kindness by inferring anything inappropriate. Reg had fought to try and get the boy support. Fought harder to make him accept it. There could be nothing worse than ignorant people casting false aspersions of sinister intent. Something which prejudiced men far more than women who showed the same compassion.

'I'm trained well enough to keep a safe distance.'

Stone caught a glimpse of Reg tapping at his knees with his forefingers. It was one of Reg's tells of anxiety.

They also discussed the connection between Luke and Amelja. It was significant enough to blow a massive hole in both investigations and created more questions than time allowed before they got to the hospital. Stone could sense Reg's knowledge of this boy was likely to become a vital part of the investigation. That meant there were more hard questions he'd have to ask Reg. Some as a detective, others as a friend.

When they'd arrived at the hospital and worked through the usual "patient confidentiality" minefield, Stone insisted the staff share all information with Reg Walters as part of the legal case. The fact that he knew a few of the staff and had performed the PM on Amelja helped break down some barriers.

There were also issues caused by a lack of surname,

and therefore any chance of getting his medical history. It didn't affect his access or rights to NHS care, but it meant the system would move slower.

Stone took out his mobile and his call was answered almost instantly.

'Boss.' Khan answered, half distracted by hammering at his keyboard.

'Harry, I need you in whizz-kid mode.'

'Oh, chuffin' heck, boss. It's only been a day,' he laughed. DC Khan wasn't a forensic IT technician, but he was DI Stone's go-to when it came to digging for information in creative ways. He was particularly good at navigating the public domain. Evidence would only count as circumstantial or hearsay, but it didn't need a warrant.

Of course, he also had access to the Police National Computer, and Stone readily admitted Khan was far better at making the best use of it.

'I want you to dig into the PNC, and anywhere in public fairy-land with the photos and info I have just emailed to you.'

'What or who am I looking for? And does it involve being naughty? And if so, what kind of pastries or doughnuts are you coming back to the office with?'

'Anything you can get me on the boy and the girl. Connections between them. It might involve knocking on the immigration door, so get Pete to help you out.'

'Going back how far, boss?'

'It's going to have to be at least nine or ten months, so let's say a whole year.'

'One major problem, though.'

'I know, but we don't have a known surname for the boy yet. Just dig into the last year or so, see what you get.'

'A year? That will make me very hungry.'

Stone laughed before he hung up. It was only when he caught a glance of Reg Walter's sullen face that the moment of levity deflated.

Reg Walters walked with the medical staff rolling a bed into the ICU. The boy had needed a second round of minor keyhole surgery.

Even from ten feet away, DI Stone could see there was no way the boy was eighteen. Just a glance at the bruises on his face caught Mike completely off guard. He'd seen the boy the night before in the ambulance, but the stark white light under hospital lights made the bruises look like a death mask.

'Have they told you much?' Stone forced his voice out of his dry mouth.

'He's critical but stable. There doesn't appear to have been any weapons used to inflict the injuries.'

Stone frowned. 'I know you can always spot that, but are they sure?'

Walters smiled at him. 'They are trauma surgeon's Mike. Yes, they know the difference. I merely get the ones they can't save.'

'What does it mean, though?'

Walters held up his hands. 'You're the detective.' He gave a weary smile that didn't quite reach his eyes.

'Either the bastards used something that didn't leave marks, or they'd simply kicked and punched him to within an inch of his life.'

A rattle of anger crept into Walters' voice. 'Then they just dumped him in the back of a fucking car to die.' He clasped his hands to the back of his neck.

'I don't know. But, DC Buchanan got in the way, and took a bullet for it.'

Walters turned to him and put a hand on Stone's shoulder. 'Sorry, old boy. All I've done is rant at you. How's your guy doing?'

'He's fine. But I have a hell of a lot of questions for him.'

Walters turned away from the ICU window and leaned up against the wall, gazing at the ceiling. 'I saw some of the wounds,' he said, sounding like a pathologist again. 'The bruises. There's something strange about them.'

Stone raised an eyebrow.

'It's what I didn't see that concerns me.' The pathologist continued his musing. 'They were too clean. I mean, not much, if any friction burns or scuffing of the skin. No signs of the contours or thread of material.'

'You can tell that? Just from bruises.'

'When the skin is damaged in an impact injury, where there is no cut or break, there's always a sign of what damaged it. A graze from concrete, or the stippling of gravel. Even the pattern of the material the victim was wearing imprints itself.'

'But, if it's not there…?'

'…the injury was likely to have been the result of a skin-on-skin impact.'

Stone paused to let the thoughts soak in. 'If all his injuries are the same could that suggest the beating happened when he was naked? Would the doctors put that in the report?'

'Not necessarily. It's much harder to see on a living body because the blood is still flowing. Unless inspecting minor wounds for minuscule evidence is your day job, you'd not have a reason to look for it. Their job is to save his life, not record evidence for police investigations.'

Stone took a few moments to weigh up what Walters was trying to say. 'How certain of this are you?'

'Certain is a big word, Mike. I'd need a proper look.'

'We have evidence photos. Can they help?'

Reg shrugged his shoulders. 'Depends how good the photographer was. Outside on a night at a crime scene? I doubt it. And we need to look as soon as possible before healing gets in the way.'

Stone went over to the nurse's station, leaving Walters to sit down and rest his head in his hands.

'I understand the boy is in a critical state, but so is my

investigation.' Stone was trying not to raise his voice.

'Sir, police or not, the patients on this ward are here for treatment, not interrogation and inspection.'

Damn it. She has a good point. Don't be a bastard.

'Look, my colleague here is a Doctor.' Stone said.

'At this hospital?'

'No, he's a pathologist.'

'Well, then, he's a bit early.'

Funny fucker. Fine, I'll be a bastard.

'I appreciate you have your job to do, and that convenience is not on either of our sides. Any information my colleague and I can gather that can help catch those who did this to him might prevent you from having to treat another one.

'I do understand, sir,' the nurse replied after a moment of thought.

'Thank you.'

'But it still doesn't make any difference. Not on ICU. On this ward, I outrank you. They will transfer him to Birmingham Children's hospital when safe to do so, when the doctor, the before-death doctor, say it is safe to.' She looked over to Walters. 'No offence.'

She ended the conversation and walked away.

'Come on, Reg,' Stone announced it was time to leave. 'We're no use here. I've got Harry digging and I think you could be a great help in that. And I need to power him up with pastry.'

Reg walked over to the ICU window and looked at Luke for a moment, shaking his head as he touched the small cross hanging from his neck. He appeared to whisper something, but the anger in his face made Stone wonder if it was a prayer or not.

Two major cases now looked like they could be colliding into one huge case. Questions were multiplying at an alarming rate. Leads remained at a depressing zero.

And he'd barely even seen a whole day.

Chapter 7

'Time for a riddle, Harry,' DI Stone said, throwing his coat over the back of the chair he'd pulled up to DC Khan's desk.

'Does that mean I get to play Watson?'

'Firstly, how is your digging into the victimology going?'

'Slow. There's nothing on social media, and since the story hasn't hit the news yet, there's no live chatter.'

'Okay, fair enough. So, how do we conduct a door-to-door when neither victim had their own door, or became victims near any doors?'

Harry leaned on one arm of the chair. The fingers of his right hand fanned out like a Chinese woman's paper fan, his middle finger rubbing the side of his nose right up into the inner corner of his eye. 'Firstly, when you say victims?'

'Yes, I know, I'm taking a leap. But for argument's sake, whether they are victims of fate or other people, let's still run with it, for now.'

Khan dropped his hand and straightened up in his seat. 'The girl. When and how did she get out of the hospital, apparently unnoticed? Then she travelled from the hospital to Galton bridge.'

'Carrying a newborn.'

'She covered a fair distance.' Khan brought up a window with Google Maps and entered the journey. 'Three miles, which is an hour's walk, at least.'

Stone frowned and rubbed at the back of his head. 'That's a lot of doors and businesses to walk past.'

'Half an hour on a bus, according to this.'

Stone's eye's wandered across the incident room to the empty whiteboard waiting to be filled with information.

Khan broke the growing silence. 'Surely staying in hospital as long as possible would have been the best thing for her and the baby.' He shrugged his shoulders. 'Dare I ask where social services were?'

Stone pursed his lips. 'That's a bloody big hole in a net someone else can worry about.' His voice softened and he spoke as if to himself. 'Why did you leave, Amelja? And why Galton Bridge?'

'Could this be an immigration issue?' Khan suggested, leaning away as if he might get a clip round the ear like a naughty child. 'If she was afraid she would be deported when discovered, maybe that's why she ran.'

'Would she really think that?'

'The Home Office has made a lot of people feel very unwelcome, especially since Brexit.'

Stone rubbed at his chin. 'No, that's too removed for a teenager. Something stronger. A direct threat. More immediate.'

'Do we know anything about her mental health? Could post-natal issues be a factor?'

'I see where you are going. I spoke to a nurse and she said there were no signs. And she would have been more likely to leave the baby at the hospital.'

They both sat in silence.

Stone let out a growl of frustration. 'None of this makes sense.'

Khan stood up and moved around to the back of his seat. 'When we have a murder, or a serious assault, the first thing we look at is the victim. The body. Right?'

Stone nodded, leaning forward with hope written all

over his face.

Khan wagged his finger, conducting the orchestra in his mind. 'The next stage is looking at the crime scene, which we don't have. And then we work outwards from that information until we find the links, right?'

Stone nodded.

'Maybe what we have to do is turn that on its head. Work from the outside, inwards.' Khan tapped his chin. 'Think of it like Google Maps, guv. We need to zoom out first, and then start zooming back in slowly picking up whatever crumbs or traces they have left.'

'It's a big world out there, Harry.'

'And I think we need to stop looking at it through our eyes and start trying to see it through theirs.'

Stone played with his tie for a moment. 'Constable, I hope you're not suggesting we start role-playing, because you know how I hate that kind of nonsense.'

Khan laughed. 'But you're so good at it, guv.' A mischievous grin lit his face for a moment. 'They were homeless. Currently, we have no leads from family and friends, teachers or carers to turn to. I've been approaching it all wrong. We need to look off-grid.'

Stone raised one eyebrow, so Khan took that as his cue to elaborate. It wasn't that DI Stone was a Luddite, he simply didn't use social media.

'Most people go through every day presuming nothing will change. They know everyone they know, have everything they own. They take most of what they have for granted.'

Stone nodded, beginning to see where Khan was going.

'Homeless people have to function one day to the next, simply to survive.'

'Okay. That's our plan. Visit their world.'

Khan's face lit up with a wide smile. 'And that is something I can show you.'

Chapter 8

Nesim Kapllani stared at the flow of people walking past his black Mercedes. A Big Issue seller on the other side of the road caught his eye and he watched how almost everyone ignored him.

He was shaken from his thoughts by a gentle tap on the front passenger window. The driver lowered the glass just enough to growl a barely perceptible instruction before the central locking clunked, and the rear door opened.

Another man dropped into the seat next to Kapllani, sinking into the soft leather. A well-built man with short, cropped hair and a rough complexion.

Kapllani didn't look at the man. 'You know what power is, English?'

The man didn't reply.

'It's not needing to know you just rolled your eyes.' He paused for a moment. 'And not having to give a fuck that you did.' Kapllani took a silver art deco cigarette case from the inside pocket of his suit jacket. He plucked a cigarette from under a velvet band and offer one to the other man.

'No, thank you. I don't.'

'Of course you don't, English.' He closed the case with a softened snap. 'You are better. No?'

'Better?'

'Than us foreign. Enlightened by your free NHS.' His voice rattled through his curled lip, making no attempt to hide his distaste.

'I don't want my breath to stink.'

Kapllani turned to the man with a glare, holding the tension until releasing a rasping laugh which broke the silence.

'Ha. That's better, English. False manners piss me off. You don't do this. I respect that.'

To his surprise, the man reached into his pocket and took out a metal Zippo lighter and flicked it open.

Kapllani kept his gaze fixed, searching as he leant forward slightly to light his cigarette. He took a long drag, sucked air in through his teeth, and exhaled the smoke across the car.

The man could see the slightest twinge at the outer corners of Kapllani's eyes. 'Still never know when a flame might come in useful.'

'Now, to business.' Kapllani took another long drag of the cigarette. 'One of our associates has gone missing.'

'I noticed.'

'He took some of our merchandise. Livestock.' His steel eyes dug into the man sitting next to him. 'Rather unlike him. But sometimes people change, no?'

The faint crackle of the tobacco burning as Kapllani took another long drag was the only sound in the car for a few moments.

'I do not like such change.' He caught eyes with his driver and gave the slightest nod. A brown envelope at least half an inch thick appeared from between the front seats. 'I want you to find my associate. And then lose him again.'

The other man took the envelope from the driver.

'But make sure you bring me answers.'

The man shot Kapllani a quizzical look, dark eyebrows dropping sharply towards the bridge of his nose.

'He has been associate for long time. Holds much information he should not have shared. Understand?'

Kapllani nodded at the envelope. 'This is advance. Treat like hand wash. Don't bring back any dirt.'

Kapllani drew on the cigarette again, hissing the smoke into his lungs.

'Also maybe get your hair cut, and wet shave. You look like shit. I tell you something, English. See this man?' He pointed to the magazine seller. 'He scruffy, dirty. But he work. He try to sell shit magazine to people who ignore him. Some stop and buy one, but most ignore him like he is shit on shoe. But still, he continue. Why?'

The man shrugged.

'People only know what they have when they know what they can lose. Most of these people do not understand how easy it is to lose everything. How close they are to stand next to smelly man and sell shit magazine. Ironic, you think? He has no power, and he knows it. They think they have power and don't know they do not. Knowledge is power. Maybe smelly homeless man most powerful of all out there.'

The other man slipped the envelope inside his coat pocket.

'English, do you know what you have?'

He raised his eyebrows, asking silently so as not to ruin a moment of great rhetoric from the strange European man.

'You appreciate what you can lose?'

'I suppose.'

Kapllani turned back to stare at the homeless man. 'When you find our associate, you do to him what you think I do to you if you ever fucking betray me. Then you know.'

'You don't need to threaten me.'

Kapllani didn't reply other than to raise his right hand, with its gold sovereign ring and cigarette poised between fingers. The central locking clunked again, and the man took this as his cue to exit.

The man stepped out into the rain and closed the door with a soft thud. He adjusted his collar and walked away.

Kapllani pressed the window button on his door and let the darkened glass slide down. He fixed his gaze on a young boy wearing a hoody over his school blazer, who took a few moments to notice. Kapllani pointed at him. The boy looked around to check that he was the one being pointed at, before approaching the car with a frown and suspicious look. He kept what he thought was a safe distance.

Kapllani took a metal clip of cash out of a pocket and counted out a few notes. He looked at the boy with a plain expression.

'You, boy. You do job for me.'

'I ain't dealing no drugs.'

'No drugs.'

'You a paedo? I ain't sucking your cock.'

Kapllani smiled. 'I have simple job for you. Come, come.' He waved the cash at the boy and noticed his eyes lit up. Kapllani held it back just out of reach. 'You see dirty man with magazines.'

The boy scanned around until he saw the homeless man. 'Yeh. You wanna Big Issue?'

'No. You take him this money. One hundred pounds.'

'Serious?'

'You tell him that man in car say he take money and fuck off for the day.'

The boy was shocked but laughed nervously at the strange man.

'You say it exactly like me.' Kapllani nodded at the boy and put a hand to his ear.

'The man in the car says take this money and,' he paused. Kapllani nodded insistently. 'And fuck off for the day.'

Kapllani's face lit up with a smile.

The boy took the money and gawped at it with

amazement, feeling the slick notes in his hand. 'Hey, mister. What's to stop me running off with your cash?'

'Two thing,' Kapllani said, holding his fingers up the Churchill way. 'One. I give you this for doing this job for me.' He handed the boy a ten-pound note. 'Two. If you take my money, I take your knee caps. And the last thing you taste will be many cocks.'

The boy sniggered at first, but his smile faded when he realised the seriousness of the man's face.

'But you do this job, take this number, maybe more jobs for you.' He handed him a white business card with just a mobile number in the centre. 'Now, go, boy. Do this job. Then you fuck off.'

The boy turned and ran straight over to the homeless man. Kapllani watched the interaction. The homeless man thought it was some kind of a wind-up and looked around as if he expected something to happen. But the boy pointed over to the car. When the homeless man smiled and waved the money in the air to indicate his thanks, Kapllani pressed the button to close the window again.

Kapllani watched for a moment and waited for the homeless man to hurriedly pack his things away and move on, probably fearing the unwelcome attention such an act could draw. He also saw the boy look one more time at the white card and made a mental note to tell another of his associates to expect a text.

The driver caught Kapllani's eyes in his mirror.

'Understand this,' Kapllani rumbled. 'Money is power. One day, this dirty man will learn his debt must be repaid. He does not know this yet, so he does not know what he has to lose.' Kapllani took another drag on his cigarette and stubbed it out in the ashtray. 'But I know what I can take from him. And that, my friend, is power.'

Kapllani gave the driver a nod and the car pulled away as the rain started to fall heavier, coating the road with a film of water.

The English man crossed the Tram Line and headed towards the Minories. The small indoor independent shopping area only had a few retail outlets, but it provided cover and a little quiet from traffic.

He dialled a number he'd memorised and waited for it to connect. 'I have the package.'

'What about the mess you left?'

'I'm about to put the wheels in motion.'

'And when do you expect to have them parked?'

The man paused to let some shoppers pass him by, conscious of prying ears. He caught a reflection of himself in one of the shop windows and realised what Kapllani had meant. He did look like shit.

'Are you still there?' The voice on the other end of the phone barked.

'It'll be done soon. I'll tell you when.'

'And where?'

'The less you know, the less you have to pretend you don't know.' He walked slowly to the opening and stood just out of reach of the rain.

The voice went silent for a moment before clearing its throat. 'And what about our other problem?'

'That's your problem. Sort your own wet work out.'

'I don't think you're in the position…'

'Likewise.' He let the moment hang as he glanced at his watch. 'Anyway, time to go. Make sure you keep a lid on your man.'

'Likewise.'

He ended the call. He removed the back cover, the battery and the SIM card and dropped the pieces into separate bins as he headed down corporation street.

When he reached the ground level of the NCP car park

he made his way to the small red van he'd bought with cash earlier that morning. It was an old van, but in good enough condition not to draw attention.

It took nearly an hour to make his way out of the city centre and over the county border towards Lichfield. His planned destination was a particular curved section of a B-road with a clear five hundred yards.

Spotting the dirt track he'd found using satellite view on Google Maps, he slowed, made one final glance for other vehicles, and made the turning. He followed the track for fifty feet before pulling up on the edge of the wooded area.

He left the engine running as he got out and went round to the back. The low-powered motorbike was light enough to lift down to the ground and wheel into the undergrowth where he covered it with a green sheet and a few loose branches.

He drove back towards the city satisfied the first stage of the clear-up was done. The second, more risky stage, would have to wait. It was going to draw attention, so the timing was essential.

And that was what he was trained to do.

Chapter 9

January
Luke

Luke lay back on the grass looking up at the bottom of the Aston Express Way. Amelja's soft features and long hair swan around Luke's mind. He relished in a rare few minutes when he could forget the rest of the world. Even the rumble of the traffic above and all around faded into background noise.

It was like being in a strange mental oasis right in the middle of the city centre, encircled by a sea of concrete.

He hoped the demand for her name might have been forgotten. Once anyone got caught up in that dirty business, there was no getting out. He didn't want that for her. The only reason he found himself trapped was the general rule that if you lost merchandise, you *became* merchandise. Part of him was screaming to drop everything and run. Run, and take Amelja with him.

By the time he heard the tell-tale shuffle of dirty old combats and hanging chains, the same older boy was standing right over him. His arrival had been masked by the traffic noise.

Luke sat up, startled, and shuffled away, his shoulders and crotch tensing at the memory of their previous encounter.

Gnome sat down next to Luke. After a moment, and a gentle shuffle, Luke felt something being put in his left pocket.

'Usual place. You know what to do. And the rules.'

Luke didn't reply.

'What about the other little bit of business?'

'Haven't seen her again.' Luke turned to look away.

Gnome let out a melodramatic sigh. Luke tried to keep his head down, avoiding eye contact. Then he felt the sudden jolt of his hair being gripped, and his head pulled back. He clenched his teeth and a growl of pain escaped his dry throat. Moving even slightly caused a searing burn across his scalp.

A backhand collided with his face, ripping into his cheek. He rolled over onto his hands and knees, spitting blood onto the ground. Luke felt like a tiny child again. It was all he could do to hold back the tears. But it was more important to hold back the fury.

Gnome stood and moved round to crouch in front of him. 'One thing pisses me off more than failure. Lies.'

'I swear, I haven't seen her.'

A punch jabbed his lower abdomen. A perfect shot, right on the sweet spot over the diaphragm. He retched and collapsed into a heap, curled up in the foetal position.

Gnome took a step back to look at his handy work and smirked as he checked around again that no one was watching. There was only one name he was expecting to hear and simply needed confirmation. But he also enjoyed reminding Luke who was in charge.

'Remembered her name yet?'

Luke shook his head.

'Shame.' Gnome made a big show of preparing to deliver a solid kick.

Luke raised his hand. 'Please.'

'Tell me her fucking name.' He flinched.

'Okay, okay.' After finally catching enough breath, he

broke his promise. 'Amelja.'

'Ameeelyahh?' Gnome mocked. 'Amel-ja. I kinda like it. And yes, well done. That is her name.'

Luke looked up at him, puzzled.

'What?' Gnome said, spreading his arms. 'Did you think I would leave something so important up to a pathetic shit like you?' He crouched down. 'No, no, my boy. You see, we already know who she is. It's just that she slipped through our little net, and now you have helped me reel her right back in.'

Gnome did a small fishing mime and he let a malevolent grin wrap around his face.

Luke wished he could let his fury loose and destroy him on the spot. But he knew the timing was wrong. Unless he killed Gnome, one phone call would be all it took to raise hell on Earth for him, and now Amelja too.

He knew he was trapped. But he also didn't know how long he would be able to hold back that fury. And when it got loose, how far it would take him.

* * *

He got his street name because he was good at hanging around and fishing for a catch. Like a garden Gnome.

It gave him a buzz exerting a little power over the new blood. If a bit of attitude adjustment was needed, he was happy to hand it out.

Different with the girls, though. He never hit them. Especially not ones that had taken such an investment for the boss. Getting Amelja away from that shithole in Albania, sorting a passport, and bringing her to the UK took time and money.

Amelja had been more troublesome than expected, though. She managed to slip from their grip, and the boss had put Gnome on task to track her down. He knew for sure he'd seen her around the city centre, based on photos, but she'd kept her head down.

In the end, it took one dumbass boy to confirmed it.

'Sure, it's her, boss,' Gnome said into the phone. 'I got this, no probs. But I think we need a proper word with the boy.' He listened for a few moments. 'Well, you let me borrow your gorillas when I'm ready.'

* * *

'Was she worth it?' Reg Walters handed an ice pack to Luke and watched him wince as he touched it lightly to his swollen lip.

Luke nodded and shrugged his shoulders at the same time. A dejected look swept across his youthful face.

'She's the most beautiful girl you've ever seen.'

'That's seen me, yeh.'

'And that's what this was about?' Reg drew a circle with his finger pointing at Luke's face, framing the bruises. 'And what about the other guy?'

Luke said nothing and looked away.

Reg opened another anti-septic wipe and dabbed at Luke's grazed cheek, holding his chin with a gentle, paternal gesture. He showed him the amount of dirt that came off his face and handed the boy a few more wipes.

'If you're worried about letting this girl down, find her. Let her see the damage and tell her why it happened.'

'How's that gonna help?'

'Trust me, one thing that women do not find attractive is two boys beating the crap out of each other on their behalf. The macho rubbish annoys them.' He paused for a moment, rethinking his point. 'Annoys the ones worth fighting for.'

Luke frowned at Reg, curling his nose in confusion. 'If I saw two girls getting into a fight over me,' he grinned at Reg.

'Wet t-shirt competitions are hardly the same thing.'

They both laughed, and Luke relaxed a little.

Reg knew he had that effect on the boy. He knew Luke was not eighteen and struggled between his need to keep Luke's trust and undertake his duty of care every time they met. Every time something happened.

He gathered the used wipes into a carrier.

Luke never took up any part of the support to rebuild his life. He was a teenage boy, always hiding from his real age, having to grow up too fast merely to survive.

Reg looked at him and sighed. 'We should see if we can get you a bed for the night.'

'I've got to find her and warn her.'

'Luke, this isn't a game you can just respawn in when you lose a life.'

'She's gonna be in big trouble if she mixes with him.'

'And you? What about the trouble or *harm* you will come to if you go chasing after him?'

Luke shrugged. His old coat was too large and sagged on his shoulders, making him look even younger. It was a dirty green colour. Or it was green with a lot of dirt. His old blue jeans were cheap and heavy with age and dirt, scuffed at the knees and along every edge.

'When you find her, bring her here,' Reg tried not to sound pleading.

'I think I know why she won't come here,' Luke said.

'Go on.'

Luke's reluctance to talk was nothing new to Reg, even though there was a certain level of trust beginning to grow between them.

'I don't know much about her,' he began with caution, scratching at the back of his neck, and lowering his voice even though no one was within earshot. 'She has an accent. Like, you know, foreign.'

'Where from?'

'Dunno. Europe, I guess.'

'Which part?'

'Not French or Spanish, I know what they sound like. And she's not German.'

'Eastern European?'

'What's that mean?'

Reg smiled at his naïvety. 'Countries like Poland, Albania, Kosovo.'

Luke shrugged his shoulders again. 'I guess so. I reckon maybe she might not be here, like…'

'Legally?'

Luke stood, temper fraying. 'Oh, I don't know. And I don't care even if she is. I ain't grassing her up.'

'I didn't mean that.' Reg got up and sat on the corner of a table so he could talk on a level with Luke. When standing, he was a clear six inches above the boy. He put one hand lightly on Luke's shoulder. 'You remember what I told you about confidentiality?'

'That you won't tell anyone what I say?'

Reg gently rocked his head side to side. 'Not quite. About respecting your privacy, and yes keeping our conversations between us.'

'Yeh.'

'Don't forget there is the condition attached to that. I can't sit by and do nothing if I know that would put someone in danger.'

Luke snapped his arm away and pointed at his face. 'You mean like this? I get into a little scrap and you fucking grass me up to the fucking social, and they…'

'Whoa, Luke, easy.' He got up and held the boy by both shoulders. 'I am not grassing you up to anyone. All I want you to understand is that if you are in danger you can rely on any of us here to help you, okay?' He waited for Luke to make eye contact. 'It's not about throwing anyone at the police or the bloody social services.'

'Sorry,' Luke sniffed. 'I just really like her, Reg. I know I only met her recently. But she's nice. She likes me. I didn't want to betray her, but I kind of already messed that up.

He said he already knew her name anyway. He just used me to get to her.'

Reg made an effort to soften his voice. 'Be kind to her. Listen to her. Show her she is safer when she is with you.'

Luke nodded.

Reg wanted to take the boy into an embrace, and would have done had Luke been a member of his own family, or a friend. But that small niggle of boundaries played at his mind, and he let the physical distance hold.

He didn't know whether it was his instinct talking to him, the universe, or some other calling of his faith. Although, his patience with a presumed benevolent God was beginning to wear thin.

But he had already decided that there was some reason this boy had landed in his life. Reg Walters was not going to give up on him.

Chapter 10

The first laborious task had been gathering as much CCTV footage as possible from key points on Friday evening. Major cities like Birmingham had multiple cameras, so even narrowing a search window down to six hours still resulted in an eye-watering amount of footage.

DC Khan had finished transferring the information from his meeting with DI Stone onto the incident room whiteboard. He'd used a different colour to write up key questions which could be turned into delegated tasks. Most of the team were fired up about one of their own being shot, so there hadn't been any trouble getting people to pitch in all their efforts.

DCI Palmers entered the room and stood back from the whiteboard before crossing to Stone's office.

'Got a minute, Mike?'

Stone waved him in as he finished scrawling on another sticky note and trying to find somewhere to stick it to the bottom of his PC monitor.

'I see you're treating the suicide as suspicious circumstances.' His tone was wavering on disapproval.

'I have, and that's why we set up a crowdfunding page, sir. Donate ten pounds, get a free fridge magnet.'

Palmers shook his head as he sat opposite. 'No need to

be facetious.'

'There are too many questions, connections, and unnerving coincidences to brush it off as a suicide too soon. The pathology report raised questions. We haven't had a coroner's verdict finding for suicide yet. Why not make headway?'

An uncomfortable silence held the air for a second too long before Palmers finally replied. 'I know it is early days for proper leads, but what's the action plan?'

'I have DC Khan working up a detailed timeline for all events yesterday evening.'

'Anything cropped up as yet?'

'Nothing specific. But now we know there is some kind of link between the two cases, and the events are overlapping. The significance of that might provide leads.'

Palmers sat back in his chair and clasped his hands behind his head. 'Sensitive question, Mike.'

'Go on.'

'I notice you've named everyone involved. But you haven't posed the question of why Buchanan was in the area.'

Their eyes met.

Stone sat back in his chair. 'We have. I just didn't want it written on the board so publicly, sir. I felt it might cast aspersions or infer something untoward going on. I don't intend to kick our people when they are down.'

'Fair enough. But you are considering?'

'Hell yes. I might not kick, but it doesn't mean I won't look.'

'I want you to take the lead on this case for the time being as I still have loose ends coming out of my ears, and half my life spent in the bloody courts coming up this week.'

Stone did not doubt that he could be the Senior Officer in Charge. Although, the cynical voice over his shoulder was muttering something about Palmers being worried the whole case could go wrong. Recusing himself of the lead role meant Stone would be left holding the hot potato, and risk dropping it in his own lap.

'Understood. Thanks for the vote of confidence.'

'We don't have endless resources, as you know, but if you need more, come to me. I want to be kept in the loop on this. No rogue play.'

Stone placed his right hand over his heart and dropped his mouth open, mocking the inference Palmers was making.

Palmers rolled his eyes.

'I'll liaise with the safeguarding team a.s.a.p.,' Stone said. 'We'll probably need their help at some point. Oh, and we will need more or uniforms or civilians to trawl CCTV footage.' Stone raised his eyebrows hopefully.

'No problem. Strategy?'

'When it comes to the girl, some good old fashioned walkabout work, sir. Officers with photos asking for any sightings. Try and build a picture of her movements between January and now.'

'Do you think that will get you anywhere?'

'Her movements are likely to be related to the boy's. Since the boy's relate to the gun incident, we could find leads by associations.'

Palmers stuck out his bottom lip and nodded slowly. 'Keep me posted, okay?' He brought his arms down and stood. He was about to start walking away when he tapped lightly on the desk.

Stone looked up at him.

'I trust your judgement, Mike. Do we need to keep Bolton away from this or not?'

'She's fine, sir. I sent her home today to clear her head and get some sleep. But she'll be fine.'

'First sign.'

'I'll kick her down the stairs to HR for a psycho-chat.'

'And Reg Walters. Your pathology friend?'

'The highly professional colleague?' Stone didn't like the suggestion of informality on the job. 'Dr Walters is fine. His insight is going to be particularly valuable in the case.'

'As long as he doesn't overstep.'

'Sir, I know what you're alluding to. Walters knows his place within procedure better than most of our officers know theirs. As for his personal involvement with one of the victims, the only way Reg's input would be recused would be if the boy died. I'm sure you share in our hope that won't happen.'

Two can play passive-aggressive, Mr Palmers.

Palmers took the hint and raised his hands in submission. His point had been made, and as a politician that meant his back was covered. And yet his little meeting meant he could still claim the credit for overseeing one of his DIs.

Palmers left Stone's office and paused as he looked around the incident room. Most of the team were still working.

'Listen up for a second.' He drew their attention with one boom of his voice. He was a well-built man and just over six feet, so he held a clear physical presence. Although he was in his early fifties, he was fit enough to appear five or more years younger.

'Tough week ahead. One of our own has been hurt. The tragic death of one kid, and a horrendous assault of another. We need to be focused.' He paused. Everyone was waiting for the criticism. 'You're all doing great work already. Keep it up. The clock is ticking, and every hour makes it twice as hard to catch the bastards responsible.' Palmers nodded once before turning and leaving the incident room.

No one knew if it had been a rallying cry, a pep talk, or a weak attempt at a Churchill moment.

Stone stood from his desk and came to his office door.

He shrugged his shoulders. 'God knows what that was about. But, to be fair, I'd struggle to disagree with him.' He couldn't quite put his finger on it, but he was sure there had been something between the lines Palmers had delivered. A niggle. A subtext just out of reach.

Stone made his way over to Khan's desk. 'Update, Harry?'

'I've sorted out some pictures for officers to carry with them.'

'Great stuff.'

'Are you busy this evening, guv?'

The guilt struck him. He was supposed to be Mike Stone, spending the weekend with his son Jack, not DI Stone chasing criminals and ghosts. His ex-wife and his son were understanding when the big cases began. They knew it meant he had to get the ball rolling as fast as possible.

But all justification aside, he would have loved to just kick that all to touch, go home and surprise them.

It's day one of the case. Cut yourself some slack, old man.

He sighed deeply before letting his face wear a smile. 'Not especially, why?'

Khan leaned forward and lowered his voice. 'Whenever I can, when it's cold, I do a bit of a walkabout in town. You know, seeing the rough sleepers, giving them a bite to eat, a quick chat.'

It didn't surprise Stone in the slightest. He knew his DC had a charitable side to his personal life. 'I take it you've never seen Luke or Amelja on your walkabouts?'

'Sadly not.' He let out a sigh, his eyes suddenly darting. The thought hadn't even crossed his mind. 'Shit, I wonder if I've passed them or just missed them.'

Stone could see he'd knocked Khan's train of thought. 'Sorry, Harry, you were saying.'

'Yes, sorry, right. I have my bag with the stuff I normally take out and was planning on doing a walkabout this evening. Just wondered if you wanted to join me.'

'Sure, why not?'

He knew that kind of work was what uniform constables and PCSOs should be doing. Not senior officers. But he also felt he needed to get into his vibe on the case. Usually, that came from revisiting crime scenes. But this case was different. If there was a chance to find even the slightest information for a lead, there was nothing to lose.

Chapter 11

DI Stone pulled up the collar on his leather coat as he walked through the city centre with DC Khan. Stone and Khan figured that a long cold night would make food a good exchange for any information.

'You realise we probably won't find out anything useful, sir?' Khan asked, rubbing his hands together.

'I know it's a long shot, Harry. But since you were planning on coming out anyway, the walk will do me good. I need to clear my head.'

Khan smiled as the two men made their way up Moor Street Queensway towards the rail station, a well-known spot for people to spend a day begging.

'I trust you're okay turning a blind eye to one or two begging laws and all that?'

'We are here to make friends, Harry.'

Khan smiled and gave him a nod.

'Besides, I can't be arsed upholding two-hundred-year-old vagrancy laws.'

'Actually, guv, it would be the Crime and Disorder Act 1998, and the ASBO which was…'

'Replaced in two-thousand-and-fourteen by ASBCP, Harry.' Stone smiled at him. 'And don't say "actually," it makes me feel violent.'

Khan raised his hands in mock submission.

'Besides, you're the second person today who I'm going

to tell I don't kick people when they're down. I'm a copper, not a Tory.'

'Lucky we're in plain clothes.'

'Makes no difference. They'll smell us a mile off.'

They both smiled at the irony.

'Any change spare?' a voice uttered, lacking hope but still affording a polite smile.

'Are you here often, mate?' Stone asked.

'Eight days a week, my friend.'

'You probably get to know the regulars.'

The man shrugged his shoulders.

Stone took a print-out and showed it to the man. 'Either of these two ring any bells?'

The man looked up at Khan as if to ask what it was about. 'What's your game? I ain't that kind of man.'

Khan chipped in quickly. 'Just asking if you've ever seen them around, sir.'

'You pervs, cops or what?'

'I'm a cop, he's a what,' Stone nodded at Khan.

The man smiled, 'I don't get called sir these days.'

'These days? What did you do before?' Khan tried to avoid being insensitive.

'Not freeze me arse off for nothing.' The man's eyes dropped towards his virtually empty cup.

Khan swung his bag round and unzipped it. 'When was your last meal?' Khan got the slightly suspicious look.

'Bit to eat this morning.'

'Are you vegetarian?'

Stone couldn't stifle a laugh and was surprised the man on the floor caught his eye and joined in.

'I'd eat roadkill if you bastards let me sort the damn young'ns out with a proper shovel,' the man sniggered.

Khan took a fat baguette from his bag, with a bottle of water and a packet of what looked like sweets. 'It's chicken salad, some vitamin tablets, and some Kendal mint cake.' Khan could see a flash of appreciation and confusion through the man's practised stern expression. 'It should be good. My wife made it.'

'You giving me your packed lunch made by the Mrs?'

Stone shot Khan a "well, are you?" look.

Smiling, Khan replied, 'no way, sir. If I don't eat my lunch, I don't get my balls back.'

'Cheers.' The man said as the two detectives walked away.

Stone rubbed the scar on his neck for a moment. 'Sorry, Harry. I shouldn't have laughed. How often do you do this?'

'Not often enough. And everyone deserves a laugh.'

Khan's generosity didn't surprise Stone. But he was moved by the forethought. It must have been planned regardless of how his day at work went.

'Why didn't you give the man the goody-bag before we showed him the photos?'

'Because giving a man food is not a transaction like paying an informant. It's not a bribe. My mother taught me it is okay to pay for a man's pride but always respect his dignity. Only cowards and weak men push a man who has already fallen.'

'What makes you say he has fallen?'

'He used to be just like us.'

'A copper?' Mike pointed his thumb over his shoulder. 'Him?'

'Professional. He had a job. A respected one. And it wasn't that long ago.'

Stone gave him a quizzical look.

Khan continued. 'His eyes dropped when I called him sir. His shoulders, too. A memory. Like we'd found him out. And his nails. Too well kept for a long-term man of the streets. His accent was local, but still well-spoken, educated, and less colloquial than he was trying to sound. He had a light ring mark still slightly indented. Wedding ring, perhaps, given up relatively recently. Many possible reasons, but could be an end of a relationship. Even a bereavement. Maybe he had to pawn it for cash.'

Stone instinctively touched his own wedding ring, which he still wore despite having separated a few years back.

'The photos.' Khan's tone softened. He wasn't showing off. 'He mentioned their age first. Observant man, compassionate, and had a flicker of worry in his tone. I'd say maybe a teacher. Youth worker, perhaps. Definitely kids in some way. As we approached him several people walked past, he asked everyone for change except the two college students. He had a life, guv. Now, he just has a sandwich.'

There was a sadness in Khan's tone as his voice trailed off. He paused for a moment before walking on a pace or two ahead of Stone.

Stone let out a deep breath.

Where the hell did that come from?

He quick-stepped to catch up. 'Harry. It's high time you were going for your sergeant's exam. Either that or a profiler.'

'I'm no profiler, guv.' Khan looked back over to the man who was already tucking into the baguette. 'But he is still a person.'

* * *

Stone hunched his shoulders against the bitter late evening air. There was a lull of activity in the city centre as most shoppers had gone home. It wouldn't be long before the Saturday night tsunami of revellers would venture out for a night of drinking and dancing, shouting and shagging, puking and pissing.

'Are there more rough sleepers these days, or are we just noticing them because we're actively looking?'

DC Khan sighed. 'A bit of both. Numbers have been

rising for years, especially thanks to over a decade of the same government that chooses to do nothing about it. But it barely scratches the surface of homelessness.'

'And that's what kids like Amelja have to survive.'

'But how did she survive nearly nine months being pregnant?' Khan shook his head in disbelief. 'She must have had help. Friends' sofas, maybe a squat. Occasionally scraping enough cash for a night in a hostel.'

'You sound almost impressed, Harry.'

'To be honest, guv, I am. But I just wish she could have escaped that life.'

Their route had taken them all around the city centre, past St Phillip's Cathedral, and through the Minories shopping arcade. As they reached the traffic island on the Priory Queensway a shiver ran down Stone's back at the thought he could have been walking Amelja's final steps. Her promising final months. Terrifying final weeks. Unknown final days.

How many chances to save her had been missed?

They turned down Bull Street and immediately saw their next potential target.

'Who's this guy, Harry?'

Khan smiled and rolled his eyes. 'Commonly called Mr Freeman.'

Stone smiled and nodded. He was a friendly-looking man that seemed to have an aura of kindness about him. And a vague resemblance to Morgan Freeman.

'No serious record. He's a long-term rough sleeper, more comfortable out and about. Kind of anti- institutionalised.'

'The Brumshank Redemption?'

DC Khan laughed as they approached the man.

'Officers.' Freeman smiled as he offered a hand to shake. Khan responded, shaking it as sincerely as he shook any other.

Stone followed suit, only to see the man's expression changed to one of suspicion.

What's wrong with my shake?

'How can I help you two fine gentlemen this evening?'

Stone got straight to the point, taking his phone out to show the man the pictures. 'Do you recognise either of these two?'

'You let me have a look here now,' the man said. He adjusted his head in the way that only long-sighted people do. The man plucked some glasses from his pocket and open the wiry frames with his mouth as he looked at the photos. That's when Stone noticed they had no lenses in the frames.

'They might seem familiar. It's cold out tonight, and what with me being quite tired and all.'

Stone saw the glint in the man's eyes. There had been genuine recognition when he saw the photos.

'My friend and I were planning on getting a bite to eat, sir. Care to join us?'

The man smiled, seemingly pleased that his subtle suggestion had worked. 'Lead the way, gentlemen. Lead the way.'

Stone led them to a smaller fish and chip shop opposite the taxi rank, avoiding the brightly lit, more public food outlets. He left Khan with 'Mr. Freeman' and went to place the order. By the time he got back, the two men were deep in the most British of all small talk.

Weather.

'The two kids, then?' Stone asked before poking the first red hot chip in his mouth.

'First things first,' Mr Freeman replied, 'I ain't wanting to get no one in any trouble.'

'That's not why we're here, sir,' Stone replied, poking at his pile of chips with a plastic fork.

'Truth and honesty matter to me, gentlemen. But the unjust repercussions of man terrify me more than the wrath of God almighty. You understand?'

'Truth never damages a cause that is just,' Khan replied,

holding up his plastic fork with an impaled chip.

'Thou speakest the wisdom of the impaled chip,' Stone mocked.

Mr Freeman frowned at Mike Stone. 'Mahatma Gandhi, my son. I see from your friend I am speaking to at least one learned man.' He let a small smile curl one side of his mouth before shovelling in a few more chips.

It was a short moment of intellectual camaraderie.

The two detectives let the man share what he knew about both youngsters in the photos. The first time he'd met them months ago was just across the city centre. It had been cold, and he'd shared food and supplies.

'How was their relationship? Did you sense any coercion?' Stone asked.

'Love,' the man said, smiling. 'Only love between those two. I could feel the warmth of it more than they could.'

Khan drowned a chip in curry sauce. 'Forgive me a pedantic question, sir, but the love of friends or…'

The man looked up and closed his eyes for a moment. 'Their love was very true.' He took a sip of his tea. 'They were very young, indeed. Too young to have been so lost in the world.' He looked down into his cup and his face softened. 'But the Lord showed me true love that day. Enough to be with child.' He threw a piece of fish into his mouth and chewed, his jaw working the food in a slow, circular movement.

'Did you see them again?' Stone asked.

He nodded. But said nothing.

'And when was this?'

'I did the Lord's work and kept watch of his flock.' His voice cracked slightly. 'I seen the boy more than the girl. Hunter gatherin' best he can, not always happy. Filled with worry and hurry and all the world's troubles on them shoulders. We spoke in passing and I aks after her, too. I share the Lord's love for them both.' Mr Freeman took a deep breath. 'His eyes so dark with worry, but just enough light for hope.' He sipped again at his tea. 'Delicate thing. Hope.'

The three men shared a silence and there was a glint of a tear in the old man's eyes like he sensed the tragedy that had befallen them.

Perhaps he knows more than he's letting on.

'I seen the girl again. Recent, like,' Mr Freeman finally said, folding up his fat-soaked papers.

'You spoke to her? When?' Stone asked.

'Amelja.' He smiled as he said her name, quietly, wafting his hand in the air.

Khan jumped in. 'You're sure it was her?'

'She was terrified.' he stood up, getting more animated, tapping at his forehead a fear entered his voice. 'It's hard to remember. The days, they just jumble up and blur.'

Khan put a hand on the man's shoulder.

'She said something about the boy. He'd been taken.'

Stone shot Khan a glance. 'When was this?'

'Luke was taken.'

'Did Amelja say anything about who took him?' Stone could feel a potential lead ringing around his ears.

The old man paced out of the shop. 'She got on a bus. Back to their special place.'

Khan followed him outside. 'Can you remember exactly when this was?'

'She was bigger. With baby.' Mr Freeman staggered and put a hand up to the shop window to steady himself. He shook his head, his tone lowered, his gestures laboured and drained him. 'She was different in them eyes. In them eyes you see. Someone got inside them eyes. Taken it all. Everything.'

Stone heard the lump in the man's throat and saw his eyes filling with tears.

'She was like Pandora, defeated,' Mr Freeman whispered, fixing his glare on Khan and then taking him by the lapels of his coat. 'That box been opened, and she'd had all the shit in the world thrown at her. She was barely clinging to the final piece.'

Stone and Khan looked at each other.

Mr Freeman noticed their look of uncertainty at the point he was making. Or understanding his reference. 'Hope.' He let out a deep sigh. A tear rolled down his cheek. 'Did she suffer?'

Stone stumbled over his own words. A lump filling this throat. 'We're trying to put together all the details.'

'What happened to the baby?'

Stone sighed, knowing he shouldn't say anything, officially. 'The baby's okay.'

A gentle smile of relief flickered before a new thought darkened his expression. He stepped right up to DI Stone. 'And the Boy?'

Stone took a deep breath. 'He's still alive.' He looked deep into the man's eyes and could tell that whoever this stranger was, beneath a surface of what came across as madness, there was a deeply empathic soul.

'Mr Detective,' he whispered, 'find whoever stole Amelja's final piece, and you have her killer.'

Stone held the man by the shoulders, partly for reassurance, but also to ease him back to arm's length. 'We're going to solve this, okay?'

Mr Freeman backed away, and looked up to the sky, blinking at whatever it was he saw up there. 'I hear it's going to be a cold week, gentlemen.'

'Why don't you pop by this place over the week, sir,' Stone replied. 'Just give the owner a nod, and remind him you're Mr Freeman. He'll fix you up a hot meal.'

Nothing more was said. The "thank you" was in his eyes.

Khan looked at the old man for a few moments. 'How did you know she was gone, sir? Full details of her identity have not been made public knowledge yet.'

'Because bad men hunt children who are trying to be

lost. Good men only come looking when it's too late, and they're already lost forever.'

His whole body sagged as he walked slowly away.

Chapter 12

Reg Walters gave Luke's hand another gentle squeeze, hoping for a response. The medical team had ended the sedation that morning after transferring him to Birmingham Children's Hospital, but he had yet to wake up.

It had taken some persuading to let Reg stay on the ward, given that he was not a family member. All Reg knew was that DI Stone had spoken to his senior officers who had made phone calls and it had been sorted. In truth, he didn't care how it had been done, he just knew Luke would need a friendly face.

'To be honest, Doctor Walters, we are just waiting for him to wake up.' The Consultant Paediatrician had been cautiously positive about the progress.

'It's not a coma, then?' Reg asked.

'No, no. He could be woken up if we reduced pain medication and actively stimulated him. But his vitals are good, and sleep is the best thing for him.'

'Prognosis?'

'At the moment, all tests suggest a full recovery. To be honest, this is an odd one.'

Reg frowned at the man.

'Well, it's a severe battering, for sure. More than once over the past week. But most of the injuries we can see are flesh deep, so whoever did it either wasn't very strong or was more interested in making a point than,' he trailed off, not wanting to say what was really on his mind.

'Right, okay,' Reg said, turning to look at Luke's bruises.

'But don't quote me on that if some copper wants to pin attempted murder on the thugs who did it.' The consultant gave a tap to his nose before turning to leave the room.

Reg looked further up Luke's arm to the bruises on his bicep. Leaning in closer, his eye was caught by bruising on his ribcage, barely visible through the gown.

Checking that no one was watching, he gently rolled the blanket down and untied the bow at the side of the gown. He lifted it for a clearer view of the purple-crimson bruises. Walters was sure he could make out the shape of a heel, the ball of the foot and the big toe at least.

He lifted the gown slightly more, to see if he could distinguish any other markings.

'What the ruddy 'ell d'you think you're doing?' A quiet, but furious voice sliced the air.

Reg froze for a moment before turning to see the ward nurse glaring at him. He knew there was no plausible white lie, so his only option was the best defence ever. Flattery.

'Excellent. I need a proper professional eye. Look at this,' he said, heaping on a tone of importance.

Nurse Frankly was seething. But she was also intrigued.

'Come on, are you a qualified nurse or not?'

'Well, yes, but…'

'Then look at these bruises.'

'The doctor…'

'Will be impressed with your sharp eye. As will the police, when you hand them an important clue.'

The nurse finally relented with a sigh. 'What're you showing me?'

Reg encircled the heel, ball and toe-marked bruises one by one. The nurse leaned in a bit closer, turning a head almost ninety degrees to see it at another angle.

'Is that a foot mark?'

'See, I knew you had the eye. Now, what else do you notice about it? Anything?' He needed her to see it for herself.

Confusion took over her face.

'Miss Frankly, what size would you say that foot-mark is? Roughly.'

It was like a penny dropping on a glass table.

'Bugger me.' She covered her mouth. 'I don't know exactly, but smaller than mine, and I'm only diddy.'

'And here,' Reg showed her the bruises on the boy's upper arm.

'That's gotta be a small hand what's done that.'

'What do you think? A woman or…'

'No, I'd say smaller. A boy.' She was getting into a stride. 'Why so certain?'

'Mr Walters, you strike me as too much of a gentleman to have experienced it. When us women get a grip, we use our nails, draw blood if we can. Ain't none of that here.'

Reg nodded, standing up and walking to the end of the bed, picking up the metal clipboard.

'Um, Mr Walters, you really shouldn't be…'

'It's Doctor Walters. And, honestly, how often have you seen this level of injury on a child?'

'Rarely this bad. Poor kid,' her voice softened.

'I need your help.'

The nurse's eyes lit up with enthusiasm.

'The thing is,' Reg tried to make it sound as dramatic as possible, 'the detective in charge of the investigation needs to know about these injuries before they fade. You know, so we don't lose the evidence to get the bastards that did this.'

He could see he was reeling her in.

'So, whilst preserving this boy's dignity, what if as you tended to his wounds, I just happened to be here, and took a few quick photos on my phone? It's done a lot on domestic violence, or child abuse cases.'

'I'm not sure about the photos.'

'If there are any questions, we can say you shared your objections. That isn't a lie, is it?'

'Bloody is.'

'Yes, but only a little innocent one.'

It took a moment, but the nurse finally agreed.

Reg already had a theory in mind. All he needed was the proof.

Chapter 13

January
Luke

Luke spent another night hidden under a bush next to the car park on Bath Street. The Salvation Army building was a matter of yards away, but he couldn't bring himself to go back inside after having made the delivery. He'd received another small reminder from Gnome's contacts how he needed to keep himself in check and was too embarrassed to go back just hours after Reg had fixed him up.

Amelja and Reg. It was like he was betraying everyone who was trying to help him.

Luke decided to hunker down, hidden away, covered by a large estate car that didn't go anywhere all night. Across the road was a well-known local pub he longed to be old enough to go inside. His stomach ached from hunger and his bruised cheekbone burnt with a touch.

Luke made his way under St Chads Queensway towards the city centre. He'd arranged to meet Amelja in the small grassy area behind Carr's Lane Church, next to the Travelodge.

It was a small square public area no more than forty feet wide and long. A few benches in the centre surrounded by a small amount of grass. It was one of those little tucked away corners between the hotel and church, on a main bus thoroughfare, and within eyesight of Moor Street station.

It had been pretty unsightly before the hotel was built, with the late-night supermarket below.

Luke tried to fight the heavy disappointment when he couldn't see Amelja. But then he'd questioned himself. Why would she be there? How long did he expect her to wait? The problem with growing up not trusting anyone was that it left you feeling harder to be trusted.

He was about to leave and go looking for her when he saw a familiar set of dirty camouflage legs walking out of the Tesco. He headed for cover behind a car parked next to the church.

Peering through its windows, he felt sick when he saw who Gnome was talking to.

An odd mixture of fear and envy caught him off guard. Gnomes smiles and well-timed expressions of concern, hand placed on his chest, caring and reassuring.

Luke clenched his fists and had to fight to control his fury. He wanted to charge the bastard right there and then. But he knew he'd end up looking stupid and risk pushing Amelja further into his arms.

Where he'd groom her. Luke knew how that worked.

Sneaky, interfering fingers. Searching. Nasty with anticipation. Piling on the compliments. Distract the mind. Touch her hair. Tell her how special she is. He knew the game. Give and give. Then give and take. Then take, take, take. Nasty fucking grooming cunt.

Luke pictured himself smashing Gnome's face into a pulp against a brick wall. The corner of it. Split it fucking open like a dirty coconut.

No fear, just fury.

His heart pounded in his chest. He had to slow his breathing to keep control as he watched Gnome stand and walked away with a casual wave back to Amelja.

But he knew, as soon as he saw Gnome take out his mobile, that was it. Just like that. Amelja was a target.

* * *

Luke waited for Gnome to be out of sight before he stood from behind the car and tried to get Amelja's attention. It took a few attempts before she finally noticed and cast him a stern look.

Staying behind the car, he waved her over again, cautious about stepping out into the open.

A few moments passed before she finally picked up the bag and walked over to the car.

'You tell him my name.' She frowned, her lips mildly pursed.

'I'm sorry. I tried not to.'

'You know I not like him.'

'I'm sorry, I had…he…'

Her expression dropped when Luke turned to face her. 'My Luke, your face. What happen?'

He looked away for a moment and caught his reflection in the car window. That's when he realised how bad he looked. It looked like he'd done a round or two with a heavyweight. Well, perhaps just one punch. But still, he looked dreadful.

Amelja reached out with both her hands, cradling his chin, and inspecting the damage. 'He did this?' One look in Luke's eyes gave her the answer. 'You need doctor.'

'I'll be fine. A friend helped me clean it up a bit.'

'Is your friend doctor?'

Luke laughed but winced when his lip reminded him it was split. 'Sort of. He cuts up dead people.'

'Ah, like you call butcher.'

'I'll tell him you said that.'

'Well, you need proper doctor.'

'It'll heal up.'

'Boys and their fists,' she muttered something in

Albanian. Probably a swear word.

Luke watched her intently. She captivated him. There was also anger lingering in her, and he knew he'd still have to answer for his betrayal. He prodded at the bruises but Amelja slapped his fingers away.

'No touch. We must keep them clean.'

He sighed deeply and looked away from her. Shame crept back upon him and an awkward silence set in.

'Luke,' her eyes settled into mild sadness, 'why did he do this?'

'He's just a horrible person.'

'Did he do for my name?'

Luke didn't reply.

'He whisper my name. I thought it you, so I turn.'

'I am so sorry.'

Amelja squeezed Luke's hand as she looked into his eyes. 'You have no sorry. I hate him.'

Luke looked at the shopping bag. 'Did he get you that?'

'Yes. And gave me money.'

'You know why, don't you?'

She looked at him with a gentle smile. 'You think we don't have girls who do sex for money in my country? I know these men. Pidhi.'

Amelja whispered in his ear. The smell of her so close made his head spin and other parts of his body stir. And he wasn't prudish, but he didn't often hear girls say that C-word.

'You must stay away from him,' he said.

'He doesn't scare me.'

Luke stood, a certain frustration in his voice. 'Well, he should. I'm serious. If you see him, turn and run the other way. Okay? You run.'

'Calm, my Luke.'

'And never shout for help. Shout, fire.'

'Fire? Why fire.'

'It's true. Shout help, and no one will come. Shout

about fire and suddenly everyone cares.'

She smiled. 'Is this another silly British thing?'

'I'm serious. I will look after you, okay. I won't let him get you involved in anything.'

'We will care for us both,' she said, softly. 'But it looks like you who need more care than me.' She reached out and hugged him. He couldn't remember anyone ever holding him. It took him a few moments to work out how to hold her back.

They both felt the warmth and safety of the embrace. Everything else floated away.

Luke wished they could stay in that bubble forever.

Chapter 14

September

The Englishman drove the black saloon out of the NCP car park and began his second journey to the same location he'd left the motorbike tucked away.

He reduced his speed a good five hundred yards from the same wooded area. It was essential there were no witnesses. When he could see it was clear from both directions, he hit the gas and felt the engine roar.

For a few exhilarating seconds, he felt the true power of the two-litre engine as the speedometer swept up to sixty in just over five seconds. The tyres glued to the undulating road as the wooded area approached.

He timed it perfectly and slammed on the brakes. Swerving into the other lane before over-correcting back to the left, the car came to rest barely a couple of feet from shooting off into the ditch below road level. Getting out of the car and opening the boot, he recoiled at the smell of decomposition set in. He'd made a point of blasting the air-con down to arctic cold before he'd parked the car.

The lump of a body weighed an inordinate amount. Placing his forearms under the armpits, he dragged it to the front and bundled it into the seat.

Returning to the boot, he took out the two petrol cans. He emptied one into the boot and removed the lid from the second, leaving it to spill. The boot closed with a gentle thud.

Releasing the handbrake and starting the engine, he pushed the car by the inside corner of the door. The vehicle rolled without too much effort thanks to the camber in the road.

He only had about six feet to move it before the left front wheel left the tarmac. The sudden small drop pulled the car along with enough momentum to keep it rolling into the ditch. Just as planned, the weight of the car hitting the drop was enough to carry the back-end over. The car rolled down into the undergrowth until it hit a tree hard enough to set off the airbags.

The smell of petrol fumes filled the air. He took a length of homemade fuse from his pocket, lit the end and threw it down towards the back of the car. It was a skill from his army days to delay ignition, giving him time to gain some distance.

It took about ten seconds for the fuse to ignite the spilt petrol. Flames leapt several feet up into the trees.

By the time he'd reached the end of the wooded area, there was a louder explosion as the extra petrol can went up in flames. It took a few more seconds for the biggest explosion of the car's fuel tank.

The fire was stretching twenty feet up the surrounding trees and acrid black smoke was filling the air. Enough to draw attention from some distance away.

He reached the bike and took the bag from underneath the camouflage. Putting on the leather jacket and the helmet, he rolled up the bike cover and put that into the bag.

The bike was relatively light and easy to stand up. It started on the first attempt, and he began his ride down the dirt track away from the road. It was about half a mile down the side of the wooded area to his left and the hedge-lined farmland to his right. He reached the next road which had him heading back towards Birmingham.

It was important to disassociate himself from even the direction of the fire so he could leave no trace of his involvement.

At least part of the events on Friday evening would be wiped out without any useful forensic trace.

As long as everyone else fulfilled their roles.

Chapter 15

Sausages, chips and beans. Mike Stone was no master chef, but when his son was staying, he tried to make more of an effort than take-away food. They'd had a good-sized Sunday carvery for lunch, so the evening fare was a lighter mission.

Jack was in the living room zone of the open-plan flat Mike had lived in for only a few months. He'd separated from his wife several years before, but events of the past year had forced reflective life changes. A reconciliation of their marriage was never on the cards, but they had come closer together.

They sold the marital home that his ex, Claire, and their son had lived in until traumatic events from the Malcolm Glenn case the previous year made it impossible to return. Equity from the sale helped them buy a smaller, two-bed house with a reasonable-sized garden where Claire and Jack lived. Mike bought a small two-bed apartment within a short bus journey.

But the biggest change was the time Mike was spending with his son. Normally, a day off only two days into a major new inquiry would be impossible, but his determination to keep to commitments to Jack made him split the weekend. Besides, the lack of solid leads meant he was able to delegate tasks.

'Grub's up,' he announced, picking up the plates and

heading over to the dining table.

Jack closed the laptop a little too quickly

'Red sauce?' the boy asked.

'You know where it is.'

Jack bounced over to the fridge as Mike slid the laptop out of the way.

Two sauce bottles appeared on the table.

'Red and brown sauce?' Mike gasped.

'Who are you? The sauce Police?' Jack smiled as he began squirting two dots and a curved line across the top of his chips. He fumbled to tilt the plate up.

'What have you been told about playing with your food?'

'Make sure you eat the evidence,' Jack replied without hesitation.

That's my boy.

'And just say your father taught you that,' Jack mimicked his mum.

'Cheeky bugger,' Mike sniggered at the perfect impression of Claire. He squirted a line of brown sauce onto a chip and held it up to his face as a moustache.

Jack grabbed his phone and took a photo.

'Don't you dare send that.'

A mischievous grin lit up the boy's face.

'Right, phones away.'

They both threw their phones onto the sofa in perfect unison. It was part of the phone-free dinner table policy Mike and Claire always adhered to. Both phones pinged a message received sound and Jack laughed, his eyes lighting up. He looked just like his dad, with dark hair and deep, inquisitive eyes.

'Now you're in trouble, dad.'

Mike grunted, mockingly. 'Finished your homework?'

'Yup.'

Try again.

'Nearly.'

One more time.

Jack didn't answer. Sometimes he envied his mates. They had parents they could tell little lies to. But his dad had a lie-radar. He thought it was cool most of the time, but not when it was used on him.

'What is it?' Mike said, spotting the twinge of tension in Jack's neck. His tell.

The boy tried to look casual. 'Just some research.'

'Sounds intriguing,' Mike raised his eyebrows.

Jack wrinkled his face into a thoughtful frown. 'I. N. T. R, um. I. G. U. I, N, G?' His voice bounced up with a little questioning Brummie accent at the end.

'Well done.'

Mike caught a glance of the laptop earlier and using a tracking program found Jack searching "nervous breakdown." He was almost sure teachers wouldn't set that kind of research for a ten-year-old. But it was dinner time, the mood was good.

I'll deal with you later.

They ploughed through dinner and followed it with the usual ice cream mountain, decorated with squirty things and a few token fruit.

The rest of the evening was quiet, spending time planning the next Birmingham City match they'd go to. They rounded it off with the usual bath, book and bed routine Jack was still young enough to enjoy.

Mike knew there was something on Jack's mind he should have pressed further. But the evening had been just what he needed to recharge himself for what would be a tough week ahead. Good-faith and grip-onto-hope batteries needed extra charging.

And they also had a rule about going to bed with a happy head.

Let the innocent lie go.

* * *

'He doesn't need both legs, really, does he?'

'Ha, bloody ha,' Claire groaned. 'I mean, how nice of you to call.'

Mike and Claire had always cut through small talk, and rarely answered the phone with a simple 'hello.'

'We're fine.'

'So…?'

'Just a quickie,' Mike was trying to keep any concern out of his voice. 'To the best of your knowledge, does he have any homework about mental health?'

'Not that I know of. Why?'

'Don't get me wrong. It's important to talk about…'

'Which homework?'

'Anything about nervous breakdowns?'

Claire paused. 'Okay. Michael. What's wrong?'

Ouch. Michael. Now I'm in trouble.

'He did a search on the web for "nervous breakdown".'

'Why?'

'That's what I'm asking you.'

'Well, I don't know, Mike, he's your son.'

Mike laughed. 'Um, our son.'

'Not the weird bits. That's all you.'

He paused for a moment, wording his thoughts carefully. 'What does he know about things.'

'We agreed what we'd tell him and when, and I've never strayed from that.' The humour had gone from Claire's tone, and concern was creeping in.

A few months after a serious car accident over five years ago Mike had suffered a major blow to his mental health. The accident was the cause of the tracheostomy scar on his neck. Claire and Jack had been in the car but escaped serious injury. After a reasonably long break from work, Mike's mental health had suffered and he'd thrown himself back into his job, one hundred per cent. And too soon. The strain on their relationship reached and passed breaking point.

They separated just early enough to still do it amicably.

It was only for the sake of keeping a relationship with his son that Mike managed to avert a complete nervous breakdown. By which time, Claire had met another man, Steve Simpson, and started to move on. But it was Steve that had been killed in the major serial killer case the previous year.

That meant Mike and Claire were both single again. And happily so. They had decided to parent Jack more closely together, but still live separately. They lived equidistant from Jack's school, and within minutes on a bus. It allowed their son more time with his dad. Even taking into account the inconsistent working hours of a senior detective.

A lot of people knew about the accident all those years ago. Their separation was no secret. But few knew about the breakdown.

'I haven't said anything to him about it, Mike. But the older he gets, the more questions he is going to ask.'

'Maybe it's just a coincidence.'

'We both know how you feel about those.' A pause hung in the air for a moment. 'What's else is bothering you?'

'Nothing,' he paused. 'Why?'

'You didn't need to phone me about this.'

'Work just got me jittery.'

'Anything I should be worried about?'

'No, God, no, nothing like that.' He even heard it in his own voice. Hardly convincing.

'You're working on that girl's case, aren't you?' Claire pressed on. 'The one that jumped off Galton Bridge.'

Very little information had been released to the press, and they had still been able to keep the word suspicious out of the media. How long that would last was anyone's guess.

'Come on, mister inspector. A girl kills herself and you start getting jittery about Jack looking at mental health information. You're a great cop, but I have something you don't have.'

'What's that?'

'Breasts.'

Mike laughed. 'Not just breasts, if I remember rightly.'

'Behave. And stop changing the subject.' She tried to sound serious. 'Look, it's possible he saw something on the news. I'll ask his teacher to keep an eye on him.'

'It's just that when you add it to everything else.'

'They said a detective saved the baby and nearly talked the girl down. Maybe Jack is worried that was you.'

'It was Sands.'

Claire gasped. 'Shit. How is she?' Her voice cracked.

'She says she's fine, but she's not.'

'She's not in any trouble, is she?'

I hope not.

'No, nothing like that. Just the shock of it all.'

'Please tell me you didn't let her go home alone after?'

'I had to force her to take the day off yesterday.'

'Michael Stone,' Claire gasped down the phone.

Uh oh.

'What have I told you? Christ. I know she's hard as a rock, that one, on the outside. But she's a mother. And you sent her home like a naughty child.'

'Are you actually telling me off?'

'Yes, I bloody well am. She needs to be with someone she can vent to. You men and your macho bottling-up crap.'

'She's got breasts.'

'Which you, sir, have never noticed.' Her voice softened. 'But seriously. I know you can't give me details but remember, in her head, she'll be projecting this.

98

Mulling it over, questioning if they will be the next ones she can't save.'

'I know you're right. How do I bring my Jedi back from the dark side?'

'Leave her to me.'

'Please don't break her. We need her.'

'I'll give her a call for a girly chat.'

Mike let out a relieved sigh. 'Thanks.'

They ended the call soon after. Their friendship had grown stronger than when they'd been together. Jack was happier. They were all happier.

But a little voice over Mike's shoulder occasionally whispered mischievous memories.

Shut up, you.

Chapter 16

By the time DI Stone got to the incident room, it was already buzzing with action. A fair number of the team had got to work sometime before the requested half-nine, and Stone was quietly impressed.

He dropped his coat on the back of his chair and picked up a pile of notes from his desk, reading as he walked back out to the incident room. DC Khan had been his ever-resourceful self and updated the whiteboard.

Stone was pleased to see DS Bolton at her desk looking somewhat more back in character, with the usual focused expression. Her hair was tied back in business mode, and she was wearing her smart grey suit with a black shirt. Stone knew it was righteously fashionable to say "don't judge a book by its cover." But that cover said kickass. And that was DS Bolton to the core.

She picked up a notepad and headed over towards him. 'Harry tells me you two went on a date Saturday evening.'

'Did he now?'

'I shan't tell you the disturbing image that gave me.'

'Please don't.'

Their eyes met for a moment.

She'd needed Saturday off work. He'd needed Sunday

off. They'd both needed time with their kids to square their heads for the start of a new week.

'Did Claire call you?'

She smiled. 'We're going to meet up and put our breasts together.'

Stone rolled his eyes. 'For pity's sake, is nothing sacred?'

She laughed and gave him a light touch on the arm. 'Thanks.'

And, back to business.

'What's this about CCTV and ANPR?' Mike held up a scribbled sticky note from his pile.

'We're just starting to make some headway.'

They were about to start the morning briefing when Reg Walters poked his head into the incident room and looked over to Stone. 'Mike, when you've got a minute.'

Stone left Bolton to start the briefing. She gave him a surprised look. 'It's time we got you leading from the front more often.'

Stone took Walters into his office and let the briefing get started. 'Is Luke okay?'

'He's doing well.'

'Is he awake?' he asked, as he closed the door.

'Semi-conscious. He's off the critical list and they stopped sedation. Vitals are good, but he's just drugged to the eyeballs and kind of sleeping it off.' Walters took a deep breath and let out a sigh, running both hands through his hair. 'I have something which could be pertinent to your investigation.'

Both men sat down as Walters took out his phone. 'I might have done something a little bit, shall we say, unofficially rule-bending.' Walters leaned forward carving the words out with his strong home counties accent.

'Should I be worried?'

'It's not exactly by the books. But I did get the pages of the book turning.'

'Reg, you are melting my brain with metaphors.'

'Idiom.'

'What?'

'By the book is an idiom, not a...' He stopped, noticing Stone's eyes glazing over. 'Anyway. Look at these photos.'

He moved his chair so they could both view the images at the same time.

'Wouldn't it be easier for you to send these to me?'

'And create a digital record? Come on, Mike, you're smarter than that.'

Stone and Walters went through the images and the pathologist shared his theory about the shapes, types and sizes of the bruises.

'Multiple sources, too.' Reg added.

Stone scratched at his stubbled chin. He felt his chest tighten with a mixture of nausea and anger.

'We need this recorded officially,' Stone said, as he opened a drawer on his desk and rifled around in the mess. It was his "I probably have one in here" drawer. He found a USB drive and handed it to Walters. 'Can you put those images on this drive, so I have an unofficial copy off the grid?'

Reg took the drive and put it in his pocket.

'You said you'd set things in motion?'

Reg sat back in the chair and crossed one leg over the other. A mischievous smile curled his lips like the Grinch. 'I spoke to the head nurse and strongly hinted that she might seem particularly forward-thinking if she contacted the social worker on Luke's case to push the police to get proper photos on the injuries as soon as possible.'

Stone looked puzzled. 'But I would have done that anyway.'

'Ah, but now no smart-arsed lawyer can try and catch you out on the stand by asking what prompted you to do that. If I told you what I know from my photos and you acted on it, you could end up with a huge chunk of evidence thrown out on a technicality of how you became aware of the injuries via an illegal search. Thereby rendering the photo evidence inadmissible.'

Stone sat back and tilted his head. He had to admit that was some rather smart forethought from the pathologist.

'You don't hold lawyers in very high regard, do you?'

Walters shrugged his shoulders. 'Some are fine. Most are money-grabbing wankers more concerned with winning than discovering the truth.'

'Well, thanks for the heads-up, Reg. I'll make a call to have a chit chat with Luke's social worker and make sure they bring up the issue. You know, make them suggest it.'

'Justice, one, loopholes, nil.' It was a rare moment of smug self-satisfaction Stone saw from the pathologist.

'I'll share the idea with the team, but won't mention photos for now. Just observations.'

The two men stepped back out into the incident room and Reg made a quick exit.

'Mr Walters.' Harry opened the door to the incident room to let Reg out.

'Detective Constable Khan. Good to see you, sir.' Reg dressed his face with his usual wide smile as they both stepped out into the corridor.

'How's the boy?'

'He's doing better. Pulling through.'

'Sounded like he got a hell of a beating.' Khan winced at even the thought of it.

'I've just given Mike some information he will no doubt get you to look at soon.'

Khan frowned at him.

Reg held up a resigning hand. 'For reference only. I know they can't be used.' He took his phone out and let Khan have a flick through the photos, watching as his jaw dropped lower and lower to the floor as he explained his thoughts.

'Holy shit.'

'Exactly. Mike's sorting out a SOCO photographer.'

'Good, we're going to need them,' Khan said, quieter, and slightly between gritted teeth. It was enough frustration for Reg to pick up on.

The two men weren't close, but they'd got to know each other a lot more over the past year.

Khan returned his look and his shoulders sagged. Their slow walk came to a stop and he leaned up against the wall. 'I know it's early days, too early to be getting solid leads, but…' he paused and shook his head.

'It's something else when it's kids, isn't it?'

'Not just that. I don't know whether I am making progress. I can't feel it yet.' Khan grunted his frustration.

'Why does progress rest on your shoulders?'

'Okay, we. But even so, I feel like I am trying to hold lentils in my hands.'

Reg gave him a quizzical look.

'Sorry, it's a phrase my mother always used. When I was a kid, I'd help her cook. Just stirring and measuring out ingredients. I'd scoop lentils from the bowl with my chubby little hands and throw them into the giant saucepan. I had to stand on a stool to reach.' Khan let out a quiet laugh with the memory. 'Anyway, I could never get it right. Some would always slip between my fingers and off the side of my hands, bouncing around the top of the stove.'

Reg smiled, nodding at the image of a mother and child together.

'She'd never tell me off.' Harry paused trying to hide a slight lump in his throat. 'She'd smile and say,' he put on an exaggerated Indian accent, 'one day my little boy will grow to be a great man, with great big hands.'

A pause lingered until Reg spoke softly. 'But even now, those big hands still let some lentils slip.'

Harry nodded, eyes fixed in another place, another time, long ago.

'If you'd reached to catch the few, you would have

dropped many more, and the dinner would have been ruined,' Reg mused. 'But dinner was never ruined, was it?'

Harry shook his head.

'Yet you still worry about the lentils you dropped.' Reg turned to face him. 'And now, as the man, with his big hands, you feel like you're struggling to hold all the lentils.'

Harry's nod was soft, barely perceptible.

'So, what was your mother's solution?'

He held out his hands to demonstrate. 'She would cup her hands under mine to catch the ones I dropped.'

The metaphor captured both men for their own reasons.

It was the pathologist who finally broke the silence. 'That's a beautiful memory, Harry. But what is it saying to you now?'

'Oh, I don't know, Reg. I'm being sentimental. And I don't like things slipping from my hands, that's all.'

'You're not that little boy anymore, constable. You do good work catching those falling lentils.'

It dawned on Harry that he'd not spoken about his late mother to anyone for quite some time. There was something about the pathologist that seemed to loosen his mind and feel comfortable. He was a remarkably good listener for someone who spent a lot of time around the bodies that would never speak back to him.

'Mr Walters.'

'Reg, please,' he replied, raising a hand.

'All this reminiscing, I nearly forgot what I was going to ask you anyway. Am I right in thinking you do charity work with the homeless?'

'Yes. I mainly work with children and young people who are or were in care. Many are homeless, sleeping on friends' sofas. Some sleep rough. A lot of them are lost in the gap left by the state that says they are too old for a place that can care for them, but too young to be treated as adults. I guess you could say I try to catch the lentils other people drop.'

'Is that work through your church?'

Reg tapped at his chest. 'I do it from my heart. If the church or the Salvation Army wants to help, and they mostly do, then that's great.'

'I'd like to learn more about what you do.'

'You are welcome to join me any time.'

'This might be a long shot, and I know you're busy, but I want to spend a little more time out and about on this case. There's something we're missing in the story.'

'Like what?'

'Luke and Amelja's connection and relationship. I feel a need to know how and why Amelja came to that end. She can't just be lost as a statistic,' he paused, choosing his words carefully. 'I trust the guv, totally, and know he trusts you. Luke isn't to blame, but I worry pressure is coming from places to scapegoat him.'

'I understand what you're saying, and I'll tell you all I can about Luke if that would help.'

'That would be great, thank you.' Khan smiled. 'I'm planning to do a bit more of a walkabout. Speaking to people. I do it as part of my voluntary work donating food to the homeless. I wondered if you'd like to join me.'

'Sure.' Reg didn't hesitate.

Reg also wanted to feel as though he was contributing more constructively to anything that could help to uncover what led to the tragedy of Friday evening.

He also had a growing feeling of guilt that maybe he could have done something sooner to prevent it.

Chapter 17

'Amelja, wait up,'

As soon as she turned to look for the voice, she regretted it.

Gnome was on the other side of the crossing.

Amelja had arranged to meet Luke at Old Square, the pedestrian area with the Tony Hancock memorial. The square has a long history in the city, transforming to serve many purposes before and after World War Two. In more recent years it became a central feature of the newer corporation street developments, including the Minories, and the sloping Priory Queensway. It functioned as a roundabout on one of the main bus routes cutting through the city centre.

The open plan nature of it made it one of Amelja's favourite places. She could be invisible, blend into the crowd, and feel protected by a steady wall of traffic on all sides.

But now the Gnome was invading it. His Cheshire cat smile twisted his bizarre face with such practised insincerity, it looked more like the earliest Jokers from Batman.

Fear glued Amelja's feet to the ground. She wished

Luke could be there, but he'd gone ahead to try and gather some loose change to get a little food.

'Great to see you again,' Gnome said, standing a little too close for comfort. His smell was an odd mixture of sweat, bad breath and damp. It reminded her of an old shed one of her uncles kept his manure-covered tools in.

'I have to go,' Amelja said, trying to turn away.

He grabbed her arm, just a little too hard. 'What's the rush?'

She snatched her arm free.

'Oh, feisty.'

'I must go.'

Gnome swerved around to block her, a taunting glint in his eye. 'No need to rush. Lucky I bumped into you, in fact.'

'Why?'

'I have a few friends I'm meeting, and I am sure you'd like them.'

'I choose own friends.' She didn't hide her scorn.

'That dirty little twat hasn't been bothering you again, has he?'

She didn't answer. Luke was still nowhere to be seen.

Gnome put his hands on her shoulders, lowering his head to her level, trying to force eye contact. 'If you want me to deal with him, I will.'

She beat his hands away and turned, but he caught up in just two strides, grabbing hard at her coat, and catching some of her hair in his grip. Amelja let out a quiet yelp, not loud enough to be heard over the traffic.

Everyone else just walked right on by, most with heads buried in their phones or suddenly interested by shop window displays.

'Now you're just being rude,' he spat his anger. 'I've promised my friends they could meet you, and I don't break my promises.'

'I don't want to meet your friends.'

A slow, gravelly laugh crept from his throat. 'Oh, but Amelja. You already know one of my friends.'

Amelja's heart pounded. She stared into his eyes. A whole new rush of fear clouded her vision.

But she caught a glimpse of movement behind him.

'Get your fucking hands off her.' Luke's semi-broken voice betrayed the authority he was aiming for. Still, he stood strong, his hand raised and pointing at Gnome.

In one swift movement, Gnome gripped Luke's hand and twisted it over so far, he buckled at the knees. He delivered a blow to Luke's chin, dropping him to the ground.

Amelja grappled with Gnome, but he wrapped his arm around her shoulders and produced a concealed knife from his sleeve. 'One step closer and I swear I'll slice this bitch.' He glared at Luke and checked no one else had noticed the scuffle.

Luke got to his feet, trying to maintain a level of confidence.

A police car approached up the hill.

Gnome's Cheshire grin returned. 'You gonna risk it? Go on.' He dropped the knife right in front of Amelja.

Luke darted to pick it up and stepped back.

Gnome let out a conspiratorial laugh. 'Oh, officer,' he mocked, 'I'm just trying to protect this poor girl.'

'We tell them you lie,' Amelja protested.

'If you like. But only Luke's prints are on the knife.'

Luke hid the knife in his pocket as the Police car passed them at least thirty feet away.

'The knife he's just put in his pocket, ripe for a stop and search.' Gnome reached into his pocket for his phone. 'Now, I've invited some of my friends to our little party.'

Luke looked around but couldn't run, dump the knife, or get help in time. There was no way he would leave Amelja.

Chapter 18

September

'This is PC Pearson, and he's got some CCTV magic that is going to blow your mind.' DS Bolton was sporting a wide grin as she presented the officer to DI Stone.

'High praise, indeed, Mr Pearson,' Stone replied.

Pearson couldn't hide the blushing of his painfully youthful complexion. 'Well, it's all conjecture, really.'

Bolton placed her hands on his shoulders in a mock Boxing coach stance behind her fighter. It could have seemed somewhat inappropriate if the humour was not so evident. 'Nonsense, constable.'

Stone grabbed a chair and tucked himself into the bay. 'What have we got?'

Pearson took a deep breath. 'Right. I was on the CCTV team when I spotted something. It wasn't until I did some digging that I realised it might be important.

Stone watched him click through screens and windows.

'Trawling some footage on Eden Street, based on the timeline, I spotted a black saloon matching the description from the shooting.'

'We weren't sure of the make or model,' Bolton confirmed.

'This car,' Pearson tapped the screen, 'driving towards the camera slightly after the call reporting the injured officer.'

Stone leaned in. 'Any chance of getting that licence plate?'

Pearson zoomed in, making the registration clearer. 'I put the plate through the PNC and the DVLA. Got a hit for the registered owner.'

'Well done, Pearson,' Stone said with a smile. 'Sorry, what's your human name?'

'James, guv. But, there's more.' His eyes didn't leave the screen. 'The registered keeper is Jennifer Wickers. Full licence and insurance.'

Stone looked at Bolton, then back to the PC.

'She lives, with her car, in London.' James paused to scratch his nose. 'I was going to let it go. You know, long shot and all. But I did a nosey and a teeny weeny follow up. I'm not sure if I should have run it by you first.'

Bolton hit him lightly on the head, her hand bouncing on his stiffly gelled hair. 'Quit blithering, Jimbo.'

'Okay. I went back to the PNC and found a crime number for a robbery she reported six months ago. Found me a contact number. So, I called her.'

Stone raised an eyebrow.

'I pitched it vaguely as a follow-up, elimination call. Thing is, she told me her car wasn't in Birmingham on Friday evening. Now, I know guv, you're gonna say this is where it turns out she doesn't know her hubby is off shaggin' some escort in Birmingham, like in the TV crime dramas, when they need a juicy subplot.'

'Where was it?' Stone interrupted.

'In London, guv. Stuck in traffic. I confirmed it with ANPR.'

Stone nodded his head slowly. 'Nice one, James. Cloned car. And clones mean crimes.'

Bolton leaned forward. 'Keep going, Jimbo, you've got him chanting slogans.' She turned to Stone, excited. 'This boy is a bloody genius.'

James clicked again. 'This bit is good. I looked again at the image and noticed the driver. We can't make out their face from the angle, but what is clear is their right arm and shoulder. They were wearing a medium-light-coloured coat. Maybe brown. I reckon that driver is a man.'

Stone squinted and leaned into the screen for a closer look. 'Okay, I'll allow that for now.'

'Working on the theory this is a cloned car, I decided to have a look at other CCTV. I worked with the same time-stamp on cameras in that area, and…' he clicked through several windows until another paused video file came up. 'Wham bam, thank you, mam. Sir.'

The new image from another camera caught a profile of the driver showing a male wearing either a grey or brown coat.

'Bloody hell, James, that's damn good spotting.'

'And, wait, wait,' he held up a finger of promise. 'Next, I went back about thirty minutes to this camera covering the road leading up to the Baxter estate and found our car again, from the rear. Definitely the same car.' He pointed at the screen.

'Holy shit.' Stone's whisper came out louder than he intended.

'A few seconds later, it turns left so I really wanted to get a face.'

'Please tell me you got one.' Stone had his hand on Pearson's shoulder, eyes fixed on the screen.

'Not quite, sorry. But, I did find something really bloody interesting.' He clicked through to a new image. 'Same car shortly before the injury call, on the way to the Baxter estate. You can't see the driver's face because of the reflection on the windscreen, but you can make out his hands and jacket.'

That's when the bomb dropped. This driver's hands were bigger and lined with jewellery.

And the driver's jacket was unmistakably black.

Holy bloody shit.

Stone looked at Pearson, then at Bolton. No one said anything for a few long seconds. 'Buchanan was adamant there was only one guy on his own. One gunman.'

Bolton leaned forward. 'James. Now show him the spooky bit.'

Stone rubbed a hand down his face and scratched at his chin.

'Well, I'd got a bit excited, guv. Scrolling back on that camera, to find when Buchanan came on the scene, I found this car. Recognise it?'

Stone squinted and twisted his head. 'That's the car Luke was found in. When is this?'

Pearson highlighted the clock. 'Arriving barely a minute or so before. Which means our black car was quite deliberately following it.'

Stone rubbed at his forehead as if struggling to process all the information.

'And for my final flourish, although I admit this is an extremely long shot, look at this.'

'More?' Stone put on his best Brian Blessed voice.

The image zoomed in on the driver. The angle of the windscreen and the streetlights also made facial recognition difficult. But what they could see was the lower arms and part of the jacket of the driver.

'I know it's a leap, guv, but doesn't that look suspiciously like the other driver of the black car? I mean, not just the coat but the way he's holding the steering wheel. It's exactly the same.'

They all paused. Waited.

Stone stood and began a slow pace, forehead squeezed with one hand, his other arm conducting an invisible orchestra.

Stone's tone was pained with thought, 'So, what you're suggesting is that we have two drivers. One drives the first car in with the boy, and dumps the car.'

Bolton moved over to the whiteboard and scrawled crude images as if playing charades.

Stone conducted her. 'He's followed in by the second car with the second driver. They are interrupted by Buchanan. Who gets shot. By driver number two.

Bolton joins in. 'But Buchanan only mentioned the one in the black in his report.'

'And a rough description of the black saloon,' Stone continued.

'Which we see being driven away by the first driver, who dumped the first car, and wore the brown coat,' Pearson finished.

'So, who is, and where the hell is our mystery second driver, who arrived in the first car?' Bolton formed it into a question.

A dumfounded pause electrified the air around the three of them.

Pearson shrugged his shoulders. 'Does this mean driver one and two were in cahoots?'

Stone continued the flow of thought. 'If they were, why didn't Buchanan see both, and why didn't they both ensure Luke and Buchanan were dead? Why leave witnesses to a body dump and a police shooting?'

Another pause.

'Boy done good. Right, guv?' Bolton said with a motherly smile.

'Boy done bloody amazing.'

Pearson let out an embarrassed laugh as his face lit up.

'Seriously, James' Stone put a hand on his shoulder. 'That was some damn fine detective work.'

'Nah, I just saw the crumbs and got the nibbles.'

'With munchies like that, I better get you piss-tested for cannabis.' Stone laughed, giving him a firm pat on the shoulder. 'We have a long way to go in this case, but you've just blown open an intriguing door.'

I.N.T.R.I.G...I...U?

'What's the next move?' Bolton asked.

'Firstly, Pearson, run all this past Pete and Harry.'

There was an air of pride emanating from the young PC as he stretched his arms and cracked his knuckles.

Stone walked over to the whiteboard and ushered Bolton to follow.

'We need Buchanan in an interview room.'

'Talk about a curveball,' she replied.

'Sodding boomerang,' Stone said as he scanned his eyes over the crazy sketches. 'Oh, and give Pearson a biscuit.'

'Wow, he did impress you.'

'You can even make it a chocolate one.'

Chapter 19

January
Luke & Amelja

No one saw Luke and Amelja being bundled into the dark blue van. No one even bothered to look. They were bound and gagged as soon as they were out of sight. Black bags were pulled over their heads and they were hunched forward, heads bowed.

Gnome followed them in and closed the door. 'Don't go pissing yourself, now,' he sniggered. His eyes searched for the two other men to join in the joke but it was clear they didn't share his sense of humour.

The van crept through city centre streets, carefully driven so as not to draw attention to itself. They continued to travel towards the southside of Birmingham. Houses got bigger, trees got taller, and roads got wider.

After fifteen minutes, the van pulled off the main road and waited at an entrance gate. There was a pause before a magnetic release freed the gates open and the van continued down a long, sweeping gravel driveway.

The property built a couple of hundred yards back from the main road. It was an expensive property, surrounded by a wrap-around garden bordered with trees, giving ample privacy.

* * *

Luke

Luke's knee knocked with Amelja's as the van finally jolted to a stop. He desperately wanted to say something to reassure. But he had no idea what to say even if he could have. The little he did know about the people Gnome was involved with was terrifying enough. Gnome's role in the outfit seemed to involve finding girls and boys who were easy targets. Usually homeless, or on the street.

Those less likely to be missed.

And more easily groomed.

Desperate for their next meal. Befriended for a while. And then vanished.

Didn't matter which foster home Luke was dumped in, or which so-called carers didn't give a shit, Luke always knew he was on his own. Even the ones who tried still didn't understand. Once you'd had a taste of freedom, the idea of going back to someplace you felt constantly like an outsider wasn't worth it.

Made to live like a second-rate with less belonging than a dog, but all the time having to be grateful because it could all be taken away with a single phone call.

Luke considered himself better off on his own.

Even before the social had taken him away from that twat who couldn't control anything without beating it to shit.

Luke could feel the rage boiling up inside.

Fury. Fury beats fear. Every time. He learnt one night when the old twat had beaten his mum to a pulp for the thousandth time and then turned on Luke.

'Come here, you little shit,' he'd said, spit dribbling down his fat stubbly chin.

He'd reached out to grab Luke by the collar and was about to lift him.

'Dirty little shit, pissin' ya pants like that again. Well, mommy won't do anything, so looks like I'm gonna have to.'

That's when he did it. Luke picked up his fire engine. Not the plastic one. The old metal one his mum found in a charity shop. He'd swung it right into the greasy twat's head. On the side.

On the soft bit.

Then he bit the stinking hand as hard as he could. It smelt of beer and smoke and puke and blood. Made the old twat scream. Bashed him on the head again and again and again with the fire truck.

Then he ran. Got to the front door. Tried to yank it open but the chain was on. The door bounced back out of his hand. He fell back on his bum. Didn't hurt. Turned to see the old twat behind him. Blood pouring down his broken face.

His chest was pounding and pounding and pounding. He was gonna get killed.

Something changed in his head. Like a switch. Fear vanished. Old bloody twat growling about killing him. But he wasn't scared. Just hot. Burning. He was on fire.

Fury.

That night he'd learned what fury was.

He charged at the old man, screaming as loud as he could. Dumb fucking look on the man's face.

Fury drove his fists into the old man. Punching harder than ever before. Harder than he'd punched the boy at school for stealing his chocolate. Harder than he punched a bully for hurting his friend. Harder than he'd punched the wall because he'd been in trouble for punching the bully and that just wasn't fucking fair.

Punched the Old Man in the balls. Watched him fall like a sack of potatoes. Kicked him in the face. Kicked him again. And again.

Shouted at the top of his voice that he was an ugly fat fucker. Fat fucking cunt.

Shouted the whole c-word.

Not him.

His Fury.

Then the door behind him opened. People stormed in. Fury turned him round ready to punch them all. But there was too many of them. Grabbed him. Held him tight. Took him outside in the cold where the world was flashing.

Wrapped him in a red blanket. Someone held him tight. Pounding slowed. Heat settled. Fury went away.

Back into hiding.

But always ready, if it had to be.

He'd learnt to remember.

Fury beats fear.

The night they took him away.

But Luke was older now. He'd had years to learn that his Fury should be kept hidden for the special moments it was truly needed. When there would be no going back.

He'd have to wait for the right moment. Not when tied up, gagged and blindfolded. Fury would be wasted on hopelessness.

* * *

Amelja

The bag snapped off Amelja's head. Her eyes took a few moments to adjust. Luke hunched forward, a few feet away, hands tied behind his back.

They were in an old English house like she'd seen on films and TV shows. Ceilings higher than normal houses, with detailed designs carved into the edges, and around the light in the centre.

Wood panelling covered the walls, and the fireplace was

a marble archway with a thick plinth. The biggest mirror she had ever seen hung above it in a detailed bronze-coloured frame. A pendulum swinging in a golden clock echoed around the silent room.

A figure stood with his back to her, smoking a cigarette. He blew the smoke right into the mirror and it bounced off before spreading around his head.

The man with the cigarette turned and fixed her with a stare. Walking slowly towards her, his eyes crept up and down her body.

She knew his look. Just like teenage boys who always walked around with their hands down the front of their trousers, squeezing themselves and licking their lips.

But this was no boy.

It was a man in expensive clothes. He moved closer and paused before taking another drag on his cigarette, blowing the smoke out the side of his mouth.

He reached a hand up to touch her hair, staring into her eyes.

Without moving his glare, he clicked his fingers. The larger of the men from the van raised his arm and smashed the back of his hand into the side of Luke's head, sending him crashing to the floor.

Amelja let out a pained yelp, calling out Luke's name. The big man waited for a nodded instruction, and then gave Luke a sharp kick in the chest.

'Please, don't hurt him,' Amelja tried to plead.

'If you did as I told you, I wouldn't have to.' The smoking man took another drag, sucking air in through his teeth. 'Amelja.'

Tears rolled down her face. She knew this man meant everything he said.

Because she knew this man.

Ever since he'd brought her from Albania, posing as her uncle. She had managed to escape when they'd been out in the open. She made herself invisible and vanished into the crowds.

But not this time. She couldn't lash out or run. Where would she run to? And she couldn't leave Luke. He'd been right. She should have run as soon as she saw that Gnome. Disgusting creature, just as Luke warned.

Amelja looked into the man's eyes and saw the darkness. The hate.

No glimmer of hope.

Just hate and the Devil.

* * *

Nesim Kapllani nodded at the stocky man to pick Luke up after the girl had been taken away. The black bag was ripped from his head, and he winced at the sharp pain. Blood matted his hair and ran down his jawline.

His eyes blinked at the brightness in the room.

Kapllani leaned in too close. 'Where is girl now?'

Luke dropped his eyes.

'You think she is girlfriend?'

Kapllani noticed the boy's focus glance over his shoulder to where Gnome was leaning up against the wall.

'Ah, yes. You could try and lie. If you think it help. But my associate remind you why lying is bad.'

Kapllani nodded at the stocky man, who rose an arm. It swung but Kapllani raised his hand just in time to stop the fat backhand from crashing into Luke's skull again. It was like watching a skilled puppet master. Luke's body shuddered in anticipation.

'I hope we clear,' Kapllani said, taking another drag from his cigarette. 'So, Amelja. She is girlfriend?'

Luke nodded with a cautious reluctance.

'Ha.' Kapllani let out a laugh. 'Good choice. She good piece of pussy. Yes?'

Luke's face reddened.

'Don't say you not felt it yet. Call her girlfriend but not

fucked her yet?'

Kapllani sucked so hard on the cigarette filter they could hear the crackle of tobacco leaves burning. He hissed the smoke deep into his lungs, held it a moment, then blew the smoke into Luke's face.

'You are just silly boy. Not man. In Albania, you could fuck girl. Not problem. Not like stupid United Kingdom.' His upper lip curled as he said the name of the country.

Kapllani reached into his pocket and took out a metal lighter, flicking it open in one practised motion. The flame danced so close to Luke's face he could feel its heat. He tried to move his head back, but Kapllani shot a look at the man behind, and Luke soon felt a hand clasp the back of his head.

Kapllani waved the flame slowly side to side. He reached into his pocket and brought out a silver cigarette case, flicking it open with one hand. The stocky man took two cigarettes out and held them up. Kapllani took one, holding it up to Luke's face.

The whole thing was playing out like a bizarre magic trick or double act.

'Smoke?'

Luke shook his head as much as he could.

'I teach you. Man to man.' He took hold of the tape over Luke's mouth and ripped it off in one go, making him grimace at the burn. Kapllani took the cigarette and poked it between Luke's lips. He touched the tip with the flame. 'Suck. Boy.' The cigarette caught and Luke's jaw stiffened. It was clear Luke had smoked before.

Kapllani put the second cigarette in his own mouth and lit it slowly, gracefully before snapping the lighter away.

'See, I could tell you know how to suck.' He snarled. 'Now, you smoke. Smoke and fuck. I make you into man.' Kapllani let out a loud, cracking laugh. 'Next thing you know, we get you drink beer also. Beer, Smoke, Fuck. Proper British piece of shit.'

Kapllani saw a change in Luke's eyes. 'You understand your girlfriend belong to me. I brought from Albania. She run away. But you help find her.' He smiled.

Luke's nostrils flared, eyebrows squeezed together.

'You think no?'

Kapllani said something in Albanian that Luke didn't understand. 'Cut on your head. Unfortunate. I give my associate chance to fix.'

Without warning, Luke felt the searing heat burning his head. The pain engulfed his entire skull, behind his eyes, and shot down his neck. His whole body shuddered. He tried to thrash away but the man behind him kept a vice-like grip on his head.

Tears exploded from Luke's eyes at the strength of the pain, and his legs threatened to give way.

Just like his bladder already had.

Kapllani turned away. 'We clear?' Kapllani waited. 'You tried to steal from me. So now, you belong to me.'

* * *

Luke woke in a dark room. His head throbbed, and a burning pain focused on one side.

He reached up to touch it, only then realising his hands were no longer tied. A dressing had been stuck roughly to the wound.

Who were these sick people? It wasn't the first time he'd had that experience, but it had been quite a few years. Burns weren't a pain easily forgotten.

What he couldn't remember at all was how he ended up in a bed. His body clock sensed that time had passed, but he didn't know how much. He could make out a slither of light from under the door. As his eyes adjusted, he noticed the curtains up to his left.

Struggling to his feet, he moved the curtain to peer out the window, noticing the old, wooden frames. The room overlooked the back of the property. It was dark outside, but he could just make out a large garden several paces beyond the flat roof below his window. A thought crossed his mind. But another one stopped him.

Amelja.

Moonlight illuminated the room in a soft, blue-white hue, revealing a sink in the corner to the right. An old wardrobe stood not far from that.

Luke looked inside the wardrobe. It was filled with a range of expensive-looking, fashionable clothing and footwear.

He moved over to the bedroom door, placing his ear against it, barely making out the sounds of people talking and laughing. His eyes crept down to the handle, but he was in two minds whether to try. For all he knew, someone could be guarding the room. Or it could be locked. Either way, he had no idea what might happen if he was discovered trying to leave the room.

But he remembered part of an old quote he'd read somewhere. Doing nothing would achieve nothing. His trainers were on the floor at the foot of the bed. But opportunities should never be missed. He went back to the wardrobe and found a pair of pricey running trainers and a dark-coloured hoody.

Returning to the door, he put one hand up to steady it in case it opened. He turned the handle.

It was open.

After a few seconds, he peered out onto the landing and the voices got slightly louder, but they were definitely from downstairs.

Luke could see there was another room to his right and one to his left. Three more doors were spaced out along the wall in front of him.

He stepped out onto the landing and approached the top of the stairs. The red carpet felt softer than any he'd ever walked on.

Sounds of a man groaning with exertion came from a room to his right, and a lock clicked further down the landing. The door opened with a plume of steam and a woman stepped out in a silk dressing gown which did nothing for her modesty.

The first door opened, and a man stood in the doorway doing up the fly on his trousers. They looked set to burst away from his despicably spherical body.

'Who the fuck are you?' the fat man snarled.

Luke looked from the man to the woman, who yelped at the sight of him standing there.

'Where you think you go, boy?' the fat man said.

Luke turned to look at him.

The man's face creased into an ugly mass of flaps resembling a giant pug.

The thug from the van appeared at the top of the stairs and marched over to Luke. There was a short pause between everyone there as if they were caught in a tableau entitled "Absurdity." Finally, Luke was guided forcibly down the staircase to the ground floor hallway.

It was a large expanse of black and white marble, probably the size of the footprint of most people's whole house. Rooms branched off it in all directions, and the large main front door sat proudly in the centre.

Luke felt a stern shove to his back pushing him in the direction of the voices.

Kapllani appeared, holding a cut crystal glass with a golden rich spirit sloshing around.

'Ah, our new recruit has awoken. Come, come, dear boy. I introduce you to our friends.' He held out an arm to lead Luke into the room.

Luke's breath caught in his throat as he felt the pincer grip of Kapllani's fingers digging into his shoulders.

Amelja was standing in the centre wearing a single piece white nightie that looked like something from the Victorian era. Luke was torn between seeing a beautiful angel with long, dark brown hair, and the disgust of how she was being paraded in front of an audience of lurid men. They were grotesque creatures sucking on fat cigars, grinning like children in a sweetie shop, excited by what they were going to buy and enjoy.

But these men all had another look about them.

Power.

'Gentleman,' Kapllani's voice boomed, proudly, 'consider this a bonus.'

Luke stood next to Amelja. They both knew not to look at each other. It was all Luke could do to keep his eyes focused on the floor. But he could still feel the eyes leering all over him. He knew the look. What it meant.

And what those eyes were doing as they looked at him and Amelja.

Kapllani clapped his hands together. What do you say, gentleman? Are we all up for something special?

Chapter 20

September

DC Paul Buchanan tugged at his collar for the third time in as many minutes. He ran his fingers through his bristly hair. But he didn't fool either detective sitting the other side of the desk, who both saw his attempt to hide wiping away the sweat on his forehead.

He was only just into his thirties, but the events of the weekend had added several years to his greyed pallor. Despite DS Bolton's offer to meet him at home, he'd opted to go to the station to clarify details from his report on Friday evening.

'I don't know what else you want me to say.' Buchanan shrugged his shoulders with a smile.

The smile didn't reach his eyes. A split-second curl of his top lip gave away a glimpse of resentment. If looking nonplussed and casual was the intention, the result was more of a petulant teenager who thought he'd outsmarted his parents.

DI Stone mirrored the shrug, but held it up, mocking it. 'All we want are facts, Paul. Nothing more.' He paused. 'Nothing less.'

'I'm not hiding anything, sir.'

'Paul,' Bolton sat at ninety degrees leaning up against the wall, her right elbow poised on the back of the chair.

'Help me visualise the situation.'

Buchanan moved his head first, but his eyes stayed with Stone for half a second too long.

'Where did you stop your car in relation to the black saloon?'

'Behind. Like I said.'

'How far behind?'

His sigh was frustrated. 'Eight, maybe ten feet.'

'And you couldn't see the car the boy was in from where you parked?'

'It was behind the wall,' the volume and pitch in his voice were rising, revealing his natural Brummie tone.

'Did you talk to him?' Bolton leaned forward.

'He was barely alive.'

'The gunman, not the boy.'

'No. Yes, I mean, of course, I spoke to him.'

Stone and Bolton looked at each other, before both giving Buchanan a stare.

'I asked for directions.'

Stone and Bolton both sniggered and broke out into a short laugh. They could see him getting more riled. Sooner or later, he'd trip over his lies.

Stone sat back. 'I think if any cop tried that one on me, I'd shoot him, too.' He let a pause hang for a moment. 'Did you see the other guy at all?'

Buchanan tried his best "confused" expression.

Yes, that's right Mr Buchanan. We know about the other guy.

'What other guy?'

'You are sure there was no one else there?' Stone pressed. 'A passenger in the black saloon, perhaps. Maybe the driver of the other car.'

'If there was, I didn't see him.'

Bolton through a mock incredulous look. 'Or her?'

'Him, her, whatever. Look, this is beginning to sound like an interrogation.'

Stone raised his hands in submission. 'Just checking the facts.'

'I don't know, guv,' Bolton interrupted. 'I'm a bit unhappy about the misogyny. He could have just as easily not seen a woman as he could have not seen a man.'

Stone raised his eyebrows at Buchanan. 'She's got a point.'

'Misogyny?' Buchanan gasped.

'A bit like sexism.'

'Don't patronise me.'

'Sir.' Stone's tone darkened. 'Don't patronise me. Sir. No one in here has dropped rank, constable. If I ask you a question, I expect a straight answer. It's unfortunate about your injury, but I know you're not telling me everything.'

Buchanan turned his head away, biting his bottom lip.

'We've given you the courtesy of allowing this chat without a cautioned interview.'

Stone stood, leaned on the back of his chair, and brought his head down to the centre of the small black table separating them. Buchanan might have been taller when he was standing, but he didn't command the same amount of space.

'Now I am going to ask you what my team asked me. Why does a gunman shoot a cop but leave him alive? Might as well stick one in his head. Leave no witness.'

Stone paused to let the thought sink in.

'And CCTV shows the two cars arrived pretty close in time. Then you happen to be in the area and drop in. One night, three cars, within a few minutes. That's one bloody huge coincidence for such an off-the-track industrial estate.' He dropped his voice almost to a whisper. 'Three cars, two drivers. Something doesn't add up.'

Buchanan glanced up at him, then darted his eyes to Bolton, and away again.

Stone leaned in closer. 'CCTV also shows us that within minutes of this incident, that black saloon you so helpfully described was being driven by someone not matching the description you gave us of the original driver and gunman.'

Stone paused.

Bolton leaned forward. 'The second man, or woman, who seems to have been forgotten in your account.'

Buchanan spoke through gritted teeth. 'I came in today in good will, despite my injury. And you are treating me like one of the scum.' The sweat had returned to his forehead. 'I'm the fucking victim here. Sir. I got shot just trying to do my job. And this is the thanks I get?'

Stone straightened up. 'What do you want? A commendation? Try the basic principle of telling the fucking truth, first.' He turned away, walked over to the door and swung it open. 'Constable Buchanan, consider yourself suspended from all duties, until further notice. Now, get out of my sight.'

Buchanan looked at Bolton. There was a nervous half-smile and a look of incredulity in his eyes. But Bolton didn't bite. He pushed his chair back and attempted to stand with defiance, but even the petulant teenager had been reduced to a stroppy toddler as he tried to march from the room.

'One more thing,' Stone had to stifle his amusement as a flash of Columbo bounced across his mind. 'I strongly advise you to contact your union rep for the interview under caution.'

Buchanan turned and walked away.

Stone let out a long, deep sigh. 'Well, that was…'

I.N.T.I.R, um.

'Intriguing.' He raised his eyebrows at Bolton.

'Bloody good fun, though,' she said, with a mischievous grin. 'You don't think we played all our cards too soon?'

'He's rattled. Now he knows we know he's a liar. He'll have to 'fess-up.'

'Or lawyer up.'

Stone nodded. 'Either that, or he's forced to use the third option.'

Bolton frowned at him.

But Stone merely patted his chest lightly. That was a card he was keeping hold of for the time being, even from his most trusted colleagues.

Chapter 21

Reg Walters and DC Khan spent nearly two hours walking around the city centre talking to rough sleepers, giving them food, simple warming clothing, and advice on where to go for more support.

They ended up at the traffic island with the Tony Hancock statue. Harry paused for a moment and looked quizzically at Reg.

'I've been wondering. Where did Luke come from? I mean before all this happened.'

'I don't know his whole history, but he'd been in and out of care for years. He'd run away more times than anyone could chase him, and fallen through more nets than have even tried to catch him.' Reg shook his head.

'I have to confess, Reg, I don't understand how it can happen. Surely, if needs be, you just lock them in a bloody cupboard for his own protection.'

'Or Police cell?'

'Touché.'

Reg smiled at the idea. 'I've been tempted.'

'Sorry, don't get me wrong. I'm not blaming you or saying it's your responsibility alone.'

'No, I know what you mean. But I am an adult to whom he turns. Repeatedly. And I try each time to engage with him. Persuade him. Thing is, for all the policies and procedures in place, written by people who never actually

137

have to deliver them, there just aren't the resources available.'

'Too many lentils, not enough hands?'

Reg let out a long sigh. 'Plenty of hands, my friend. Just too many fingers in too few oversized pies, at meals where only the fattest people are invited.'

Harry smiled at Reg. 'Did you ever meet the girl?'

'No, sadly. He told me about her, and I saw the effect she'd had on him. But the first time I met her was...'

Reg couldn't bring himself to say it.

Khan knew not to push it and the two men walked in silence for a few contemplative minutes. They headed down Corporation Street, turning to follow the road down to the same place Khan had introduced Stone Mr Freeman a couple of nights before.

The evening had been a typically quiet Monday after the rush hour footfall had cleared. The cloudless sky gave no warming carpet and a bitter air had dropped like a cold slab. A disturbance outside fast-food outlets caught Khan's attention, and he wasn't surprised to see who one of the men was. This time he appeared to be taking on a tired-looking old woman.

'Come on Reg, I'll introduce you to someone.'

'Who?'

'You'll see.'

Harry raised his hands, smiled, and adorned his most placatory mediator voice. 'Now, what's going on here?'

The dishevelled old woman appeared to have the upper hand.

'Crazy woman,' Freeman growled.

'Let's all calm down, shall we?' The old woman was ranting and flailing her arms around, gripping her head. She didn't seem to be saying anything that made sense.

'Iz-toonaah. Toonah, iz-toonah,' she gesticulated, then placed her palms together in prayer.

'What the hell is going on here?' Harry pleaded

with Freeman, raising his shoulders much like the classic Hollywood Italian pleading with his mother for overcooking the pasta.

Freeman's eyes lit up, believing he had an ally. Until the woman ran at him again and he batted her arms away. But he pushed her too hard, and she fell back. Had it not been for Reg's feet, she would have hit the concrete.

Harry fronted up to Freeman and ushered him away. 'That's enough. Back off.'

'She attacked me.'

'Back away, sir.'

'You saw it.'

'I saw you push an old lady to the ground.'

'Oh, I get it. You arrest the black man.' He laid on a strong Jamaican accent.

DC Khan responded with his strongest Indian accent. 'Don't you start on me with your racism bullshit.' It was met with a stunned look, just long enough to knock the fire out of him and diffuse the situation.

Reg reached down to help the woman up, but she flailed at him, ranting her bizarre nonsense words.

'Come on,' Reg tried to placate her, 'here, come and sit down.' She was in a bad state. Her clothes were an array of mismatched brown, green and grey. Gloves without fingers barely covered her arthritic hands, which she used to rhythmically scrape at her tangled grey hair. Her head was squashed into an old woollen cap over a tightly wrapped cloth somewhere between a bandanna and hijab. Both had seen better days.

Reg looked back over to Freeman. 'Do you know her?'

'Everyone does. You aks anyone around here.'

Reg and Harry caught each other's eye for a moment, both as lost as each other.

'You can't go pushing old ladies over, no matter what.' Harry spread his hands as if to plead. 'You're a sensible, worldly man. A man of God. Whatever you desire for men to do to you…'

'You shall also do to them,' Freeman finished. 'Matthew, seven, twelve.'

'Exactly, and the last thing I want to do unto you is arrest you.'

His eyes settled from the tightened anger as he scratched at his sandpaper chin. 'She totters about the place like even the Devil himself has had his fill with her.' There was more pity than cruelty in the man's voice. 'See it in her eyes. Her soul is twisted, crushed, blown away by the cold winds an age ago.' He let out a deflating sigh. 'Only time I see her look or sound human, when I hear her sing or cry.'

Reg looked at him. 'Excuse me, sir, but do you understand what it is she's trying to say?'

Freeman shot Khan a glance, his eye-widening as he nods towards Reg and whispers. 'Who's the toff? What you done with the other guy?'

Khan rolled his eyes.

Freeman turned back to Reg, attempting to match his accent. 'No one knows, dear fellow. But I tell you, all her iz-toonah,' he mocked the woman, 'got folk thinking she's ranting about tuna fish all the damn time.'

Khan looked back at the woman for a moment. 'What do you think she means?'

'Buggered if I know. 'Scuse the French. Maybe she just really likes fish.'

'What set her off tonight?'

Freeman's mouth curled down as he shook his head. 'No idea. She's been out and around a lot this week. And louder, too. Used to just ramble to herself, but she just been…different.'

'How so?'

'Like she's trying to tell us something. Warn us.' Freeman softened, his figure sagged, and his eyes began the water over. 'God bless her soul, she probably is missing a marble or two. But that's fear in them eyes.' His voice cracked slightly. The man appeared to genuinely feel pain for her. He spoke with quiet pity, and eyes gathering just a few more lines. 'Fear and sadness.'

Khan followed the man's eyes and saw what he meant. 'Remember the arrangement that nice Mr Stone made for you? At the chippy? Get yourself something to eat.' He smiled. 'Any problem, this'll sort it.' He slid the man a five-pound note.

'No, no, stay sat down,' Reg continued his battle with the woman.

Khan walked back over. 'Got anything from her, Reg.'

'I know one thing,' he said. 'I've had cadavers who…'

'Don't, Reg. Don't go there.'

Reg's smile curled his face with mischief. 'Can't get any sense out of her, though.'

Khan took out his phone. 'Let's try something.' He flicked through to the photos of Luke and Amelja.

'Oh, come on, old boy. Do you really think it's worth it? Or appropriate? What do you expect her to say?'

The woman didn't respond to Luke's picture, but her eyes fixed on the screen when she saw Amelja. She drew her hands to her mouth and mumbled in another language.

'You know her? Have you seen this girl?'

The woman looked up at him, then at reg, her eyes glistening. One of her hands reached out for the phone, but with a slow tenderness with the back of her fingers as if to stroke the girl's hair or cheek.

'You know her?'

The woman nodded 'I see.' She tapped at the screen.

'Amelja.' He pointed again.

The woman frowned, and looked at him, waving a finger to correct him. 'Ammeel-ya.' She sighed. Her voice softened as she looked at the picture again, a tear rolling down her cheek. 'Amelja.'

'When did you…'

'I see her. Gone. Gone.' The tears ran and a sob engulfed

her as she turned away.

Reg stood and scratched at his head. 'What do we do with that?'

'I don't know.' He shuffled for a moment. 'We can't just leave her here. She looks really unwell, Reg.'

'I agree. I'll take a picture and send it to some people I know. They do some outreach work.'

The temperature had dropped several degrees over the hour and was feeling like it would be falling throughout the night.

'I think it's time we called it a night, Reg,' Harry said, his voice quietened by an edge of regret.

The pathologist nodded. 'You want a lift home?'

'No, that's okay, thanks. I'll grab a black cab, after diving into one of these fine culinary outlets.'

'Well, it's been a pleasure, Harry.'

The men parted for the evening, Reg walking up Bull Street, and Harry going to get a quick fix to devour before getting home.

As he stepped out into the cold again, hot food in hand, he crossed over to the taxi rank. He gave a nod to the driver at the front of the line of black cabs waiting in the bay.

The driver nodded back, and Harry climbed inside. Harry sent his wife a text to say he was on the way home before sitting back to watch the city glide by.

There was something about the woman's reaction to Amelja's photograph that bothered him. He knew she could easily have said nothing of significance, but his gut felt uneasy about dismissing it entirely. Recalling what she had said, "I see her. Gone" kept running circles around his head.

He snapped out of his thoughts when the taxi pulled up outside his house. Paying the driver with a card, he got out on the driver's side with his phone still in his hand, and a thought struck him.

'Before you shoot off,' Harry said, 'I wonder if you could help me with something.' He took out his ID to show the driver. 'Don't worry, your driving was excellent.' It hadn't been, but flattery almost always built rapport.

Harry opened his phone to the pictures again. 'Have you seen either of these two before? Maybe seen them around town. Even if you have driven them. I know it's a long shot, but you never know.' He shrugged his shoulders.

The driver looked, but his cheeks wobbled with the shake of his head. 'No, never seen them,' the driver replied, shrugging his shoulder. 'Sorry.'

But Harry saw recognition in his eyes. 'You're sure? Have another look, sir. Really, even the slightest thing might help.'

'No, sorry. Is that all, officer? I should be going.'

'Yes, yes. Thanks anyway.'

Harry let the driver pull away and do a U-turn on the road to head back towards the city centre. He also saw the glance from the driver, his eyes much darker than when he'd been picked up.

That's why Harry had been fast enough to snap a picture of the licence plate.

Chapter 22

The dark ceiling was trying to spin round but kept bouncing back like an old-style dial phone each time he blinked. It was a nauseating experience.

He turned his head to the side.

Wardrobe.

Sink.

Same room, like before?

The day before, or just earlier?

Time was blurred.

Luke tried to get his bearings and attempted to sit up, counting to three and heaving his body round in one motion.

The heaving from his stomach was so intense, when he tried to stand to reach the sink in time, his legs buckled.

He collapsed back onto the bed with pain coming from where it should never be. A sense of panic was building. The last thing he could remember clearly was being walked into the big room with all the men and…

Amelja.

Where was she?

Luke squeezed his eyes shut and rubbed them with the heels of his hands, desperate to recall anything. He tried standing again but nausea and dizziness dragged him back down to the bed. After a few deep breaths, he managed to calm his body enough to stand, realising just in time to drag a sheet with him to protect his modesty.

For a few moments he felt his breathing shudder, his lip curl over his chin, and he wept. He couldn't remember the last time he'd cried in that way. Feeling like a helpless, lost little boy, waking from a terrifying nightmare he couldn't remember, but could still feel. All he wanted to do was to call out for help.

After half a minute, he rubbed at his eyes, surprised to feel how many tears had flooded out. He even had to wipe his nose but ended up with a long line of mucus down his bare arm, rather than into a sleeve.

The ridiculousness of that moment made him snigger and smile as he tried to open his mouth. But cracked lips and a nose filled with burning bile stopped him.

He needed water.

Taking more care for the second attempt, he rolled over and onto his feet and stood with one hand using the wall to keep steady.

There was no glass at the sink, which was already coated in vomit. The smell made him gag and convulse.

Cupping his hand to scoop the water, he drank and splashed his face, trying to wake up.

A key rattled in the door and the handle moved. Luke retreated to the bed, clutching the cover as the door opened.

A figure took half a step into the room. It was one of the men that bundled him into the van with Amelja. But it wasn't the violent, stocky one. This man was more reserved. He walked over to the bed and crouched down to look Luke right in the eyes. Then he dropped a two-litre bottle of water on the bed.

'Drink that. Slowly. Don't down it, you'll chuck it back up.' His voice was too quiet, barely above a whisper. He dropped a couple of fruity breakfast bars on the bed. 'Get them down you. Blood sugars will be low. But get dressed. You're wanted downstairs. Ten minutes. No pissing around.'

'I need a shower first.' Luke replied, dryly, feeling the roughness in his throat.

Frustration crept into his voice. 'Just do as you're told, okay? Don't piss them off.'

The man waited for a moment to see that Luke had got the point.

By the time Luke had dressed and made his way down to the ground floor, he caught the unmistakable smell of bacon crisping in a grill.

The man who'd brought him the water was standing to the right. He took out a packet of cigarettes and held one to Luke, nodding at him to take it. Confused, but thinking compliance was probably the best course of action, Luke took it and carried on walking into the room he'd been taken to the night before.

His eye was drawn to the large chandelier hanging in the centre which glistened in the morning sunlight. The entire room seemed almost twice the size.

Luke tried to work out if he should stay standing or sit down. He noticed a frail figure hunched over in the corner of the large sofa.

'Amelja?' Luke managed a raspy whisper.

She didn't respond.

He looked over his shoulder to check he hadn't drawn anyone else's attention. 'Amelja, it's me.'

Her hair was tucked inside an oversized red jumper, and she seemed engulfed by oversized blue jeans.

Luke moved closer and reached out to touch her on the shoulder but stopped when he saw her shudder.

'Amelja? It's me.'

A few seconds passed and she turned her head to look at him with one eye.

One red, puffy, terrified eye.

And a flash of anger.

'Ah, it is Luke. Once, a boy. Now, the man.' Kapllani's arms were outstretched like a ringmaster as he walked over to Luke, inhaling deeply. 'You still stink of alcohol. English drink a lot. But can handle little.'

He exhaled smoke into Luke's face.

'But you handle, how we say?' He mocked a quizzical look. 'Quite rough. Not appreciate beauty.' He paused to let the confusion build in Luke's eyes. 'Surely you remember?'

The fearful doubt written across Luke's face made Kapllani grin.

'Sit.' The command was sudden.

Luke sat on the sofa but kept his distance from Amelja. Why was she so terrified at the sight of him?

Kapllani held a smartphone out in front of him.

'Watch. Now you are a fucking film star.' Kapllani announced it with reverence.

Luke's hand shook as he took the phone, the video already playing.

It only took a few seconds, but it was clear. The noise. The picture.

The violence.

He doubled over, dropping the phone to the floor.

Kapllani laughed as he crouched down to pick up the phone and move right next to Luke's face. 'Video show how rough you get.'

Luke shook his head. 'No, I didn't do that.'

'Yes, boy. Yes, you did. All here. You want to watch whole thing?'

Luke shook his head, tears beginning to flood his eyes.

'We could put it on big screen if you like.'

Luke wanted to crawl away from the man whose hot breath stank of cigarettes and greasy bacon, mixed in with too much sickening aftershave.

'Your porn movie show how you treat nice girl like whore. People pay good money for this.' He stopped to take a drag from a cigarette that was almost burnt out. 'Girl, she not say much, but try scream "no" a lot.'

Luke was breathless with disbelief.

'You want me to keep your dirty secret?'

Luke looked at him.

The man produced his cigarette case again and gave one to Luke. He placed it between his shaking fingers and flicked his lighter open.

Something clicked into place in Luke's head. He lifted the cigarette to his lips and let the man bring the flame to it as he sucked in the air.

'Good English. You fuck, then you suck.' His laugh was maniacal. 'I leave you alone with your girlfriend now. Want breakfast? You like bacon, yes? I get you some.'

Kapllani left the room with the man standing just outside to keep an eye on them.

Luke stayed on the floor shaking for a moment, taking another drag on the cigarette. His mind was still blank on the night before.

But the video was clear.

And was it. The end. He had no idea who those people were, but why him? Why Amelja?

He sat up and let his head steady before moving over to the fireplace. An enormous mirror hung above it, but he avoided his reflection. Something dark and hot stirred inside him. He knew what it meant.

When all is lost, and there is no escape, don't be afraid.

Fury beats fear.

Chapter 23

Chief Superintendent Carter winced as she scanned across the incident room whiteboard. DI Stone noticed her from his office. She usually only came into the incident room to deliver bad news or to hunt him down.

Something seemed different, and Stone couldn't put his finger on it. He always reported up to DCI Palmers and CS Carter. But he couldn't help the little voice over his shoulder telling him to keep an eye on her.

Getting paranoid. This is stupid.

Finally, Stone stood from his desk. 'Good to see you here.'

Her sideways glance and raised eyebrow was a reminder that she also had a bullshit radar. She held out a piece of paper without looking at him.

'DNA results. A match has come up.'

He read the report slowly, jaw lowering by the time Carter turned to him.

'Tell me about Amelia, Mike. What was really going on with her?'

'How has this match even been made? Why was the comparison even done?'

'All that matters is what it tells us.'

His expression darkened as he read again that DNA samples taken from Luke, the victim currently in hospital, matched the DNA collected from the rape kit started on Amelja in January that year.

DS Bolton walked over to join them. She gave Carter a respectful nod.

'A new development?'

Carter folded her arms and straightened her back. 'We need to ask ourselves some serious questions.'

'Because all we've been doing so far is having a laugh?'

Carter gave Bolton a steely look, but Stone swallowed a snigger trying to escape.

'What exactly was the nature of the relationship between Luke and Amelja?' Carter continued.

Stone handed the results to Bolton. 'Boyfriend and girlfriend.'

Carter took a deep breath. 'You saw her in January, sergeant. Was she alone?'

Bolton nodded slowly as she read the results twice.

'On her own, after having been raped, then running away from the hospital. What kind of boyfriend was he?'

'You're suggesting there are two ways to look at this. Either Luke is a victim of abuse, or he's implicated in her rape.' DI Stone watched Carter carefully.

Carter's eyebrows raised. 'A bit bloody more than implication.'

'You can't be serious?' Stone retorted.

'Perhaps only statutory rape, but still…'

Bolton folded her arms. 'I saw the state she was in. It would be hard to argue statutory to the CPS given the physical injuries. You'd have to either go for rape or not at all.'

Stone didn't hide his incredulity. 'Luke's a victim.'

Carter raised her voice. 'And yet the evidence could be suggesting...'

'DNA shows they had unprotected sex. Pathology

shows more than one sexual attack. The space between is called reasonable doubt.'

'Don't condescend me, inspector,' Carter barked back.

DI Stone nodded to his office and all three took the conversation behind closed doors.

'All I am saying,' Stone tried to lower his voice, hands placed firmly on his hips, 'if we go in all guns blazing, even a junior defence clerk could tear a rape case to pieces.'

Bolton looked at Stone. Part of her knew how important it was not to ignore evidence of sexual assault. She'd seen the state Amelja was in back in January. She'd also been the last to look here in the eyes.

Carter leaned on Stone's desk. 'You're defending him?'

'I'm bloody protecting innocence until proven guilty, yes. He's not even a suspect.'

'Maybe he needs to be.'

'If he raped her, why did their relationship apparently gain strength after?'

'Care to assist, sergeant?' Carter raised her eyebrows at Bolton.

'Because I'm a woman?'

'Because you're a detective. And you have seen the evidence.'

Bolton looked at Stone, who was pacing, clearly trying to avoid an argument. 'I agree with Mike. This is a DNA match. That doesn't necessarily make it evidence of an offence on Luke's part. Especially out of context.' Bolton didn't want to share Amelja's final words in case they hadn't been filed.

'What context?' Carter snapped.

'Take the two necklaces, and Reg Walters' statements.'

Carter cleared her throat and sat on the edge of Stone's desk as she brushed her hair back. 'We need to consider him a suspect for the rape. Gifts? Come on, you know how grooming works. At the very least, the boy needs to be classified as a person of interest. I want you to pursue that angle at the same time as trying to establish what happened to him.'

Stone raised a hand to rub at his temple and forehead, closing his eyes. 'Just to be clear, your agenda is that he raped Amelja, then groomed her well enough to bring a child to term, then got beaten up, and now we blame him for it all?'

'Don't be so bloody obtuse. Especially not with such an insubordinate tone.'

Stone held up his hands. 'No, no, you've given your orders. When Luke is fit enough, we'll interview him.'

'And I don't think it is appropriate that Dr Walters' be your primary source of evidence on the boy.'

Bolton threw an arm up as she turned away.

Stone moved between the two women. 'Fair enough.' He kept his voice flat enough to get between his gritted teeth. 'What if this whole thing is far bigger than we even thought? Bigger than Luke, Amelja, Buchanan.'

'Buchanan?' Carter frowned. It was her turn to be wrong-footed.

'Yes. I am afraid to say, after our initial debriefing, I had to suspend him from duty pending further inquiries.'

'Playing a bit above your paygrade, Mike. When were you going to tell me about this?'

'I cleared it all through DCI Palmers.'

Carter's eyes narrowed. 'Well, I'll check with him, of course. But why is he suspended?'

'Because he's lying about the events on Friday evening. And we can't have insubordination, can we?'

It was Bolton's turn to hide a snigger.

'He was injured in the line of duty, Mike. I think some leniency might be allowed as a matter of professional courtesy.' Carter looked deep into Stone's eyes, and there was a flicker of anger hiding somewhere in their darkness.

'Look at everything happening on one night.' Stone moved round to his chair and sat down. 'When you consider the firearms element, this isn't just petty criminals or wayward teenagers. It's not cops and robbers. Buchanan is picking the wrong time to tell lies or, in the best-case scenario, get things a little blurry.'

'I don't think we have enough to bring ROCU in yet.'

The Regional Organised Crime Unit was a collaboration between West Midlands, West Mercia, Staffordshire and Warwickshire police. Their remit was the most complex crime and criminal outfits across all regions. In one sense, it was supposed to be strategic, but most saw through the politics to a fine piece of cost-cutting at the frontline level. A lot of top brass were still getting higher salaries for hours of meetings.

'Are we going to need to give the press more to chew on?' Bolton said, looking at Carter.

'I'll deal with the PR, thank you. You just get the leads and evidence. People will want to know what made that girl jump. What or who. And at the moment, all we have is one potential suspect, and his DNA to prove it.'

Carter turned to leave the office.

'Amelja,' Stone said.

Turning back, a scowl creasing her reddening face, 'Inspector?'

'That girl.' He turned to look at her. 'We use our victim's names down here.'

Carter marched out of the office and the incident room.

A long silence hung in the air.

Stone gasped. 'What the hell was that?'

'Permission to speak freely, sir,' Bolton asked.

Stone raised both hands in submission.

'She's turning into a serious bitch.'

'Sands, you know I can't agree with you saying…'

'I know…'

'…"turning into".'

Bolton laughed as she sat down at his desk. She leaned forward and rested on her elbows. 'I just don't like the feeling of being manipulated. You know?'

Stone listened to the voice over his shoulder reminding him she wasn't the first person to say the same thing in that case.

Chapter 24

January
Luke & Amelja

Luke stepped back from the mirror as he felt his hands begin to shake and his chest tighten. He squeezed his eyes closed and open, closed and open, and tried to slow his breathing. Using the first cigarette that was almost burnt out, he lit the one the man in the hall had given him.

He threw the used butt into the open fire and watched the flames for a few moments.

But it was coming. He could feel it.

The Fury.

And that was when the idea came.

He picked up a copy of the morning paper from a side table and rolled it up. Holding the tip of the cigarette to the edge, the paper quickly caught a flame.

A book from a shelf was next, replacing it on the shelf to spread to the others. He ignited another book and put that on the floor under some curtains, hoping they were old enough to catch.

Luke knew he had no more time left. The smell would be lingering.

Thick black smoke was rolling up the bookshelf and curling into the white ceiling. The shelves filled with old books were catching like a bush fire.

Luke had expected the man in the hallway to come straight in, but he wasn't there, so he wedged what was left of his newspaper lantern into the sofa between cushions, throwing another paper next to it for added ignition.

Amelja finally broke from her trance-like state. 'Luke, what are you doing?'

That's when the man showed in the doorway. But he didn't call to alert everyone or run in to stop Luke. It had only been a couple of seconds, but Luke saw the hesitation in the man's eyes.

Another voice came from the hall.

'What the fuck? Fire.'

The man at the door shouted over his shoulder. 'Get water, now.' Then he fixed his eyes on Luke and nodded at the French doors.

Luke followed his eyes, and then looked back.

'Fucking go, kid.'

And he did. Luke grabbed Amelja by the wrist, but she snapped back, fear filling her eyes. He understood why. He picked up a dark wooden chair and with the strength only pumping adrenalin could muster, he launched it at the glass doors.

The Fury was in charge.

Flames had already consumed the bookcase, and the old sofa was beginning to smoke, forcing Amelja to her feet.

The man in the doorway turned to grab the water being handed to him, fumbling with it. Another voice from the hallway shouted, 'don't let the fire alarm go off.'

'Amelja, come on, we have to go, *now*,' Luke shouted at her as he grabbed her by the wrist again, squeezing much harder. He knew she might hate him for it, but that didn't matter.

Stepping through the shattered window and out onto the pavement, he noticed Amelja had no shoes on. Luke pulled her through the window, bent down and grabbed her by the knees, lifting her into his arms. He stepped across the path and dropped her on the grass.

He paused for a moment, desperate to get some bearings. The choice was clear. Head towards the unknown bushes or flee along the path and leave by the gate.

The gate swung open and Luke saw another man in a black suit running their way. The Fury took control and turned to attack. The man's confidence wavered as Luke charged straight towards him, apparently unafraid.

When he was merely a few feet away, Luke leapt towards him, aiming one foot at the man's crotch, and the other at his ankle. It was like performing the most dangerous tackle a footballer could.

Luke's body was virtually horizontal when his feet connected with the man. There was a snapping sound as the man's ankle gave way, and a loud grunt as Luke's other foot connect with genitals. The man doubled over.

Another guard appeared, running towards them.

'Come on,' Luke shouted back to Amelja, as he got back to his feet and started to run at the second man.

But the second man slowed and reached inside his jacket. He drew out a black pistol and was rounding to aim at Luke.

Amelja cried in terror.

Luke instinctively ducked, and in one burst, drove his shoulders into the man, knocking him off balance a split second before he could pull the trigger. The momentum carried Luke forward and on top of the man, crashing him to the floor with a heavy thud. He hit the man's gun arm away and landed a punch in the centre of his face. Bone and cartilage crunched and blood rushed out.

But the man fought back, caught up in his own red mist. Luke landed a couple more punches on the chin and the side of his head. As he lifted his right hand again, he flinched as something appeared from his right.

A terracotta pot crashed into the man's skull, covering

him with black soil.

Luke turned to see Amelja standing to his side.

Footfall coming from behind them launched Luke back to his feet, clambering over the motionless body, grabbing Amelja's wrist with his bloodied hand.

They made their way through a gate and out onto the gravel drive at the front of the building. Still powered by pure adrenaline, now across the crunching gravel, they pushed on until they were clear of the building.

Luke had to keep tugging on Amelja's arm as she was lagging behind.

'Luke, you must slow,' she cried out.

'We can't slow down.'

'My feet, Luke.'

He knew the gravel must be hurting her feet. But slowing down meant almost certain capture.

She cried out again. 'Luke, wait, please.'

'I know it hurts, but we've got to get away. Put these on.' He slipped his trainers off.

'But what about…'

'Just put them on.'

Amelja slipped her feet into the trainers, which were at least two or three sizes too big. Luke reached down to pull the laces tight, hoping they'd hold on.

They heard voices and the sound of a revving engine. Luke tugged Amelja's arm, and they ran again. The gravel cut into his feet as he heard footfall closing in and a car turning around.

The front gate was in view, and it was closed. But it was only about six-foot-high, so Luke was sure he could get one of them over.

It had to be Amelja.

'When we get to the gate,' he shouted, panting through a dry mouth, 'I'll lift you over first. Don't argue.'

Luke turned as soon as reached the gate, dropping to one knee and ushering Amelja up. She stepped onto his knee, pulled herself up with the black iron spikes and lifted her second foot into a space in the ornate design. She winced at the pain screaming from her foot.

And the pain from the previous night.

As Amelja swung her second leg over the gate, Luke took one more look behind him and saw he'd run out of time.

Throwing his weight towards the square column holding up the gate, he ran two steps up the brickwork whilst gripping the top of the ironwork. His manoeuvre swung his legs up and over the gate in one go, inches away from the grip of his pursuers.

The gate clicked and began to open as Luke jumped up and pushed Amelja away. Traffic was coming from both sides and Luke knew that they needed to lose the pursuers amidst as many witnesses as they could.

Turning right, they ran towards the oncoming traffic, gaining what lead they could. Amelja struggled to run, the pain and large trainers fighting back. Luke kept up, driven by the Fury.

In the first stroke of luck that had come their way, he saw a black cab taxi dropping a passenger a hundred yards ahead. Luke ran into the road waving at the taxi with both arms.

He could feel the men behind him, hear the snarling, swearing, and threats. He could see the taxi driver's eyes widen at the pantomime being played out before him.

Luke felt a hand grasp at his top, but he snatched his shoulder forward and dug deep into the sprint, keeping himself between the men and Amelja.

He made a snap decision and screamed to Amelja. 'Run.' Then he swung round and barrelled into the two men, crashing all three of them to the ground.

Amelja reached the taxi and hammered on the bodywork and driver side window. 'Please, please,' she said, her mind clouded by panic.

'Get in,' the driver replied, opening his driver door, his expression of shock replaced with anger.

Luke was grappling with the two men when he heard the shouting.

'Hey, you leave him,' the driver hollered. 'Let him go.'

'Fuck off,' one of the men shouted back.

The driver ran over to the tangle of three bodies, his stature growing with each step. 'Let him go.'

One of the two men stood up, ready to square up to the driver until he noticed the man was somewhat thicker built than he expected. 'This is none of your damn business.'

Ignoring him completely, the driver pushed past, grabbed Luke by the back of his top, and lifted him momentarily clear off the tarmac. Luke felt his body being thrown around like a ragdoll and heard the driver bark at him to get in the car.

The driver squared up to the two men.

'You two want to come with them? We all go to the Police station just down the road.' He glared at them.

The men froze in a stand-off for a few long seconds.

Finally, the two men turned to walk away, holding a glare at Luke as long as they could.

Luke saw the confrontation from the car and took a moment to stick his middle finger up before the driver turned around.

The driver returned to the car let out a loud sigh. He caught Luke's eye in the rear-view mirror.

'If your aim was to piss them off, son, I say you achieved that.'

Luke shrugged his shoulders. 'Can't please everyone.'

The driver's laugh cut through an awkwardness in the atmosphere as he started the engine. 'Where to?'

The Fury had retreated again. Amelja looked him in the eyes and she took his hand in hers.

They had nowhere to go.

'I figure you two probably don't have the money for

a fare, right?' He looked in his mirror, but there was no anger in his eyes. It had been clear the boy had been trying to protect the girl from the two men, and all things considered, he should phone the police.

But he also knew the futility in that. After all, what exactly would he say?

'I'm heading back into the city centre anyway. How about I drop you there and we speak nothing more of it?'

'Thank you,' Luke replied, unable to come up with anything else.

Nobody spoke on the journey back to the city centre. There wasn't anything that could be said without delving too deep into a long story.

When they finally pulled up at the taxi rank on Dale End next to all the fast-food outlets, an awkward silence filled the cab. None of them quite knew how to get out of the situation without embarrassment.

Luke opened the door and helped Amelja down onto the path. He turned back to the front passenger door to thank the driver properly. Their eyes met and they simply gave each other a nod. But as Luke turned to walk away, the driver called him back, waving at him to move closer. He held out his hand. Pinched between his forefinger and middle finger was a couple of folded notes.

'You, and the girl, take this.'

Luke stared at the money. He knew they needed it desperately, but he felt wrong taking it.

'Get yourself some shoes. And both of you have something to eat.'

Luke tried to reply, but he noticed the man's eyes filling. He couldn't understand what had moved this man so much for strangers. Most would have driven away. He'd waited, acted.

He fought.

For them.

'Thank you,' Luke said. 'But why?'

The driver cleared his throat.

'You just look after that girl, you hear me?' His voice cracked enough to betray his otherwise commanding presence. 'Never. Go. Back.'

As the taxi drove away and Luke stood with the thirty pounds in his hand, the horrific events of previous days and nights started seeping back.

The video. The fire. The escape. And an unexpected hero appearing from nowhere.

The rest of the world was just white noise.

And he was just a little boy again. Completely alone. His whole body burnt but felt numb at the same time. And a voice called from a distance. And again. Closer.

Amelja tugged at his arm.

Luke looked into her eyes and swallowed hard before walking away, pushing his way between the busy morning footfall. He reached the wall and put his face up against it, sliding down to the ground as if his legs had deflated.

He felt Amelja's hands gently rest on his shoulders, but he moved away. His breathing was shallow and fast.

'Luke. You need shoes back.'

He held out his hand and gave her the money the driver had handed him. Amelja's eyes lit up with surprise and confusion.

'Where did you get?'

Luke glanced at the taxi rank.

'Why?'

Luke's voice cracked, 'He said we should get some food and, um, you need some new shoes.'

'Why me?'

'Those are too big for you. You should buy new ones.'

Amelja paused for a moment before taking a breath and standing, summoning a reserve of energy.

She switched to a pragmatic tone and nodded as she spoke. 'I do that now. You wait here, I get shoes.' She turned to look around for inspiration. 'I go Primark.'

Luke thought he smiled at her slight mispronunciation of the well-known store. But he couldn't tell.

'You wait here.'

She turned and walked away with a determined pace as Luke picked himself up and limped over to the nearest bench he could find.

* * *

'Did you get what you needed?' Luke asked when Amelja reappeared less than thirty minutes later.

Amelja took a simple pair of casual shoes out of the bag and waved them at him.

'Is that it?'

'These all I need. No fuss.' She reached down to take off the trainers and winced at the pain in her feet.

'Here, let me look.' Luke lifted her leg onto his lap and gently took the shoe off her right foot. The sight of blood made them both gasp, drawing a few unwelcome glances from passers-by. None of them stopped to help.

'I not realise,' Amelja said. 'They hurt, but I not think of blood. I am sorry.'

'It's not your fault.' Luke looked around, trying to find inspiration. 'We need to get you to a doctor or hospital or something.'

'No, Luke, no. My feet will be okay. First, we go away from here. People are looking.'

She was right. A thought struck Luke and he grabbed the bag from Primark. Tearing it open down the edges, he made a small, narrow rectangle of paper, doubled over. He squeezed that carefully inside Amelja's new shoes, creating a paper pocket to slip her foot into.

'There, try to put your foot inside.'

She winced flood slid inside, but then smiled. 'You are smart, my Luke.'

Luke let a small, embarrassed smile flicker before

pulling up her other leg and repeating the process.

'Now, see if you can stand okay.' Luke stood first, ignoring the pains in his own feet, and held her hands. She frowned and hissed through her teeth at the pain, tensing. But after a few seconds, she relaxed into it.

Amelja sat back down, tore more of the paper bag off, and got to work folding with a prowess Luke hadn't seen before. She fashioned an envelope shape that looked like a shoe itself. Pushing it inside his trainer, it appeared to line the whole interior.

It made his little bit of folding look quite pathetic.

'It looks like you are the smart one.' He slipped his foot into the shoe, and it was only then he realised just how much his feet were hurting, too. The socks he'd been wearing soaked up the blood from his feet.

'Have you got the rest of that money?' Luke asked.

Amelja handed him twenty-two pounds.

'You only spent eight pounds?'

'These shoes all I need. More for food.'

He resigned himself to her logic. 'Come on, we need some supplies.'

Amelja's were far worse than Luke had expected. The cuts were deep and Luke's worried that she might need stitches. His gut told him she had to see a doctor or at least a nurse.

After getting some food and first aid supplies, Amelja showed Luke the underpass behind WH Smiths, near the Britannia Hotel. Most of the old retail units were out of use, so there were barely any people walking through. But it was as a good spot as any to get out of the rain and feel a little safer.

Luke focused on wrapping Amelja's feet with the white square dressings, with some antiseptic cream he hoped would keep germs out. He fixed it with the furry of sticky tape, pulling it tight to hold it.

Apologising when she winced at the pain.

They had both taken two paracetamol each, after first wondering if they classed as an adult. In the end, they decided to only take a single tablet later.

Amelja kept nagging at Luke, insisting she looked at his feet. But he was determined to sort her out first.

Luke had no idea if Amelja knew about the video recording he had been shown back at the house. He had no idea what to do about it.

The words of the taxi driver were still ringing around his head. "You just look after that girl, you hear me?"

No matter what he had to do, fights he had to fight, or lies he had to tell.

He had to protect her from something far more dangerous and terrifying.

The truth.

Chapter 25

September

The press briefing room hummed with anticipation. The rumour mill had been working hard over the weekend, digging for information on the suicide on Galton Bridge. It was nothing short of a miracle that no significant leaks had surfaced. Chief Superintendent Carter put that down to the fact that few people even knew the girl's name.

She took her seat at the table, adjusted her dress uniform, and shared cursory nods to the various grey faces around her.

Lenses pointed, cameras rattled test shots before dipping to check screens. It looked like a bizarre warm-up for a dance group.

Hush swept across the room as the Assistant Chief constable called for silence and opened the briefing with the usual platitudes and tone-setting sombre declarations. He handed the proceedings to Carter.

'Emergency services were called to an incident on Friday evening of what was initially reported to be a girl on the bridge. The caller was anonymous.'

There was a flurry of questions that had to be calmed with a polite but insistent raising of her hand. She waited for silence before proceeding, much like a teacher asserting her authority over a regular unruly class.

'We would like to speak to the caller. They are not in any trouble, and their help with the investigation would be…'

'Do you have reason to believe the caller is involved?' The voice brought an unwelcome barrage.

'Is this more than just suicide?'

'What was the girl's name?'

'Was she homeless?'

'Has anyone tracked down her parents?'

Carter raised her hand again. 'At this stage, we have no evidence to suggest the death was suspicious. But that makes it no less tragic. We are investigating the circumstances leading up to the incident because we want to get a clearer picture. If lessons can be learnt…'

The killer phrase, like a blood drop in a pool of sharks.

'Where is the baby?'

'What have social services got to say?'

'Is the hospital being investigated?'

Carter sat up in her seat and raised her voice over the noise. 'Birmingham City Hospital staff are assisting us with all elements of the inquiry. We are asking for anyone who might have seen the girl on Friday evening, or thinks they know her, to please contact West Midlands police.'

'What was her name?'

Carter turned to the Assistant Chief Constable for one final check that he was sure it was the right way to go.

'At the moment we know her name to be Amelja Halil. We believe she is of Albanian descent and may have come to the UK quite recently.'

'Was she an illegal immigrant?'

'Is this just more misuse of NHS care?'

'Is this a human trafficking issue?'

They were baying for blood and hyperbole, each one after the best scoop or quote.

'Anyone can contact West Midlands police directly, or

via Crime Stoppers. Further statements will come in due course.'

Carter stood to make it clear she would not be taking any further questions. The usual barrage still came thick and fast.

As far as Carter was concerned, they'd given the media enough to chew on and speculate with for a few days. Social media would explode with armchair experts fighting out their theories about youth suicide. And then it would vanish as fast as it appeared when something else deemed more tragic took its place.

There had been nothing to gain by raising the issue of rape until they had a viable suspect. A badly beaten fifteen-year-old boy would create a confusing moral ambiguity. Carter knew public opinion couldn't cope with moral grey areas.

It was rarely able to cope with the truth.

And she knew all too well that this case would probably carry a truth that no one was going to want to hear.

Chapter 26

'Inspector Stone, I think I have something of yours.' DCI Palmers' voice bounced down the corridor.

Stone turned to look at Palmers, trying hard to hide the welcome interruption from going to see Carter.

Palmers nodded towards his office door a few windows further down the green mile. The morbid nickname for the corridor was a nod to the film and its reference to the final walk to execution. Strange green-grey carpet tiles covered the floor one up from where all the real work was done.

Already standing behind his desk, hands balanced on his hips, Palmers held out a hand for Stone to take a seat on the opposite side of the oversized oak desk.

'I need an update anyway,' Palmers said, leaving enough pause for Stone to jump in. But he didn't. An awkward pause stretched until Palmers opened a file as he sat in his bizarrely oversized leather chair. It was the size of a first-class seat on a plane, minus the cup-holder.

'What am I meant to have lost, sir?'

'A black saloon, by chance?' Palmers handed him a photo of a badly burnt-out vehicle in a wooded area.

'Okay, I'll bite.' Stone gave him a wry smile.

Palmers relaxed back into his chair like a leather sofa.

Do they have some kind of budget for those?

'We got the call from traffic when they went out with the reds for a torched car. Then it became a car with a body. To the layperson, the car must have skidded off the road, rolled, and crashed into the woods. The airbags went off and it burst into flames.' He made a mock-explosion sound and action with his hands. Just like a child would.

Stone raised his eyebrows at the final comment.

'Exactly.' Palmers wagged his finger at Stone's surprised expression. 'And drivers don't tend to take their foot off the brakes a yard or so from the edge of the tarmac.'

'Meaning?'

'I've got an expert out there now, but he has already told me that judging from the marks on the road, the car skidded to a full stop. Then got slowly rolled off the road.'

'Did it have help going…?' Stone mimicked the explosion sound and gesture.

Palmers nodded. 'According to the fire crew, the smell of petrol was simply too strong, even after the fire had been all but snuffed out.'

Stone held out a hand for the file and Palmers nodded for him to take it.

'Plates on the back of the car were burnt out, but we were lucky that the front one mostly snapped off when the car rolled. We checked the number.'

'False plates. And the car was cloned from one in London.' Stone mumbled the remark and saw Palmer's eyebrows rise.

'The last ANPR hit was Sunday, which showed it driving out of the city roughly in the direction of where it was found.'

'Driver?'

'ID from dental records. And a likely cause of death.'

Stone flicked through the file. Two bullet wounds to the torso, and one to the head.

'Double-tap and top hat,' Palmers said with a little too much self-satisfaction in his wordplay.

'Safe enough to say the shot to his head was the probable cause of death.' Absent-minded, Stone began scratching at his stubble. 'Goes by the name "Splint". Is that important?'

Palmers' expression and tone changed as he sat forward 'Very important.' His deep sigh announced the bad news. 'He's a known associate of Nesim Kapllani.'

The realisation struck DI Stone in successive blows, each adding painful new weight to his investigation, and his shoulders. 'Holy…'

'…exactly.'

'If Splint was burnt out in that car two days after the Buchanan incident, that means he was possibly our shooter. But that also means our mystery third man must be the one who dumped Luke's body and killed Splint.'

They both paused, stuck on the same thought.

Stone stood and paced with the file. He often preferred to walk and think. 'More importantly, if these two are both Kapllani's men, why did our third man kill and dump Splint?'

'Worse than that, Mike. Luke is connected to Amelja, who, at pretty much the same time that evening, was jumping off Galton Bridge.'

'Which drops Luke and Amelja right in the middle of organised crime.'

A long pause extended between them as Stone walked over to the window overlooking the city. The murky day seemed to accentuate the shadow over the whole case. Stone knew that it was going to get a lot more complex before it got solved. If it got solved.

'Why didn't they just kill Luke?' Stone asked over his shoulder.

'I think we need might have a lot to learn from Luke. And about Amelja. And exactly how they got tied up with Kapllani.'

Stone turned to Palmers. 'Carter's pushing us to consider Luke as a suspect for Amelja's rape.'

Palmers let out a frustrated sigh and shook his head.

Stone picked up on it, but decided what it meant was probably above his pay grade. 'When it comes to Luke, Reg Walters is our best source.'

'And Amelja?'

'Luke is probably the best source we have.'

Palmers got up from his seat and joined Stone over by the window. 'Be honest with me, Mike. Do you seriously think Luke assaulted her?'

Stone shook his head without hesitation. 'But how did the kids get involved with Kapllani in the first place?'

They looked at each other. Neither wanted to say it out loud, but Kapllani was suspected of having connections with the Albanian sex trafficking trade.

'And how does a pregnant teenager fit into that scene?'

It was Palmers' turn to look grey. 'Badly'

'What are we still waiting on from SOCO for Friday?'

'Various pieces. Having it all sent to me and Pete Barry at the same time.'

Stone nodded as he turned to leave the office. 'If you don't mind, sir, I'd like to send DS Bolton out to our scene from Friday. Fresh pair of eyes.

'Seems a good idea. How's she holding up?'

'Working is doing her good. She dwells if she stays off.'

'Bloody good detective.'

Far better than you think. Far better.

Chapter 27

DC Harry Khan's knock gave away how much caffeine he'd already consumed that morning. He bounced into Stone's office and dropped into the chair by the window.

'I spent a bit of time last night doing a walkabout.' He raised an arm to halt the admonishment. 'Not on police time. This isn't a bill for overtime.'

'Good, because now you've sat down, you can't shove it where I'd tell you.'

'It was with Reg Walters, actually.'

'Did he mention how Luke is getting on?'

'He mentioned that he's doing well. A little bit fuzzy, but he's pumped full of funky painkillers at the moment. The kid's probably never been so high.'

Stone rolled his eyes.

'Anyway, on the way around, we met a couple of people. Firstly, came across our friend Mr Freeman again. Nothing new from him. But he did introduce us to an old woman who appeared to recognise a picture of Amelja.'

Stone sat back in his chair and listened more intently.

'I showed her Luke's picture and got nothing. But when she saw Amelja's picture, something clicked.'

Stone leaned back in his chair for a moment, scratching at his stubble. 'Could she be worth bringing in?'

'Forgive the stereotype, guv, but even though it's interesting, she's unlikely to be a viable witness.'

Stone dropped his head again to look at Khan. 'So, what you're telling me is more of a hunch, not something for evidence?'

'As you always say, rule of thumb, it's not evidence if it can't stand on its own two feet in court.'

Stone nodded and smiled. He liked it when his DCs listened to him. And it was true. If it couldn't be used in court, it wasn't much use for the file. But that still didn't mean it was useless.'

DC Khan continued. 'All she said that I could make out was "I see her, gone".' Harry paused to let Stone think for a moment. 'It could mean anything or nothing.'

'That's a bloody long shot, Harry.'

Khan looked a little deflated, like an apologetic puppy caught with the mangled remains of a slipper.

'Good work, though. And include it in your notes as a possible lead. Maybe get the bobbies and PCSOs to keep an eye out for her.' Stone paused and raised his eyebrows, asking if that was all.

'Now the good bit.' Khan reanimated, fluttering at another piece of notepaper in his hand. 'When I got the taxi home, the driver let something slip that perked up my Spidey-sense.'

Stone rolled his eyes again.

Keep the caffeine away from this man.

Khan leaned closer. 'I know it wasn't official, what with me being off duty, but I did tell him I was an officer, showed him my ID to prove it, and then showed him Luke and Amelja's photos.'

Stones look turned to a glare. A mad old homeless woman was one thing. But a genuine potential lead was another.

'I just showed him the pictures and asked if he recognised them. And he did.' Harry pulled his chair closer to Stone's desk, leaning on the edge. 'He recognised them. And there was fear in his eyes. He looked like he was suspicious that

I happened to have chosen his taxi.'

'But you did.'

Khan shrugged his shoulders. 'He didn't know that, did he?'

'What did he say?'

'Denied ever seeing them. But made a bloody sharpish exit.'

Stone leaned in. 'And this is where you tell me…'

Khan waved the paper with the licence plate and taxi number on it. 'Both gained with my eyes, so no naughty magic buttons of unauthorised PNC checks.'

'That's my boy.' Stone couldn't resist laughing at the childish enthusiasm. 'Let's see if we can turn this into a lead, shall we?'

'You're going to want to see this, Mike,' DS Pete Barry said, standing in DI Stone's office door, leaning up against the frame with a tablet in his hand.

'Will my life become more peaceful and zenlike?'

DS Barry smiled back at him, amused that it would be the polar opposite.

Stone grunted. 'Give me a one-sentence taster.'

'Blood evidence from Friday evening.'

Stone paused and thought for a moment as he put his coat on. Bolton was busy tapping away at her computer, so he called her over, noticing a sigh of relief.

'You busy, Sands?'

Her eyebrows twisted as she tilted her head to the side. *Stupid question. I get it.*

'I had a chat with DCI Palmers earlier about our missing black saloon. Pete, did you get the update?'

He tapped the tablet and nodded.

'Right. Pete, bring Sands up to date with the blood evidence and the saloon info. Sands, you take a tablet with you out to the shooting scene. I want your fresh eyes looking over it. I need to take Harry out for walkies, so you take the puppy.'

She frowned, clearly missing the point.

'Pearson.'

Bolton smiled and nodded. 'Sure. I like him.'

'Behave. He's almost young enough to…'

'Don't you bloody dare finish that comment.'

'Mr Pearson,' Stone called over to his desk. 'Look smart. Auntie Sandra is taking you out to show you how to use your light-sabre.'

Chapter 28

January-Luke & Amelja

Luke knew Amelja was trying to hide her pain. Always being on the move but never having enough food or being able to clean properly was a terrible cocktail. He knew going to Reg was the best thing to do, but he knew the state they were in, Reg would have no choice but to report them urgently.

Amelja looked up at Luke. 'What are you thinking,'

'Nothing.' He tried to sound nonchalant, but his fixed frown had grown deeper over the week.

'Tell me.' She wrapped her arm around his and leaned into him.

His eyes darkened and narrowed. 'You're not well. Your feet are still bad.' Luke might not have known much about first aid, but he had seen infection setting in before.

'They get better.'

'No, they aren't. It's been nearly a week. You need to see a doctor.'

'We can't. You say.'

He stood and gripped his head by the sides. 'I know what I said.' Pacing and tugging at his hair. 'I was wrong, okay?'

'We get more pills.'

'Don't you get it?' He snapped, turning to her with

such a jolt she flinched.

Her eyes crumpled with shock. It was the same expression Luke saw just before they'd run.

'I'm sorry.' He knelt in front of her. 'If they get infected you can get really bad. I saw it on Casualty.'

She looked blank.

'Please, Amelja. It's my job to look after you.'

'What if they call police? Should we call Casualty?'

Luke couldn't stifle a small laugh. 'What about we get you to a nurse. If we tell them you are sixteen, there are rules. They can't tell people then.'

'Confidentiality.' She corrected him. It was a word she had heard and learnt from somewhere she couldn't recall. But she understood it.

Luke was impressed, as he'd heard it many times. 'Yeh, that's what I mean.'

Amelja looked unconvinced.

Luke struggled again, searching for a new plan. 'Well, even if they do say they must call someone, pretend to agree. They will have to treat your feet as we wait.' He smiled at her. 'Then, when they aren't looking, we slip away.'

Amelja smiled back. 'Misdirection.'

They had been developing their skills over the week, using them to steal essentials, as well as food. One night they managed to steal a small bottle of vodka and giggled at the idea of becoming travelling magicians.

Luke stood Amelja up and held her in his arms. The rain was falling heavier but he'd been scared of a rift between them forming from his outburst. He needed the embrace to fix it. Like a wound.

She returned the embrace, wrapping her arms around his waist, and they stood in the rain for a few moments, sharing each other's warmth.

Turning towards Colmore Row, they began the journey to perform their next trick.

* * *

It hadn't taken long for a bus heading towards the hospital to appear. A little acting about Amelja needing to see a doctor. Luke used the tearful, wallet-losing panic act.

A single generous member of the public had taken pity on them and paid their fare. Hook, line and sinker, the good Samaritan offered to pay for their evening tickets. Since they were also going to the hospital, too, they could show them where to get off.

When they arrived at A&E they followed the plan to the letter. Luke's feet had healed far better, and he insisted that they didn't complicate the story with both of them needing treatment.

It only took thirty minutes for Amelja to be taken to triage for her first assessment. As expected, the nurse was concerned. She figured that Amelja was homeless. The fake surname bought extra time when they couldn't find medical records.

Amelja played along with the nurse's concern, let them take blood for tests and give her advice so they felt like they were helping. She even accepted the offer of a cup of tea and a sneaky chocolate bar from the vending machine.

The nurse even went to the lengths of offering to find Amelja a cheap pair of jogging bottoms and some new underwear. Amelja could tell the nurse was another good person and felt bad taking advantage of her good nature.

Luke had moved seats in the waiting room so he could just about see the cubicle, ready to make his move if needed.

It seemed like everything was going to plan, even if it was taking longer than they had hoped.

They just had to keep their cool.

Chapter 29

'What are we looking for, boss?' Pearson asked, with a little too much enthusiasm. 'This is so cool,' he gasped when he realised he was driving the route he'd been staring at for hours on CCTV.

DS Bolton was flicking through the file photos and answered without looking at him. 'I want to see the evidence in context.'

'Walk the grid.' He nodded confidently.

'James, we're not in a film.'

'Sorry, boss.'

'Call me Sands, please.'

'Okay, boss-Sands. But that's what we're doing. Getting inside the mind of the killer.'

'It's also not Hannibal Lecter.' She let out a sigh.

'You worked on that Malcolm Glenn case with the guv-boss, didn't you?'

She looked at him with her sternest 'no more chit chat' look.

Their car pulled up into Baxter industrial estate, which was still marked out by remnants of police tape.

She handed him the tablet. 'Have a scan through that lot. I've bookmarked most relevant points.' She walked over to the walled area the car with Luke had been hidden behind. 'You should find a mighty coincidence. Start with the boy, Luke. Consider only the fresh evidence from his

185

clothes or at least those collected at the hospital.'

Pearson tapped at the screen, bringing up the relevant sections. 'Were they not his?' He asked.

'Lab techs don't think so. They were rather new, still had that factory new smell.'

Pearson grunted 'That's hardly scientific. Can just hear that in court.' He mocked a thick Brummie accent. 'I swears y'ronner, I sniffed them up proper and they was well new.'

'You'd be surprised how handy your nose can be, James. Don't be so quick to dismiss it.' Bolton walked over to where Buchanan's car had stopped. The blood patch still showed in the gravel.

'Blood evidence is the boy's.' Pearson confirmed before, looking between the tablet and down to where Bolton was crouching.

'Three sources,' she replied, without looking up.

Pearson's eyebrows bounced up, and he swiped back and forth.

'Some blood from the boy, which is hardly surprising.'

'The second blood source?'

'Second known blood, according to type and DNA belongs to a Detective Constable…'

'Paul Buchanan,' Pearson announced with a flourish.

Bolton nodded first. 'Where was that sample taken from?'

'Only small amounts taken from the boy's clothes.'

'He said he checked Luke's pulse before calling it in. So that should make sense, right?'

'You'd think.' Pearson frowned and scratched his head. He walked over to stand next to the bloodstain on the ground. 'When the ambulance arrived, he was lying on the ground next to his car.' He pointed down at his own feet. 'Where he'd been shot.'

Pearson and Bolton looked at each other, a question hanging in the air between them.

The constable opened. 'But how did he walk twenty feet or so, and back…'

'Without leaving a trail of blood drops?' Bolton finished.

'Sands. Are we here investigating the guy with the gun, or…'

'Keep that thought to yourself, for now, James. But you'd agree something isn't adding up, right?'

'Sorry, it's just that I don't get why he would bother walking back to his car to call it in.'

Bolton shrugged her shoulders. 'Maybe he left his phone in his car.' She moved over to the second bloodstain in the gravel. It was about ten feet away from the first and was marked on the photos as approximately where the black saloon car had parked.

'Buchanan had a through and through shoulder shot. Gushing blood. How did he only leave a trace amount of blood on the boy but a small lake here on the ground?' Pearson held his chin in his free hand.

Bolton stood over by the second blood patch. 'James, tell me where the PM estimated the points of entry were for the second gun victim. The one in the saloon.'

Pearson flicked through the files until he found the information. His jaw slipped open. 'Two in the torso, one in the left side of the head.' He looked up to see Bolton pointing at him with a mimed gun hand.

'Are you firearms trained, James?'

'No. But I'd like to be.'

'No, you wouldn't.' DS Bolton was a skilled and trained firearms officer, despite not being on any of the teams. It was rare for her to carry a weapon, and she didn't like doing it. Most of the officers she knew dreaded the day they would ever discharge their weapon. And most of them go an entire career never doing it outside training.

She held out her right arm full length, which is how untrained, usually criminal shooters liked to hold the weapon. She looked down at her chest and pointed to the left side of her head with her left hand. Then she looked back at Pearson.

A few moments passed.

They both turned to look to Bolton's left. Pearson walked across the gravelled area to stand approximately the same distance from Bolton.

'Our mystery extra man had a gun,' Bolton said as Pearson lifted his hand like a gun and took three imaginary shots.

'Two to the body, one to the head. That's a pro.'

'Yes, it is. Armed forces style'

Pearson looked back at the tablet and then walked over to Bolton. 'Here's something odd. The third blood source on the boy has been identified and is likely to be our mystery driver. But look what the PNC says.'

'Sealed? Above our paygrade, then.'

'Is it a double-o agent or something?'

She laughed.

'So, that's it? Brick walled?'

Bolton smiled at him. 'Not entirely, no. It means we now have good reason to call our friend Buchanan back in.'

Pearson smiled. 'That's the best bit about coming up against a brick wall.'

Bolton gave him a puzzled look.

'Gives us a chance to blow some shit up.'

Chapter 30

DI Stone knocked on the door of the terraced house in Small Heath and it opened after a little hubbub he couldn't quite make out. Big, bright eyes only four feet from the floor peered up at him.

'Hello?' said a young boy no older than seven or eight. His voice mixed somewhere between polite and nervous.

'Hello there. Is daddy in?'

The door slammed shut, possibly harder than the boy expected. Stone could hear the conversation on the other side of the door. Who was it? A man. What man? Old man.

Old man? Cheeky little sod.

Stone smiled at the peephole, pretty certain it was being used. A moment later the door swung open and a man stood in a narrow hallway. He was shorter than Stone but by no means a small man. Stocky, but with a spreading midriff beginning to suit the man's profession.

His eyes narrowed. 'Can I help you?' The man asked, nodding up as if pointing his question with his chin.

'My name is Mike Stone.' Stone let a moment hang to allow the man his innocent lack of recognition. 'Detective Inspector Mike Stone, from West Midlands CID.'

The man's face dropped.

'This is my colleague, Detective Constable Harinder Khan.'

Khan turned right on cue.

The man's eyes widened with a tightening of the jawline. He turned to check that no one was behind him and then stepped outside, holding onto the door. 'I spoke to your colleague yesterday evening.'

'I understand,' Stone kept his voice calm, 'but I have one or two more questions.'

The man didn't move.

'Do you think we could come in?'

It took him a moment before he finally relented and let them inside. He ushered them into his living room on the left in the simple two-up, two-down, pre-war terrace. The living room was dulled by the brown décor, which swallowed what little light battled its way in through the small bay window.

It was also immaculately clean and smelt of the spices from the previous night's family meal.

The man invited the detectives to sit on the sofa before calling out to his wife in what Stone thought he recognised as Bangladeshi. But couldn't be sure. He made a mental note to ask Khan later. Then cancelled the mental note.

Remember the cultural sensitivity workshops, Mike.

Stone started. 'I'll get straight to the point, Mr,' he let the moment hang, waiting for the man to confirm his name.

'Masood.'

'Masood, yes. I understand you met my colleague last night. He was very complimentary about your driving, by the way.'

The man looked puzzled. Not sure if that was meant as a joke.

'Anyway, do you recall he showed you a couple of photographs?'

He nodded, tensely.

Taking his phone out and opening it to the images, Stone turned the screen around and showed him Luke's photograph first, without saying anything.

The driver's eyes darted from the picture, then down, then between the two detectives. Stone and Khan got what they needed. It was the glance down that mattered. Subconscious, fast, but definitely there.

'And this one, too.' Stone did the same with Amelja's picture. The man's eyes fixed on the image for a second longer before fixing on DI Stone's glare.

'Now, Masood, my colleague asked you if you recognised them.' He paused for a moment. 'But I am asking where you recognise them from. How well you know them.'

Masood shook his head.

'Can we skip that stage, please, Masood? We're not here because we're investigating you.' He paused long enough for "yet" to fill the space. 'We need your help in our inquiries into what happened to them.'

The man's swallow was heavy, and his palms rubbed his knees before he clasped them together.

Stone held the photos up again. 'Because this is Luke, and this was Amelja.' Stone intended the past tense to sting.

Masood's expression changed. There was a flare of anger in his eyes. 'Okay, look,' his voice lowered almost to a whisper, 'I recognise them, okay. I drove them in my cab.'

'Just the once?'

'First time, I dropped them off in town, Dale End, Bull Street. I took pity on them. I've done nothing wrong.' He was pleading, his shoulders raised, palms up to the ceiling in a gesture of contrition. 'I admit I gave the boy some money.'

Stone glanced at Khan, which unsettled the man.

'Nothing sinister, for goodness sake. Just for food, and to buy some damn shoes.'

'Buy some shoes?' Stone was caught off-guard by the comment. 'You mean, new shoes?'

Masood shook his head and his frown drove deep into his forehead. 'The boy had no shoes. And the girl appeared to be wearing trainers too big for her.'

Khan continued to scrawl the new information down in his black book.

'Do you remember when this was, sir?' Stone asked.

He shook his head slowly. 'Long time ago. Months and months ago. Not long into the new year, I think.'

Stone knew it was probably too long ago to expect CCTV to be recoverable. Most systems cleared after six months. 'Where did you pick them up from?'

The man's faced darkened as he shrugged his shoulders. 'I don't remember.'

'Sir, please. We were doing so well.' He raised his eyebrows. 'I mean, this could have been nine months ago.'

The man grimaced. 'Somewhere down Bristol Road. Quite some way out of the city centre. That's why I remember it. Seemed odd they were out there. Especially without shoes. Cold day. I took pity on them.' He jabbed a finger at the detectives. 'No shame in that. I have done nothing wrong.'

Stone raised a hand to cut the man's protestation dead. 'But that wasn't the only time you saw them, was it?'

Masood rubbed his hands together again and lowered his voice. 'Look, from time to time, if I see them out and about, and it's cold and wet. When I didn't have a fare, I give them a ride if they needed to get somewhere. You know, just get them out of the rain. For a short while.'

'You knew them well, then?'

Masood shook his head. 'No, not well. Just by name and a smile, you know. Occasional bit of loose change, or some food.' He frowned at Stone and a glint of anger came into his eyes. 'I am a man of faith. Doing a good deed is not as hard as you might think for everyone.'

Stone let the pause hang for a moment, watching the man intently. 'Do you often drive young people, or anyone else, out to the same address on Bristol Street?'

'I go where my fare asks. I stay on public roads. My work, Mr Stone, begins and ends in my cab.'

He stood and offered his hand, which the driver took clumsily as he rose at the same time as Khan. They were both taken aback by the sudden end of the conversation.

'I'd like to thank you for your help today, Mr Masood. And please, if anything jogs your memory,' he shrugged his shoulders as he handed the man his business card, 'say, perhaps an address, call me. Confidentially, of course.'

The three men bundled themselves out into the hallway. Stone noticed a picture of a girl in school uniform on the wall facing into the doorway to the front room. It was positioned as if to be a focal point for anyone leaving the room.

She was a very pretty young lady. A wide, bright smile sang in her eyes. Perfectly straight, long black hair draped softly over her shoulders.

'You're daughter, sir?' Stone expected the man to smile with pride like fathers always do. But he seemed reluctant, and the short pause before his reply gave away the falter in his voice and expression.

'Yes, yes it is. Just a school photo. She was thirteen when that was taken.'

Stone heard the past tense in the man's voice. 'What was her name?'

Masood's eyes glistened just short of filling and his voice came out as a dry whisper. 'Yasmina.'

'Very pretty girl, sir.' He looked at Masood, struggling to meet the man's eyes. The atmosphere of the hallway felt like it was pressing against his head. When their eyes did meet, Stone was sure he could see right down into the blackened depths. And yet, at the same time, a kind of lingering anger was holding onto him. He'd seen it so many times. But it was almost always in the eyes of those who had been forced to do the worst things his job sometimes called upon him to do.

As they stepped out onto the front doorstep, Khan walked out onto the path and Stone turned back towards the man.

'Mr Masood, thank you again for your help. But, a word of advice.' He didn't wait for an invitation. 'You may not have done anything wrong, but even the smallest of lies, no matter how innocent, only makes us come back and ask harder questions. Sometimes unwelcome ones.'

The man stood stock still as the two detectives walked away, his top lip curling at one edge and a frown drawing darkness into his eyes. But as his heart began to pound and his breathing shallowed, he retreated into his house and closed the door.

The two detectives didn't speak until they both got back in the car. Stone took a moment before starting the engine.

'I want to know more about him,' Stone said, rubbing his chin before feeling his hand slip down to the scar. It was his reminder of the first time his family was put in grave danger, and he'd been left him breathing through a tube. He closed his eyes and regretted it straight away as flashes of the second time tragedy had nearly knocked at his door. Malcolm Glenn's face was etched into his memory.

'You alright, guv?' Khan asked after a moment.

'Did you see the photo of his daughter?'

Khan swallowed heavily and dryly. 'Yes.' He paused. 'She looked a bit like…'

Stone's glare cut off the end of Khan's sentence. 'Let's go for a drive.'

'Bristol Road?'

Stone nodded.

'What are we looking for?'

'I don't know. But there's something, or somewhere out there that Masood didn't want to tell us about. We might need Luke's help to find it. He might come through and tell us. But for now, let's just go for a quick recce.'

'More importantly, on the way back to HQ we could pick up some essentials.'

Stone looked at him. A slight smile crept back to his face. 'You and you're damned stomach.'

Chapter 31

Nesim Kapllani looked at the screen on his burner phone. All it showed was an X, which meant the call was coming from the only phone that had his number.

It annoyed him how many foolish low life criminals made the same mistakes. Lying in wait for the one call, they answered numerous wrong numbers from spam or cold calls. When it came to forensic data scrubs, this gave a pattern to any number, including burner phones. In his view, a true burner phone should be used to connect once. And only once.

'Speak.' He answered it quiet and fast. Impossible for voice analysts to sample.

'We have a problem.'

Kapllani didn't answer. He just waited.

'Press statement? Anonymous caller means a possible witness,' the voice replied.

'Do you have a solution?'

'The witness has already said something to at least one detective.'

'That isn't what I asked you.' Kapllani didn't bother hiding the annoyance in his voice. He wondered what it was with the British. Were they all so incapable of answering specific and direct questions?

'You can't just vanish a person of interest without drawing unwanted attention.'

'Redirecting unwanted attention is exactly why you are on my payroll, is it not?' He waited. 'If you cannot give me solution, makes you a part problem.' Kapllani let the suggestion hang. 'Then I get someone else solve problem.'

The voice on the other end of the line didn't reply.

'Glad we cleared that up,' Kapllani smiled. 'Who is witness.'

'Mad old homeless woman.'

He sighed. 'The problem with mad old women is they don't know how to shut up. And they don't know how to stay shut up.'

'I have no intention of doing your wet work for you.'

'Find a solution.'

'You can't threaten me.'

Kapllani let out a deep laugh. 'You and I both know that is something I absolutely fucking can do.' He ended the call and handed the phone to his driver. A small nod was all that was needed to say exactly what needed to happen to that phone.

Kapllani looked out the window and swore under his breath. Too much was at stake, and the last thing he needed was distractions like witnesses.

Chapter 32

Luke's body lay on the stainless-steel workbench in front of the pathologist. His greyed skin made the bruising glow.

A bright overhead light appeared to flatten his features.

The silent freezing mortuary air was disturbed by the faint murmur of sound growing from a distance. It formed around the pathologist's ears.

Soft sobbing echoed off the clinical walls.

He held his breath in fear of the cold touch he knew was coming. Every part of his body locked into stillness, but his hand acted against his will. Touching the boy's hand, his fingers. Taking them in his grip.

A single ice-cold tear coursed down his face and he tasted its salt on his tongue as it hung from his jawline.

A faint whisper pressed through the sobbing. Rasping into the shape of a word.

'*Reg.*'

Dry, forced.

'*Reg.*'

Desperate.

'*Reg.*'

The pathologist squeezed his eyes shut, wishing the sound away.

'*Reg.*'

When his eyes opened, he saw the boy glaring straight at him, blood tears were crimson in the cold light, pouring onto the steel bench, oozing from his nose and mouth.

'*Reg.*'

* * *

Reg jolted awake and took a few seconds to regain his bearings. Sitting next to Luke's bed, his hand holding the boy's, he felt the tears wet on his cheeks. As he wiped them away, he felt the squeeze on his fingers and heard a raspy voice sounding out his name.

'Reg.' Luke could barely sound it out from his swollen wounds.

Reg stood and leaned closer to Luke. 'Luke, I'm here.' A small, nervous giggle slipped out. 'Oh, mate, it's so good to hear your voice.'

The boy had regained consciousness two days before, but to keep him still and let his body heal, doctors had him on heavy doses of painkillers, and semi-sedated to stop him aggravating the process.

Luke tried to speak, 'Wher'm I?'

'Hospital. Birmingham Children's hospital. Don't worry, they're taking great care of you.' He turned to see if there was a nurse around, considered calling out for one, but decided against making a scene.

Luke tried to sound out something else, and Reg had to lean in to listen. He knew he should just tell the boy to rest. But he was acutely aware he might be trying to say something vital.

'It's okay. They have you on some funky drugs. But you're safe.'

'Amelja,' Luke whispered, before coughing at the effort, and then wincing from the cough.

Reg was almost caught off guard. He'd been so worried about whether Luke would even pull through he hadn't considered how and when to tell him about Amelja.

He pulled the chair he'd been using closer to the bed

and sat down again. 'You've got to focus on getting better, Luke. Okay?' He placed a hand lightly on his shoulder. 'You can trust me. I'm here.'

Everything from his training said he was crossing a line. But as far as he was concerned, no child deserved to be beaten to the edge of life, and then be told they are alone.

'Don't try to speak, you need to rest. Whatever you need to say can wait.' He waited for a reply. Luke frowned.

Luke's head moved, slow, awkward, side-to-side.

'Just rest. Rest.'

But he shook his head slightly more, letting out a small groan. Reg wondered if he should alert the nurse in case Luke was in more pain.

'Do you want me to call someone?'

He shook his head again, and then moved his hand, letting go of Reg's fingers. It took Reg a moment to work it out, but he realised the boy was miming for a pen. He fumbled in his jacket pocket for something to write on, pulling out an envelope he'd yet to open. Taking a pen from his shirt pocket, he placed it in Luke's fingers and guided it to the paper, not sure if that was what he'd meant.

It had been.

Slow and unsteady, he watched as Luke did his best to make four scrawled letters on the paper before dropping the pen. Reg held the envelope up to try and read it. He had no idea how reliable it could be. What if a brain injury had disrupted his ability to write? The shapes began to suggest characters.

'Luke. Are these numbers?' He didn't reply. 'Okay, listen. Don't say anything, but squeeze my hand once for yes, twice for no. Are these numbers?'

Luke squeezed once. Reg waited. Just one.

'Two, three, three, four.' He waited. Waited. 'Is that right, Luke? Two, three, three, four?'

Luke squeezed once.

Reg waited. It was just once.

'What is this, Luke? A door number?'

A harsh whisper cut the air like a knife.

'What do you think you are doing, Mr Walters?'

'He's awake.'

The nurse glared at him with such incredulous displeasure he could have combusted on the spot.

'Well, I can see that. We've told you already, he's getting better, floating in and out. But the poor boy doesn't need you here badgering him, does he?'

'I wasn't. He spoke.'

'What this boy needs is rest. And he is going to get it because you are going to leave.'

Reg stood and looked at her. He straightened up a little, wanting to protest. But he looked back at Luke and sighed.

'I'm sorry,' he said to the nurse. 'You're right. Thank you for all you are doing for him.'

The nurse softened her scowl and rolled her eyes. 'You are a good man, Mr Walters.' She touched him on the arm. 'But, please, bugger off for a bit.' She picked up Luke's chart and began making notes of vital statistics.

Reg picked up his coat and gave Luke's hand one more squeeze. He felt the slightest squeeze in return before he let go and left.

He looked down at the numbers in his hand and wondered how small the needle was, and how massive the haystack could prove to be.

Chapter 33

'Bloods are back for your homeless girl, Janine,' the head nurse said, handing the print-out to the young trainee nurse. 'Looks like you need to have a chat with her. Do you want extra support?'

'No thanks. I've got this.' Janine was keen to impress and wanted to show her initiative. She went back over to the cubicle and opened the curtain with a soft smile that curved her whole face and made her eyes twinkle.

Young patients usually only gave false details when they were scared. Foreign accent. Inconsistent story. Suspicious wounds. It was too easy to say, 'illegal immigrant.'

'Sorry about the wait, Amelja. I had a problem with our computer. Can I check the spelling of your name?'

Amelja gasped. 'Oh, no. I make mistake. These two letters, wrong way. So sorry I have waste time.'

Janine smiled. 'Easily done. I'll get these rechecked in a minute.'

'Raining outside. I think cold freeze my brain.'

'My poor lovely. Don't you worry one bit. We'll sort it.' Amelja smiled.

Janine moved closer and lowered her voice. The next question was a little more private. 'I do have another question, Amelja.' She waited for the girl to nod. 'This is a little personal to ask, but are you sexually active at the moment?'

'You mean, I have sex?'

'I'm not here to judge. We just need to be honest about these things when getting treatment, okay? And remember what I said about confidentiality?' She watched as Amelja looked down and then back into her eyes.

'It is not good for me to be doing that right now.'

'You aren't in trouble. But your blood test results show you are pregnant.'

Amelja's complexion greyed instantly, her eyes filled as they darted from side to side. She brought her hands up to her stomach and her entire body tensed.

'Is there really no one I can call?' Janine said, keeping her voice down. 'The father?' she let it hold as a question nuanced with many possibilities.

Amelja shook her head roughly.

'Remember what I said. I am here for you. To make sure you get the help you need.' She waited for the girl to nod. 'I tell you what, I fancy a cup of tea. What about you? I could go get us a cuppa, and we can have a little chat.'

Amelja nodded.

Janine patted her on the hand and then quietly left the cubicle. She was now almost certain from the fear on that girl's face, the name was not the only lie she'd told. She was prepared to bet there was no way the girl was seventeen. Or even sixteen, for that matter.

* * *

Amelja

Amelja felt her whole body tremble with panic. Her head filled with fog.

This wasn't part of the plan. They'd agreed she go along

with all the treatment offered, then sneak out.

But she couldn't make sense of her thoughts. Pregnant? Could they be wrong? Surely not in a hospital with all the experts.

Before that night at the horrible house, she had never had sex. And she was sure they had all used a condom. She was sure. It had been a rule she heard the man who called himself 'uncle' say. They made jokes.

There was only one she never saw.

And he had been so drugged, out of it, not knowing what he was doing.

It had been different with that one.

* * *

Janine

'Hey, Sands.'

DS Sandra Bolton saw her and walked over.

'Little Neens. Long time, no see.'

'I know. How are you? You're looking good. What you doing here?' Janine always blistered out questions when she was excited. It was one of the things that DS Bolton liked about her.

Bolton was almost old enough to be her mother and was often referred to as her aunt Sands when she needed advice.

'It's just a disagreement between human bodies and cars and raids going a little bit squiffy. What's up?'

'Couldn't bend your ear a sec, could I?'

'I have a couple of minutes.'

Janine took a breath. 'I'm not saying this really, what with…'

'Blah, blah,' Bolton waved off the confidentiality spiel. 'Schtum as a princess and her Brussel-sprouts bum.'

Janine took a breath before launching in a staccato

barrage. 'Girl comes in. Homeless. Says she's seventeen. Complaining of foot pain. Feet cut up awful and badly dressed probably a week or so ago. You know the score?'

'Sticky-taped, not stitched, right?'

'Exactly. Infection setting in. Anyway, that's not it. Old bruises on her wrists and neckline. Maybe collarbone, too.'

Bolton winced and shook her head, knowing exactly what the nurse was heading towards.

'But there's more. She sounds Eastern European. False name. I doubt she's even sixteen. Her bloods came back and she's pregnant.'

'Bloody textbook. What's she like?'

'She's talking a bit. But if she goes back out on the street this way we both know how this could end.'

They both knew there was no option but to report it. The question remaining was more about the best way to achieve the best results. 'Follow safeguarding to the letter, avoid mentioning immigration.'

'Damned Home Office will jump at the chance to drop-kick her into some prison, or send her to Windrush plane, wherever that is.'

DS Bolton smiled at her naivety. 'I have a contact in safeguarding I know I can trust. I'll prime them for the call. But you, Neens, you go by the book. Right?' You're too close to qualifying to balls-up on a case like this. When I give you the nod, we'll move on it.'

'Okay, auntie Sands.'

'But first thing's first, get your SANE down here and make sure you get the girl's clothes, sealed and signed.' Bolton knew that having a Sexual Assault Nurse Examiner's expertise was vital to collecting evidence correctly if there was any chance in securing convictions later down the line.

'Will do. Cheers, Sands.' Janine planted a kiss on Bolton's cheek and went to get a cup of tea for Amelja, as planned.

DS Bolton took out her phone and made a call. She

was determined that they would not let another one of these girls slip through the net.

* * *

Luke

He'd watched the nurse treating Amelja talk to the other woman. No doubt about it. She was a cop.

She also looked kind of scary. A bit kickass. They clearly knew each other personally, though. All hugs and kisses. But their chat was definitely about Amelja, from the way they looked over to the curtain. What happened to all that confidential shit they talk about?

Surely, Amelja knew they needed to get out of there soon. The cop was already on the phone. He wondered what Amelja had said.

He had to get out of there.

But the nurse was coming back with two cups in her hands. Were they having a cosy drink together? He'd said to go along with the treatment, but, Christ, that was a bit much.

What was it about girls and having a fucking drink together? Like they were always going to the toilet in pairs or groups. Maybe that was because of all the tea they drank.

An ugly thought crossed his mind. He didn't want to consider it and tried to push it back. But it lingered.

He had to find out what was going on. Was Amelja pulling off the greatest ever misdirection, or had she been tricked into turning on him?

*   *   *

Amelja

Everything was taking too long. Normally the cup of tea would have been a welcome treat. But why was she doing it?

And where was her folder? She was being chatty like a friend would. Like she was trying to bide time or distract Amelja from something else going on.

Was she trying her own misdirection?

The nurse had folded up Amelja's clothes and put them under the bed. It had sounded liked they were put inside a bag or something, too. She worried she wouldn't get them back, as all she could see now was her coat on the chair with the jogging bottoms and spare underwear she'd got.

Luke would be waiting, getting more and more worried about what was taking so long.

But he also didn't know what she'd been told.

The curtain was pulled back slightly and a woman popped her head in. Something about her seemed strange to Amelja. She looked important, strong.

'Sorry to disturb you. Quick message.'

The nurse looked at Amelja, then at the other woman.

Amelja could see they knew each other well. Her heart pounded.

'Are we still on for later?' The woman seemed to be arranging their social life.

Amelja thought that sounded unprofessional.

'I made that call but Safia will be delayed. So, she says you'll have to put up with me first, alright.'

The nurses nodded a little too certainly, and Amelja felt like something else was being said. She knew a couple of girls called Saffia or Sohpia. She'd never heard Say-Fia before.

The nurse just nodded.

Amelja could sense it in the air. Something was being organised. She was beginning to worry about Luke. Had he already gone without her? She didn't want to think about him leaving her alone.

What if someone had caught him? Seen them come in together, found out their secret, and given him to the police.

She felt sick.

'Amelja,' she softened her tone, 'I know the pregnancy result came as a shock, so I think it would be a good idea if we did a quick check to see if everything is okay. Down there.' She dropped her eyes and nodded as she whispered the last two words.

Amelja knew she couldn't say no without making them more suspicious, and Luke had told her to go along with all the tests, so she nodded.

'I tell you what,' the nurse said, 'I'll just get a colleague of mine to help. Nothing to worry about.'

But Amelja was more than worried. Everything was getting out of control. She let the nurse leave the cubicle, and got down from the bed, standing awkwardly at first. Her feet felt much better. She opened the curtain and after some looking, she could see Luke.

Amelja waved a few times to catch his eye. Could she tell him then what she knew? She had to get him to get out of the hospital.

'Luke, you must go. Now.'

'We go together.'

'No, you must go now. They might catch you.'

Luke scratched at his head.

'Go now, and I will follow soon.'

'But what if you need me?'

'I find you.'

'How will you find me?'

Amelja tried to think of the closest place to find each other, but far enough away to be safe. 'Big Tesco shop,' she said, eyes wide with the idea. 'We pass the Tesco shop on the bus here.'

Luke nodded, reluctantly.

'I will find you.' She kissed him quickly on the cheek. 'Now, you must go.'

Amelja watched Luke turn and walk away just as the nurse came back around the corner with something in her hand.

Another test.

More questions.

More lies.

Chapter 34

'Hope I'm not disturbing you,' Reg Walters oozed his accent into DI Stone's office.

'I am beyond hope.'

Walters entered the room and closed the door behind him. He paused for a moment before turning around to face Stone, taking a deep breath. He was out of his normal uniform of a three-piece suit and instead wore a pricey pair of casual jeans, and an expensive leather coat.

Stone jumped in first. 'I've had SOCO take a full set of photos. Took some string-pulling, but it's sorted.' Stone suddenly remembered why Reg was probably there. 'Shit, sorry. What I meant was, how is he? How are you?'

'He's been awake a couple of days, but dosed up on funky painkillers, so pretty out of it.' Reg let out a sigh of relief. 'Initial tests suggest no brain damage, and the internal bleeding is under control.' His whole body visibly sagged.

Stone sat back in his seat.

'He's still struggling to move or talk much, but that's okay. The consultant says he's doing remarkably well.

'Poor kid.' Stone looked at Reg, a hopeful expression on his face. 'Has he managed to say anything to you so

211

far?'

Reg took a piece of paper from his pocket as he spoke. 'The only thing he tried to say was to ask where Amelja was. I didn't have the heart to say anything to him, yet. In truth, I don't know how I am going to do it.'

'There's never going to be an easy way.'

Handing the piece of paper to Stone, he let out a deep sigh. 'He scribbled this down in one of his less lucid moments.'

Stone took the piece of paper and looked at the four scrawled numbers. 'Was it just the four numbers?'

'Just the four. I wondered if it was a door number or a partial phone number. I started listing possibilities but I just got lost.' Reg wiped his hand across his face. If it was an attempt to wipe away the tired look, it failed.

Stone fiddled with the paper in his hand for a moment. 'It could be a taxi number or a bus number. This will have to be one for the hive mind. I'll put it up on the board and get people to search for any local reference. All we can assume is that there is some importance to it and he thought you would understand it.'

'That's what frustrates me, Mike. I want to be able to help him, and the only thing he's given me so far, I can't make head nor tails of it. I feel utterly useless, really I do.'

Stone raised a hand to calm Reg's demons.

'And he's still got to contend with being suspect-number-one in a rape case.'

Stone rocked his head and groaned, raising a placatory hand. 'Let's come back to that.' He changed the pace of the conversation, refocusing the pathologist on his expertise. 'Tell me more about the injuries and bruises.'

Reg went through the details of a number of the bruises he'd observed and photographed with the help of the nurse.

Stone leaned forward. 'More likely a woman or a child?'

'Children.'

'A group attack?'

'At least two, maybe three. It was hard to tell as I had to be quick taking my pictures. But there are different shoe sizes for sure. Plus, some bruises look like knuckle abrasions. One set of four is definitely narrower than another. The human hand is unique in far more ways than just fingerprints. You know, if we took more prints around the hand, so many more crimes could be solved.'

Stone's eyebrows raised with a slight smile at Reg catching a second wind of energy. 'Age of the attackers?' Stone knew he was asking an almost impossible question.

'I would say most probably pre-adolescent.' Reg sat forward to and leaned on Stone's desk. 'Individual blows seemed to lack the power advanced muscle growth gives teenage boys.'

'Is there any way we could substantiate this with evidence?'

Reg stopped for a moment before clicking his fingers and slapping his forehead with the heel of his hand. 'Luke has relatively few fractured ribs, which indicates a limit to the force he was hit with. Had these been older, stronger boys, or women, his ribcage would have been pulverised.'

Stone rubbed his stubbled chin and scratched at his ribs, subconsciously responding to the idea. 'Ironically, the only thing that possibly saved him was the tragic fact that these were younger attackers?'

Reg nodded but frowned and titled his head to one side. 'But when could this have happened? A group of young boys beating a naked teenager.'

Stone leaned forward. 'And why didn't he fight back?'

'Exactly. He's no wimp, Mike. Good kid, but he's had to learn to protect himself. When he blows, he can do serious damage, even to adults.'

They both sat back.

Stone tapped at his chin. 'Reg, let me sound something out to you.'

Reg waved both his palms open before putting them back together at the fingertips. It was a scene often played out in his own office when the two minds came together to bounce ideas and sound out the kinds of thoughts that might not be welcome in a senior police officer's presence.

'We have physical evidence that Amelja was raped.' Stone raised a finger to count each factor. 'We have DNA that shows, almost indisputably, that Luke had sex with Amelja. But you are pretty sure he could never have raped her.' He was careful not to pitch it as a question. Or worse still, an allegation.

Reg stared at DI Stone. It was a look of utter defiance, and there was a tightness in his face the detective was not used to seeing. He knew Reg cared for the boy and didn't want to overstep their trust. But at the same time, he couldn't evade asking the question, not with the pressure from Carter to investigate the possibility.

'Luke did not rape her, Mike.' He spoke quietly, a man biting back rage.

'Okay. My hunch. What if he was forced, or coerced?'

Reg's breathing deepened and his hands gripped the arms of the chair. 'That boy is lying in hospital.'

'I know.'

'Beaten and left for dead.'

'Reg.'

Reg bolted up from the chair and turned to face the door. His breathing was heavy as he raised a fist and pointed at DI Stone. His mouth opened and Stone sat back in anticipation of an outburst.

But it never came.

The pathologist retracted his hand and marched to the office door, swinging it open before walking out and leaving the incident room.

The air fizzed with unspent, explosive anger. Mike Stone let out a deep sigh.

What the hell is this case doing to us all?

DI Stone walked over to the whiteboard in the incident room and wrote the four numbers under Luke's name, circling them a few times.

'Right, people, gather round.'

There was a general hubbub of calls being finished, office chairs being wheeled over, and desks creaking under a little too much weight being applied to the corners.

'First thing. Luke is awake and early signs show he's escaped brain damage and serious long-term injuries.'

There was a release of sighs across the room. Even amidst all the uncertainty in the case, knowing at least one of the children involved was alive brought some relief.

He pointed to the four numbers. 'This could be a lead, a hint, or even a pointless garbled message. But it is unlikely to be a deliberate red herring. Stick it in your heads. Make it your muse. Luke scrawled these numbers to Dr Walters. We don't know if that factor is important, though.'

'What's next, guv? Sudoku?' a constable laughed at his own joke.

'If you like, constable, here's your very own puzzle.' Stone wrote 'P45' in big letters. 'Let me know in writing if you want any help with that.'

A disapproving and bitter groan was directed at the DC. Humour was commonplace and welcomed. But timing mattered.

'Is there a prize, Guv?' another voice called out, attempting to lighten humour again.

Stone held up both hands. 'If anyone solves it, I will personally buy them a beverage, and a tube of smarties.' His heart sank at the number of blank younger faces looking back at him. 'Jesus Christ, kids. Google Smarties.'

DS Pete Barry waved a hand.

Thank God, a sensible voice.

'Are we assuming it is a four-digit number, or could it be a different arrangement of the four numbers?'

'Good question. The only thing we can be reasonably

sure of is the order of the numbers. How they are grouped is also not clear. Pete, could you handle the collation of our collective genius?'

DS Barry grinned. 'Genius? I'll be off home for the day, then.'

The room returned to its usual hubbub but there was a palpable fresh energy that even the slightest new lead always brought to a case.

* * *

'That's a bit bloody cryptic, boss,' DS Bolton didn't hide the scepticism down the phone.

DI Stone had spent the rest of the afternoon doing mundane paperwork in a bid to distract himself, hoping he could dupe his subconscious into solving the numeric code.

Page numbers from a book.

He'd scrawled the idea down.

Idiot. What teenage boy reads a book with that many pages?

He'd scribbled it out and written 'duh' next to it.

'That's all he wrote on a piece of paper when he woke up.'

'Best call Arthur.'

'Who?'

'Conan Doyle.'

'The Barbarian.'

Bolton sighed. 'Just ask Jack. He'll probably know.'

'About the numbers?'

She laughed. 'Bloody hell, where is your head at? No, Arthur Conan Doyle, who wrote Sherlock.' She paused. 'But now you mention it, why not ask him about the numbers? Kids think like kids.'

Stone tried to rub the tiredness from his face. 'Well, we've all spent the past few hours hammering the numbers into everything, and no one has solved it yet.'

Silence hung on for a few moments before Bolton's softer tone crept in. 'How's Reg holding up?'

'He's struggling.'

Bolton paused and bit her lip.

'I heard that, Sands.'

'What?'

'That Jedi silence.'

'Look, I respect Reg completely, and I know he means well, but I have to ask you this.'

'I have thought the same, don't worry.'

Mike Stone had wondered if his friend Reg Walters might be too close to Luke for his own good.

'I don't mean creepy-pervert-close, Mike.'

'No, it's okay. I see your point. I share it.'

'And I also realise the irony, that it's a little pot-kettle-black for me to say it.'

Stone smiled. 'No, it isn't. You were knocked for six by a traumatic event. And don't you dare try to minimalise it.'

'Reg knows Luke. Seeing him that way would be traumatic. A big part of me wants to just shrug it off.'

'Your instincts are bang on. But, Luke has no one else. If Reg is going to be the bridge that helps us to help Luke, then we need to give him that support.'

'It's just the evidence.'

'Yes, I know. But let's not forget Reg knows how child protection investigations go. And remember, all we have is information and facts. It is only interpretation that makes them 'evidence'. Only when you start writing the narrative.'

'Does he know how to handle when the boy might be a suspect, too, though?'

It was Stone's turn to pause and listen to the voice niggling over his shoulder again. 'What if that's something you look out for?' Stone asked.

'In my devil's advocate, bitch-cop role, you mean?'

Stone laughed, feeling himself relax. 'If this all goes to shit, it's my head on the block. Can you keep an objective eye on Reg's part? It allows me to be his shoulder without causing a conflict of interest.'

'Your head and shoulders?' She sniggered. 'I think I have a shampoo for that.'

'The way this is going, I think it would be better to go for some masculine grey hair remover.'

'Bloody hell, Mike. I don't want images of you two lathering up together, recolouring your silvery bits.'

'Detective Sergeant Bolton,' Stone laughed down the phone. 'That's a whole new level of insubordination. And on that note, I expect a full page of possible ideas on this number riddle by morning briefing. Annotated. In triplicate.'

Bolton continued to laugh.

'Bugger off, will you?'

'I'll give the girls a good night kiss from Uncle Mike, shall I?'

They ended the conversation a little more relaxed.

As he put his phone back in his pocket he could see the mood in the incident room was beginning to get sluggish. Walking over to his door, he raised his voice to the rest of the room.

'I should demand we stay here all night, but if you're on day shift, that's enough for today guys. Get home to your better halves and miniature selves.'

'And inflatable partners, too, guv?'

Just as a sigh of relief and a synchronised dropping of many pens kicked off a round of yawns that seemed to hit the room like an epidemic, PC Pearson entered the room and stopped in the doorway.

Stone nodded at him. 'Young PC Pearson, are you on nights?'

Pearson nodded and gave Stone a mock salute to

accompany a smile so sincere it was difficult to get annoyed with the inappropriate way of greeting a senior officer.

'That, I am, guv, boss, sir. That I am.'

'Well, I'm about to go home. Classwork and homework are on the whiteboard. If you finish all your work, practise your spellings, and do some private reading.'

Pearson smiled and made his way over to his desk, glancing at the whiteboard.

'Aw, chuffing heck, sir,' his voice was loud but mocking. 'Not bible studies.'

'Bible studies?' Stone raised one very confused eyebrow.

'No disrespect sir, equal ops and all. But I'm an atheist.'

'Pearson, what are you blithering on about?'

He pointed at the board, waggling his finger in a way that could only be described as slightly camp. Stone wondered if he was trying to mimic the character from the nineties sitcom with Rowan Atkinson. Then he remembered Pearson was too young to know that.

'Yeh, bible studies, boss. You've got it right there. Luke, twenty-three, thirty-four.'

'Bible?' Stone felt his heart rate rising. As yet, no one, not even Reg, the devout Christian, had mentioned the bible. 'What is Luke, twenty-three, thirty-four?'

'Holy shit,' another voice said.

At least two computers gave out the noise of hammering keyboards and mouse clicking. Stone was sure Google was about to earn its brownie points.

Pearson continued. 'Yeh, I think it goes something like, "forgive them for they know not what they are doing," boss.' He shrugged his shoulders. 'Something like that. Christ's last words on the cross. Look it up.'

Stone looked around the room, waiting for confirmation. He caught the eyes of the fastest Googlers in the room who had already scoured, found the reference, and looked up at him. Nodding, awkwardly.

'Well, what the hell does it mean?' Stone felt himself

almost shouting.

Pearson continued. 'It's the bit where he's asking God, his dad, to forgive the men for punishing him, and beating him and, well, chuffing well executing him in a pretty nasty way. That's the whole thing, you see. Jesus took his death to be the sacrifice for all their sins that.' He paused and tilted his head like a thoughtful dog.

'He's right, guv,' another voice said.

'But would Luke know enough of the bible to make that reference?' Stone asked, out loud but more to himself than to anyone else.

Pearson perched on the end of his desk. 'Who did he say it to?'

'He wrote it on a piece of paper to Reg Walters, the pathologist.'

'Mr Walters is a Christian, right?' Pearson looked around at all the nods in the room. 'Well, if the kid knows Reg, and with him being Christian, maybe he assumed Reg would cotton on straight away. I dunno.'

'Pearson,' Stone pointed at him as his voice boomed across the room loud enough to make the PC sit upright. 'If you have just sodding well walked in here and worked that out in one go, when we have all sat here and not clocked it for the past two hours, I am going to slap you.'

Pearson's mouth carved an upside-down smile out of his chin.

'And then I am going to kiss you.'

'Now, boss, I can tolerate a slap, but I won't be having no sexual harassment.'

There was a palpable change in atmosphere as the incident room erupted with laughter that was probably the first in the whole week.

'Perhaps not, Constable, but if you are right, I owe you a drink and a tube of smarties.'

'Smarties, boss?'

'Google it, smart arse.'

DI Stone went back into his office and was about to call Reg to ask his opinion, but decided to give him some much-needed space, and sent it as a text instead.

Pearson appeared at his door with a confused look on his face. 'Got a sec, boss?'

'Sure, come in.'

Pearson came into the office and stood to attention in front of DI Stone's desk.

'Relax, James, please. How can I help.'

'It was just, well, I hope I haven't tread on anyone's toes, sir. I didn't mean to seem all arrogant coming in like that and just shouting my mouth off. Boss. Sir. Guv.'

Stone's mouth dropped. 'You don't need to apologise. No one has even mentioned the bible. There are one or two out there tugging at the collars and blushing slightly at their oversight.'

Pearson's shoulders relaxed. He didn't mind pissing off a few of the more seasoned detectives, but it was clear he wanted to stay in Stone's good books.

'I value initiative and outside-the-box thinking. And given your stellar work on the CCTV, you're earning your stripes all good and fair.'

'Yes, sir. Thank you.'

'While you're here, Pearson,' Stone changed his tone just enough to let the young officer know it was the end of that subject. 'I haven't had time to sit and talk with you about your plans. Where you see yourself going in the force.'

'Well, I do want to think about going for sergeant positions when I'm ready. Not sure I can even grow a moustache yet. A good sergeant needs a moustache, I reckon.'

'I'll be sure to tell DS Bolton you said that.'

Pearson tried to stifle a snigger.

Stone rubbed at his stubble. 'Have you considered training as a detective?'

Pearson's face lit up. 'Seriously?'

'Look, I won't start saying positions are available and making promises I can't keep, but I really think you should at least look into it.'

His smile almost reached his ears before he pulled it back a bit to try and rescue some humility. 'Yes, I will do. Thanks, sir. Thank you.'

'Now, you go and work some more of your magic, and I'll keep you posted if this turns out to be something.'

Pearson left Stone's office with a childlike spring in his step, and DI Stone couldn't shake a warm, fuzzy feeling. He could be a grumpy old man at times, so when it came to genuinely acknowledging his team, he liked doing it.

And he was getting to like PC Pearson.

As for the religious reference, if his theory was right, the young officer had hit the nail on the head.

The only thing he couldn't understand was why Luke would want Reg to forgive those who had hurt him.

Stone took his phone out and called DCI Palmers.

'Mike? What's new?'

'Just a couple of things, sir.' He paused for a moment, glancing into his own eyes in the reflection of his office window. 'I think it is about time we put some very serious thought into the organised crime group angle.'

'Something else happened?'

'More like some pieces are beginning to fall together in ways I can't make sense of unless I think of this whole thing like an OCG.'

'And you're thinking Kapllani? Albanian, right?'

'I don't see how we can't at least give it due process. Get the whole team on it.

'Right, go on then. I'll handle the fallout for now.' Palmers let out a sigh loud enough to be heard down the line. 'This is one of those times I hope you are wrong.' The line went dead.

Chapter 35

The gothic, red-brick library stood prominently on the street corner in Spring Hill. Luke wondered why it wasn't the building that had stuck in their minds. Closer up, it was impressive and imposing in equal measure. It seemed odd that someone had joined a Tesco to the Victorian Terracotta building, no longer using the impressive entrances at the front.

Luke smiled at the idea of asking the Queen to enter Buckingham palace by the back gate. But then he realised he'd never actually seen her on the front steps of the Palace either. Maybe the front doors were all just for show. Especially for the rich.

Luke's stomach rumbled, and that gave the answer he needed. Certain landmarks stayed in the mind depending on what we needed or used them for. He like big buildings, and even liked libraries. But they didn't settle hunger.

Luke kept moving in and out of the entrance to the supermarket, sheltering from the bitter crosswinds, but still keeping an eye out for Amelja.

'You alright, bab?' A voice thick with black country drawl interrupted Luke's solitary thoughts.

He turned to see one of the staff from Tesco had come

outside and was talking to him.

'It's just, well, you've been out here a long time,' the woman said. She looked kind. Soft, wrinkled skin and silver hair. Pudgy, but not fat in an ugly way. Luke thought she looked like a lovely little grandma you only ever saw on TV.

'I'm just waiting for my girlfriend,' he replied, putting on his best voice again.

The woman looked back over her shoulder, then at her watch. Then she raised a finger with a beaming smile and pointed at him. 'You wait here. Back in a mo.' Turning on her heel with impressive speed, she waddled like she was close to falling forwards. Each step seemed to catch her body just in time.

Luke returned to looking down the road, longing for Amelja to appear. Almost ten minutes had passed when the same woman came back with a Tesco carrier bag, looking over her shoulder repeatedly.

'It's cold out here, bab. Too cold for you to be hanging around.' She tilted her head to look up at Luke, as he was a few inches taller than her. 'Why don't you go home, out of this rain, eh? Catch your death, you will.'

Luke took a little too long to reply. 'It's okay, I have to wait.'

'Like that, is it, bab?' Her face warmed and Luke could see the expression he knew all too well.

Pity.

She reached out and took his hand, and Luke surprised himself as he let her do it. There was something in her manner that was not at all threatening. Not even patronising. Her skin was softer than he had ever felt a hand before. And warm. She slipped the handles of the bag into his hand and closed his fingers around them.

'You must look after yourself, bab. It's cold. Little bit of grub for those hungry eyes. And for that girl of yours.'

Luke felt his chin and bottom lip tighten, secretly

beginning to quiver. Here, again, a stranger helping him. And with such expectation that he cares for Amelja. If only they knew the truth. Would they help him then? He mouthed a "thank you" but wasn't sure if any sound came out.

But he knew she heard it.

'No need, bab. Besides, she ain't half beautiful, your girl.'

Confusion gripped his face as he looked at her.

The lady nodded over his shoulder to a figure stood just twenty feet behind him.

Luke turned so fast he almost dropped the bag as he called to Amelja. It was only after a couple of steps he thought to apologise and thank the old woman again. But she raised a hand and smiled.

* * *

Amelja detailed the whole escape from the hospital to Luke as they walked back towards the city. She told him what they had said, how they had examined her and that the police wanted to interview her.

She told him everything besides one key detail.

Heading towards the Jewellery Quarter, they cut through Brookfields Cemetery and finally found their bearings on Vyse Street, one of the main roads in the area.

Several buses passed them on the route, but they couldn't work out fast enough if they were heading in or out of the city centre. Tiredness, pain, and a level of irritability was clouding their judgement.

But they were running from the police, too.

'Luke, let us stop. My feet.' Amelja pleaded. She was still pale, clammy and her eyes seemed to have greyed.

Luke scanned around the area, looking for somewhere to sit. Hands on his hips, he folded almost double.

'Luke, the train.' Amelja pointed over to the Jewellery

Quarter train station less than fifty feet away. If nothing else, it would be somewhere to sit down.

They found a second burst of energy and ran towards the station, laughter coming from somewhere deep inside them. That place children go to when the horrors of the world are suddenly forgotten.

The familiar sound of screeching metal filled the station.

'This way, Luke, a train.'

'No, Amelja, not…'

But she had vanished down the steps towards the platform, knowing Luke would follow. And he did, getting to the bottom of the steps to see her leaning out of the train door and waving him on.

'Get off the train, Amelja,' he shouted, barely sounding the words from his rattling throat, gasping breath, and laughter at the situation.

'No, you get on,' she shouted back, 'before it shut door and shoot off without you.'

'But, Amelja…' his voice trailed off as the alarms for the door began. He jumped onto the train and Amelja laughed out louder than he'd heard her laugh in quite some time. Luke moved closer, putting his hands on her sides as she wrapped her arms around him.

'You're slow,' she said.

'You're an idiot.'

'How dare you say?'

'We're on the wrong train.'

The train started to roll gently and Amelja turned to look out the window.

Luke whispered in her ear. 'We should be going the other way.'

Amelja covered her mouth in shock, but a quiet giggle betrayed any concern she might have wanted to express. Turning to Luke, their eyes met. She looked at him carefully, breathing a deep sigh, and for a moment Luke thought he saw sadness.

'This means all the walking we did is about to be wasted,' Luke said.

'Maybe it is fate.' Amelja shrugged her shoulders. 'We were meant to go this way.'

'Well, we don't have tickets either way.'

'Let's go. New place. Adventure. Just you, me, and…' she paused as the words got trapped in her throat.

'And?'

A booming voice came from the other end of the carriage. 'Tickets, please.'

'Shit,' Luke hissed. The moment of panic screwed up his face clear enough for the ticket inspector to notice them. There was no point trying to hide, they'd already been clocked. He approached with a perverse amusement on his face, clearly enjoying his little bit of power.

'Tickets, please.' His round face twisted with a smug grin.

'We're going to get one at the station,' Luke tried to sound apologetic.

The fat inspector's eyebrows raised. 'You were just at the station.' He stretched his words all out of shape, desperately trying to hide a strong black country accent.

'Er, no. The next station.'

'Which is?' Tilting his head, leaning in towards them.

Amelja cut in. 'Scotland.'

Luke sniggered.

The inspector frowned and rolled his eyes. 'Very funny.'

'I only buy ticket from man with skirt,' Amelja blurted out, straight-faced.

Luke looked at her.

The inspector looked at Luke. 'You clearly think this is all just a joke.'

'No joke,' Amelja shook her head, stern and defiant, but polite. 'I respect man who wear skirt. I buy from him. You no wear skirt. You are…*i zhburrëruar*.'

Taken aback by what he assumed was an insult, the

inspector adjusted his belt and rolled his shoulders. 'If you do not present a ticket you will be issued with a fine.'

'A fine?' Luke replied, calm and polite. 'But we don't have enough money to pay a fine.'

'Well, you'll be getting off at the next station anyway,' the inspector fumbled for a reply. He had been flustered by the lack of intimidation he'd managed to achieve over two children.

Amelja played on the man's apparent fluster. 'Which station is next? Is it long time to Scotland?'

'Normally it would be the Hawthorns, but the station is closed for safety reasons. You will have to get off at Smethwick Galton Bridge. Just a couple of minutes away.'

The inspector took a moment to wait for a reply, but when he got nothing, simply shook his head roughly as he moved to stand just inside the door.

He looked sternly at Luke and Amelja as the train pulled into the station. Trying to assert his authority, he gave his belt a shuffle, straightened the lapels of his company blazer, and attempted to look as tall as he could.

'Thank you,' he said, somewhat passive-aggressively, opening the door and holding his arm out to wave Luke and Amelja off the train.

Amelja turned back to him. 'My Luke is right. You do not have balls to wear a skirt.'

The whole episode left the teenagers giggling at the ridiculousness of it all as they waved to the man when the train pulled out of the station. Everything about the day had tired them, pushed them over the edge and they held each other.

'Where to now?' Amelja asked as they climbed the steps to the station exit.

'I guess we make our way back to the city centre.'

The dread of walking for much further screwed Amelja's face up. Luke saw the look but felt there was more to it than just the walking.

'Don't worry, I still have the bus ticket. We can use that.'

'What is this?' Amelja pointed away from the main road and across to the canal that she could just make out between the trees. Without waiting for Luke to reply, she darted off.

He called after her, but she didn't turn back.

By the time Luke caught up, Amelja was standing at the middle of the bridge, arm wrapped around the lamppost as her head rested on it. Amelja stared down the length of the canal. Her eyes were fixed on the vanishing horizon swathed in the setting sun.

Luke placed his hand on her shoulder around the lamppost, but the physical obstruction spoke volumes to him.

'It is beautiful, this place,' she said, her voice quiet and sad.

Luke nodded.

'I think it is special.'

'It's just a bridge, isn't it?' Luke frowned. He zipped his hoodie up a bit higher to his neck, trying to shield from the bitter breeze catching them out in the open.

'Bridges bring people together,' she said. 'You have saying about not burn bridges, yes?'

Luke had heard that many times. He remembered Reg talking to him about them some time ago. Even then he'd thought he had no bridges left in his life. Until he'd met Amelja.

'Do you believe in fate, Luke?'

He rubbed his head through the hood. 'Dunno. I guess if there is such a thing, I wonder why it is so shitty.'

Amelja's face darkened and she pushed away from the lamppost, and him.

'You think this is shitty?' Her outburst was sudden. 'Fate brings us here, together. We make bridge. You think that is shitty?'

'No, I didn't mean us.'

'What if there was more?'

'More what?'

'More on our bridge? Would you want that?'

'I don't understand.'

He moved towards her, raising a hand to her cheek. But Amelja slapped it away.

'No, Luke.'

'What happened? I just wanted you to get your feet looked at.'

'I know.'

'And, now you're like this.' He raised his hands and shrugged his shoulders.

Amelja walked into the centre of the bridge.

Luke slapped the railing with his hand, gripping it and pulsing his hand as if trying to squeeze the metal. After a few moments, he pulled himself away. 'Amelja, what is it? What did I do?'

Her voice came from somewhere dark. A growl of anger. She spat her words out. 'You know what you did.'

It cut Luke like a knife. They stood frozen in silence.

Tears filled Amelja's eyes and she pointed over and beyond him, back across the city. 'And now they know.'

'Who?'

'At hospital. Nurse and police, Luke. They know.'

He brought his hands up to his head.

'They looked, they see bruises still here,' she said, stabbing at her wrists, at her neck. She shoved Luke in the chest. 'And then they look here. Take blood and samples.' She vaguely indicated lower. She punctuated every word with another slap to his chest. 'They. Know. You…'

Luke staggered back with each hit, refusing to defend himself. 'I did, and I'm sorry. I want to take it back. Wish it all away. How can I do that?'

He dropped to his knees, holding his head to her abdomen, the sobs beginning to fill his voice.

'They asked me,' she said, pulling his hood down fully. They did tests. I say nothing. I tell them nothing.'

'It's okay. You couldn't lie about that.'

'Don't you see what they think?'

He nodded.

'I fear for you.'

He paused a moment as the words of the taxi driver flashed into his mind. And those of the woman from Tesco. 'I must keep you safe. Just tell me what to do. Anything you want.'

'Luke…'

'I love…'

'I am pregnant.'

Chapter 36

'How come he's never been on our radar before?' Khan said, as he chewed away at the end of a pen and tilted his head to look at the new name on the board.

Nesim Kapllani's name had finally been added to the board after DI Stone got the green light from DCI Palmers.

'He's always on the radar, in the background,' Stone replied. 'But being a part of an Organised Crime Group, he doesn't come within in our remit. However, now we know he's linked to one of our cases, we get to play with the big boys.'

Bolton brushed pastry crumbs from her shirt. 'And it's this Splint character who has linked us up this time?'

'By getting killed,' Khan smirked.

'By a second gunman,' Stone waved his sausage roll.

'Who has a top-secret name.' Bolton thought twice about any more greasy food.

The three detectives had done their best to uncover the identity of their second driver, and since the ID was above even DCI Palmer's pay grade, and CS Carter was out at meetings, they'd all felt a shuddering pause in the case being enforced on them.

'Boss,' Khan sat forward, 'why can't we crack Paul Buchanan for more information? I realise it could become an elephant in the room, but either he knows who this guy is, and is covering his own back, or he has been ordered to keep it that way.'

'We still don't know why he was there.' Bolton jabbed her finger at the whiteboard, not bothering to hide her distaste for the man. 'Buchanan's not working any undercover angle.'

'That we know of.' Stone mumbled. 'And if he's somehow involved in a killing, even undercover, he could be bent, or rogue.'

Bolton nodded to the photo in the corner of the whiteboard. 'Who's that Masood bloke?'

Khan sat forward. 'Taxi Driver who knows Luke and Amelja.'

Stone corrected him. 'Well, he'd given them free rides on occasion. Charitably, it would seem.'

'Sounds fishy to me,' Bolton raised an eyebrow.

Khan raised his hand. 'He's on the system, but not for anything shifty, Sands.'

She looked at him, then Stone, then back to Khan.

'His daughter was sexually assaulted, battered, and left for dead six years ago.'

A Bolton swallowed heavily and sat up straight, steeling herself.

Khan continued. 'We never caught the bloke,' he paused. 'She took her own life two years ago.'

Stone took over. 'Mr Masood is almost definitely not shifty, but he is someone we need to keep an eye on.'

The three of them let the air settle, unable to avoid the feeling of observing silence.

A silence broken by Stone tapping on the whiteboard.

'My organised crime buddies have told me to keep an eye out for this fella. Martin Sketchford goes by the street name, "Gnome".'

'Prick in a red hat?' Khan sniggered.

'Known associate of Nesim Kapllani. Record as fat

as his left arse-cheek. Mostly petty rubbish, but drugs, violence, theft, and so on.'

Bolton frowned. 'What's he doing with the big boys, then?'

'Word has it he is one of Kapllani's runners. Drugs and, we strongly suspect, grooming for Kapllani's sex trafficking network.' Stone's eyes darkened. 'I want him.'

Khan sat up with a jolt, a thought striking him square in the forehead. He got to his feet and paced, one hand to his head, the other rolling over and over in the air like he was struggling to conduct an orchestra.

Finally, he spoke piecemeal thoughts. 'Luke. We need to talk to Luke.'

Stone replied first. 'Because?'

'Think about it,' Khan said, picking up a marker and scrawling his thoughts on the whiteboard so fast they were illegible. 'This whole thing. All organised. Kapllani, known for trafficking. Amelja, Albanian. Luke getting beaten.'

Bolton sat forward. 'Come on Harry, stick it together.'

'We need this Gnome guy. He's working for Kapllani. Luke was beaten by, what you and Reg say, was a bunch of kids.'

Stone twisted his head to look at Khan's scrawling. 'And Luke, twenty-three, thirty-four. Forgive them. Them. He's not talking about the people who took him, he's talking about the kids that kicked the shit out of him.'

'Were forced to,' Bolton added, catching up with the line of thought. 'And maybe that lack of wanting to do it meant they held back a bit.'

'Luke doesn't want us to blame a bunch of kids who were also rounded up by the likes of Gnome.' Stone got his phone out of his coat pocket. 'I need to get hold of Reg. If Luke can pin something on our Mr Gnome, we might find our way to go after Mr Kapllani.'

'We could always bring the garden critter in,' Bolton mused.

Stone paused as he considered it. 'Let's wait on that until we have something solid enough for an arrest warrant.'

'I bet there's one out for him already. Unrelated. Could bring him in on that, then have a nice friendly chat.' Bolton let a mischievous grin creep up to her eyes.

'That's a bit sly, sergeant Bolton,' Khan smiled.

She looked at him with a raised eyebrow.

'Which is why I'll gladly see to it.' Khan rolled his chair over to his computer. Both Stone and Bolton knew he'd find some way or reason to drag him into the station.

Stone searched for Reg's number, hoping he'd pick up a call. He didn't want to disturb him when he was with Luke, and certainly had no intention of harassing an injured boy into an interview.

He only stopped when he remembered that until Luke knew what had happened to Amelja, he needed to be left well alone.

Bolton tapped on Kapllani's name on the whiteboard. 'He's going to be high up in the OCG, which means he will have good protection.'

Stone nodded.

'Which also means if we start rattling too loud, too soon, he could get even the likes of Gnome lawyering up and going silent.' She paused for a moment. 'We need to play our cards carefully, Mike. The worst thing about these people is they know how to vanish underground very quick.'

'When you say underground, I think of moles.'

'And when you say moles, certain names start popping into my head.'

Chapter 37

February
Luke & Amelja

Her hands were on the inside, palms wrapped out the mug. His hands enclosed hers, warming them from the outside. They took it in turns to sip at the tea. If it had been a milkshake they would have had two straws, but that seemed a bit silly with tea.

Amelja's eyes were grey and puffy. The nightmare she had endured was written all over her face, even if no one knew the details. The past couple of weeks had been so mixed. Some days her stomach churned so badly she had vomited several times.

Luke had the idea of going into a pharmacy to ask for advice, and say he was worried about his mum. He was surprised at how helpful the lady had been, giving him booklets and leaflets and some advice.

They'd both walked slowly through the centre, begging just enough loose change for a single cup of tea to share between them.

Their coats were drenched, and even though their hoods were up, the edges of their hair had caught enough to drip.

Luke had thought to warm two napkins on the cup for a minute or so, and then use them to wipe their faces dry.

Amelja's legs bounced involuntarily under the table. A combination of cold and constant anxiety. Luke held her knees together with his, trying to keep her warm. When she flinched, he recoiled, letting go of her hands. He slid his chair away and stood as the metal echoed around the whole café. His face tightened and his dark eyebrows curled down so much they touched in the middle. When he could no longer stand to keep eye contact, he turned and walked out of the café, letting the door slam.

It took a few seconds for the shock to wear off, but Amelja put the cup down and followed him outside. Luke ignored all of her calls for him to wait.

'Where are you going?'

'I don't know. Nowhere. Anywhere.'

'Why? You cannot leave me. I need you.'

When he turned she still thought she could see his tears amidst the rain as if they were a different bright colour.

'Don't you see?' he shouted, voice cracking halfway between anger and tears. 'I caused this. Everything. None of it would've happened if you'd never met me.'

'No, not you, Luke.'

'What I did was bad enough. But we're just kids. This can't happen.'

'I love you, Luke. This is all that matters, no?'

He backed away from her a few more steps, beating his fists at his temples. 'I've ruined your life.'

Amelja caught up with him and took his head in her hands as she stared into his eyes. Luke placed his hands over hers, gripped to the sides of his head as he shook it side to side. She planted a fast kiss on his lips.

Luke took her by the shoulders and pushed her away, shaking his head more violently. 'I have to get away. I need to think about everything.' He turned away, walking faster, and breaking into a jog. Then into a run. He knew leaving her behind wasn't protecting her, but he had to get away. His mind was stirring. Fear was mounting.

Fury beats fear.

He couldn't let his Fury take hold around Amelja. He knew how dangerous the Fury was.

The sound of her voice calling after him faded under the thickness in the air and his heart pounding in his ears.

* * *

Amelja

It took all her strength not to panic. For a moment she had just looked around, uncertain what to do.

Had Luke left her? How could she convince him she loved him more than ever before?

She felt weak and sick from the fear of being alone, not knowing where to go, or who to turn to.

In the time she had been in the country, and even in the city, she'd not spent much time totally alone. When first arriving in the UK she had been brought across by that man who claimed he was her uncle. He'd taken her from Albania, making promises that she would get a job and earn good money to send back to her family.

But the uncle had been talking to the other men about a house. She heard the way they spoke about girls like animals or toys. Things to be enjoyed by men. When she had been allowed out of the vehicle to stretch her legs. When they were not looking, she had run.

They looked for her but ran past her as she hid around a corner. Waiting for the right moment again, she ran in the opposite direction.

There were shops and restaurants and people everywhere. Shiny bags of all colours. Huge glass windows. The tallest buildings she had ever seen. Cars filled the roads. People filled the paths. Shouting and noise filled the air.

But Amelja knew she could hide in that noise. She had seen a coat lying over some bags on the floor. A woman was shouting into her phone. She vaped a sickly-sweet smoke. Amelja crouched down as though she was tying her shoelace, and stood up, taking the coat with her. It was long and dark brown, and expensive. She took her hair out of the ponytail and draped it over the coat, walking away swinging her hips like the women on catwalks did.

Using her new coat and walk, Amelja blended in well as she came to a large shopping centre, passing through to the other side only to be faced with a large statue of a bull. Almost all the English she'd picked up had come from listening to people speak. "Bullring" was a new word for her vocabulary. Learning new languages didn't worry Amelja, but English was an unusual one.

More shops filled the pedestrian zone called New Street selling sportswear and clothes. There was even a cinema tucked away between tall buildings with almost entirely glass fronts. A bank ahead of her was opposite a large hotel whose name was unclear but said something like Britain.

That's when Amelja had noticed another small walkway and decided to go down there, trying to get herself out of sight. Everything was so large compared to her hometown in Albania.

Her plan had worked out well on that day, and it hadn't taken her long to meet people and make friends. Girls, of course. The boys in the UK were as bad as those in Albania.

Sometimes she'd stay with friends on a sofa or in a big place with rooms filled with bunk beds.

But a lot had happened since then.

She met her Luke. He was nice. And had kind, beautiful eyes. Funny nervous boy, getting his words wrong.

But then the older boy she didn't like, who made Luke tell him her name. He hurt Luke and took them both back to the man who called himself her uncle.

And then everything had gone horribly wrong. Luke blamed himself when he shouldn't have. She knew the truth.

But she was alone again. Soaked through in the rain, and standing in that alleyway she'd turned down near the hotel. The same place she'd brought Luke when they needed to rest and sort out their injured feet. The same place again. It was out of the rain, but just as cold.

Amelja wished she had the coat she'd stolen that day. But someone else had stolen it from her. Which only seemed fair. In a way.

She was alone.

He armed crept down to her belly as she leant up against the wall before sliding down until she was sitting on the floor.

Amelja dug her hand into all her pockets, looking for whatever change she might find. Not enough for even a hot drink.

Her mind was filled with sadness. And anger. Not at Luke. She didn't even have enough energy to be angry at what they made him do.

Amelja's thoughts turned to what it meant. She had a baby in her. A life, growing. There was nothing she could do to change that. In less than a year she would be holding a new baby, still a child herself. The thought terrified her.

But not as much as the sadness and hopelessness of being alone. No life would be worth living if always on her own.

She heard horror stories of being locked up in prison before being sent back to her own country. Maybe without her baby. The thoughts Amelja made pull her knees to her chest, put her head down, and hide from the world.

Hoping, for Luke to return to her.

Or just hoping that there could be any hope at all.

Luke

Luke kept running on autopilot, not knowing where he was going. He ran across the city centre and down past Snow Hill Station and the large business buildings. When he reached the crossings opposite St Chad's cathedral he didn't bother waiting for the lights and gave only a cursory glance for traffic.

There was no one he thought he could go to. No one to trust. The hole he was in was getting deeper and deeper and he was drowning. The Fury was taking over, but it was attacking him.

And he deserved it. There was no going to the police. Not when that video of him existed.

He finally slowed, staggered, and collapsed onto a bench next to the cathedral. He took a deep breath and opened his eyes, realising where his instincts had drawn him. Luke had never been one to believe in God, but he figured something in his instincts had brought him back.

Possibly the only person he could turn to.

If not Reg, who else?

It took him a few more minutes to regain his breath and walk up to the place Reg usually was. No guarantee that he'd be there, but maybe someone could call him.

Luke pushed at the door and almost fell inside, causing everyone to look over at him. An older woman with tightly pulled back grey hair and obscenely large glasses looked over, her mouth dropping open. She leaned over and said something quietly in another woman's ear before walking towards Luke as the other woman vanished out of sight.

'You look like a drowned rat. Inside.' She spoke with a soft Irish accent and despite her stern look and thin frame, she sounded like a cuddly old granny. In his delirium, Luke's mind flashed back to the nice old lady at Tescos.

Was there some kind of organisation or army of them?

The lady radiated warmth. 'What on earth are you doing out there in the wet. You'll catch a death.'

It was at that moment that Reg Walters appeared around the corner, wiping his hands on a tea towel, blue apron around his waist covered in flour. His face was a crumpled wrinkle of concern.

Their eyes met for a fleeting moment before Luke collapsed into the man's arms and sobbed. Reg looked at the woman, who looked back and shook her head in bewilderment.

'It's okay, I've got this,' Reg said, gathering the boy up and guiding him to a pair of chairs in the foyer.

It took nearly five minutes for Luke to calm down and regain his breath. He wiped at his nose with a soaked coat sleeve, so Reg handed him the tea towel to dry his face.

'What's happened?' Reg tried to keep the desperate concern out of his voice.

Luke just shook his head.

'Come on, mate. I've never seen you like this. What's wrong?'

Luke turned and sat with his face in his hands, shaking partly from the cold, since the adrenaline had faded.

'Wait here. I'll get you a towel to dry off, and then we can have a chat, okay?' Reg waited for Luke to nod before he stood to walk back into the main room only to find himself nearly walking head-on into the same woman.

She held out a large towel and a can of coke. 'Figured he needs drying up, and by the looks of him, could do with some sugar.'

'Thanks.' Reg let out a sigh of relief through a familiar smile.

'You sure you don't need any help?'

Reg looked at Luke for a moment and lowered his

voice. 'Leave him with me for now. Let me find out what's going on. Then we'll go from there.'

The woman placed her hand on Reg's arm. She was warm, tender, and as maternal to Reg as she was to Luke.

Reg sat down next to Luke and helped him take his coat off before wrapping him in the towel. The strong smell of fabric softener tried to fight the damp, acrid smell that had followed Luke in the door.

'Here, drink this,' he said, opening the can before giving it to the boy. 'You're going to need to tell me what's going on.'

'It's all gone to shit.'

Reg was familiar with the melodrama that adolescence creates out of minor events, his instincts told him something worse had happened on this occasion. He let the silence hang.

After a sip of the coke, Luke stared down at the floor. 'I can't take it back, Reg.'

'Okay,' Reg could feel his experience and training working in his head. 'Why don't you tell me just one thing first, and then let's work from there?'

'I've hurt her too much.' Luke's voice caught and he had to fight a lump in his throat.

'Hurt her?' Reg knew all too well that he was in dangerous territory when it came to disclosures and had to be careful not to lead the conversation. For all he knew, what Luke was about to disclose could turn out to be nothing, or it could end up being a serious investigation.

Luke nodded. 'She says she still loves me.'

Reg fought back a sigh of relief as one of the nightmare scenarios in his head had dissipated.

'How can I look after her if I can't keep her safe?'

'Where is she?'

Luke shrugged his shoulders and drank from the can again. 'I was afraid I might lash out in anger. I had to get away.'

'Sometimes the best thing to do is to walk away if that means diffusing a bad situation.'

'I'm a coward.'

'You're not a coward. It takes greater strength to walk away.'

'I ran away. That's what cowards do.'

Reg started drying Luke's hair, noticing the change in colour to the towel. 'But you came here. How did that happen?'

Luke shrugged his shoulders. 'Just ran without thinking. I stopped to sit down, and I realised.'

'Something in your head told you to come here.'

Luke looked up at Reg. 'I guess I hoped you'd be here.'

Reg gave him a soft smile. 'And here I am.' It suddenly struck Reg how paternal he was being without even second-guessing himself. 'You came here for help.'

Luke took another sip of the drink. His shoulders were relaxing and his whole body was sagging.

'Cowards run away from their responsibilities. Asking for help embraces them.'

'Even when you know there's nothing you can do to make things better?'

Reg let another moment of silence hang between them, and he gave Luke's hair another quick rub before placing a hand on the boy's back. 'If I can help, and trust me, I want to, I'll need to know how. Talking is important, but it's the action that makes a difference.'

Luke let out a deep sigh. He still didn't think he could tell Reg the whole truth. Not everything. He knew he couldn't ask Reg to keep it all secret. And if the police were called, that was it.

'Is she safe?' Reg asked, carefully measuring the concern in his voice. 'I mean, physically safe?'

'I left her in town. She'll be cold. Wet.'

'Can I make a suggestion, then?'

Luke looked up at him.

'Bring her here. I'd love to meet her. Maybe we can all work out a way for you to be safe.'

Luke shook his head. 'I can't bring her here, Reg.'

Reg felt his spine tingled with fear. Betraying Luke's trust was the last thing he wanted, but he would do it in a heartbeat if he knew the boy was in danger.

He shook his head and let out a sigh. 'Then take me to meet her? Perhaps?'

Luke didn't reply. His furrowed brow gave away that he was considering the option. 'I just need to know how to win her back.'

'What makes you think you've lost her?'

'I failed her.'

'Then fight for her. You've shown me here, right now, you have the courage to get help when you need it. Convince her to do the same. Do it together.'

He could see Luke weighing up the options.

'Focus on the most important thing. You need a place to stay which is safe. And to know that place is yours. Will you try? For her sake? Maybe that is your role in her life. To convince her to have the courage to ask for help.'

Luke sat up and nodded. 'You believe in God, right? All that stuff?'

'Yes, I do.' Reg swallowed hard and dry. He didn't believe in pushing his faith onto children.

'And you believe we are all his children, and he loves us all? That's what people say, isn't it?'

Reg nodded, wondering where Luke's interest in religion was suddenly coming from.

'Does he forgive people when they do wrong?'

'Absolutely. Christians believe that Jesus sacrificed himself to free them of their sins.'

'Even though he wasn't the one who did the sins?'

'Yes. Such was his love for his people. But that is also why it is most important that when we make mistakes in our lives, no matter how bad we think they are, we must do two things.' Reg paused and looked at Luke, who met his eyes. 'First, you must repent.'

'Say you're sorry?'

'To truly repent you must not only say you are sorry but show it. Maybe not put things back, that might not be possible. But to put them right.'

Luke nodded. 'And the second thing?'

'That's often the hardest of all.' Reg saw the worry clouding the boy's eyes. 'You must forgive yourself.'

'What about forgiving other people who have done wrong? Do I have to forgive them?'

'If they knew what they were doing was wrong, and weren't forced into that wrong, they were not innocent. It's not your place to forgive them. They must repent.'

Reg noticed a change in Luke's posture. Subtle, but present. An air of resolve.

'Do you think the men who nailed Jesus to the cross repented?'

'Well, Jesus gave his life for them. His final words to God were, forgive them, for they do not know what they are doing.'

'Is that really true?'

Reg smiled at Luke. 'Even if the event cannot be proven, the meaning of the story still matters. We can't blame a man for mistakes he is forced to make.'

'Does that count even if someone does something truly terrible, but they weren't aware, or were being forced?'

'I believe that their innocence is intact. Yes.'

Reg watched Luke's eyes drop, taking the words in, and he wondered what the boy had done that was so terrible he needed such reassurance over.

Luke stood from the chair, ruffled his head and neck with the towel one more time, and handed it back to Reg.

He picked up his coat and put it back on, feeling the heavy weight of the rain. 'I have to go.'

Reg jumped up. 'No, wait, you can't go out like that.'

'I have to find her.'

'It's too cold.'

'All the more reason I have to find her.'

Reg suddenly felt a weight back on his shoulders. 'Let me come with you.'

'I can't. Like you said, if I am going to do that repent thing, I have to put it right. Not you. No one else. Me.'

Reg held up his hands in submission. 'Oh, bloody hell. Wait here for a second.' He turned and disappeared around the corner for a minute before returning with a small, waterproof drawstring bag. The kind of bag that people used for their swimming kit many years ago, but became the fashionable general schoolbag for teens in the noughties.

'There's a few thermal blankets in there, a couple of sets of gloves and hats, something to drink and eat.'

Luke took the bag with a faint smile.

'And take this, too.' Reg took his wallet out and handed Luke all the cash he had.

'No, Reg, you've already helped.'

Reg gave him a stern "don't argue" look as he clasped Luke's hand between both of his, pressing the money into a thumb grip. 'Get something hot to eat and drink, and in a hostel for as many nights as you can.'

Luke let out a sigh with a nod, and before Reg could do or say anything else, he turned, opened the door, and walked back out into the misty rain.

Reg watched as Luke picked up his pace into a jog, and then to a run. He gripped the cold handle of the door and rested his head against it, rocking side to side. He clenched his other hand into a fist and thumped at the door.

He knew there was little the authorities could or would do. The vastly overworked system was not going to run around town looking for a wayward teenage boy trying to find his girlfriend. It wasn't a question about compassion on an individual level. It was about the systemic failure resulting from chronic, long-term underfunding.

He just had to keep praying the day would never come where he came across Luke or the girl in his professional capacity.

Praying when it was already too late.

And then praying again.

But for what?

Chapter 38

September

'I've kept the news away from him. TV and papers. But the lad isn't stupid, Dr Walters. He's going to work out sooner or later something is wrong.'

Reg looked at her and placed a hand lightly on her arm. 'You've done a wonderful job with him. Thank you. But I think it's time.'

She nodded and smiled, sympathetic to the pain she knew he was about to deliver. 'If you need any help…'

'Thank you.'

Reg placed his hand on the door and took a deep breath, looking through the narrow window at a boy who appeared to be sleeping peacefully. Some of his bruises were yellowing and the swelling was already going down.

He opened the door and slid into the room. He had a quick look at the medical chart and the distinctive metallic sound of it hanging back over the bed frame chimed around the room.

Luke opened his eyes and took a few moments to refocus his eyes to the foot of the bed. At first, his frown only showed confusion until he recognised who it was.

Reg was sure he could see a gentle smile niggle at the edges of Luke's lips, and he walked around the left side of the bed.

'How you holding up?'

'Going for a run in a bit.'

Reg felt a weight evaporate with the stupid joke. Even the slightest touch of humour was a massive relief.

'The nurse says you are doing really well.'

'I feel like a roll of Sellotape.'

'Wrapped you up good and tight, have they?'

Reg put a hand on his shoulder and didn't hide the sigh.

'Where is she?' Luke's voice cracked with tiredness and worry.

Reg tried to look puzzled, desperate to deflect the question he'd been dreading.

'Please, Reg.' He swallowed hard, and his dark eyebrows pinched together over the bridge of his nose.

Reg closed his eyes and fought to control his breathing. He'd met so many people engulfed by the ferocity of grief, but he'd never had to deliver the message. He wished he'd asked Mike to help.

A sudden squeeze from Luke's hand opened his eyes and locked into the boy's stare. It was all he could do to keep his composure.

'I'm sorry. I'm so, so sorry.'

'No.'

'She's gone.'

'She can't be.' Luke began shaking his head side to side.

'She died.' He knew he had to use the word. He hated the word more than ever before. But there was nothing to be gained with platitudes or ambiguity. No other word would lighten the hammer blow. Only certainty could deliver the painful, horrific truth.

After squeezing his eye's tight shut, Luke's eyes shot open again. 'Baby. The baby. What about…'

'She's fine, mate. Beautiful.'

'But Amelja?'

Reg shook his head again.

'How…but how? What, happened?'

Panic exploded into Reg's mind. He'd been so worried about delivering the message he'd not prepared for that question. An accident or medical issue or something would be one thing. But the truth was even more terrible.

'How did she die?' Luke's voice snapped him out of the panic. There was no room for an innocent lie, even just to hold back the pain a little longer. Luke was bound to find out soon enough.

He lifted the boy's arm and gripped his hand as he turned to sit on the edge of the bed.

'Listen. Amelja escaped whoever did this to you. She wasn't hurt and went into labour without complications. The baby is a couple of weeks premature, but is perfectly healthy, and doing fine. But Amelja,' he had to pause to breathe. 'She must have been convinced that you were gone. Forever. That thought would have been too much for her to bear.'

'No, no.'

'I'm sorry. I truly am. She got the baby to safety. But she took her own life.'

Luke froze for a moment, his breath stopped dead. His eyes clamped shut as he squeezed Reg's hand so tight it caused pain. His head began rocking side to side as his entire face contorted. A deep, guttural growl worked its way up from his chest and he let go of Reg's hand, clasping his face as his head rocked side to side with increasing force. Howling sobs engulfed him with such violence Reg had to hold Luke down by his shoulders.

Reg smacked the alarm button on the wall, and it took less than ten seconds for a team of nurses to come crashing into the room as if they were expecting to perform resuscitation.

'What the hell happened?' one of the nurses had to raise her voice over Luke's.

'Sedate him before he hurts himself, Reg shouted.'

The nurses looked at each other blank and confused until the ward nurse he'd spoken to just ten minutes before marched in, right on cue. She set a vial down on the side before opening a syringe, filling it, and then administering a dose of something to the drip. She squeezed the bag, pushing the drug into his system.

'What was that?' Reg asked.

'When I heard the alarm from Luke's room, I knew what it would be. It's a sedative. Not a strong one, but fast-acting. Give it about thirty seconds.'

Reg nodded, holding Luke down, feeling the fight ebb away, listening to the sobbing fade until all they could hear was Luke repeating her name.

After five minutes, Luke had calmed enough that his eyes were lulling between barely open, and not quite closed. The occasional slight sob tried to escape, but there was no strength in it.

Reg sat next to the bed for another half an hour as Luke lay with eyes half-open, blinking slowly, a tight grip in his hand again. Eventually, the boy's eyes slipped shut and the grip loosened. There was no peace as his subconscious took hold to deliver its darkness.

Reg heard the door open and turned to see the nurse standing with a blanket and a pillow.

'Thanks,' Reg replied softly.

'As far as I'm concerned, you're all he has right now.'

'He's going to need a lot more, very soon.'

'Perhaps, but just for now, not being alone is what matters most.'

* * *

It was surprisingly easy for him to blend in. All he needed was a meaningless story just in case he was stopped and questioned.

If another parent asked, then he'd say he was there to

see his son and just needed a few minutes to himself.

How is your child doing?

Oh, how awful.

Be strong.

They are good here.

Stock phrases appease people.

If a member of staff asked, he'd merely hold up the padded envelope with the courier order sheet and ask them for the doctor that didn't exist, quoting the wrong hospital name in a foreign-sounding accent. He'd been practising. The staff member would tell him that he was in the wrong hospital. Embarrassment and profuse apologies would be enough.

Poor criminals get caught most often through poor planning of their exit strategy, not the crime itself.

But the English man, dressed like a courier, had already achieved what he needed. He'd found the boy, and now who the boy trusted. Which meant he knew exactly how to get closer.

As soon as he stepped outside, he took a phone out and dialled a number he'd memorised. The call was answered within a few rings.

'Speak.' Kapllani used the single word devoid of feeling, accent, or tone.

'The boy is doing well, physically. Likely to recover.' He paused to listen. 'No police. Just that pathologist.' The man walked towards his bike. 'Yes, I have it with me. Consider it delivered.'

He ended the call and looked at the package in his hand. Part of his cover story, but also precious contents.

The man tapped out a short text message and sent it to another memorised number, before turning the phone off. He took the back cover off the phone, removed the battery and the SIM card, and went over to the bin. Dropping the phone and battery in, he paused with the SIM card in his hand.

More questions were going to be asked, and he wanted to stay on the right side of some difficult answers.

It was time he kept some insurances of his own.

Chapter 39

'I hope I haven't burnt our bridge.'

Amelja opened her eyes and looked up to see the shadow of a figure covered in a strange plastic poncho. She sprang up and wrapped her arms around him.

'I'm sorry I left you.' He held her tighter, feeling a warmth in his heart that was not there in his damp flesh and coat.

Amelja leaned back and looked him in the eyes. 'You never can burn our bridge.' She smiled and kissed him on the cheek. 'Not in this rain.'

'Maybe wobbled it a bit.'

'Where did you go? And why are you wearing bin bag?' She tugged at the single-use poncho. Luke loved her ironic humour, given that they had made makeshift ponchos from bin bags on many occasions.

'I went to see a friend. He helped me get my head straight.'

'About baby?'

Luke nodded. 'You tell me what you want to do.'

'We are so young, Luke.'

'I know.'

'But I have strong belief. If this has happened, then it

is meant to be.'

Luke knew Amelja was Catholic.

'All I need to know is I have you.'

Luke smiled at her. 'No matter what. Me and you.'

She nodded, smiled, and wrapped her arms around him again.

They spent the rest of the evening going through the bag of items Reg had hastily thrown together and planning how to use the money. The rain continued to fall, and the temperature continued to drop, so they used part of the money for a couple of nights in a hostel. They could wash and dry their clothes in a laundrette.

Neither of them had any real idea what faced them, but they knew that once again, they'd fought some of the worst, and still they were surviving together.

Chapter 40

DI Stone welcomed the knock on his open office door as a welcome distraction from paperwork.

'Enter. Come into my realm, child,' he said with his best Disney evil tone.

One eyebrow rose high on the face of young PC Kelly Saunders. 'Um, I have some post for you, sir.'

Stone saw her expression and instantly regretted what would probably turn into a 'little chat' with HR at some point. 'Since when is it your job to deliver my post?'

'Well, this was delivered by courier and it's marked, by hand. Sergeant Gibbon thought it was a bit odd, so he sent me up with it on the off chance it was urgent.'

'Thanks,' Stone replied as he reached for the small brown envelope. 'Tell Gibbon you can both have a biscuit for the initiative. And you can have a chocolate one for extra effort.'

Stone flipped the envelope over in his hands noting it didn't appear to even contain a full piece of paper. But down in the corner, he could feel the shape of staples and a small rectangle.

Go with your gut. Something is wrong with this.

He reached into his drawer and took out some blue

259

nitrile gloves. He also grabbed a pencil and scrap of paper.

Using the old tracing technique everyone learns on tree bark at school, he scribbled over the outline of the small plastic shape.

A full-sized SIM card.

He sliced his way into the envelope and tipped the contents onto his desk. A small piece of paper with a SIM card in a plastic clip bag stapled to a blank piece of paper.

Stone held the paper up to the light, but there was no sign of hidden writing, nor were there pen marks from a writing pad. The plastic bag appeared to be new, but he decided not to open it and took out his phone.

'Something odd. I need your skills.'

'Should I be concerned this isn't coming through proper channels?'

'Do I ever ask you to do anything shifty?'

'Like a dog with a dirty arse on grandma's beige carpet. I hold you personally responsible for my blood pressure.'

'I have received a SIM card, delivered by hand, in a small plastic baggy.'

'Sounds like your local dealer is getting very confused.'

'Before I open this bag, I'm looking at the metal chip on the card and even I can see there's a print on it.'

'And you want me to take that print and run it? But you want this doing off the record, right?'

Stone stood up and let out a sigh.

'Look mate, I'm worried something is going on here, on a case I am working. I'm not just talking a gobby leak or even a single bent cop.'

'Something bigger?'

'The case is veering into major organised crime, and I get an unidentified SIM card delivered in an envelope by hand.'

'CCTV on the delivery?'

'Well yes, and that's even weirder. Why not just post it? It's as if they want to be seen dropping it off.'

'So, why the favour? Surely you want to keep everything you do totally above board?'

Stone considered his point.

'Problem is, I think this SIM came the way it did because someone is telling me not to use the proper channels.'

It didn't take Stone much to convince his contact to meet and help with what he needed. The dirty word 'corruption' was not something he wanted to shout too loud, but it was prickling the hairs on his neck.

When his internal phone rang and CS Carter was calling him to her office to discuss a sensitive matter, his gut couldn't avoid a slight turn at the coincidental timing.

* * *

'Where did it come from?' DI Stone looked suspiciously at the USB drive before checking CS Carter's reaction.

'That's only a small part of the problem, Mike.'

DI Stone looked at the laptop with the paused video on the screen. 'I'm not going to want to see this, am I?'

'It is one of the worst things I have ever laid eyes on.'

Stone sighed deep, steadying himself.

He struggled to keep his eyes on the scene playing out before him. The image quality was frighteningly good, which made the violence even harder to watch. One male, one female, and it was clear there was nothing remotely consensual about the footage.

The hardest part to take wasn't even the apparent ages of the boy and the girl. It was the fact that their identity was made very clear.

He paused the video after less than a minute.

'I can't watch any more of that.'

A heavy and painful silence filled Carter's office.

'When did you get this?'

'Today,' Carter replied. 'Delivered by courier.' Her eyes were fixed somewhere in the distance. Stone couldn't quite read them.

'Are we going to presume it was sent to you on the back of the press conference?'

'I doubt this will be the only copy.'

'We'd better hope to God it's not online.'

Carter's glare was serious, and her eyes darkened. She passed him a piece of paper in a plastic evidence bag.

Stone read it out, wanting to hear the threat as much as read it. 'Judge in court, or judge in public. Your choice.' He flipped it over to look at the back and the front, at the same time wondering if he should mention the SIM card.

'First the DNA, now this video.' Stone said. 'Someone is going to great lengths to see this boy charged with rape.'

'No, Mike, what we have here is proof that he did rape her.'

DI Stone's tone hit incredulous. 'You're having a bloody laugh, surely.'

'I'd like to remind you of rank, Inspector, before you cross the line of insubordination.'

I'll give you fucking insubordination.

He stood suddenly, knowing he needed some physical distance. 'Not only is there no proper chain of evidence, so you can't use this. Both of the children in that video are victims.'

'Would you like to explain that to Women's Rights?'

''It's child pornography and you damn well know it.'

'That might be true, but she is clearly his victim.'

'Clearly? He could be drugged. Coerced.'

'Inspector Stone, if you are not capable of investigating the case objectively, I will gladly recommend that DCI Palmers takes over.'

'If you plan on throwing "innocent until proven guilty" out the window, you're very welcome to.'

'We already have DNA evidence that makes Luke suspect number one. Can you imagine what will happen if we didn't even question him?'

'You're worried about bad press?'

She stood up to meet his eyes. 'What other leads do you have?'

'Why are you so desperate to believe he raped the girl he loved?'

'Why are you so sentimental not to?'

The stand-off between them held for several uncomfortable seconds.

'How far away is the boy from being fit to interview?'

'As a victim or a suspect?'

'Either.'

'I'll speak to Reg.'

Carter scowled and rolled her eyes.

'And I don't bloody care whether you like that or not. That boy has been a victim of abuse his whole life. I will personally go right above your head if you command me to presume guilt.'

Carter sat back down. 'Do whatever you need to do. Just close this case.'

'What the hell does that mean?'

'A girl was driven to suicide after giving birth to a rape child. People want someone to hang.'

'Oh, trust me. People are going to hang.'

DI Stone turned and walked towards the door.

'Inspector, I haven't dismissed you yet.'

'Sorry, ma'am. I was in a hurry to go and order a child-sized noose.'

He turned and left the office not caring about a reprimand for insubordination. He knew that if he stayed any longer, he'd say something an apology could not repair.

As far as DI Stone was concerned, she was wrong. Morally, ethically, and procedurally. This was not how investigations should be conducted, and he resented the way his hand was being forced. He even questioned why DCI Palmers hadn't swooped in to take control.

Stone knew he was capable, but the whole thing felt

worryingly above his paygrade.

He knew there were bigger fish to fry even if Luke was made to look guilty of rape.

Why was Luke being set up as a scapegoat?

Or is it meant to be me?

Chapter 41

True to his word, Mike Stone had spoken with social services and the safeguarding team and convinced them that given the sensitivity and potential danger of the case, standard emergency foster care would not be appropriate for Luke.

He pointed out that unless they could find carers equipped and prepared to allow round-the-clock police protection, Luke would be safer in a police cell. When he told them the budget would need to be met by them, they agreed to follow his recommendations to discharge him into Reg Walters' care. He was the only logical short-term solution. Luke trusted him, and given the voluntary work he already did, he'd satisfy safeguarding checks anyway.

Two days had passed and Luke's road to physical and emotional healing had begun.

Standing at the edge of Galton Bridge, feeling the chill of the wind down their neck's, Reg and Luke shared a moment of respectful silence.

Reg placed a hand on Luke's shoulder as they walked halfway across the bridge and stopped to look at the collection of flowers and other token items placed around the base of the lamppost. Some of the flowers were fresh and it looked as though someone had been taking care of them like a temporary shrine.

'Why do people spend more money on expensive flowers for a dead person they barely spared a few coins for when they were alive?' Luke's voice had an edge of anger.

'I think they want to pay their respects.'

Luke shrugged the idea away. Reg had no intention of arguing the point because he agreed.

'She would've liked you, Reg.' Luke knelt to read some of the cards and their messages. 'I should've tried harder to get her to meet…'

Reg leaned on the railings and looked out across the water below. For a moment he considered saying a prayer, but something inside him felt uncomfortable with the idea. But a question suddenly sprang to his mind.

'Do you remember writing those numbers the other day?'

Luke stopped moving. After a moment of pause, he stood and leaned on the railings, wiping his eyes with his sleeves. And then nodded.

'What did you mean?'

He shrugged his shoulders and struggled to clear his throat. 'It wasn't their fault. The kids what done it. I know they were made to.'

'Where did you learn the verse number?'

'Some old bloke we met. He was religious, like you. It stuck in my head because it was the same as you said.'

It occurred to Reg that the old man he was referring to might well be Mr Freeman that DC Khan had introduced him to.

'That's why I don't want no cops arresting them or anything. You told me that we have to find a way to forgive ourselves. They can't do that if someone is arresting them.'

Reg looked at him. 'You continue to astound me.'

Luke didn't reply, but Reg could see his mind had suddenly jolted off to a distant thought.

'What's going to happen to the baby?'

'Honest answer?'

The boy looked at him, his eyes still fighting the cold breeze and a terrible chasm of sadness.

'In the short term, she's safe and healthy. The long term simply doesn't need to be your worry right now, okay? One thing at a time.'

Luke nodded but wasn't convinced. His complexion was grey, and although the bruises were beginning to fade, and most of the swelling had gone down, his soul was still so wounded.

He walked to the centre of the bridge and turned to face down to one of the ends. His hand reached up and he pulled a leather necklace with half a heart out to rub it between a finger and thumb. Reg had managed to get it back for him and had promised that he would return Amelja's as soon as the police would let him.

Luke closed his eyes and appeared to lose himself in a memory.

Reg knew it had been important to take Luke to the bridge. It had to be real. But it didn't need to be sustained, so it was time to leave.

Nothing more was said between them as they walked away. Reg had to admit he was still taken aback by just how deeply Luke and Amelja had fallen in love. And not just a teenage infatuation, or the fickle hormonal trick of adolescence. More profound than he'd previously ever given young people the credit for.

He also wondered about how strong a paternal instinct was going to be for Luke. But where would the old African proverb apply for him, that it takes a village to raise a child? What if the child's only living parent is still just a child, with no grandparents, family or village to speak of?

Reg looked up for a moment and frowned at the sky. Thought to himself, as if to ask his God, 'where is your love for these children?'

Luke turned back one more time. 'You would have liked her, Reg.'

One day, Reg was going to have to explain that he did meet Amelja.

Once.

Luke closed his eyes and took a deep breath as if he could still smell her there with him.

Chapter 42

March
Luke & Amelja

The sun was setting on the warm spring evening as they ran up to the centre of the bridge and wrapped their arms around the lamppost.

'Let's play a game,' Luke said, a wild and excited smile brightening his face and eyes.

Amelja laughed, but she couldn't hide her confusion. 'What game?'

'You go to one edge of the bridge, I go to the other. We close our eyes and walk towards each other.'

'Our eyes are closed?'

'Yes,' he nodded with excitement.

'This sounds dangerous.'

'No.'

'Yes.'

'It's fun.'

'It is silly. People will see, and they will laugh.'

Luke laughed. 'Let them.' He took Amelja by the hands and pulled her in to kiss her on the cheek. 'There's no one else I would rather be silly with.'

Starting to step away from her, their arms outstretching, Luke nodded to her with a mischievous grin.

A little embarrassed, Amelja looked around.

'Count ten steps away, so you know how far to come back,' Luke added.

She walked backwards, counting ten steps, still a little confused by the strange English game.

When they reached ten steps, Luke waved at Amelja and signalled to put her hands over her eyes.

He shouted over to her, 'Ready? Count to ten.'

She nodded.

'Go.'

And they did.

Luke kept looking through his hands at her, and he could tell by her unsteady walking she was doing it honestly. Luke put his hands into a pocket and took out a small box with a crumpled piece of paper. Hiding it behind his back, Luke kept his eyes covered with one hand and made his walk look unsteady because he knew she would be glancing once or twice.

As they got closer to the centre, Luke began to veer in her direction to ensure they ended up right in front of each other. In his final few steps, as she slowed, Luke stepped forward and dropped to a knee right in front of her.

'I am here, Luke,' she giggled nervously, 'where are you?'

'I'm here too.'

Amelja heard his voice from below her and opened her eyes. Her mouth dropped open when she saw him kneeling, holding a small jewellery box up to her. After a moment of confusion and nervous excitement, she clasped her hands together, her fingers at her chin.

'Amelja,' Luke began, his voice croaking slightly with nerves, 'we might be too young to get married, but we're not too young to be in love.' He lifted the box a little closer, nodding at it for her to take it.

She took the soft, dark blue necklace box and carefully opened it. A crudely cut and filed metal heart, cut into two pieces. One half had a stamped "L", the other, a stamped

"A". Both pieces had a simple leather lace.

Luke bounced up, nervous to see if she liked them.

'It is our hearts, you see. The "L" is for you, and the "A" is for me. We always share half our hearts for each other.'

'You make this?'

A flash of worry glanced across his eyes. He knew he was hardly a jewellery maker. 'Um, yeh, I kind of tried to shape it and file it smooth.'

'They are beautiful.'

Luke couldn't hide his surprise.

'Beautiful because you make these.'

'Let me help you.' Luke took the "L" necklace out and put the lace over her head. Then he let Amelja do the same for him. The lace was long enough so they could hold the pieces out and connect them in one heart.

Amelja looked him in the eyes as she smiled. She put her arms over his shoulders, wrapped around his neck and pulled them into a tight embrace.

After a few moments passed, she whispered in his ear. 'Silly English game, you clever English boy.'

Luke held her tight and they both stayed in the embrace in the middle of the bridge, forgetting the whole world as the sun went down.

Chapter 43

September

'Well, that has to be one of the most horrific things I have ever seen,' Khan said, turning Stone's laptop away.

Bolton was standing by the side window of the office so they could view the screen without anyone accidentally walking in on it. Her arms had started folded but soon moved subtly so she was clasping her upper arms, openly wincing at the recording.

'Carter wants me to use this solely as evidence against Luke,' Stone sighed, running a hand through his hair.

Khan looked incredulous. 'But this is top category child pornography. Regardless of what it shows, both children are victims.'

'No one is questioning that, Harry,' Bolton added.

'And let's not forget someone is filming it.'

Stone brought his hand down over his forehead, pressing hard over his eyes.

Bolton straightened up, dropping her hands into her pocket to search for some chewing gum. It was a habit of hers that she used to prevent grinding her teeth. 'Does Luke even know this exists?'

A knock at the door got a grunted reply from Stone. After a short pause, it was opened by a sheepish PC Pearson.

'If it isn't my favourite little uniform,' Bolton said with a wide smile.

The atmosphere must have been palpable as Pearson seemed reluctant to enter. 'Hey, bosses. Have you got a quick second?'

'Make it happy, or I might throw something at you,' Stone groaned without looking at him.

A nervous laugh faltered from him. Not sure how serious the threat had been. 'Well, thing is, you know you're trying to track down that Gnome guy?'

Stone locked his eyes on Pearson.

'I was in a newsagent yesterday evening, called out to a shoplifting. I did the standard statements and so on. Anyway, whilst I was there, two things cropped up.'

He moved around the door and stood inside the room. No one replied, so he read that as his cue to get to the point.

'Firstly, I thought it was worth just showing the shopkeep Gnome's photo whilst I was there. Turns out he recognises him. You know, a local troublemaker. Likes to intimidate, and all that.'

'I'm trying to get excited James,' Stone grumbled.

Pearson wagged his finger in the air. 'Well, apparently our Gnome doesn't tend to go in there himself much. He usually turns up with a younger kid, waits outside while he sends them in to do the job.'

He paused again.

The others all swapped unimpressed glances.

'I know that doesn't help much, but something else he said perked my ears up. I let him go on a rant about the youth and blah blah blah.' Pearson looked down at his notepad. 'Like that poor girl what jumped off that bridge.'

Stone sat up slightly.

'He said it was so sad, but then whispered to me he thinks her and her boyfriend stole from his shop.'

'Was he sure?' Bolton asked.

'I showed him the photos. He says quite some weeks or so back, but definitely her.'

All eyes in the office danced around each other, trying to work out how relevant that could be. Could it be a lead?

Pearson closed his notepad and began backing away to the door. 'I don't know it's any use to you, just thought it might be a potential lead.'

Stone nodded. 'Thanks, James. Send us the shop address, and write your report up in full.'

'Sure thing, bosses.' He left the room and closed the door behind him.

'What do you reckon, Sands?'

'I think we need to keep Pearson away from caffeine.'

Khan sniggered. 'I think we should piss test him for crack.'

Stone rolled his eyes.

Bolton smiled at him. 'Let's check it out. If nothing else, we can prod him about Gnome, and see what he says about these two,' she pointed at the laptop.

'Yes, but there's something I need to go over with you two before we go.'

Bolton and Khan looked at each other and then at Stone.

'Something I need to share with you that must be kept on the hush for now, understood?'

They nodded.

'Yesterday, I got an envelope delivered by hand and all it had was an old, full-size SIM card sealed in a small plastic baggie.'

Khan frowned first. 'That's a bit obscure.'

'A contact I have in SOCO printed it. He's emailed me today.'

'Intriguing. Is this connected?' Bolton asked.

'Firstly, no usable DNA anywhere on the SIM, the baggie or envelope. The only thing he found was a single, crystal-clear forefinger print on the metal chip. Apparently, you can get DNA from prints, but it is harder to do. And much harder to do on the quiet.'

'That print sounds deliberate,' Khan added with a tilt to his head.

'The print,' Stone let the moment hang for the tension, 'The account was sealed.'

'Holy shit,' Bolton whispered, reading the tension in the room. 'Did the print match the other mystery one?'

'He couldn't run a direct comparison through the system. But I sent him a copy of the prints we already have and we got a visual match. It's our mystery man again.'

Khan nearly lost his eyebrows. 'What about the data on the SIM?'

'The only thing he has been able to confirm is that the SIM itself has only contacted two phone numbers.'

'What do we do with this?' Bolton asked.

'Harry, I need your magic whilst Sands and I go out to see this shopkeeper.'

Khan's face lit up with a devious smile.

'See what you can do about identifying the numbers. It could just be a burner phone, but something tells me this guy wanted me to have his print. He knows the print is useless, which means there's something about the numbers.'

Bolton tapped Khan on the shoulder. 'And let's see if we have the pretty little face of whoever delivered it by hand on our CCTV.'

'My thoughts exactly,' Stone added. 'Look, you two, the reason for the cloak and dagger on this is because I am getting increasingly concerned about this sealed record thing. Keep this close to the chest, please.'

Khan gave him a boy scout salute. Bolton gave a nod.

Closing their meeting, Stone picked up his coat and left the office with Bolton. Khan returned to his desk to do a little covert digging.

Chapter 44

They both scanned the area around the shop for a few moments before Stone pushed the door open and turned back to give Bolton the nod. Confirmation of their usual approach. He would make the introductions and she would go for a recce of the shop.

'Good afternoon, sir,' Stone said with a smile and pleasant tone. It didn't stop the shopkeeper from meeting him with a slightly perplexed expression.

'Bit high-brow, isn't it? Two detectives for a shoplifting? Or are you here to find out where I hid their bodies?'

Stone smiled. Then showed the man the photo of Amelja on his phone. 'Do you recognise her at all?'

The man's face turned grey. His bravado deflated. 'That's the girl from the bridge.' He choked on his own words.

Stone nodded. Then he swiped to a picture of Luke. 'And him?'

'Yes, him too. They were together.' He cleared a lump in his throat. 'Look, I'm sorry about that bodies joke.'

Stone raised a hand. 'I take it from your reaction these are the same two from a shoplifting incident you reported back in May?'

'Pretty sure, yes.'

Stone leaned casually on the counter. A more casual tone to the chat was likely to get more out of the man. 'Can you remember what they took?'

277

'Look, I don't intend pursuing this.'

'Bear with me, sir, if you would.'

He took a moment to think. 'They went over to the drinks cabinet over there and were hovering.'

Stone continued. 'How were they behaving? I mean, were they arguing at all?'

The man frowned and tilted back away. 'Oh, no, they were in on it together. Looked like they were counting pennies. Still ain't no excuse. If you can't afford something, you can't afford it. No right to steal from me.'

'What did they do next?'

The man tried his best thoughtful expression. 'He sent her outside.'

'Could you tell why?' Stone looked at the man as if he was a behavioural expert. The man leant on the counter to share his psychological opinion.

'Nah. He kissed her. Just a peck on the cheek. Then sent her outside. Like he wanted her to keep watch.'

'Anything specific you can tell me about the girl?'

The man softened. 'Pretty girl. But seemed a little sad.'

Bolton came to join Stone and the man at the front of the shop.

The man continued. 'She stopped at the door for a moment and looked back. It was a bit like she didn't really want him to do it.'

Stone looked at Bolton.

Bolton rolled her eyes.

'Then what happened?' Stone asked.

'He takes a drink out the fridge. Can't remember which. Walked around a bit more. Then came down here almost up to the counter.'

Bolton interjected. 'Did he look you in the eye, sir?'

The shopkeeper paused, partly caught out by Bolton suddenly cutting in. But his frown revealed his confusion. 'How the hell did you know that?'

'Do you have children, sir?' she asked.

278

'I do.' He looked back at Stone, hoping for some help with the odd new line of questions.

'Think about when your kids have done something wrong, or they're about to. Is that what you saw?'

The penny dropped. 'Yes, he looked like that. Guilty. Looked sorry.' The man paused. 'You know, I think that's why I remember him. He actually looked sorry.'

The man closed his eyes for a moment and gently shook his head. 'He also didn't steal the usual stuff kids steal.'

'Such as?' Stone pressed him.

'Kids nick junk and fizzy drinks. Energy drinks especially. But this boy took water, cereal bars, even fruit.'

They were interrupted by the shop door opening. A boy entered confidently but slowed as he walked past Bolton.

Stone brought up the picture of Gnome on his phone.

'According to one of our officers, you recognised this chap.'

'Now, he's a damn nuisance. Always getting kids in and out of here. Weird name.'

Stone raised his voice slightly again.

'Wouldn't be 'Gnome,' would it?'

The boy turned suddenly at the mention of the name, glancing around the end of the aisle.

Bolton saw it.

Stone took the cue, her Jedi powers working on him. He raised his voice just loud enough to be sure he was heard.'

'Well, that should be everything we need, sir,' Stone said, giving the nod to Bolton. The shopkeeper looked between the two of them, wondering what they were saying, unsaid. 'You've been a great help today.'

Bolton opened the door and they left the shop smiling at the owner.

'You stick the car just around the corner, Sands. I'll wait here for our friend to come out.'

Stone waited with his back up to the wall, just out of

sight from the opening door. And the CCTV camera. He dialled Bolton's mobile and waited for her to pick up.

'Keep your phone on speaker and listen out for my cries of pain.'

The shop door opened, and there was a pause. Stone assumed the boy was taking a quick look outside before leaving.

'How do you know our friend, Gnome?'

The boy looked him straight in the eyes, then turned on the spot, dropped his bag, and ran.

You little bastard.

'And he's off!' Stone said, loud enough to be heard on his phone.

The boy shot across the road and Stone made chase, trying to keep a running commentary between his gasps for air.

The boy headed down an alley between two houses, climbed a fence with some ease then started hopping from garden to garden.

Stone was twenty yards behind when he stepped up onto a low brick wall for extra lift to swing his legs over the fence. He knew the move had been a mistake. He hit the ground hard, rolling to soak some of the force. The boy had gained an extra garden on him.

'Stop. Police,' he shouted, mainly to alert house owners.

As he approached the next half-height fence, he heard shouting from two voices. One was higher-pitched and using far more expletives than the other.

And both were coming from his phone.

He scaled the rear fence of the next garden and deliberately paused at the top to get a look. Bolton had made it round in time to catch the boy and have him face down on a small grass area a hundred yards away.

Stone ran over to Bolton and the boy pinned to the ground. The image was similar to that of an entomologist holding an insect down for examination.

'Get the fuck off. I paid for that shit.'

Stone took a moment to rest his hands on his knees and catch his breath.

'You alright, sir?' Bolton asked, with a wry smile.

Shut it, you.

Stone nearly collapsed on the grass. 'Sit him up, sergeant.'

'I ain't done nothin'. This is shit, man.' The boy was thirteen or fourteen and a small build. An unhealthily pale complexion with scruffy brown hair which looked beyond redemption. Everything he was wearing was a murky mixture of greenish-grey or faded black. It was dirty, creased heavily and unevenly.

Stone turned so that he was sitting next to the boy, whilst Bolton still had hold of his wrist and shoulder.

'Hands off, bitch.'

'Hey, hey.' Stone raised his voice and pointed right in the boy's face. 'You show some damn respect, or I won't order my sergeant to loosen her grip. Got it?'

He finally relented.

'That's better. Now, we're going to sit here nice and quiet for a moment.'

'Fat little piggy out of breath?' the boy laughed.

'You're not going to do anything stupid like try and run off and make me arrest you.'

'How do you know?'

Stone reached to his belt and unclipped the cuffs he carried. He snapped one around the boy's wrist and the other around his own.

'You can't arrest me.'

'I'm not. But if you really want to run, you'll have to drag this fat piggy with you.'

'I'll sue ya.'

'Fine by me. I'm still sitting down for a minute first.'

'Whatever.'

Stone gave Bolton the nod to let his other arm go. She

took her cue and went to lean on the bonnet of the car.

Stone broke the silence. 'Sorry about that. She's a bit kick-ass. That's why I know better than to piss her off.'

'Bet she could kick your ass.'

'Totally,' Stone let out a slight laugh. He took his ID from his pocket and showed the boy. 'My name is Mike. DI Mike Stone.'

'You don't need proof. I can smell you.'

'I'm just identifying myself. It's a mark of respect. Don't be a dick about it.'

The boy paused. He kept his frown as he rubbed his wrist, packing in all the melodrama he could.

'Show me some respect and I'll take these cuffs off.'

The boy thought about it for a moment. Sighed. There was a shift in his expression. Years of experience interviewing people had taught DI Stone a lot about watching all the tiny non-verbal signals.

This boy's expression gave away a flash of fear. The filling eyes, bottom lip protruding slightly. A split-second pinch of the eyebrows in the centre. It was gone as fast as it had appeared. But Stone had seen it.

'So, let's start again. I'm Mike.'

The boy's eyes dropped. 'Matt.'

'Okay, good.' Stone softened his tone. He un-hooped the cuff from his own wrist, which he'd never actually clasped shut.

Matt looked at him open-mouthed.

Stone handed him his keys. 'Have a go. Find the key for the cuffs.'

Matt paused for a moment, utterly confused why this copper was handing him his keys.

Mike Stone knew exactly what he was doing. Build bridges, no matter how wonky. He watched Matt find the right key, then fiddle about with the lock until the cuffs clicked open.

'Cool.' Matt's smile was genuine. He held up the keys.

282

'Can I keep these?'

'Well, hang on to them for a minute.'

He didn't expect that answer.

'Matt. Outside the shop, I really did just have a couple of questions I wanted to ask. I know you haven't done anything wrong.'

'I know you lot. You'd accuse me of nicking.'

'Not this time. You see, we're working on something special, and we think you might be able to help us.'

Matt looked at him.

'Then you made me run my fat piggy arse off.'

The boy laughed, freely. 'That was funny.'

Stone nodded. He got his phone and swiped the screen a couple of times. 'Matt, I'm going to show you a photo of someone and ask if you recognise them. But before I do that, let's get something clear.' Stone waited for the boy to look at him to acknowledge that he was listening. 'I'll know if you lie.'

Stone showed him the photo of Luke. Matt's eyes widened.

Bolton saw it, too.

'Nev' seen him.'

'So, who is Luke?' Bolton added.

'I dunno.' He flinched, darting his eyes between them both.

Stone lowered his voice conspiratorially. 'We call her the Jedi.'

Matt glared at Stone.

'Damn sure she can read minds. So, you take another look. Have a little think. This time, I'd like to know how you know Luke.'

Matt turned away as if to assess the situation for an escape route. He looked back at the phone. He drew his knees up closer to his chest and fixed his eyes on the picture. His frown deepened and his complexion was reddening. Three fast blinks, a tightening of the chin, and

Stone knew he had the boy where he needed him.

I've got him but this is not going to be nice.

'When was the last time you had a proper, hot meal, Matt?' Stone softened his voice enough for the boy to notice the change in character. All he got in return was a resigned shrug of the shoulders as the boy's eyes fixed on the picture.

'Listen. Matt. You're not in trouble. You could run now, and I would probably just let you go. But I don't want to. What I want you to do is to come with us. Talk to us where you are safe. Not out here where you can be seen. Where they can find you again.'

Stone waited. He could see the boy was fighting an internal battle between desperately wanting to go with them but also being terrified of the consequences.

He looked around again.

'And mainly because I'm getting pretty bloody hungry, too.'

'I never had a choice.'

'Well, I am giving you a choice now.'

'You gonna lock me up?'

'No. I want your help.' He waited a moment. 'But if you call me piggy again, I'll let my Jedi here kick your ass.'

There was the slightest flicker of a smile from the boy.

'What d'ya say?'

Matt nodded.

Without speaking, Stone stood and offered a hand to help the boy up. The gesture wasn't completely altruistic. Stone felt the boy's hand was clammy with fear and his knuckles showed faded bruises and grazing.

Stone showed the boy to the back of Bolton's car, sitting him on the driver's side so it was easier to keep an eye on him. As he shut the door, Bolton smiled at him.

'You are such a big softy, Mike Stone.'

'Shut it.' He walked around the front of the car. 'We'll need to knock this to Safeguarding a.s.a.p., but let's get some grub first.'

Bolton shot him a disapproving look. 'You're going to get your fingers burnt if you delay too long.'

He gave her a shrewd nod. 'He's coming with us willingly. We suspect he is homeless, and therefore vulnerable. As officers of Her Majesty's constabulary, we have a duty of care to exercise powers of loco parentis, without need to arrest. PACE doesn't apply. Yes, it's close to the line, but we're on the right side of the blurry edge.'

They got into the car and Bolton checked Matt had his belt on in automatic mother mode. Stone adjusted the smaller rear-view mirror Bolton had in the top left side of the windscreen, positioned specifically to keep an eye on anyone sitting behind the driver.

Stone caught the boy's eye again as he sat in the back, playing with his set of keys. It was a moment that carried an unspoken conversation.

'I've done something bad.'
'I know.'
'I'm in trouble, aren't I?'
'No.'
'Can you help me?'
'I'll try.'

Chapter 45

May
Luke & Amelja

The cold wind caught Luke's cheeks and rolled down his exposed neck. He'd long since given his scarf to Amelja, who had wrapped her face so that her eyes barely showed above it.

Having been told to leave Snow Hill station walkway, they'd turned down the top of Livery Street and walked down the hill towards the ring road. Luke knew there was an underpass often frequented by rough sleepers.

It was late afternoon and he thought it might be a good spot to catch a few workers heading out of the city centre as they went home.

But by the time they turned the corner and were halfway down the steps Luke stopped. There was already someone there. Intruding on someone else's patch was risky business.

'Bit wet to be walking around up there,' the man from below spoke in a deep, warm voice. He was an old, black man with short wiry hair and a rough complexion. 'You two come on down here, get yourself out that wind.'

Amelja tugged on Luke's arm. But something about the man made him seem safe.

'You're more likely to catch ya death up there than off

me,' the soft, rough tone said.

Luke looked at Amelja and shrugged his shoulders. The old man began to struggle to his feet, awkwardly twisting around to steady himself and stand up against the wall. He was wearing torn old black gloves. He took his right glove off and offered his hand to Luke. He paused a moment, but Luke shook the old man's hand and felt warmth he'd not experienced in days.

The old man's face seemed to sink. He immediately put his second hand over Luke's. 'My lord, lad. You're frozen to a cube.'

Despite Luke's initial flinch, the man held tight, reassuring. Softened by kindness. The man then took Amelja's hand. 'A young lady of your beauty, should not be out here.' He covered her hand with his second and gave them a gentle squeeze. 'Now, come, you two. Rest those weary legs as my guests.'

The old man bent down to his stand of cardboard and spread the several layers so Luke and Amelja had space to sit. 'Please, please, come and sit.'

'Thank you, sir,' Luke surprised himself with the formal slip.

'Sir? The Lord as my witness,' he laughed. 'My friends call me Freeman. Those who He aks to sit with me, be my friends.' He looked up and crossed his chest.

Luke and Amelja sat down close together and they drew their knees up to their chest.

'First thing's first,' Freeman said, 'It's time to enjoy a good paper.' The man opened a bag and took out several copies of the Metro and placed them between him and Luke.

'Go on, son, help yourself.'

'Thanks,' Luke said, handing a copy to Amelja. They both already knew the benefit of adding layers inside their clothes to keep the warmth in.

Freeman nodded, impressed with the apparent

288

knowledge of the two youngsters. 'Give the paper a bit of a scrunching up, like this, so it's not so flat.' The old man showed Luke how to insert papers between layers of clothes. 'Best to keep this stuff as crisp dry as possible. No use when it's wet.'

The teenagers then spent another ten minutes or so, under instruction, adding a few more layers to what few clothes they had on under their coats. After they'd finished, Luke fidgeted around for a moment.

Amelja smiled. 'You sound like bag of crisps.'

Freeman let out a loud laugh. 'Ha. That he do.' He reached into his bag again and produced pairs of small, one-size-fits-all style gloves. Luke looked at the man, doubt and delay in his eyes. 'You need to keep yourselves warm.'

'But don't you need them?'

'Me? Lord, no. I have these.' He held up his scruffy old gloves with holes in them. 'Do you know how long I've had these gloves?'

Luke shook his head.

'No, neither do I.' The man let out another loud laugh. He handed the gloves to Luke.

'Thanks.'

'I love the Lord, my saviour. But our mother, she has a lot to answer for.'

'Your mother?'

'Mother Nature. A beautiful lady.' Dropping his voice to a whisper. 'But she can be a bitter old bitch, sometimes.'

Luke grunted a small laugh without even noticing it.

'Nothing warms the heart like laughter.' He paused, looked at Amelja, and then back at Luke. 'And love.'

Amelja smiled.

'Lord, forgive, where are my manners? I have yet to ask your names. If you wish to share them.'

'Amelja,' she replied quietly, almost a whisper.

'Luke.'

'Luke and Amelja.' Freeman gasped like quenching thirst. 'A fine gospel name. And if memory serves me right, Amelja means striving. Never gives up. Fine names, both.'

At that moment a loud clicking of heeled shoes came down the steps. Luke and Amelja tightened whilst the old man remained calm as he took out a small cap from beside him and dropped it on the floor in front of them.

A smartly dressed woman in a tight red coat appeared around the corner halfway up the steps. She was carrying a small umbrella which seemed more of a fashion accessory than for fending off rain.

'Good evening,' Freeman said in a smooth tone. 'Spare change for my two friends?'

The woman skipped a step and first looked as though she would scurry on by. But her eyes rested on Amelja a little longer. Reaching into a matching small red bag, she drew out her hand and gently curtseyed, dropping a few coins into the hat.

'God bless you, ma'am, God bless you indeed.'

Her mouth smiled. Her eyes winced. And her legs moved on quickly. It was hard to tell whether it was out of fear or embarrassment. Or the guilt that maybe she could have left more.

'First one today,' Freeman said, matter-of-fact. 'Anyway, it's time to get food inside us. What d'ya say?'

Luke was caught off guard and instantly worried. He had no money or food, and he didn't know how to say it.

He'd spent years learning to suspect generosity. All too often people wanted something in return. But at the same time, he secretly chastised himself for being so unfair. He had met a handful of people whose kindness had been genuine.

Freeman shuffled around in another bag and produced small packs of sausage rolls.

'I insist that you join me as guests of my castle. For I feast on the rare treat of company.' He handed a pack of sausage rolls and an orange each to Luke and Amelja without giving them a chance to try and refuse. 'All three of you are welcome.'

Luke paused. Did he hear the man right? Or was it a slip of the tongue? Luke looked at Amelja and she had also looked worried.

'I noticed the way you stood, free hand protecting the young. Worry not, my friends. Your secret is safe with me.'

Luke smiled at Freeman again.

'I may not know where's y'come from, nor wheres y'heading. But right now, the Lord has placed you here with me. He has his reasons, and I heed to his will. No matter what your beliefs might be, my Lord bids me by the second commandment.'

He dug out a small copy of the bible and opened it at a marked page. Handing it to Luke, he tapped on the line. 'Love thy neighbour as thyself.'

Luke repeated it as he read the words.

'I take it this is not a book you study?' Freeman kept his tone to one of acknowledgement than a chastisement.

'I think I only know one line,' Luke strained to remember what Reg had said to him. 'It was Jesus on the cross saying something about forgiving because they didn't know what they were doing.'

Luke felt the book being taken from his left. Amelja gently, but quickly, leafed the pages and then tapped on the lines as she handed it back to him.

'Here it is. In Luke. Luke twenty-three, thirty-four.'

Luke read the line just as Reg had spoken it to him what seemed so long ago. Luke, twenty-three, thirty-four.

Freeman reminded Luke of Reg Walters, even though Reg was less preachy. It hurt him to think of the lies he had told Reg, believing that he did it to protect himself and Amelja. But he was meeting the same kindness again and he wondered, once more, why did he always keep running from those who meant him no harm?

Chapter 46

September

Mike Stone got into the back of the car with the large, brown paper bag and a holder with three cups.

'Shove over, kid, I'm hungry,' he said, handing the drinks tray to Matt after he'd moved.

'She's not a real Jedi, you know?' The boy announced with a triumphant tone.

'DS Bolton? She bloody is,' Mike insisted, closing the door, but keeping a close eye on the tray of drinks. Two soft drinks and one coffee.

Matt's eyes lit up with anticipation like he hadn't eaten a full meal in days. 'Nah, I tested her. She's faking it.'

Mike tapped on the coffee and pointed at Bolton, indicating to the boy to pass her the drink. 'Careful with that,' he said it softly, but parentally, as he would speak to Jack.

'What's this I hear, Sands?'

Bolton waved a dismissive hand in Mike's direction. 'You don't need to know.' She took her drink from the boy and flashed him a conspiratorial wink.

'I don't need to know,' Mike reflected instantly, looking down into the bag of food.

The boy looked between the two of them, let out a quick laugh at the strange double-act before trying to regain his composure.

Mike took a large, multi-layered burger out and dropped it into one of the free cupholder spaces. He did the same with a large fries, before taking his drink.

The boy's eyes lit up.

Stone then took out a handful of paper napkins and dropped them into the remaining space, together with a handful of sauces, several wooden stirring sticks, a few sachets of salt, pepper, white and brown sugar, and several straws.

It was deliberately farcical. And it got the response he was after. The tension lowered a little more.

After retrieving his selection of food, he passed the bag to Bolton, who noticed the extra burger hidden at the bottom. Unofficially buying some help from an adult informant was one thing. But from a child witness?

'What do I need all this stuff for?' Matt asked, picking at all the sundries.

Miked shrugged his shoulders like a petulant teenager and took a bite of his burger to make sure he answered with a full mouth. 'Freebies.'

'I never get away with this much.'

Mike tapped his nose. 'I just grabbed them. What they gonna do? Call the cops?'

The boy laughed at the ridiculousness. He shot Bolton a look as if to ask, 'is this guy serious?' She just rolled her eyes.

Matt took the burger out of the box and delved into it with lion-cub like ferocity.

Mike and Bolton caught each other's eyes and agreed to let the silence run its course. It was comfortable. Neither of them was especially hungry, but collective eating was a good leveller. It also served as a reminder to Mike Stone as to just how easy it was to buy compliance from a child. Too easy.

After a few minutes had passed, he decided to break

the silence.

'Matt, we're not supposed to spend our working day just munching on food. We do actually have to get some work done, or our boss gets stroppy.'

'Even popo gotta eat, though, right?'

'We do indeed. But still, when we aren't going by our Telltubbies name, work is work. So, do you think you might be able to help us out?'

'Yous two want me to help you not get an ass-kickin' from your boss?'

'Totally.'

The boy smiled.

Mike looked at him and dropped the joking tone for a moment. 'Just a couple of questions. No pressure, and not accusing you of anything, okay?'

Matt shrugged his shoulders in an attempt to seem nonchalant. But his eyes still held the same worry.

'You recognise Luke. I know. But when did you last see him?'

Matt shrugged his shoulders.

'Did you speak to him?'

Shook his head.

It was Bolton's cue, and she slid her finger across her phone screen to show Amelja's image again. 'Do you recognise her?'

Matt leaned forward to look closer. He nodded, wearily.

'Did you ever see them together?'

'She's deffo his girl.'

'And when did you see them? Together.'

'That was ages ago. I dunno.'

'Where did you see them?' Bolton asked.

The boy looked out the car window. They'd parked on Dale End, just down from Bull Street with all the fast-food outlets. Mike knew it was a key spot in town that attracted a lot of young people.

It also kept cropping up a lot in the investigation. More

coincidences.

'I saw them around here once.'

'Ever see them with anyone else?' Mike was keeping as casual as he could and had turned half with his back to the door, one knee up on the back seat, looking more casual. He'd watched the boy mimic his body language, which was a good sign they were connecting. The boy's subconscious communicating a lot more than he realised.

Matt nodded, more cautious. 'That other guy. Hangs around talking to other kids.'

'What other kids?' Bolton asked, tending her fries.

Mike registered the boy's discomfort. He'd finished the food already and lost that defensive wall. Without needing to be asked, Bolton responded on cue.

'Hey, Piggy, who's this extra burger for?' She passed it to him.

He looked at Matt, whose eyes had met his, and then looked with a hungry wanting at the box, without realising. Mike held it out to boy.

'Thanks.' It was a quiet reply, but it was just about there. And it was understood. 'Does this make me an informant?'

Mike smiled. 'Totally.'

'If I grass, I'm dead.'

'You're not a grass. This is like a job. And that's your pay,' he pointed at the burger. 'Now, tell me about this older guy, and the other kids.'

'Kid's like me.' He took a bite. Saw the cop was waiting for a bit more than that. 'Homeless, runaways, care kids. You know? Us kids what could vanish and no one would give a sh…'

The boy's voice cracked and his eyes glistened. He filled his mouth with a couple more bites, desperate to shove the bad feelings back inside. Deep down inside.

'People do care, Matt.'

He scowled at Mike. 'No, they don't. They shout when

we cause trouble. Ignore us when we don't.' He bit off a couple more bites. One too many.

Mike reached out a hand and gently tapped him on the knee. 'Hey, slow down. It's really hard explaining "busy doing body dump" to the boss.'

For a moment, Matt turned to look out the front window, trying to avert his eyes. He let out a deep sigh and paused to breathe between bites. His whole body sank into the corner between the seat and the back door.

The rain outside began to rumble on the roof and windows, but it also made it feel warm and solid. Safe. And it had the fast-food-fat stink.

Matt spoke quietly. 'But the older kid. He gets us doing small jobs.'

'Small jobs.' Stone knew well enough to reflect the statement without throwing it back as a question. It was a technique used to help a nervous person, especially children and young people, process what they have said.

'Like taking. Things. To people. Deliveries.'

Drug mules. Stolen goods. Burner phones.

'But he also looks for certain types. You know?'

Bolton let out a cough. She looked at DI Stone and mouthed "ABE" at him. A gentle reminder to leave the push for the Achieving Best Evidence interview. "It's what the kid said in the back of a car over a burger, your honour," did not go down well in court.

Matt took another bite and another sip of the drink. But it couldn't stop the tears welling up.

After a long pause spent weighing up his options, Matt spoke quietly. He's the one called Gnome.'

Mike nodded and swiped at his phone screen a couple more times. He saw the boy's eyes widened with a fearful recognition when.

Mike nodded gently to him. He leaned forward to gather up all the rubbish, stuffing it into a crumpled old carrier bag from the floor except for the napkins, which he threw gently at Matt again in a soft kind of hint. The boy took it and scrunched his fingers through a couple somewhat ineffectively.

Mike turned back round to sit properly on the seat.

'I thought you were looking for me,' Matt said, almost as quiet as a whisper. 'At the shop.'

Mike and Bolton looked at each other for a moment, confirming a thought they'd both had.

'Thought you were after me.'

'Why?' Mike said. Waiting for a moment. 'Why would we be looking for you?'

'What I did.'

'Matt, we're not interested in drugs or other deliveries.' Bolton waited for any sign that what she had said sank in.

Mike heard that voice over his shoulder again and remembered what he'd noticed about Matt's hands. 'Do you know what happened to Luke?'

Matt paused for a moment before he gave a reluctant nod and he spread his fingers and looked at his bruised knuckles.

Mike held one of the boy's hands until they made eye contact.

'Luke's okay,' Mike nodded, giving a gentle smile.

Finally, the floodgates opened.

Chapter 47

September
Day Ten ~ Monday

DI Stone and Reg Walters had agreed to give Luke more time over the weekend to refocus after the shock of Amelja's death before interviewing him. As far as Stone was concerned, it was more important to get the ABE done with Matt first.

He was still angry at having been pressured to treat Luke as a suspect, and he knew in the long run any skilled defence barrister would tear apart evidence collected under mental duress when it came to children.

Stone dropped his coat over his chair, opened the drawer on his desk and took out a piece of paper. DC Khan had been the first to get to the office that morning, and Stone watched with yearning envy as he clutched his morning sausage sandwich.

'Morning, guv. Good weekend with your lad?'

'Took him to see something too bright and too colourful at the Odeon.' Mike Stone loved taking his son to the cinema, which they did quite regularly. But he found the high coloured, noisy kids films nauseating.

Khan pointed at his computer. 'You're not even logged in yet.'

Stone paused and looked up at him. 'Why? What have

you got? Or done.'

'Right, well, don't be angry.' Khan swallowed hard, putting the back of his hand to his mouth and wincing at clearly trying to eat too quickly. 'I didn't want to disturb you over the weekend. But those numbers.'

'Don't choke on my behalf.'

'Good news and bad news. Oh, and confusing news.' He sat down as Stone's PC booted up and he opened his emails. 'Bad news is neither one is registered to a name.'

'Burner phones? Hardly surprising.'

Khan wobbled his head side to side. 'No, they've been used more than once, they just aren't tied to any name or address that I can find.'

'But my clever little constable...'

'Haves hims locations.' He tapped at the paper. 'Emailed. Approximate triangulations of where the numbers were used. The first one is out on Bristol Road.'

Stones eyes widened. 'That's a tasty coincidence.'

Khan nodded, but his expression darkened straight away. 'The second number is a little closer to home.'

'You have got to be kidding me?' Stone dropped his head into his palms as soon as he read Khan's email. 'Are you sure?'

Khan shrugged.

'Is there any way of getting a more accurate position?'

'Not unless I trace a live call, and even that would only show part of the building, not a specific room or floor.'

Stone was faced with the worrying reality that the second number he'd shown DC Khan was being used from somewhere in their station. Which meant it was a high probability it was a police officer. And whoever was using that phone was in contact with an address on Bristol Road that could be at the centre of organised crime.

He felt his stomach churn.

'Next email, guv.'

Stone took a deep breath, opened the email and clicked

on the CCTV link to a small file.

'Got the face of the courier. Only, I don't think it is a courier.'

'Pray, tell, constable.'

'You watch it. See if you see what I did.'

Stone played the file and spotted it straight away. The face was one of the clearest CCTV shots he'd seen in a long time. The man looked straight into the camera and gave a slight, but perceptible nod. Not a taunt. But a recognition that he wanted his face to be seen.

The voice whispered over his shoulder.

How did you know I would come looking for that CCTV?

A knock at the door distracted them both, and Bolton walked in with Reg Walters close behind.

'Sands, come and look at this,' Stone waved her over to his desk.

'Good morning to you, too.' She joined him on his side of his desk and watched as he restarted the video file. 'That's something we don't see very often.'

Stone cast a glance to Reg. 'Where's Luke?'

Reg raised a hand to calm the concerned edge to his voice. 'I left him with a nice breakfast in one of the family rooms.' Reg then nodded at the computer. 'Bit early to be watching amusing kittens on YouTube, isn't it?'

'I wish,' Stone snorted. 'Just trying to work out if someone is leaving breadcrumbs.'

There was a pensive pause in the office before Stone sat up in his chair and invited all the other occupants to get comfortable.

'Right. First thing's first, Reg. How is he, all things considered?'

'Holding up. He could do without being grilled about what has happened. He needs time and therapy, not police investigations.'

Reg saw all three detectives look at each other and fidget uncomfortably. Khan nodded. Bolton sighed. Stone scratched at his stubble. The elephant in the room had a bowel movement.

'Worry not, I've gone over the procedure with him. In a way, he kind of wants to help.'

'Thanks, Reg,' Stone replied.

'But let me be clear that I have told him what you told me to emphasise. He's not under arrest or suspicion.'

'He's helping with our enquiries. Carter is pressuring me to go in tough, using video evidence, but this is my investigation.'

Everyone nodded in agreement.

'I've spoken to DCI Palmers, and we have his backing.'

Reg turned to look out the window. 'And I am intending on being in the room as the appropriate adult.'

Stone looked at Bolton, who nodded. 'We are fine with that. That would change if he is arrested because you did the PM on Amelja.'

Bolton looked at Reg with quizzical eyes. 'Reg, does he know you did that?'

Reg let out a sigh and ran a hand through his hair. 'It hasn't come up yet.' He turned to look at Stone. 'Level with me, Mike. What are you going to show him?'

'Harry has taken some stills and cropped them so that they only contain the faces for ID. Besides that, we'll show him images of Buchanan, Gnome, and Kapllani.'

Khan sat up. 'Random thought, guv. Why not show him the picture of our mystery guest, too. On the off chance he recognises him.'

'Good idea. Get me a still of his face.'

Reg felt his phone buzz in his pocket and took it out, expecting it to be Luke. But the text came from another number. He frowned at the screen, tapped out a fast reply and looked at his phone for a moment.

'Everything okay?' Stone asked, keen to let Reg leave as he wasn't needed for the briefing. But he'd also noticed Reg had been caught off guard. 'Get yourself downstairs and we'll try to be quick.'

Reg made no eye contact, his mind elsewhere.

'I'll send you a text when we are on our way down.'

Reg got his focus back. 'That would be great.' He was about to leave the office when he turned back. 'Guys, I appreciate all you're doing. Just try to remember he's grieving.' He nodded before leaving the office.

Stone waited for the door to close before he spoke. 'Okay, Sands, let's plan our approach.' He turned to Khan. 'Harry, get Buchanan in. I want him at arm's reach.'

Khan left the office, and Bolton came round to it in the seat.

'Talk to me, Mike.'

He looked at her, their eyes meeting under furrowed brows. 'I think I'm being backed into a corner.'

She tilted her head. They knew each other well, and it was rare she ever saw him looking genuinely worried. 'You know I've got your back.'

He smiled, but it didn't reach his eyes. 'This interview could start a snowball that is going to achieve one of two things.'

'Luke will be fine, okay? Your head and heart are in the right place.'

'But this case is either going to have to destroy him or cause serious damage to a lot of jobs and careers. And maybe some people we work closely with.'

'Remember what I told you Amelja said to me?'

Tell him I'm sorry.

'And remember the first thing Luke said when he came round?'

Forgive them.

'Mike, I remember you teaching me a long time ago that good cops do the job to catch the bad guys, and to protect and serve justice.'

But the best of us do it to protect innocence.

Chapter 48

The smell of Amelja's hair lingered softly as he stood behind her, holding his hands over her eyes. She tried to sound impatient, but her nervous giggling betrayed her tone.

'Where are we? What are we doing?' Amelja shrugged her shoulders and held his wrists.

'Just a few more steps.'

'This is silly. You are silly.'

'Okay, we're here.'

'Now can I look?' Amelja laughed, lifting his hands away from her eyes.

'Tadaa,' Luke revealed his surprise.

'What is this place?'

Luke ran around in front of her to reveal his presentation. The tired, red-brick, terraced house with boarded upper windows and lower windows clamped shut with steel sheets. Several weeds and small plants sprouted out from various cracks in the brickwork. The gutter was dripping from several places, and white lintels were stained with decades of stale rainwater.

Amelja's face sank beneath a mild scowl. 'What is… this?'

'Just imagine, one day this will be ours. Without the boards.'

'But it is half plants.'

'We can get rid of them, easy.'

'It is falling down.'

'Nah, it survived the war.'

Amelja laughed. 'Which war?' She turned to him pecked a quick kiss on his cheek and laughed. 'I love your fantasy.'

Luke took her hand and pulled her towards the house. 'Come on. I'll show you around.'

They pushed through the front gate hanging on by one remaining rusty iron hinge. Battling through the thickly over-grown front yard to an equally rotting side gate, they ducked between low-hanging branches.

'Where are we going?' Amelja laughed nervously as she was pulled along.

'There's a way in, round the back.'

'Is it safe?'

Luke's youthful optimism dragged them into the rear garden. The wall of a murky brown, shabby old extension barely attached to the rear wall of the property had a door also fully boarded up.

Luke pulled at the board, opening it just enough to squeeze himself inside and then poke his hand out again for Amelja to follow him in.

'We are not supposed to be in there.' She tried to protest.

His head reappeared. 'It's fine. Perfectly safe. Don't worry, I checked with, er, the landlord.'

Amelja folded her arms and cocked her head at a disapproving angle. 'Now you tell lie.'

He smiled. 'Well, I checked with the future landlord.'

'Who is this?'

'Me.' He laughed, slightly proud at his twisted logic. 'Come on. You'll love it. It's dry.'

She let out a deep sigh and relented.

The first small room was attempting to be a kitchen, but barely had the units and cupboards to show it. There was a kitchen sink, but not the plumbing to go with it.

A damp, musty smell filled the small space, black mould creeping from every corner of the sagging ceiling.

They passed through into the middle room which couldn't have been more than twelve feet wide.

'This could be our dining room,' Luke gestured grandly, miming a table in the centre of the room. 'We can have a large mirror on this wall, see. Makes the room look bigger.'

'And now you design house?'

Luke shrugged his shoulders. 'I saw it on a TV show.'

He dragged her into the front room. 'In here, we can have an open fire, and a Christmas tree in the corner. TV over here in the other corner.' Luke stood at the wall like a weather reporter. 'And you can sit here in the window, Madame,' he attempted a French accent.

Amelja laughed and played along with the fantasy. 'Thank you. But I might want more comfortable seat.'

'You can have your own chair. And I can lay back on the sofa, here.' He spread his arms with a flourish against the wall opposite the fire. 'I can admire you.'

Amelja gently placed a hand on her increasingly showing bump.

'And little one will roll around and play and laugh and smile as we watch.'

Luke reached out to her again and Amelja ran her fingers through his dishevelled hair, before wiping the sweat from his forehead. 'You need to wash your hair.'

He stepped back, straightening their arms and grinning with mischief. 'Let me show you upstairs.'

Amelja gasped, covering her mouth.

He turned back and paused, looking at her with innocent confusion written across his young face. It took him a moment to realise the Freudian slip, but he pulled her along, running out into the hallway.

The stairs were old and cracked, bare wood. Luke ran up them two at a time.

'Be careful, Luke. How you say? Poshtë, poshtë.'

'Nah, I'm not posh,' he laughed and put on his best English accent he'd learnt from Reg. 'But one can be if madame wishes.'

'No, silly. Poshtë. Down. Get down. Come down.'

Luke bounced down the stairs again. 'Posh?'

'Poshtë.'

'Posh-t. Down?' He frowned at her. 'No, let's go up.' He grabbed her hand and led her up the stairs. Each one creaked and groaned as their feet clattered up halfway, then turned the corner, up a few more stairs and onto the landing.

He whisked her into the first room. A small window let in barely a sliver of light, but it was just enough for them to make out its limited features. The floorboards were in a bad state and old wallpaper was peeling from the walls.

Luke played the part of interior designer again. 'There'll be a cot in the corner with a dangly mobile over it. Twinkly stars lighting up on the ceiling. Nice chair to sit in to rock her to sleep.'

'How you know it will be girl?' Amelja smiled a playful inquisition.

'Because she'll be as beautiful as you.'

'But what if he's a silly boy like you?'

'He will need a racing car track on the floor.'

'Shelves in the corner for all the books.'

'And he…'

'She will learn to read and write and speak…'

They both embraced again and spoke in unison. 'English and Albanian.'

Luke grabbed her hand again and led her back onto the landing.

'Luke, slow down.'

'Come on, let's see our room.'

They ran into the front bedroom, which was in an even worse state than the other room. The window let strong shafts of light in through the same cracks in which small weeds had crawled their way through the masonry. The smell of damp clawed at their throats as they scuffed on the dusty, cracked floorboards.

Sleeping bags lay on top of some old foam camping matts in the back corner. Terracotta plant pots were dotted around the room with a variety of tealights and cream-coloured candles of all sizes.

Amelja gasped. 'You make all this?' She picked up one of the candles. 'Where do you get such things with no money?'

'I have my ways,' he replied, with an edge of pride to his voice. 'Do you like it?'

'And this bed.'

'Look. Warm new sleeping bags.'

For Amelja, Luke was her innocent little thief. She held him by his cheeks and kissed him on the forehead. 'You are my own little Enji tonight.'

Luke mimicked her. 'Onjee.'

'In Albania, Enji is God of fire. It is you. My own little Enji.'

Luke took a lighter from his pocket and started to light the candles.

'Why the pots?'

'I saw it on a film once. The candle heats up the pot and you hold it. Warms your hands.' He handed Amelja a small pot with a lit candle inside. 'And it's safer because they can't fall over and start a fire.'

Amelja grinned at him.

'Because I am your On-jee,' he said triumphantly.

'You look like Statue of Literally in America.'

Luke laughed and held up another burning candle. 'I am the Statue of Literally.'

They looked around the room at all the candles they had managed to light. In reality, it was a meagre number. But in their minds, they were floating into the Phantom's lair under the opera house.

'I have another surprise for you,' Luke said, Cheshire grin lighting up his face.

'Not more stealing?'

'Nope, I did a deal with a market man, all fair and square.' He reached into his pocket and brought out a small digital radio. 'It works, too. I checked.' He handed it to Amelja and showed her how to switch it on, and which button to press.

It was tuned to a local station playing popular music.

The DJ made some poor jokes and short introductions before playing the next track.

"Rule the World" by Take That squawked from the speaker with considerable volume for its relatively small build.

They held each other close and balanced the speaker between their chests. Amelja guided Luke's hands to hold in the right place for a slow swaying dance, rocking side to side with the music. Amelja rested her head on his shoulder as they danced around the room, lost in the music and flickering candlelight.

Luke whispered into her ear. 'One day, all this will be ours. The house, our little, baby boy…'

'Girl…'

'And I will protect you.'

'My very own Enji.'

'We are going to rule the world.'

Chapter 49

Reg had done a good job making sure Luke understood he wasn't under arrest and was simply helping the police with their enquiries. Ground rules were established, and the atmosphere was as relaxed as it could have been.

That didn't stop Mike Stone from feeling more nervous than he did in front of some of the most dangerous people he'd interviewed in his career.

Luke identified Gnome and briefly explained the activities he'd had to engage in. He also identified Matt as one of the boys forced to carry out the physical assault.

He struggled to keep his cool when Stone had shown him the picture of Nesim Kapllani, who he identified as the 'boss.' A flash of hatred in Luke's eyes when he'd seen Kapllani's picture was all it had taken.

DC Paul Buchanan's photo drew a blank, but that was considered hardly surprising given the state he was in when found.

But the surprise came with the new face.

'I want to show you another person, Luke,' DS Bolton showed him a still taken from the station reception CCTV.

The recognition was instant. But the reaction was very different.

Luke looked up at Bolton, then Stone, then Reg. 'I

know him.'

All three adults shot glances between them.

'Yeh, he's one of them. From the house.'

Stone leaned forward to get Luke's eye contact. 'Stupid question, I know, but what do you mean by 'one of them'?'

Luke rubbed at his eyes. 'He's the one that got me out the house.'

'When, Luke?' Stone fought to keep the urgency out of his voice.

'First time we escaped. And, after they made the boys…'

Bolton raised a hand. She didn't feel the need to make him say it again.

But Luke continued anyway. 'He carried me out. Took me in a car and kept saying I was gonna be okay.' Luke shrugged his shoulders. 'He saved me.'

DI Stone leaned forward. 'Did you ever hear his name?'

Luke pressed his eyes with his palms again as he shook his head.

Reg placed a hand on his shoulder. 'Do you want a break?'

Luke shook his head and steadied his breathing.

Stone and Bolton looked at each other to confirm they'd both seen it. That was not the kind of self-control Mike Stone ever saw sexually violent rapists ever bothering to learn and use.

'This is all more helpful than you realise, Luke. You're bloody brilliant. Thank you.'

It took him a moment, but Luke gave him a puzzled look.

'I have had a room of twenty detectives looking at that picture, trying to work out who he is. First time I showed you his picture and, boom. Hole in one.' Stone could see the slightest relaxation cross the boy's shoulders. 'So, forget about him for now. I'll find out his name.' Stone then raised his eyebrows and reached for the folder. 'Now, there is just one more picture I want to show you, just to check I have got the right people. But first, if you don't mind, I need a drink. What about you?'

'Can I have some water? Please.'

Stone smiled and shrugged his shoulders. 'Sure, if you like. Was gonna offer you a beer, but…'

Luke let a thin smile slip into a confused look.

DS Bolton stood up on cue. 'Behave, Mr supposed-to- be-an-Inspector Stone.' She looked at Luke. 'Ignore him. Sometimes he comes out with terrible dad jokes. Just water?'

She was closely followed by Reg Walters. He felt his phone vibrate in his pocket and took it out to read the text that had come in. 'I fancy a coffee, too. Mike, would you like one?'

'Thanks, yes.' Stone replied.

Stone made a note on the audio recording as the others left the room.

They spent a few minutes just swapping small talk as they waited for the others to return. The entire break had all been a staged affair to allow the atmosphere to settle. The opposite of sweating out a real suspect. Stone was well aware that Carter would want to see the recording and know exactly what he had done.

When Reg and Bolton returned, she handed the water to Luke and turned to give Stone a nod. The signal was subtle. A tried and tested check on the atmosphere. If one of them left and then returned it was easier for them to sense a change.

Reg saw the quick exchange between the two detectives but chose to ignore it. He knew they were known and respected for how well they managed the interview process.

'Okay, Luke,' Stone continued. 'What I am going to show you is a part of an image. We've cropped it just to focus only on the faces of who is in the image. That's all that matters. It doesn't matter what the whole image is about, just that I make sure I am right about who is in it.'

Stone turned the photo over and Luke froze.

He glared at DI Stone, face tightened, his breathing getting more rapid, and his eyebrows dropped into a wolf-like frown. His nostrils flared and he gritted his teeth.

Stone kept a composed tone, knowing even the slightest thing could trigger the rage he could see boiling up in front of him. He pointed at the male in the shot.

Everyone knew the answer, but they waited.

Luke's face reddened and his hands curled into fists.

A rasping sound, barely a whisper, said, 'me.'

Stone pointed at the girl. 'And her?'

Luke's eyes locked on Mike Stone's. Not blinking. Pupils dilated. Every ounce of the boy's being warning him off. It was like a bull and a matador, and DI Stone was dressed in red.

'Where did you get that?' Luke spat the words through gritted teeth.

'This is a cropped image taken from a recording.' Stone saw no point in lying. Luke clearly knew the answer.

Stone wanted to glance at Reg, but knew he had to hold Luke's stare. Not to win a battle, but because he had to let Luke choose self-control, to know he could back down from his rage.

'You've seen the recording, haven't you Luke?'

He nodded.

'Did they show you the recording?'

He nodded again.

'And told you what they'd do with it if you ever told, right?'

Luke didn't nod, but tears suddenly filled his eyes and streamed down his cheeks. But he still fixed his eyes on DI Stone.

'Mike...' Bolton whispered.

And Mike Stone knew he'd just crossed a line. He'd just asked two leading questions and potentially put future interviews and evidence into jeopardy.

He had all the proof he needed. And he would fight so that no one was ever allowed to show that boy the video again.

Protect innocence.

Finally, Luke blinked and then squeezed his eyes shut.

Stone looked at Reg, then at Bolton, and they agreed. It was time to call that interview to an end.

Reg placed a hand on Luke's shoulder. 'Come on. We'll finish up here. You've done great. Really, really, great. Amelja would be proud of…'

Luke shot to his feet and hurled his drink across the room. He picked up the image and ripped it in half before crumpling it between his hands and throwing it at Mike Stone.

Then he turned and shot both hands so hard into Reg's chest it emptied his lungs in a painful gasp as he slammed into the wall.

Stone and Bolton instinctively flinched backwards for a moment.

'Don't fucking say her name,' Luke screamed at Reg.

Luke's right hand battered his chair away and into the back wall.

'Don't say her name,' came out as a garbled snarl, drowned by sobs as Luke turned and retreated to the corner of the room, arms covering his face, and ramming his head into the wall.

Stone and Bolton were about to move in to restrain Luke, but Reg raised a hand to ward them off as he clambered back to his feet.

Luke dropped to the floor and sat, knees up to his chest, arms over his head, sobbing, and battling the Fury.

Reg moved around to Luke's side, so the boy would be less threatened by the sense of someone behind.

Eventually, Luke's arms loosened, and his head rested on the wall. His hands came down to clasp his knees, revealing half his face.

A hoarse whisper strained out. 'I loved her so much.'

Reg moved closer and slid down the wall to sit on the floor within arm's reach.

He sighed. 'I know, buddy. I know you did.'

'It was my punishment.'

'Punishment?' Reg turned to look at him. 'For what?'

'Trying to save her.' He coughed and rocked a couple of times. 'It was my fault they found her in the first place.'

Reg looked at DI Stone, a pleading in his eyes.

Stone crouched down next to Reg. 'The people who brought her to the UK already knew her name. She escaped from them. They used you.'

The boy took a deep breath and looked down at the floor. 'I can't even remember doing it.'

A dark cloud filled Reg's mind as he wondered what drugs they had plied him with.

'I loved her.'

'I know,' Reg nodded.

'Her Enji.'

Luke thumped the wall as he repeated it, the sobs growing. The thumps became a sudden, powerful punch.

'And I killed her.' Luke's voice deepened as he pushed himself up, punching the wall with increasing force. And then with both fists pounding. 'I killed her, I killed her.'

Reg leapt to his feet and dragged Luke away from the wall, which was smudged and marked with flickers of his blood. At first, Luke struggled and fought, pummelling at Reg's back, but this time Reg stood his ground.

Luke's thumping died down with exhaustion, but Reg held firm until the sobs began to fade enough that he knew Luke, and only Luke, would hear what he was whispering in his ear.

'You didn't kill her, Luke. Not you. But when I find who did, when I find them, I'm going to kill them.'

Chapter 50

'Luke, wake up,' Amelja whispered, nudging him with her feet, then rolling over on the makeshift bed and shaking him by the shoulder. 'Luke.'

His eyes opened and took a moment to register Amelja's face right up to his, her forefinger pressed up against her lips.

There was little blue moonlight coming into the room between the boards covering the window. Picking up on the tension, he listened for any other noise.

They heard a crunch.

Luke had scattered broken glass around the hallway, stairs, and landing to alert them to anyone approaching.

He helped Amelja up to her feet. Heavily pregnant, all movement was awkward and cumbersome, let alone trying to move in silence.

They moved to the corner of the bedroom avoiding the creeks marked out on the floorboards with a piece of chalk. A discarded old wardrobe stood close enough to the door to either push over to block it or hide inside. Luke handed Amelja a solid piece of wood the size of a cricket bat, spiked with rusty old nails, before pushing her into the wardrobe.

He put a finger to her lips and then pointed down, whispering. 'Poshtë.'

Another crunch of glass, this time on the stairs.

Luke knew the police had to announce themselves, so he hoped it was just another rough sleeper or squatter wanting to find somewhere to sleep.

But this was someone who knew they had to sneak. Someone who knew they were upstairs. That meant they were no friend or innocent stranger.

Luke's heart pounded as he whispered his mantra. 'Fury beats fear.'

He chanted the mantra in his mind. No matter what happened, he had to protect Amelja and his child. The more the baby had grown, the more Luke's instinct to protect like a father had developed, despite his age.

A floorboard creaked just eight feet away. But he also heard more crushed glass a little further which meant there were at least two intruders.

His eyes rose to the brick carefully balanced on top of the door. That was wrapped with tape holding shards of glass intended to cause maximum possible injury and shock.

Luke picked up the second piece of wood. He also had a half piece of brick, sharp at one end. Light enough to swing and heavy enough to throw.

Finally, there was his last weapon. One he wasn't so proud of making but would use if he had to.

A small plastic bottle filled with a toxic mix of vinegar, salt and loads of scotch bonnet chilli sauce. No long-term damage, but enough to slow anyone down.

The door started to open, and the Fury steeled itself for action. There was no doubt that danger was imminent.

Luke moved back from the door to give himself the best space to swing, visualising his movements.

A black leather-gloved hand reached just a few inches in, and then stopped. They were planning their entry.

With a sudden movement, a figure crashed through the door. The brick dropped, catching the attacker on the leg, and distracting him.

The Fury took the opportunity.

He swung the brick shard with all his strength, catching the figure on the shoulder and glancing off the top of his head.

'Fuck,' a voice shouted.

The Fury swung his homemade mace crashing down on the knee that had present itself, hearing the owner scream. He then ripped it back to try and cause as much damage as he could.

No sooner had he done that, a second attacker pushed his way past and into the doorway to be met with the second swing crashing into his shoulder.

'You little...' a voice tried to start, but Luke's Fury drowned it out with a terrifying scream.

His Fury was in control and Luke was watching from above as he bounded into the second attacker. The large, stocky man at least twice his weight hadn't expected such an explosive attack. He fell backwards into his partner who tumbled onto the landing as Luke stamped on the leg of the first man.

Luke shouted over his shoulder. 'Amelja, run.'

They had discussed this at great length, and she did as commanded, without pause. Appearing at the door, she came up behind Luke, brandishing her mace.

The second man pulled himself back, only to find the boy in front of him brandishing a clear bottle. And he knew what it meant.

Luke squeezed and thrust the bottle at the same time, splashing fluid all over the man, who bolted into the room, desperately covering his face. Luke knew he would be thinking it was acid.

The man on the floor kicked out at Luke's lower leg, buckling it at the knee. But this act was met with a crashing blow from Amelja's mace digging into his arm.

'Bitch,' the man growled.

'You little cunt,' shouted the man from the room desperately wiping at his burning eyes.

Luke jumped onto the first man and landed the most powerful punch he had ever delivered. Blood exploded from his nose.

'Amelja. Run. Now,' Luke screamed.

There was just enough space and time for her to pass the mess of limbs.

The Second man appeared at the door again, as Luke landed another punch into the bleeding lump on the floor.

'Amelja…'

'Luke, no…'

'Run…'

Luke leapt up and threw his entire weight at the waist of the second man, crashing him into the door frame. Hands and fists crashed down on Luke's back, grabbing his coat, lifting him off his feet. The man hurled Luke around, sending him clattering into the landing floorboards.

'Run,' Luke gasped.

Her flight instinct finally kicked in, running down the stairs, leaning on the bannister. The second man loomed over Luke and reached down to grab him.

Luke kept throwing punches, but his attacks were parried before he was swung into the wall.

'I could kill you, kid,' the man spluttered as he lurched forward, only to see Luke move to his right, towards the stairs. He caught the boy's arm but only found himself being dragged down as they both tumbled.

Barely keeping to their feet, their bodies battered against the banister and the wall as they careered down the rest of the stairs.

Amelja turned to see the mess of limbs and bodies crashing towards her and she jumped clear just in time for the bodies to hit the floor.

'Get off him,' she screamed.

Amelja looked up to the top of the stairs to see the second man with blood pouring down his face.

'Amelja, run.' There was frustration in Luke's voice as he rolled over onto the man and pummelled at his chest, going for speed rather than strength.

The Fury was in full control.

Amelja turned and ran through the house to the back door.

Luke continued his onslaught of the man lying on his back, arms up, parrying each blow away from his face.

He growled in anger, 'get off me, kid,' landing a punch to Luke's kidneys and rolling them over again.

'Fuck you, fuck you, fuck you,' Luke's Fury growled and hammered, anything to hold them back from Amelja.

The man found a second wind of strength, dug his feet in, and in one heave, lifted Luke by the collar. He slammed Luke into the hallway wall, holding him off the ground.

Leaning in close, his rasping voice cutting through the throbbing of heartbeats, 'you're lucky the boss wants you alive.' Luke tried to hit the man's arms at the elbows to free himself. 'Well, when I say lucky,' the man sniggered.

He drew a combat knife and held it to Luke's neck.

The other man disappeared through the house in pursuit of Amelja, but she had already reached the end of the path and crossed the road.

Amelja saw the two men coming out of the gate with Luke. She wished she could help him. But they had discussed the plans and possible escape rules. And they had agreed above all else, they had to get the baby to safety.

No matter what happened.

Amelja turned and ran, following the planned escape route, clutching her extra weight, vision blurred by pouring tears.

The two men dragged Luke to the back of a black saloon.

Luke allowed himself a wry smile, knowing Amelja had escaped. He felt his weight being dropped into the boot, heard the thud as it closed.

And the world turned black.

Chapter 51

His nose curled at the stench of urine, cheap alcohol, and the damp mould of the underpass. Gnome did most of his work in such places because they provided good cover and a lot of clients.

As the figure entered the tunnel from the other end, coat pulled up tight around his shoulders, scarf wrapped tight around his face, Gnome almost laughed out loud at how obvious the guy was making himself look. Not a punter of his, of course. But, Christ, he might as well have had 'I want to buy drugs, but I am new to this' in neon on his hat.

The other man kept a steady pace, but Gnome knew not to make eye contact. It was never easy to tell what nutters lurked around each corner.

Gnome cast a final glance at the figure, just in time to see movement in his peripheral vision.

A vicious strike crashed into Gnome's chin and threw him back into the concrete wall. The entire tunnel lurched as he was grabbed by the shoulders and slammed into the opposite wall. A leather fist smashed into his eye socket, his nose, and jaw in a blistering triple attack. Too fast to take a breath.

Gnome tried to kick out, but his legs flailed and slid on the dirty floor. He coughed up a mixture of blood and phlegm just before a kick drove so hard into his chest it threw him onto his side.

He tried to curl into a ball but a brutal kick to the kidneys slid him across the floor up to the wall.

His collar was gripped from the back and he was dragged up to his knees, choking the air from his throat. The heel of a boot kicked him in the chest so hard he sat with his back to the wall and the pain felt like his inner organs were exploding.

Delirium was swamping his mind as he felt his attacker lift him to his feet by the collar.

'Give me your fucking phone,' the voice rasped through the scarf.

Gnome reached into his pocket with his shaking hand and found his phone. He tried to hand it to the man but got a knee in the crotch.

'Think I'm fucking stupid? Unlock it.'

'Who the fuck are you?' Gnome spluttered as he unlocked the phone with his thumbprint. 'What do you want, man?'

The attacker grabbed the phone and backhanded Gnome across the ear. Scanning through the phone, tapping on options, he crouched down on one knee and held the phone up to show Gnome a photo.

'What's his name?'

Gnome grimaced in defiance, his face covered in blood, and his hair dripping with the same wet, stinking urine he'd turned his nose up to just moments ago.

The figure slapped the side of Gnome's head again.

'Luke, it's Luke.' He coughed. 'Fucking hell. Luke.'

'Wrong.' Another punch crashed into Gnome's jaw. 'Say his name.'

Gnome barely spat the name out. 'Luke.'

'Try again, you snivelling little cunt.'

Gnome groaned as a sob rocked his shoulders.

'Give me the fucking name.'

'It's Luke. Luke.' He tried to push himself up onto his elbow.

The man brought his fist down on top of Gnome's head. 'What. Is. His. Name?'

'I don't know.'

'That's right. You don't know.'

The man lifted Gnome halfway up the wall then dropped him back down onto this backside. He took the phone and scrolled again until he found another image came up. 'Her name.'

Gnome fixed his eyes on the image, then the man's eyes, and he felt his bladder empty.

'Look, it was business.'

Another punch cracked into his jaw, and Gnome could feel teeth breaking. He spat out blood and pieces of teeth, choking for air. He wiped at his nose, covering his sleeve in blood.

'Amelja,' Gnome coughed. 'Her name was Amelja.'

The figure grabbed him by the hair and pulled him up to his feet, smacking his head into the wall. He hammered the phone into Gnome's head, over and over until the glass shattered completely.

Finally dropping the battered phone to the ground, he held Gnome up with both hands and kneed him in the groin.

Gnome doubled over and started to vomit. The man delivered one final kick to his ribs and he collapsed into a battered mess curling into the foetal position.

'Ever see that boy again, you walk the other way. No, fucking run the other way. Because, I swear, I will hunt you down and won't stop until your whole body is soft enough to pour down the shithole you crawled out of.'

Gnome spat out more blood and felt his head fall to the solid, cold concrete.

The figure stood back, turned, and walked out of the underpass. He stopped and looked across the road. A motorbike revved its engine and its rider gave a single, discernible nod.

The man nodded back and then watched the rider speed away.

Chapter 52

Amelja had run and never looked back. She'd had no idea what time was when they were attacked in the house. Night blurred into morning and a dirty orange hue bled across the sky. A ghostly feeling washed over Amelja as dawn set in, and everything seemed like a bad dream she couldn't quite wake from.

The noise of traffic and city life rising finally gave Amelja a sense of reassurance. She knew how to hide amongst the crowds, to blend in.

But she was so tired.

After crossing a couple of roads and under the railway bridge, she remembered where she was. She recognised the archways with the train on top and not far from the place they'd met that kind man.

Part of her hoped he would be there.

She tried to say a little prayer to herself, but her head was spinning and unable to focus.

'My, oh my, is that not a beautiful sight?'

Amelja froze.

'Amelja,' Freeman's voice warmed the tunnel.

Amelja quietly thanked God and turned to him.

'How good it is to see you again,' he eyes smile and eyes

beamed with sincerity. 'Where is that boy of yours?'

Amelja was overcome. Her stomach heaved, her burning throat was sandpaper dry, and she would have crashed to the ground had Freeman not caught her in time.

He embraced her sobbing body before holding her cheeks, straightening her hair, and searching her eyes with his.

'Where is your Luke?'

Amelja wiped her nose on her sleeve 'Beaten. Taken.'

The old man frowned, a flash of anger creeping into his eyes.

'My Lord. Who took him?'

'Big men.'

The man's confusion was growing with each answer.

'We hide from them, long time.'

'What people?'

'They take him. Take my Enji.'

'You are here now. The good Lord has brought you back to me.' The man held her hands, warming them one at a time with his gloved hands. 'Tell me, Amelja, when did they take your Luke?'

'Last night. Break into house. But my Luke was too clever.'

'He's a smart boy.'

'He fight them. He save me.' She stroked her belly.

The old man stroked her hair again and look down at her large pregnant belly. 'He saved you both. And you kept the little one safe. But you look so tired.'

Amelja shrugged her shoulders. 'So heavy and I get so hungry. But Luke is gone.'

'First thing's first, my child. Let's get energy into you. Then we talk about what to do next, okay?'

* * *

Freeman walked Amelja into the city centre after they'd

328

eaten through his supplies and he'd added more layers to warm her up. Her legs ached from all the running the night before.

She was too thin and pale. Her heart was heavy with worry for Luke. Every time the baby inside her kicked, she felt joy, until her mind flashed back to the kicks she saw being delivered to Luke.

Neither Amelja nor Freeman could help but notice the looks from passers-by, curling lips at the very young, heavily pregnant girl with an old Black man. Generous in judgmental contempt, but none prepared to offer help.

Freeman laughed. 'They can't even work out which prejudice matters most. The age or the colour.'

They were on Corporation Street when Amelja remembered the number of the bus she and Luke had caught a few times.

'I must go,' she said to Freeman. 'I must go to our special place.'

She started walking over to a number eighty-seven bus.

He tried to chase after her before his chest fought him back with a deep, gravelly cough.

Amelja reached the bus and prepared her best tearful routine, which worked especially well to garner sympathy from the driver. She'd get on confidently searching for her pass, apologise, and then let the tears flow. A wince and, holding her pregnant bulge, another apology. She'd tell the driver she would get off, not wanting him to get into trouble, and wince some more.

The driver told her not to worry about it.

Worked every time.

The bus drove past Freeman, and Amelja waved, mouthing a "thank you" to him.

* * *

Amelja stepped off the bus at Galton Bridge. Taking her

329

time to cross the road, she felt the strain on her aching calves, swollen ankles, and at the bottom of her back.

She got to the edge of the bridge and felt kicking from the baby.

'I know, little one. He should be here with us.'

Amelja stepped over the invisible threshold onto the bridge, walked to the centre, wrapping her arm around the lamppost. The gentle wind teased her hair.

As she cradled her unborn, Amelja began to sing a soft lullaby to herself.

"Tregon gjyshja nga herë
Na ishte se na ishte
Na ish një herë një djalë
Si veten shokët kishte."

It was only as she got to the end of the verse that she heard a voice joining her. Standing to her right, some ten feet or so away, she saw an old lady. Dirty, unkempt, clearly as homeless as Amelja.

But she also knew the song and was singing it in Albanian. She didn't look anything like Amelja's real grandmother, but there was a warmth about her.

The old lady turned and smiled nervously at Amelja, her head tilting slightly to the side. Her face was filthy and rough with age.

But her eyes shared a sincerity in their glint as she started to sing the second verse of the song. 'Dhe unë duke dëgjuar.'

Amelja joined her, soft and uncertain, as they sang the second verse.

The Old Woman approached Amelja, raising her hand to stroke her hair. She held out her second hand and Amelja took it, placing it over the unborn child. Her touch was light and reassuring.

Then her look changed. As if she had been alerted to something. The Old Woman seemed surprised and nervous at the same time. She kept her hand on Amelja's belly, but took Amelja's other hand and placed it next to hers. Nodding, urgent and excitedly.

'Sonte,' she said. 'Sonte. Sonte është nata,' the woman began to ramble. She looked around at a couple walking past, shouting the same at them.

Amelja shook her head, panic building inside her.

The Old woman held onto Amelja's, smiling, but then frowning. 'Sonte.'

Amelja looked out from the bridge down the length of the canal. Her heart pounded in her chest, and she tried to slow her breathing.

That's when a sharp pain engulfed her abdomen.

How could the Old Woman have known?

Another woman appeared to her left.

'Oh, dear, babs. Are you alright?'

Amelja frowned and tried to stand up straight, but the sharp pain buckled her knees.

'Are you going into labour?' The woman said. 'We'd better call an ambulance.'

'No, it is fine,' Amelja protested.

'Don't be silly, babs.' She took out her phone and dialled. 'Do you know this lady?' She asked Amelja.

'No, I only met her now.'

'What is she saying? Do you know?'

Amelja nodded, wincing at the pain.

'What is it?'

Amelja gasped at a breath. 'The baby. She say it coming. She says it's tonight, it's tonight.'

The old woman nodded frantically, repeating in garbled English.

'Iz toonah, iz toonah.'

Chapter 53

He swung the door to Chief Superintendent Carter's office open and marched in without bothering to shut it.

'You can bloody forget pinning rape on the boy.'

'Inspector Stone,' Carter tried and failed at incredulity. 'How dare you presume to storm into my office.'

'Me? How dare you?' He had to pause just to measure his breathing.

'I demand respect of rank.' She held his glare for a moment. 'And if you intend to even try insubordination, bloody well close my door.'

Stone marched back to the door and shut it just on the safe side of a slam. He gripped the handle for a moment to steady himself.

'I take it you have interviewed Luke?'

'We've spoken to him, showed him photographs to identify.'

'Don't patronise me, Mike.'

'No, I haven't. And I'm not going to.'

Carter stood as tall as she could. Not a large woman, but she was well built enough and had an imposing physical presence.

Stone and Carter had a complex history. They

had mutual respect on most issues, but their working relationship had been strained since the Malcolm Glenn case. Trust had been tested when it was revealed that she played a part in the demise of Arnold Stone. Mike's father.

The relationship between Mike Stone and his father was transformed into a childhood of hatred marred with deliberate scapegoating created by organised crime and sexual abuse.

'What the hell do you mean?' Carter barked.

'He will be interviewed by safeguarding as a victim and witness.'

'I ordered you to investigate him.'

'And that is what I did. But there is no evidence.'

'There is DNA.'

'Proving two teenagers had sex.'

'There's a fucking video.'

'Recorded by an abuser guilty of making category A child pornography.'

'Jesus Christ, Mike. What more do you need?'

Stone walked over to her desk. 'A reason.'

Confusion filled her reddening face.

'You know as well as I do that any good defence barrister could collapse this case. But you also know no homeless kid on legal aid will get the best. I'm not prepared to throw him to the wolves of privilege. But I wonder why you are.'

They both stood stock still, holding the glare. An accusation was floating somewhere in the air between them.

Carter lowered her voice, almost to the point of a threat. 'The girl jumped from...'

'The girl had a name.' He could feel the heat rise in his face, his nostrils flaring with heavy breathing. 'Two kids, abused kids, snared by child traffickers survived long enough to bring a baby almost to full term. One jumped. And now you want to throw the other.'

'Don't be so melodramatic.'

334

'But it's your style, isn't it?'

Carter's eyes filled with fear but settled on anger.

'And I want to know why.'

She moved only slightly back away from him, behind her desk.

'I should suspend you from duty with immediate effect.'

'Go on then. Let's do it properly. Union rep, my direct senior officer. I'll write my handover in full for DCI Palmers. Hell, I'll even book my own damn tribunal.'

Her eyes fixed on his. 'Are you really prepared to end your career like this?'

'Yes.' He leaned across her desk, fists pressed into the glass top. 'Are you?'

She matched his glare and spoke almost in a whisper of venom. 'Get out.'

Chapter 54

September
Thursday ~ Luke

It was dark. The room was uncomfortably hot, but Luke
was shivering. His skin felt clammy and was sticking to the
floor. His whole body ached, and as he tried to move, he
realised he was naked.

The rattle of a lock broke the silence and a shaft of light
cut across the darkness. The only shape Luke could make
out was a chair in the corner of the room. Heavy footsteps
paused in front of him. Very shiny black shoes waited for
a moment until one of the feet pushed at his shoulder,
rocking his body.

Perhaps he should have played dead.

'He's awake,' the voice said.

'Good,' replied a more familiar, scratchy voice his mind
tried to place.

The shoes moved over to the chair in the corner of the
room and turned, followed by the heavy landing of what
must have been a very large body. Luke didn't want to
snatch a glance.

'In you go, boys,' the scratchy voice spoke again.

There was a light patter of small feet coming into the
room. Luke squinted his eyes and tried to count the ankles
he could see. Four? Six? Eight? No, only six. He couldn't

be sure. But he knew it must have been at least three boys. Bare feet, bare shins, and legs.

'Now, boys, we have something very special for you today. We're going to offer you a chance to be rewarded for hard work. And if you work hard, and you please me, well…' he paused for a moment. A puff of smoke blew out across the room.

Luke saw the boys' toes curl as the man sitting in the shadow adjusted his heavyweight in the chair.

'Our friend, here,' he said, walking over the stand right next to Luke's head, 'made a terrible mistake. He betrayed me. Stole from me. It cost me a lot of money. He needs to be taught a lesson. Don't you agree?'

Luke knew exactly what he'd stolen.

'My friend over there is going to keep an eye on you all. I tell him if any of you not try your hardest, he can do his hardest with you. But if you do good, I let you have special reward.'

And that was it. All he could do was hope he had saved Amelja and their baby.

But Luke knew he had no choice.

He must not let the Fury loose this time.

Two. Three. Three. F.

* * *

Amelja

The ambulance had only taken a few minutes to arrive, but they had been the most painful and terrifying minutes of her life.

The pain shot through her entire body. Everything felt cramped and spasmed, squeezed and stretched.

Onlookers rushed over. Said things. Offered coats. Most just got their phones out.

She had collapsed when a sudden gush of wetness

drenched her inner thighs.

When the ambulance arrived, they bombarded Amelja with questions she couldn't understand. Pain made her forget her English when they spoke too fast.

'How far along are you?'

'How old are you?'

'What is your name?'

'Are you alone here?'

'Have you seen a doctor?'

'We need to take you now.'

Everything was moving too fast.

More questions in the ambulance. She was lying on her back, knees up. The medic in green had gloves on and was touching her. The pain just kept getting worse. Gas made her blurry.

All she could think about was her baby.

And all she wanted was Luke.

Chapter 55

'Is he here?' Stone slammed through the door into the incident room and looked over to Khan's desk.

'Your office, guv.'

'Harry, I have a job for you.' He took a cheap mobile phone from his pocket and handed it to Khan.

'Please don't tell me this is a burner, boss.'

This time, Stone didn't smile. 'Harry, it is time to start playing dirty. I want you to take those two numbers we have, and I want you to use this burner phone to contact them. Use it to keep the lines live and then use that magic stuff you do to get the numbers to ping pong…'

Khan raised a hand and smiled. 'I know what you mean. I'll get onto it. Do you want me to call or text?'

'Both. But don't get into a conversation at all.'

Khan was about to swing back round to his computer when he stopped. 'How is our esteemed Chief?'

Stone let out a deep sigh, not sure how to reply.

Khan left it. 'Is Reg back in the building?'

Confusion shot across Stone's face. 'Back? When did he leave?'

'He just said he'd grab something for late lunch on the way back from a quick errand.'

'Did he take Luke with him?'

'No, he's in a family room. Reg left him playing games with one of the guys downstairs.'

A thought flashed through Stone's mind, but he shook it off. He had bigger things to deal with in his office. He opened the door about as forcibly as he could to find Paul Buchanan sitting in the chair at his desk.

Stone shut the door behind him and flicked the Venetian blinds shut.

'How are you healing up, Paul?'

'Doing fine, sir,' with bitterness in his tone.

Stone stayed standing over by the door. 'Last time I called you in for a chat it ended on a rather negative note.'

Buchanan looked at Stone, then turned to stare straight ahead, chewing at the inside of his cheek.

Oh, yes. Keep biting, Paul.

Stone walked over to the corner of his desk, took out his phone, and found the photo he needed.

'Who's this?'

Buchanan looked at the photo. There was the slightest twinge at the edges of his eyes. Recognition.

'You're not a petulant teenager, Paul. Don't make me ask again.'

He fixed Stone with a glare.

'Okay. You keep playing your silence thing and I promise to bypass tribunals and just go straight to perversion of the course of justice. Maybe conspiracy to murder.

Buchanan smirked, sitting back in his chair and wincing slightly at the shot of pain his injury still gave him.

'Look, you deceitful piece of shit. I've had enough of all the lies, the subterfuge, and whatever you're tied up in. I know you didn't find Luke's body, and I know this guy was there. That makes you an accessory after the fact. So, you can either come clean now or…'

'His name is Steve Chambers.'

'Who is he?'

'All I know is he's a cop. And he's ex-army.'

Well, that's hardly a surprise.

'What was he doing there?'

Buchanan fidgeted and ran a hand through his hair, scratching at the back of his neck.

Stone's glare hadn't moved.

'I pulled up behind the other car. I didn't know Steve was there until the other guy had pulled his gun, and Steve comes out the shadows with a gun.'

'Steve? You didn't just know who he was, you knew him.' Stone didn't bother pitching it as a question. 'Who called you to the scene in the first place?'

Buchanan avoided eye contact again as he said the name.

The name Stone had been expecting and fearing at the same time.

Chapter 56

Every part of his body throbbed. Even breathing hurt. His face felt fat and heavy like he had toothache, but all over.

Light tried to dig its way through one of the two squash balls sitting on either side of his nose.

Painful breathing led to a dry, wheezing cough.

Coughing set fire across his ribcage.

His stomach rolled and gurgled, constantly feeling on the edge of vomiting. His bowels and bladder felt the same. On the edge of emptying. Again.

A breeze brushed over his swollen skin enough to tell him he was naked.

But the light increased around his head, and he sensed a presence in the room. Movement to his side. A voice whispered in his ear.

'Hey, kid.'

Too quiet beneath his pounding pulse in his ears.

'Can you hear me?' The voice waited. 'Luke?' The voice seemed to plead with him, but he couldn't speak.

All Luke could do was summon up the slightest gravelly groan.

'You're gonna be okay, kid. Right?'

Was the voice real or a dream?

He felt his left leg being lifted, then his right. More movement and something pulled up his legs. Pain seared through his left arm, right arm, and whole body as he felt his weight pulled up to sitting. Something wrapped around him.

The voice whispered, frustrated. 'Come on. Help me, Luke.' His body was heaved up against someone's chest, trousers pulled up and the cold breeze vanished.

Luke's arm was wrapped around the voice's shoulder, lightning shooting through the joint. It tried to walk him, but his legs were too heavy.

'Come on, kid, please. I need your help. You're gonna be okay, but we gotta get going. One last push.'

Luke groaned. All he wanted to do was lie down, go back to sleep and let the world wash away.

There wasn't an inch of his body that didn't hurt.

His life hurt…

The voice dragged him over to the door.

'No,' Luke gargled.

'We gotta go, kiddo. Come on.'

'No, please.'

'Come on, where's that fight gone? Think of the girl, Luke. For Amelja.'

Deep down inside, he found just enough energy to barely help follow along with the voice.

For Amelja.

* * *

It took nearly five minutes to battle down the stairs. The two guards who would normally have intervened had gladly taken the offer of a cool beer. The slip of something extra had helped them drift off for a little while.

The house alarm was disabled, and after a few steps, the door was open, and they were outside, struggling down the white stone steps. He dragged the broken body across the gravel drive, over to the car. He opened the back door and rolled the body onto the back seat.

'What the fuck you doing?' A dark growl came from behind him.

Steve Chambers paused for a moment. The stocky figure of Splint was looming over him.

'Boss told me to dump the little fucker's body,' he answered, with confidence packed into his voice. 'Somewhere away from the house.'

'Never said anything to me.'

'No. Because he asked me. And you're not my sitter.' Splint was all brute and absolutely no brain. 'Now, fuck off. I don't want this sack of shit stinking out my car.'

'Maybe I'll give him a call.'

'Whatever. But he's busy. You wanna piss him off, go right ahead.'

Splint took out his mobile and started to tap the screen.

A decision had to be made. If Splint placed that call, he and Luke were as good as dead.

He whipped the mobile clean out of Splint's hand and delivered a left-right jab combination to the lower chest, followed by an uppercut that crunched into his jaw. Splint was caught out more by the speed of the attack than the power, and fell back against another car, rolling to the ground.

Chambers reached down to pick up Splint's phone and got into his car, hitting the engine start button in one swift motion. The gravel kicked up and caught Splint in the face as he stumbled to his feet.

It took just seconds for the car to reach the main gate. Splint's phone was one of few that had the app to open the gate because he drove Kapllani around the most.

He checked his mirror to make sure Splint was following, no doubt tracking his car with GPS.

'Come on, you fat fucker.'

347

* * *

Chambers parked the car out of sight behind an old redbrick wall in the disused Baxter industrial estate just outside the city centre. Slightly hidden away, but still within easy reach of emergency services.

Still sitting in the front seat, he pulled a Pay as You Go phone from his inside pocket. There were no numbers stored in it. He dialled a memorised number and waited for the call to be answered before he spoke.

'It's done.' Assured, emotionless. 'Critical, but alive.' He paused for the other voice to make the decisions. 'Needs treatment. Urgent.' His voice was quiet, and he kept scanning the area in his rear-view mirror. 'Baxter. Tell him to get a move on or this will get messy.' He hung up and dismantled the phone.

Chambers got out of the car and moved round to the back door. He reached in just far enough to check the boy still had a strong enough pulse to leave him.

Only just.

'You're gonna be okay, kid.'

Reaching into his inside pocket again, he pulled out a business card and checked its details. Screwing it up slightly and then flattening it out, to take the new shine off it a little, he slipped it into the front pocket of the boy's hoodie. Then he took out a leather necklace with a crude metal half-heart shame and put that with the card.

He closed the back door of the car, walked away, and crossed the road. Finding a place behind a wall in complete darkness, and waited.

Two people were coming.

One friend. One foe.

All he had to do was wait and hope it was a friendly who got there first.

***

The black saloon pulled into the industrial estate and slowed to a stop. It was not Chambers' preferred scenario, and he knew it was likely to get messier before it got sorted.

He watched as Splint got out of the saloon and looked around to check he was alone. GPS locating was good but couldn't pinpoint much better than a ten or twenty-metre radius.

Splint pulled his gun and the slick black cylinder of a suppressor. He screwed the two together and pulled back the slide to chamber a round. He was about to start searching for Chambers when the sound of an approaching car made him stop. He tucked the elongated barrel of the gun into his side pocket, keeping a firm grip on the handle.

The second car pulled around the corner, slow and steady. Its bright LED headlights had been dipped to sidelights only, but they still lit Splint and his car up. It stopped, engine running for a few more seconds as the driver weighed up their options.

'Fuck, fuck, fuck,' Chambers hissed under his breath, reaching down to his right ankle for the pistol. He clicked the safety off and brought the pistol up to his second hand. He knew if he was going to use it, he needed to be accurate.

The driver got out of his car and stood just behind his door.

'Excuse me, mate. My satnav has had a hissy fit. Sorry, I'm not local. Do you know the quickest route back out into the city centre?'

'Back the way you came.'

'Oh, right.' The driver tried his hardest to sound nonchalant. 'You, okay, by the way?' He loosely pointed at his own face with a circling finger.

Chambers whispered under his breath, 'get back in your car and fuck off. Don't play the hero.'

Splint curled his lip into a menacing half-smile. 'Walked into a door.'

There was a silent pause. But it was enough.

Both men knew the other was lying.

Splint pulled his weapon from his pocket and pointed it at DC Paul Buchanan.

A split second later, Chambers stepped out from the shadows, gun aimed at Splint's head. 'Drop the gun.'

Splint's eyes shot open for a second before recoiling back into a scowl. 'There you are.'

Buchanan glanced over at Chambers and back at Splint, feeling very conscious as the only one without a gun.

'Steve? What the fuck are you doing here?'

'Shut up, Paul,' Chambers said. 'He's nothing to do with this, Splint.'

'Well, Steve, problem is, he's seen my face now. And you gone told him my name.'

'He's a cop, he'll know your name anyway. He's nothing to do with this, let him go.'

'Why would I do that?'

Indeed, thought Chambers. Why would he do that?

'What the hell…?' Paul started.

'Let me handle this,' Chambers barked at Buchanan, still keeping his eyes firmly fixed on Splint.

'You ain't handling shit,' Splint said with a cold snigger. 'I knew you were bent. Turns out you're double bent.'

'Drop the gun. You know you can't hit us both.'

Chambers moved a step closer, gun trained on the large, central body mass.

Splint grunted a single wry laugh and curled his lip as he glanced at Chambers.

And that was the moment.

Buchanan swung round and down in one swift movement.

At the same time, Chambers stepped forward as Splint fired two suppressed rounds. They were followed by two louder shots from Steve, both hitting Splint's torso.

He dropped to his knee but tried to swing his weapon around as he pulled the trigger. Both rounds hit Buchanan's door, one shattering the window.

Chambers responded with a viciously accurate shot to Splint's head. The lump of a man hung in the air for a second before collapsing to the ground.

Buchanan lay down, a hand clutching his shoulder. Blood oozed through his fingers.

'Shit, Paul.' Chambers ran over and crouched down. He quickly checked the wound, one front and back meant the bullet had gone through, so blood loss was the biggest risk.

'Steve, what the hell is going on?' He winced in pain, his face already getting the clammy and pale look of someone losing too much blood.

'I don't get it. Were you called in for this? Shit man, why are you armed?'

'Shut up. You here for the boy?'

The officer gritted his teeth through a burn of pain as he nodded.

Chambers stood and turned away, trying to square his thoughts. He couldn't call in ambulances as there was a body that would be too hard to explain. He needed to clear the scene.

'Right, I'll shift the other guy into his car. I'll vanish his body. As soon as I take off, you call it in. You got me? Call this in as officer down.'

'No, Steve, I can't.'

'You have to. I know who sent you. Let them carry the can. He took a few shots at you. Next thing you know, you're spilling blood, and then his car drove off. You checked on the kid and called it in. Okay?'

Chambers took Buchanan's tie off and wrapped it

around the DC's hand. 'Press this here.' He stood up and made his way back over to the car he'd arrived in. He opened the back door, hoping the boy was still alive.

He was barely moving, and when Steve held two fingers to his neck there was a faint, but fast pulse.

Steve looked down to see the boy's eyes slightly open. 'You're gonna be alright, kid. Hang in there. Amelja needs you.' He reached inside the hoody and took out the business card, pinching it to leave a pair of clear prints. He didn't know yet how that might help, but it would at least raise some eyebrows.

He closed the door behind him and ran over to the dead weight of the man he'd shot just minutes ago. Grabbing him under the arms, with all the strength he could muster, he dragged the body to the rear of its car, popping the boot open.

'You fat fucker.' It took all his strength just to fumble it inside and close the boot.

Buchanan was in a bad way, with shallower breathing and fading consciousness. He already had his phone out, trying to dial.

'Give me that.' Steve Chambers dialled emergency services and said the key phrases. 'Not breathing. Doing CPR on a police officer. Gunshot wound. Gun-shot-wound. Second victim. Boy, in a car, behind the wall. Two victims.' He gave the location and ended the call.

'Steve, what the fuck is going on man?'

'I gotta go, Paul. I'm sorry. The kid is in the car, still has a pulse. Okay. Stay awake.'

Steve got up, ran to Splint's black saloon, and got inside. Turning the air con to the coldest setting, he drove away, knowing that he was leaving behind a lot more than two victims and a whole load of evidence.

He'd just passed the point of no return.

Chapter 57

'It's not that bad,' Luke said to Reg, as they stepped out into the damp early evening air.

'Trading standards should shut these places down. You can't honestly call that stuff food, can you?'

'Grumpy old man.'

'Oy, less of the old,' Reg said with a smile. Then paused. 'Okay, but less of the grumpy.'

Reg was fine being the butt of the jokes as it was good to hear it from the boy. They'd arranged to meet with Mike Stone and decided to get a bite to eat first.

The weather was grey and dreary so their initial plan to take the reasonable walk was looking far less appealing.

'We should get a taxi,' Luke suggested.

Reg was about to make a 'cheeky little bugger' comment when his young shadow crossed the road, waving to a taxi driver.

A driver who seemed to know the boy.

'Masood.'

'Luke, my friend,' he lifted his arms and then shook his hand.

Reg noticed the curious way the man held one of Luke's hands in both of his. There was genuine affection. Then he saw sadness across the driver's face. It didn't take a genius to connect the dots.

'You call me, yes? Any time.' Masood handed him a business card.

Luke turned around to see Reg standing behind him. 'This is Masood. I've seen him around loads.'

Reg smiled and decided to offer the driver a hand to shake. Building bridges with the few adults Luke felt comfortable with seemed a good idea. He decided to store what he'd seen and talk to Luke about it some other time.

Masood took his hand as Luke introduced them.

'This is Reg. He's a friend.'

'It is my pleasure to meet you, Reg,' Masood said, giving a single, sharp nod of the head. 'The boy says you are taking care of him.'

'I think it goes both ways, to be honest,' Reg shared a mild laugh with the man. But both men were searching each other's eyes.

'Where are you heading?'

'Won't we get you into trouble jumping the queue?' Reg asked, concern for taxi rank etiquette.

Masood dismissed his point with a wave of his hand.

'Do you know the Gunmaker's Arms?'

'I do, yes.' He opened the door for them to get in.

The drive was a short one and Masood refused to take any money for it. But he told Reg it was good to meet him, a softer look in his eyes that time. He gave Luke a knowing, and affectionate nod as they got out of the cab.

* * *

Mike Stone had already finished his half a pint of lemonade and made good headway on his pint of real ale when he heard a taxi pulling up outside the Gunmakers Arms.

He and Reg both frequented the pub as a kind of neutral zone between their respective workplaces. It was the perfect place. Still in the city centre, within easy distance to Police HQ and the pathology labs where Reg did his work. Being just a nudge outside the main city centre, it sat in a nice quiet corner. Reg also liked it because it was in the same area as most of his Salvation Army work.

And of course, they both simply loved the pub and the vibe there, especially the whole small brewery and proper real ales local pedigree.

'Beats sitting in a crass chain pub owned by a Tory,' was Mike Stone's official critical viewpoint.

Mike was sitting in a small alcove, tucked away in a corner but in view of the entrance. As Reg entered, he lifted his pint and shook his head with a grimace. Universal code for 'I'd love one, but shouldn't.'

'Cool bar,' Luke said, mouth dropping open to the natural wood bar which was a well-known feature of the pub.

'Yes, but that's the bit you're not quite old enough to enjoy yet, young man,' Reg replied.

Mike caught Luke's eyes and Reg nudged the boy to go and say hello. He'd had a chat with the staff before they'd arrived, explained as much of the situation as possible and they'd given him the nod on the quiet that the boy could be there, if supervised, and kept away from the bar. Who else was better to do that than a copper?

Luke couldn't resist running his hand along the natural contour of the bar as he walked over towards the detective. It then dawned on him that he'd slept rough barely twenty yards from the place and could remember at the time wondering what it was like inside.

'Is Reg behaving himself,' Mike said, pulling Luke back from his memory.

Luke let a small smile slip, but there was still a wariness around a detective. 'He's okay.' He sat with a teenager's thud, then winced at having caught a bit of bruise yet to fully heal.

'Make sure he doesn't try and feed you anything weird. Like quinoa.'

'I just made him eat a cheeseburger.'

Mike snorted and had to wipe the dribble from his chin. 'I bet you later he dabs his forehead with a hanky.'

Luke smiled.

Reg appeared with two tall glasses of coke. 'Not the healthiest beverage, but it will do.'

Mike and Luke both looked up, then at each other, and laughed.

'Should my ears be burning?'

'When you get to hell, you greasy sinner.'

It was Luke's turn to wipe coke from his nose and chin.

The atmosphere seemed to relax. Reg had been concerned about how Luke might react to seeing Mike so soon again after the interview.

Technically, he should not be socialising with Luke, but Reg trusted Mike not to manipulate such a situation. He also needed Luke to grow his safety net and Reg thought it was best to start with people he could trust.

Luke was too young to know the pub atmosphere. But at the same time, there was a kind of male bonding point that could be made by an amateur psychologist.

Mike looked across at Luke's hand, noticing the dark red that would develop into bruises over the next couple of days.

That's when his eye was caught by a similar marking on Reg's knuckles. Not as severe, but his hands certainly looked more laboured than their usual manicured tools of the trade.

Reg was the first to break the silence that was threatening to grow uncomfortable. 'Luke wants to know if they make guns here.'

Mike nodded. 'Between serving drinks.' He pointed at Luke's glass. 'You should always check the bottom of your glass for a bullet.'

Luke frowned in disbelief.

Mike still caught the boy's glance down into the bottom of his glass and then smiled, which earned him a roll of the eyes from Reg. 'It's where the term "my round" comes from.'

'Really?' Luke's eyebrows sprang up.

Reg dipped his head, smirked, and then turned to Luke. 'No.' He turned to back to Mike. 'Stop it. Behave. Anyway, I don't know the full history of this building, but we're in the gun quarter of the city. For some time, it was one of the biggest gun-making places in the world.'

Luke's eyes widened. 'That's cool.'

Mike jumped in. 'More importantly, this place also makes its own beer and is part of the Two Towers local brewery. That's the two Towers that inspired Tolkien, as well.'

Reg wagged a finger as he raised his chin, a clear sign his education was about to speak for him. 'As some believe.'

'Philistine,' Mike said, laughing at Reg. 'Besides, we were talking about guns.'

'As guns got more technical and advanced,' Reg said, 'this was a thriving area of the country. It's no coincidence that the canal runs right through the gun quarter.'

Luke frowned. 'On canal boats? That would take bloody ages, wouldn't it?'

Mike and Reg laughed. There was no way someone of Luke's generation could comprehend how much life had increased in speed.

'Oh yes,' Mike mimicked Reg's finger-wagging, which Luke recognised immediately. 'How do you think Amazon delivered all your parcels back in Victorian times?'

Luke laughed, apparently relaxing more into the seat. 'Do you carry a gun?'

'Good God, no. I'm not trained for that.'

'DS Bolton is firearms trained, isn't she?' Reg asked.

'That's the Jedi one,' Luke smiled.

Mike nodded.

'So, if she can carry a gun and a light sabre, how come you outrank her?'

There was a pause. Mike feigned a confused look.

Reg smiled at Luke, then at Mike. 'The boy's got you there, Mr Inspector.'

He answered with a smile, not wanting to get into the reasons he hated firearms and had always refused the training. 'Closest I get is a blasting-by-Nerf from my son. I'm even rubbish with foam bullets, as it is.'

'Isn't she the one who,' Luke paused, trying to avoid finishing the question he'd begun.

The mood cooled in an instant.

Mike looked at him and nodded.

The boy let out a deep sigh. 'That must be have been really tough for her.'

Mike couldn't help but glance at Reg, surprised by Luke's empathy. Reg returned his look with a more knowing nod.

'What happened is tough on everyone,' Mike said as carefully as he could. 'Which is why it's important for all of us to say so. No good putting a front on. Even my boy knows the saying, "it's okay not to be okay".'

'Not everyone cares.' Luke's top lip curled, as he stared into his drink. 'Some don't care, and never have to face any consequences.'

An air melancholy washed over Luke in an instant and he reached up to rub his necklace between his finger and thumb. He looked up at Mike.

'Do you think you'll ever catch them? Make them pay?'

'We're working on it.'

Reg's frown began to deepen as he cut in. 'The most important thing for us to focus on is getting you back to full fitness.'

'Or will they just get away with it?' Luke cut Reg off.

Mike looked back at Luke. 'They will not get away with

it. Not from me and my team. We make sure people care, or if they don't want to, we make them scared.'

'Make them care, or make them scared,' Luke whispered. 'I like that.'

Reg shot Mike a disapproving look.

'It's hot in here. Can I go sit outside for a bit?' Luke asked Reg.

'Sure,' Reg said, indicating to Mike he was going to show him the courtyard area.

When Reg returned, he sat down with an utterly deflating sigh.

'Is he okay?'

'He's just up and down. All over the place.'

'Sorry, Reg. I think I sounded a little vengeful, and that would not have helped.' Mike glanced at Reg's hand. 'Something I need to know about?'

'Nope.'

Mike finished his drink. And looked Reg square in the eyes. 'Nothing that is going to come back and bite you, or me on the ass?'

Reg shook his head.

Mike Stone thought for a moment how sometimes truth wasn't all it was cracked up to be. There were times that lonely truths simply didn't tell the whole story.

Reg cleared his throat and ran his hand through his medium-length hair. 'So, your mystery man was this Steve Chambers?'

Mike nodded.

'What if he is playing both sides?' Reg shrugged.

'He's killed, Reg. This isn't the movies. There is no licence to kill.'

'Perhaps not. But when it comes to saving lives, or protecting innocent people, are there no mitigating circumstances?'

Mike glanced again at Reg's knuckles. Then back to his eyes.

Reg folded his arms and leaned over the table to lower the volume. 'And what about that Buchanan chap? Beginning to sound like one hell of a conspiracy.'

Both men sat silently as they let all the ideas sink into the remainder of their drinks.

Mike listened to the voice over his shoulder again. 'Why do you think Amelja didn't take the baby with her?'

'To be honest, because Sands did a bloody good job making her think like a mother.'

'But she couldn't feel enough hope for herself.'

Reg shrugged his shoulders. 'I am just trying to support Luke however I can.'

'Sounds like you're doing a damn fine job so far.' Mike heard the gentle and watched the slight shake of Reg's head. 'He looks up to you more than I think you realise.'

Mike saw the gentle squeeze of his friend's fists and the slightest guilt creep into his eyes.

After letting silence sit for a short while they decided it was time for Mike to get back to work, and Reg to get Luke home to rest and wind down properly.

They both stood, and Mike returned the glasses to the bar before they headed out to the courtyard to collect Luke.

But he was nowhere to be seen.

'Oh, shit. That's not good,' Reg said, running to look outside on the road, Mike following closely behind.

'Where's he gone, Reg?'

'I don't know, dammit. Fuck.' He gripped his hair and turned back and forth a couple of times, pacing to engage his mind. 'Think, what did he say.'

Mike cast his mind back over the conversation. 'He said some people get to not care and never have to face consequences.'

It took a moment, but as if choreographed, the two men froze, eyes fixed on each other.

Mike thumped the heel of his hand to his forehead.

'Then I had to open my bloody mouth and say that shit about making people care or be scared.'

'No, that's not your fault, Mike.' Reg nodded. 'But, yes, he's gone to make people care. This is on me. I started this.'

'What does that mean? Started what?'

'Luke's going to make them pay.'

'For fuck's sake, Reg, where has he gone?' Mike shouted, but only heard his voice fade into the night as Reg Walters ran towards the city centre.

Chapter 58

September
Friday ~ Amelja

Where was her baby?

Amelja tried to move but her body ached all over. Searing pain shot up her spine. But she felt a yearning from deep inside. An ache in her heart like a huge part of her was missing.

A nurse entered the room with a gleaming smile that brightened her entire being. The young black woman had smooth dark skin and striking white teeth.

'You are awake,' the nurse said with a singing, Jamaican accent that reminded Amelja of the nice old man. Warming and safe.

Amelja's eyes shot open wider.

'She's fine,' the nurse said with the lightest touch on Amelja's arm. 'Beautiful little girl.' Her soft voice elongating her words with a hypnotic effect.

'I want to be with her.'

'No problem, Amelja. She safe and sound, waiting for momma.'

The birth had gone well and the baby was healthy, despite being a couple of weeks premature.

'Help me,' Amelja, sitting up, making it clear that she was going to see her baby.

Uncertainty flashed across the nurse's expression. 'Let me just check it is okay for you to go now.'

'My child. I say it okay.'

Sensing there was no point trying to stop Amelja, she relented. 'Okay, but first I take your drip off. Then and I'll fetch you a dressing gown and some slippers.'

Amelja flashed her a quick smile, but she willed the nurse to hurry up when the thought of Luke exploded into her mind. She had to see her child with her own eyes to be sure she was safe.

* * *

There was a darkness in the man's eyes which unnerved the receptionist even before he spoke. She had no idea who Nesim Kapllani was, and just how dangerous their conversation was.

'I am here to see niece,' he said as if there would be no doubt of it happening.

'Name?'

'Amelja. Amelja Halil.' He stared at the receptionist.

She tapped at the keyboard a few times. 'Can you tell me which ward?'

'Maternity,' he said, quietly. 'She have a baby.'

She matched his stern look. 'And you are?'

The man blinked too slowly. He took a deep, calming breath. 'Her uncle. Jansson.'

Everything about him prickled at her instincts. 'We don't have your name here as…'

Nesim Kapllani knew his fake ID would hold up to inspection. He'd paid enough for it. But he'd still wanted to avoid using it.

He glanced at her name badge. 'Carla, I am sorry your system not up to date. This is not your fault. Perhaps this will help ease your mind. Amelja asked me to look after it.' He handed a passport to Carla.

Amelja's photograph and name were clear, and although the receptionist couldn't help but feel something wasn't right, she could hardly deny the man's politeness. Why would he have her passport if he didn't know her? Records showed she'd had no other visitors.

Carla handed back the passport and gave him directions to maternity. She noticed he was tall, but stooped, looking down. Maybe he had a bad back.

As soon as he was out of sight, he was out of mind.

* * *

Amelja

She didn't like the whispering between the nurses when she got to the room with all the babies in the plastic boxes. The doctor came over and said lots of things that didn't make sense, besides the three Amelja wanted to hear.

'Healthy baby girl.'

But why were they in plastic boxes? Other mothers were holding their babies. Her baby was lying on her back with her arms and legs spread like a flat chicken on the grill. Her tiny face kept moving between fat and sweet, to scrunched and wrinkled.

She was beautiful.

Baby let out a yawn so big and her eyelids opened for a moment.

'I hold her?'

The smiling nurse nodded, reached inside the plastic box to gather the tiny body up, laid her on a white blanket, which she wrapped like the most precious Christmas gift.

'There you go,' the nurse whispered. 'Remember, like we showed you. Support her neck, and let her face touch your skin. That's good.'

Amelja wanted to tell the nurse she knew what to do, but she knew she was just being nice.

'Përshëndetje. Hello, little one.'

'She is so beautiful,' the nurse said. 'Have you and the father thought of a name yet?'

Amelja felt the heat rush to her head, the tears collecting in her eye.

The nurse sensed she'd touched a nerve. She knew the likeliness of the father being a positive factor was low. Then she'd privately chastised herself for being so judgemental.

'I take her to my room?' Amelja looked at the nurse.

'Not just yet, love,' the nurse was careful to explain without sharing the real reason why.

'But you say she healthy.' A shiver of panic crept into Amelja's voice.

'She is, she is. We just want to be extra safe with her. Check she's got all her strength.'

The nurse rested her hand on Amelja's arm. 'We just want to keep an eye on her for a little while. No rush, love. You stay here with her all you like. This is the safest place for mummy and baby. This is your special quiet time. If you need to pop to the loo or stretch your legs, we are right here for you.' Another soft smile, all the way up to the eyes.

Amelja nodded in agreement.

There were other factors concerning the team.

'Now she's drifted off to sleep again,' the nurse said, 'why don't you get yourself something to eat? Get your strength back up?'

Amelja had to admit she was feeling rather hungry. It felt odd to be hungry only for herself.

'I am hungry, yes. But I have no money with me.'

The nurse let out a quiet laugh. 'Now don't you go worrying about that, my love. Pop back to your room and we'll bring you some breakfast.' She leaned in. 'And I'll sneak a naughty treat when no one is looking.' The smile and conspiratorial wink gained a smile from Amelja.

Thoughts of Luke filled Amelja's mind as she returned

to her room. What would happen to her and the baby? Did the nurses recognise her? Were they going to call the police? She trying to banish the heavy feeling of hopelessness from her chest.

She didn't feel like eating, but when the nurse had suggested it, she knew it was best to play along.

* * *

He'd avoided the cameras as he made his way to maternity, glimpsing into each room.

'Can I help you, sir?' A face smiled, but the eyes were suspicious.

'I look for Amelja Halil. I am uncle.'

The flash of a frown on her head gave her suspicion away. Nesim cut in before she could speak again.

'Carla at reception say to come here. This is maternity? But she not say which room for Amelja. Sorry.'

'She didn't mention her uncle to me.'

'No?' He smiled, apparently hurt. 'Oh, Amelja okay, yes? Baby good, yes?' Kapllani was going for an Oscar-winning performance.

And it worked.

'Yes, they are both fine. Amelja is in room eleven.'

'You are angel. All of you here are angels.' He made a quick cross and clasped his hands together. 'Thank you, thank you.' He turned and walked away.

When he found the right door, he peered through the window. Amelja stood by the bed. He wondered why the baby wasn't with her.

He placed his hand on the door and gently pressed down the handle, keeping his eyes fixed on the girl.

The door clicked open and he stepped inside.

* * *

Amelja

Amelja heard the door and readied herself to look pleased and thankful for the food.

She turned and saw the man and her heart stopped.

'Amelja,' he said through a tight smile. 'I was worried about you when you didn't come back with,' pretending to forget his name, 'Luke. Yes. That was his name.'

Her mind spluttered like a car engine failing to spark. How was he here? How could he have known?

Kapllani interrupted her confusion. 'It's such a shame you didn't come with Luke. You could have seen how much care we took of him.'

'What did you do to him?'

He shrugged his shoulders and curled his bottom lip, holding out his hands. 'He stole you from me, Amelja.'

'He loves me.' Amelja willed her feet to move away.

'Do you know what happens to people who steal?' Taking out a phone and giving it a few swipes, he held it for her to see.

Amelja's breath stuck in her throat.

He forced her to watch for a few moments. 'It was unfortunate. But I can't have people thinking they can steal from me. Not even a little whore like you.'

Amelja winced.

'Now, I tell you what to do and you will do it.' He stared hard at her. 'You will do it.'

She raised her eyes, trying not to move her head. What did he want? Was she supposed to say yes, or no? Her mind was spinning.

'Get that bastard whore child of yours and bring it out to the front of the hospital. I wait across the road. I'll be watching. Any sign,' he leans in and whispers in her ear, 'any sign that you tell anyone, I will make sure you never see the child again.' He stared at her. 'Understood?'

Amelja could barely move but managed the slightest nod. His hand stroked her cheek as he tilted his head like a curious dog.

And he laughed.

'If you weren't so fucking pathetic.' He let the thought linger.

Kapllani turned away and left the room.

A few seconds passed before Amelja finally exhaled, only then realising she'd been holding her breath.

Hopelessness overwhelmed her.

The nurse came back into the room wheeling a small trolley with an array of food.

Amelja turned away, desperate to dry the tears.

'Oh, bab. It's all a bit much isn't it?' She was warm, and the opposite of the man who had stood there moments before.

Amelja conjured up a few words, keen to keep the dark secret. 'I am sorry, I am feeling up and down.'

'All those hormones, love, they haven't gone away, yet. I'd be a mess in the corner of the room. But not you, bab. You are strong as an ox.'

'Ox?'

'Yeh, you know. Like a cow.'

'You say I am cow?'

'Oh, no, I meant strong. It's a silly English saying.'

Amelja faked a smile. 'It is okay. But I don't feel strong.'

'And that is why you need to get some food in you.' The nurse framed the trolley like a magician's assistant. 'I got you some proper hospital gruel and some secret little extras.' She winked.

'Thank you,' Amelja said, quiet and timid. She still struggled with other people's kindness.

The nurse fluffed a pillow and placed it on the back of the chair next to the bed. 'Here you go, bab. You sit here, take your time. Then we'll go spend more time with your beautiful little girl.'

Amelja thanked her with a smile. She noticed the nurse hover about flattening blankets, wiping a surface. She presumed the nurse was waiting to see her start eating before she left. Amelja spread a little jam on the corner of some toast, and then made all the right sounds people do when they get to eat something tasty.

The nurse smiled and finally left the room.

Amelja had been right. But the toast was rubbery, and the jam was bitter. She decided to eat the banana instead. And the smuggled bag of crisps. It would give her a few moments to think about what she had to do next.

Chapter 59

DI Stone picked up the phone on his desk and dialled Chief Superintendent Carter's extension. There was no answer after a few rings. He tried her mobile, but that also went straight to voicemail.

The voice over his shoulder was shouting at him, but he didn't want to listen to it. Marching to his door and swinging it open, he gave DC Khan a wave.

'Harry. Got a sec?'

Khan responded straight away. The urgency written across Stone's face had 'drop everything' in neon.

'I'm going to order you to do something,' Stone said, taking a deep breath.

'That's a special talent you have, guv.'

'Don't be facetious,' Stone smiled. 'I'm going to order you so that if you are ever asked about it you must not deny it, and you just say exactly what my order was.'

It meant he was about to be asked to do something that technically he really shouldn't do if rules were his main concern.

'I can't get hold of Carter, and I need to know where she is.'

'And you want me to fix that?'

'Get me the information.'

'Is she in her car?'

'I don't know.'

DC Khan scratched at his forehead.

Stone continued. 'This is a matter of potential police corruption, and it's in urgent nature. That is why I am choosing not to follow strict, normal procedural. You're not getting all the details, so you'll have some plausible deniability, just in case I am wrong. Got that?'

Khan laughed. 'Wrong, guv? Pull the other one.'

'I also need you to track those two phone numbers as best you can and keep me updated by text or email.'

'Guv, what are the chances of a pay rise?'

'How about a bag of nuts and a pint?'

'No, I mean for the private healthcare I want to pay for when I finally get the massive ulcer I am destined to get.'

'Two bags of nuts?'

'Sir, you know I have your back.' The humorous tone was put aside.

DS Bolton knocked on the door and entered as Khan returned to his desk. She looked at Stone, slightly wincing. 'Guv, we've got a big problem.'

Stone let his head fall back, looking at the ceiling. Every time he looked up, he swore he found a new odd contorted face staring right back at him.

Bolton didn't bother waiting for a reply. 'We just got a call from a PCSO asking for you. Specifically, you.'

Stone rolled his eyes and groaned loud enough for most of the incident room to dip their heads lower to their desk. He picked up his coat with the urgency his sergeant's voice had done enough to communicate. He held up his phone as they left the office and got to the incident room.

'Harry. Call me.'

A wolf-whistle.

'Piss off, Pete.'

Chapter 60

September
Friday – Amelja

Amelja had all her clothes on, with space for the baby in a simple makeshift sling. It was just as her grandmother had taught her.

She opened the door and peered down the shining corridor. When the coast was clear, she slipped out and walked to post-natal care. She'd planned her story.

Amelja knocked on the glass of the door and held up her wrist to show her medical band, but the nurse recognised her anyway.

'Hello, love.'

The misdirection began. 'I've had a good breakfast and I feel so much better.'

'That's good to hear.'

'I want to say sorry.'

The nurse looked confused. 'Whatever for?'

'I think earlier I seem rude.'

'Not at all.' She smiled.

'I was tired, but I feel much better now. Thank you for looking after my little girl.' It was working. She could see flattery warm the motherly woman. Amelja knew a little kindness and good manners went a long way.

The nurse ushered Amelja over to the little plastic cot.

'She is so beautiful.' She sensed that mummy wanted to be alone with her baby. 'Here's a nice, clean blanket.'

It was at that moment the nurse noticed Amelja had dressed and put her coat on. 'Are you cold, love? Got an awful lot on there.'

Amelja had planned for this question.

'You will think it silly if I say.'

'Really?' There was a tiny air of concern in the nurse's voice.

'It is usual tradition in Albania. My grandmother say it good to have baby smell things like mother's clothes. Babies remember smells forever. I know I look silly, but this is favourite coat.'

The nurse looked slightly sceptical.

'Am I wrong?' Amelja kept the act going. 'Have I broken rules?'

'You know what, Amelja, I've never heard that before, but I think it sounds beautiful, and you have a wise grandmother.'

The little lie was working. 'She tell me it is important like skin to skin. Get all senses working. My first baby. I only know things grandmother teach me. So, I think I try them.' Amelja shrugged and smiled.

The nurse smiled back before leaving them together. When the nurse was far enough away, Amelja safely stowed her baby in the secret sling. She then held the folded white blanket as if that was the baby.

Misdirection. Just as Luke taught her.

She spent a few minutes pacing up and down, staring at the empty blanket whilst tending to the real baby in her sling. She was still asleep, and she needed to stay that way for a moment more.

The nurse came out of the station again to make more notes on one of the other babies. She smiled at Amelja.

The plan would now work or fail.

'Mummy is just going to have another wee, and be

right back,' Amelja said as she very carefully laid the empty, carefully shaped blanket back in the cot. The nurse merely glanced over her shoulder, and Amelja made sure she placed her kissed fingers on the baby's head.

'I be right back,' Amelja whispered to the nurse across the room.

The nurse smiled and nodded, glancing over the cot to see the baby safely wrapped, and the mother cutely waving at her.

At least she thought she did.

Amelja opened the door and closed it quietly behind her. Making sure to stand upright as if she wasn't carrying a newborn hidden under her coat.

As soon as she was out of sight, Amelja looked around for the lifts. She pushed the button and stood back. If anyone was in the lift, she would have to change her mind.

The lift chimed and the doors opened. It was empty. Amelja entered and pushed the 'door close' and the Ground Floor button to hurry it along. The lift made its way down two floors before grinding to a halt and chiming.

It was the first floor. As the door opened, two nurses and someone else in a suit were standing waiting to get into the lift. Amelja dropped her arms and bolted out from the lift, turning left.

Checking over her shoulder, she pushed the stairway door open and made her way down to the ground floor.

Fairly sure the fire exit would set off an alarm, Amelja opted for some more confident misdirection and stepped out into the front lobby. Keeping her arms by her sides and walking briskly, she left the building by the front exit without drawing attention to herself.

The cold air hit her from the side as soon as she left the brightly lit building. A misty rain was falling and Amelja felt a buzz of exhilaration as she moved away from the building.

Until she looked across the road at the long car with

black windows standing out amongst all the others.

Amelja thought for a moment about running, but she knew that she couldn't. Not with the baby.

She folded her arms across her chest, shielding the newborn as she crossed the road aware of the sound of a disturbance developing behind her.

The alarm must have been raised.

A door at the front of the car opened and a large man got out. Amelja recognised him from the big house. He opened a rear door and she got inside. When it closed she felt dark eyes digging into her. She kept her eyes down on the baby, which was beginning to stir.

'I am impressed,' Kapllani said with a cruel, mocking laugh. 'You are a resourceful little whore.'

She didn't answer.

'Such a waste.' He took out a phone. 'Excuse me for a moment.' His voice changed when the call connected.

'I have something you need to see. Fifteen minutes. If you aren't there, you'll find out what you missed on the ten o'clock news.'

He ended the call without waiting for a reply, before tapping a dividing window to let the driver know it was time to go.

Amelja had to force herself to breathe.

'Now, is uncle Nesim going to get to see his little one?'

* * *

Amelja kept her eyes on the baby for the whole journey, resisting the desire to look up as the car lurched to a stop in a gravel yard. The few lights outside didn't give much away about their location.

The driver got out and opened the rear doors for Kapllani and Amelja. The cold air hit her again, and she clutched her baby safe inside the sling.

A tight grip squeezed her right arm and she felt herself

being forced to walk. He spoke much louder and more determined than he had inside the hospital.

'Let's see if you recognise this place.'

They came out of the yard onto the road, and she was swung to the left. When she saw where they were, her heart ached.

How did he know?

'You see, I never let anyone who belongs to me truly out of my sight.'

'I do not belong to you,' Amelja spat out the words.

'I brought you here, to this country. I gave you everything you had.'

'You are evil.'

'No, I am not evil. I was your only hope, Amelja.'

She looked over her shoulder, across Galton Bridge. The lamppost in the centre threw a gentle light on the walkway, slowly getting lost under a film of rain.

'There's nowhere you can go. Nowhere for you, or the child.' He shrugged his shoulders and spread his evil smile. 'Maybe we just let the police take baby from you. Put it in care. Never knowing her real mother. No, worse. Calling someone else mama.'

Another car approached, pulling up on the side of the road. Kapllani took a few large, fast steps and grabbed Amelja by the shoulder, swinging her in front of him and pushing her a few steps forward.

A figure got out of the other car but was hard to see through the glare of the headlights. It walked forwards a few paces and stopped about twenty feet from their position.

'Glad you could make it,' Kapllani said to the woman, as he took a small revolver from his pocket and placed the barrel to Amelja's head.

Chapter 61

September
Day Ten ~ Monday

Luke

He'd run all the way from the pub in the Gun Quarter until he'd reached the tall office blocks around Snow Hill. Finding his way to the tracks for the tram, Luke followed Bull Street down to the bottom with Dale End and the taxi rank.

After a few frantic minutes of searching for Masood's taxi, he begged another driver to let him use their phone to call him.

'It's Luke,' he kept his voice low.

'What's wrong? You okay?'

'I need your help. Now. Right now.'

Luke could hear the expletives in the background. 'Where are you?'

'At the taxi rank. Can you come now? It's urgent.'

After another pause, he heard the driver's voice. 'Stay there. Ten minutes.' The call ended.

Reg

Reg knew if Luke didn't want to be found he was resourceful enough to blend in like a social chameleon. But this time Reg was especially concerned. Luke had lost almost every reason to worry about survival. He'd been backed too far into a corner and the only thing left was for him to lash out.

Reg reached Colmore Row and broke into a jog until he had to stop and sit on a bench in Pigeon Park, resting his elbows on his knees and dropping his head. He cursed himself for doing what everyone does with their new year's gym membership by the middle of February. The chase was futile, and it would be far easier to find Luke on CCTV cameras than it would be running around in circles until he collapsed.

A part of him admired Luke's tenacity and ability to survive. But he also knew what Luke wanted was revenge.

Justice was the lie adults told each other to protect their conscience under the cover of righteousness. Much in the same way religious doctrine did to the purity of faith.

Reg stared at the Cathedral in front of him and felt only anger. There was no forgiveness or love to be found when injustice was allowed to betray innocence. Should he sit in awe and say a prayer? For what? To whom?

Why pray to a God who had already shown his hand by laying it down on the cold metal slab in his mortuary?

Reg let the thought fade to black as he stood and turned his back on more than just the self-aggrandising bricks and mortar. It was time to stop thinking like a man who relied on the servitude of piety and think like a boy who believed he'd lost every reason to hope.

*   *   *

Luke

He'd been waiting for more than ten minutes when the hand gripped his shoulder. Luke swung round, but relief turned to confusion as Steve Chambers stood right in front of him.

Luke took a step back, dry-mouthed, and unable to speak. No words would form. The sound of a car horn cut through the disorientation, and he saw Masood's cab pull into the taxi rank. Luke ran out into the road and straight towards it.

Chambers called out to him to wait, but Luke clambered into the taxi, slamming the door shut, and shouting at Masood to get a move on.

Breaking into a run, and getting close enough to hit the side of the taxi as it pulled away, Chambers cursed in frustration.

'Wait, Luke. Don't go back there.'

The commotion attracted the attention of a pair of PCSOs who came running over to hold Chambers back.

'You need to call this in,' he protested.

'Sir, just calm yourself down.'

Chambers raised both his hands in submission. 'Detective Inspector Mike Stone. You know him? DI Mike Stone?'

The officer looked blankly at Chambers, and then each other.

'Well, do you? DI Mike Stone.'

The smaller of the two PCSOs summoned up her most condescending tone. 'Sir, I'm not going to waste a detective's time.'

Chambers growled in frustration. Then he paused, a

calculated thought crossing his eyes. He looked at the bigger of the two officers.

'Tell him Steve Chambers wants his SIM card back.'

Then launched his fist and buried it into the officer's jaw, dropping him to the floor in the single blow.

He leapt over the dead weight, leaving the other PCSO shocked by the heap of her colleague on the ground as she put in a call for DI Stone.

Chapter 62

September
Friday ~ Amelja

The woman stood casting a long shadow from her car headlights.

Amelja held her baby tight up to her. The gun barrel squeezed painfully into the side of her head.

'There's no need for this,' the woman spoke. 'She's holding a child, for Christ's sake.'

'You know me, Chief,' Kapllani replied, sounding too relaxed. 'Business is business. What was it you said about doing my own wet work?'

'Let her go.'

'I want to know who is on the inside. Who have you got sniffing around, Carter?'

'No one. I'd never sanction it.'

Kapllani shook his head. 'Okay. We'll get Amelja to decide.'

He squeezed her left shoulder so hard she let out a small scream, waking the baby.

'I want you to make this girl a promise.'

'Kapllani, stop this.'

'Look her in the eyes and promise her that you don't have a video of lover-boy raping her.' Kapllani leaned into Amelja's ear. 'A video proving your baby will always be a child of sin.'

Carter shouted, but without confidence. 'You know I can't make promises.'

'She is not worth saving?'

'I can't make this all go away until you let her go.'

'English police, Amelja. More corrupt than Albanians.'

Amelja looked at the woman in front of her. Her heart burnt for Luke. Gone forever. She'd heard stories of babies taken from young mothers. The evil man who would never let them go. The hopelessness.'

Carter looked back at Amelja holding the baby, avoiding her pleading eyes.

Kapllani pulled the hammer back on the revolver, knowing the sound would add urgency.

'What's it going to be, Chief? Is this girl, and her baby, worth the price of silence?'

Carter's eyes met Amelja's. They held the gaze for a few seconds.

A few too many.

* * *

The wrinkled hand reached for the large, black receiver and brought it down to her head. She crouched, hidden in the phone box.

One button, three times. Waited. A voice spoke. She didn't understand what they said. She just replied.

'Iz toonaah, toonaah,' she whispered. 'Now.'

The voice kept speaking.

'Now. Girl. It now. Pliss. Pliss. Help.'

The voice kept repeating things she didn't understand.

'Girl and, and, foshnje. Foshnje.'

The voice sounded a little annoyed.

'Foshnje. Baby. Now. Pliss.'

The old woman let the receiver drop to her side, dangling on the end of its cable, the voice squeaking from it. The woman crouched down, trying to stay out of sight. Watching.

Quietly humming the Albanian melody.

* * *

Luke was gone. She would never see her home again. Her Grandmother would never meet her child. Her child would grow to know only pain and suffering.

And there it was.

Amelja knew that all hope had gone. No promise. Nothing. Not even the attempt at misdirection.

The air filled with the wails of the tiny child stirred up with approaching whining of sirens.

Kapllani turned his gun on the woman. 'Walk away. Get back in your car. Make this all go away.'

She didn't answer him. She didn't even move for a moment.

'I'd say you have about thirty seconds, Chief. I assure you, I'm not the one going down for this.'

Amelja took the moment and the chance and turned, running from Kapllani and Carter out onto the bridge, wrapping her arm around the lamppost.

Kapllani's driver got out of his car and called over.

Releasing the hammer on the revolver carefully, Kapllani kept his eyes fixed on Carter as he spoke.

'Make this go away. That little whore is collateral damage. A bad investment. But remember, I know every privileged cunt you protect all these years.'

Kapllani walked over to his car. Moments later, it rolled away.

Carter took another look at Amelja, who looked back, empty, hollowed by everything. There was no way she could explain being there.

The sirens were close enough to show the blue and red lights flashes spreading through the misty air.

Carter turned and walked back to her car.

She paused before she opened the door, looking over to the phone box on the corner. The cowering old mess of a woman was unreliable at best, certifiable at worst.

A problem for another day.

Carter swung the car down a side street just as the first marked police car came into sight on the other side of the bridge, and another further down the road.

Amelja looked over the canal knowing she was alone.

Albania, home, was but a distant dream.

Luke was gone.

Everyone had walked away.

And hope had vanished.

She took her necklace off and felt the "L" engraved into it. Squeezing it in her palm, Amelja climbed and sat on the edge of life itself.

Ice-cold wind rocked the girl as she sat on the railing, clutching the lamppost with one hand.

Her other arm cradled the newborn.

Tears rolled down her face as misty rain drenched her from head to toe.

Chapter 63

'What do you mean, he got away?' Stone snapped at Bolton.

'PCSO's saw a man arguing with a boy at the taxi rank.'

'Luke?'

'They think so.' She gasped in frustration. 'By the time they get over, the kid breaks away, jumps into the back of a taxi which screeched off.'

'What is this? Jason Bourne Six?'

Bolton looked at Stone. 'I bet we know who drives that taxi.'

'Masood. Get Harry on the ANPR.'

Stone swung the car out onto the ring road. It might have been easier to run to Dale End, but he knew they would need the car.

'Call handler said the PCSOs mentioned you by name.'

'I told you, Sands, I'm famous.'

'Matt Damon is quaking in his boots.'

It took a moment for the pieces to fit, and a quick whisper from the voice over his shoulder. He started pounding the steering wheel with the heel of his hand.

'Shit, fucking bloody shitting,' Stone growled the sentence to an end of a frustrated outburst.

387

'Something wrong, Mike?' Bolton asked, without hiding the sarcasm.

'The other man. Did he give a name?'

'Message was, "tell DI Mike Stone Steve Chambers wants his SIM card back."'

Stone growled. 'Get the PCSOs on radio and tell them not to move. We will be there in one minute.'

Stone pulled off the roundabout onto James Watts Queensway and covered the yards before the turn to Dale End in seconds.

* * *

Masood drove out of the city centre to get some distance before pulling over. He rested his head on the steering wheel, letting out a deep sigh before turning in his seat to look at Luke.

'You going to tell me what is going on?'

Luke was still wired on adrenaline. 'I have to do something, but I can't do it on my own. No police.'

'Sounds to me like you probably should.'

Luke looked away, frowning, nostrils flaring. 'You told me to look after her.' His whole body shook from the adrenaline and emotion. 'I failed her.'

'I know what happened to her.'

'She didn't kill herself.'

'But, the bridge.'

'No, it was something else. Someone made her. Forced her.' Luke sat back in the seat, hearing the stretch of the leather as his weight sagged into the cushion. 'You don't know what they made me do to her.'

Masood paused for a moment, rubbing his hands together as if to warm them on a cold winter day. 'Will you tell me something?'

Luke nodded.

'You loved her?'

'Yes, totally,' his reply shot out with a flare of the Fury's aggression behind it.

Masood shook his head and waved off the answer. 'No, you don't get my meaning. How can you truly know love? Hmm? What experience of life do you have to know that you loved her with all your heart?'

One of the tears lost its grip and plummeted down Luke's cheek as he stared out the window, gritting his teeth at a burgeoning mix of anger and pain. Far more damaging was feeling he knew too well, and Amelja had been the first person to free him from it.

Loneliness.

'I know I loved her because of how much it hurts to lose her.'

Masood nodded, understanding written across his furrowed brow. 'And what is it you want now?'

Luke's head dropped. He wanted to save the others. But he also wanted something darker.

Masood turned a little more, to get Luke's eyes back on him. 'What do you want to do about it?'

'I want justice for her.'

'Justice? What is this justice you want?'

'I wanna burn that place down to the ground. Every last fucking piece of it.'

Masood shook his head as he closed his eyes. 'No, Luke. You want revenge.'

'Call it what you want.' The defensive petulant teenager reared its head. 'It's all the same to me.'

'No, Luke. The difference is that with justice you wish to right a wrong. You wish to put the world back to good, to act without hatred and anger.'

Luke was sure the man was never going to help him. He'd just picked Luke up to get him away from trouble.

'Revenge is what you seek.'

Luke opened the door and got out.

Masood got out of the front and rushed around the

front of the car and stood in front of Luke, who tried to push his way past.

'Let me go. If you aren't going to help me.'

'Say it. Go on Luke,' he pushed him up against the car.

'Let me go. Fuck off.'

Masood pushed him harder, slamming him into the side of the cab. 'Come on Luke. Say it. Tell me again you loved her, they took her, and you want revenge.'

Luke pushed back, but Masood was too strong, and slammed him back into the car, holding him by the shoulders.

Masood leaned into him, inches from his face. 'Tell me you wanna kill those mother fuckers for all they did.'

Luke was taken aback. 'I loved her.'

Masood shook his head gripped Luke by the jacket, pulling them face-to-face. 'Say it again.'

'I loved her.'

'No,' Masood growled. 'Mean it. Believe it.'

Luke felt the Fury boiling up inside. His face tightened and his eyes dried of all tears and filled with blood. He shouted, 'I loved her. And. I. Want. Revenge.'

They froze with eyes locked.

The man put Luke down and nodded a single, powerful nod. Then he marched around to the back of his cab and opened the boot. The strong smell of petrol poured into the air from the two filled cans sitting next to a bag of heavy tools, ropes, bottles and various paraphernalia that would cause anyone to feel concerned.

Luke's jaw dropped and he almost let out a laugh. 'What the hell?'

Masood slammed the boot shut. 'Now I know you mean it, let's go burn those fuckers down to the ground.' His hand shot out. 'For Amelja.'

Luke nodded. They shook. And both got back into the cab.

Chapter 64

It hadn't been hard to find the old woman. A few instructions were sent out to a range of contacts. A message had come through on a burner phone.

Slipping away undetected had been easy enough. The harder part was always going to be getting the old hack into the car without being seen by anyone.

In the end, the offer of some hot food and a nice little walk was all it had taken. The old woman stopped for a moment, searching her mind for recognition of the car.

Leaning up against the boot sipping at the hot tea, the old woman shot a double-take before dropping the drink from her shaking hands. The boot opened, and she looked inside before the mighty crack of weight against her head tipped her world sideways and the ground vanished from beneath her.

Carter had been waiting tucked into the small industrial area a hundred yards away from Galton Bridge. Kapllani's car swung into the gravel area and the driver swung it round to face the exit before coming to a stop.

There was an awkward pause. Both were waiting to see who would get out of their vehicle first. In the end, Carter relented.

The first power move lost to Kapllani.

She stood in the cold air as his door opened. When he didn't step out, she walked up to the open door.

'There's no way I am climbing into my coffin quite yet.' Carter knew it was a gamble calling his bluff. But that was the only language he understood.

Kapllani got out the other side, straightened his coat, pulled on some leather gloves, and stared at her.

He walked around the back of his car to stand in front of Carter.

'You've left us with quite a mess to tidy up, Chief.' Kapllani's certainty that there was no way anything could be pinned on him made her want to risk trying it.

'Perhaps if you didn't spend your time making so much that needed to be hidden, it might be easier.'

'You whine like a bitch.'

'And you bitch like a woman.'

He nodded at the boot of Carter's car.

Carter nodded. 'You don't need to worry about this.'

He stared at her. Waited.

Carter could see his mind working, trying too hard not to play all his cards in one go. She wondered how well he could read her, too. She placed her hand on top of the boot.

'I have this, Kapllani. What have you got?'

Chapter 65

Stone pulled up into a spot in the taxi rank, resulting in several horns blaring. He left his sergeant to placate them with the wave of a badge as he marched over to the flustered looking PCSOs.

'Right, no pissing around.' Stone didn't bother hiding his anger as he held out his phone. 'Is this the boy you saw?'

The PCSO nodded.

'And this,' he swiped the screen, 'was the man?'

The same response.

'For fuck's sake, don't you pay attention to daily briefing notes?' Stone stood with one hand firmly on his hip. 'Did you even see which way they went?'

The PCSOs looked at each other, the larger of the two rubbing at his chin, which was glowing red and beginning to swell.

The smaller one spoke. 'All we got from him was your name.'

'Well, I'm already bloody familiar with that.'

Bolton appeared next to Stone and nearly folded her arms until she noticed they looked like a dreadful eighties American cop show.

'Mike, this is getting us nowhere.'

Stone felt his phone vibrate and answered it with a bark 'What?'

DC Khan replied. 'Reg Walters is here.'

'Tell him to stay there.'

There was a muffled loud voice. 'Um, he's just said no blinking way. But he didn't say blinking.'

Stone rolled his eyes. He knew there was no way he could stop Reg from leaving the station without DC Khan locking him in a cell. 'Okay, Harry, listen up. Get a marked car here, pronto. I'm sending Sands to the Bristol Road address. Take Reg with you but keep him on a tight leash. Use cuffs if you have to.'

'Right, okay. Does Sands know the location?'

'She will when you send it to her, dimwit. Meet her there and don't do anything until I arrive. Wait and watch. Am I clear with you on that?'

'Yes, boss. But where will you be?'

'Officially speaking, I am ensuring things are wrapped up here, okay?'

DC Khan knew when not to argue. The less that was said, the less he had to lie about. That's when he also sent the other GPS location he'd been asked for.

Stone ended the call, and the nod from Bolton was enough to know she'd picked up the plan.

Chapter 66

Kapllani walked round to stand next to the boot of Carter's car and she took the keys from her pocket, holding them up.

He nodded almost respectfully, sighed, and took one more drag from his cigarette before dropping the butt on the ground right in front of her.

Then he swung his left hand to slap Carter hard across the cheek and grabbed her wrist with his right hand.

She grasped her jaw as Kapllani snatched the keys from her hand. He watched her straighten up and wince. Then he released the tight grip on her wrist.

'You seem to like wasting my time. It is time that I do not have to waste.' He pressed the button on the fob and the boot hissed open. The woman inside murmured behind the tape over her mouth.

Kapllani tutted. 'This can't be regulation police custody?'

He leaned into the boot and grabbed the woman by the arm, recoiling at the stink which had filled the boot. He pulled her up to her knees and waited to see her eyes.

The woman squinted at the light for a moment, looking around to see where she was until she recognised the two faces.

Kapllani put a finger to his lips. 'My dear, my dear. Who did this to you?' he said, picking at the tape and peeling it away. He tilted his head in mock sympathy.

The woman smacked her lips, gulped at breaths.

'She's not going to speak to anyone, Kapllani.' Carter's uncertainty was given away by the quiver in her voice.

Kapllani let go of the woman's arm and shot a glance to his driver, who was standing watch. The driver walked around to stand behind Carter.

'Someone else coming to do your wet work, Kapllani?'

He smiled back as he took out the same revolver he'd used the last time they met.

The old woman gasped, shaking her head. She began to mumble. 'Tonight. Is tonight.'

Kapllani looked at the woman. 'Tonight? What is tonight?'

The woman glared at him. She knew what was coming. But hidden under resignation was defiance in her eyes.

Kapllani laughed. 'What is tonight, you mad old hag?'

The woman fixed her eyes on his and with all the force she could muster, screwed her expression up and spat in his face.

Kapllani took out a handkerchief and wiped the putrid saliva away. He held up the gun.

She barked at him in Albanian. 'Hakmarrje.'

* * *

DI Stone switched the headlights off as he rolled his car the last couple of hundred yards. He got out and pushed the door shut silently.

There was movement in the industrial yard to his left. Keeping out of sight, he took out his phone and switched it to video.

They were too far away to hear what was being said, but the boot of Carter's car was open, and someone was inside. She had her back to Stone's position and Kapllani stood facing her.

Something escalated in the interaction and Stone fought to capture it on the camera, unable to get a better angle. He zoomed in a little more and kept the camera steady.

Part of him knew the situation looked hopeless, and he was trying to work out how to approach it.

But when Kapllani produced the gun, his options were reduced.

He stopped the video and opened up his messages.

It was time to get the Armed Response Team out, and he needed Bolton to contact someone senior enough to make that happen. Someone who had the rank to authorise it.

And he knew where they would need to be going.

* * *

Kapllani shook his head as he let out a low rumbling laugh. 'Revenge?' He looked at the woman, then at Carter. 'It is a strange world where a tied and gagged old witch spits in your face and cackles about revenge.'

With the slightest upward nod, he passed an instruction to his driver.

Carter felt the grip on her left arm as it was dragged behind her and pulled up her back. She fought to keep her composure. Her right hand was gripped and pushed forward, out in front of her. Kapllani forced the pistol into her hand. He squeezed the handle into her palm and held her finger against the trigger guard.

'Don't you fucking dare,' Carter protested through gritted teeth.

'Dare?' He stared her in the eyes and saw the weakness.

Another glance into his driver's eyes and her hand was twisted into place.

The old woman squirmed, trying to turn away.

The driver placed his finger over Carter's, pushing it back onto the trigger.

She didn't have the strength to fight and watched the hammer draw back.

Kapllani's wry smile dropped as something caught his sight. Fast-moving, dark, flying towards them.

The gun fired.

A dull thud of a large stone colliding with the driver's upper back followed a split second later.

Kapllani turned to see the old woman's body collapse back into the boot, a hole in the side of her head. At the same time, he heard a loud growl from his driver as he threw Carter forwards to the ground.

'What the fuck was that?' the driver spat out.

Kapllani took a plastic bag from his coat pocket, picked up the gun. 'Now, Chief, it looks like it is time for me to go.' He dangled the bag in front of her face. 'And this is a little insurance.'

Carter dragged herself to her feet as the doors slammed on Kapllani's car and the gravel kicked up. Dust stung her eyes as she tried to refocus on the hunched mess in the boot.

She took her phone out, struggling to hold it in her shaking hand. But there was no one to call until she had time to work out what she was going to do.

* * *

DI Stone had been a split second too late to prevent the gunshot.

Another life lost. Taken.

Stone watched as Kapllani sped away. He sent a message ahead to DC Khan and Bolton that Kapllani was likely on his way and was definitely armed.

He ignored the reply and put his phone back in his pocket before walking up behind Carter. He waited for her to close the boot and notice him.

She gasped. 'Mike? How long…'

Shaking his head, he tried to rattle the thoughts into order. 'I'm not sure how much I want to know.'

Carter's eyes searched for a grasp on the situation. 'There was nothing I could do.'

Stone laughed, but without humour. 'You drive out to an illicit meeting with an organised criminal, and you say there was nothing you could have done.'

'This is way above your pay grade.'

'Fuck pay-grades, Sue. This is simple right and plain, damn wrong. A woman just got shot in the face in the boot of your car.'

'You saw?'

'What did I see?' His voice rattled with anger. 'Go on, you tell me what I saw.'

Stepping forward, attempting to hold more ground. 'Every complex case has collateral damage.'

'Collateral damage?' He reached up and scratched his head. 'Is that what Amelja was, too?'

'This is a major operation.'

'Which you dragged across my lap, remember?'

Carter took a moment. Her face and voice softened, and the air began to fill with light dusty rain. 'I trust your judgement, Mike. I trust you.'

'You want to talk about trust?' He moved to stand face-to-face with her. 'All you've ever done is covered your backside. And then you want me to be grateful for your trust?' He turned around, raising his arms and dropping them heavily by his sides.

'I had no choice.'

'We always have a choice.'

'He was blackmailing me.'

Stone turned, his eyes sharp with anger. 'With what? Hmm? Years of standing by and watching God knows how much corruption and abuse went unchallenged only because you kept your friends' secrets?'

Carter straightened her back and inched closer.

'Come on, Sue. What skeletons are really in that closet? Who is Kapllani?'

He stared right into her eyes.

'And who the hell is Steve Chambers?'

Chapter 67

Masood's taxi pulled up a hundred yards from the house on Bristol Road, close to where they had met all those months ago.

'Ready?' He kept his glare forward.

Luke said nothing. His whole body was begging him to lie down and rest. Except for his heart, which thumped with anger and adrenaline. He opened the door and stepped out into the misty rain.

Masood opened the boot and got out of the car, walking round to meet Luke at their arsenal.

A thought crossed Luke's mind. 'How come you had all this stuff in here, Mass?'

The man let out a deep sigh. 'You aren't the only one who has thought of revenge.'

They took the waterproofs first, pulling up the hoods in a moment of unison. Luke held up his hands which were buried in sleeves, and he smiled.

The feeling shook him. The last time he'd had a flicker of innocent amusement had been with Amelja.

Masood noticed and pulled back the sleeves over Luke's wrists, refastening the Velcro straps tighter.

Luke looked at him. 'Why are you helping me like this?'

'I have my reasons.' His tone wasn't dismissive, his eyes dropped at the sides. He took Luke's hand in a thumb-grip and placed the other on the back of the boy's neck, nodding a final confirmation.

They picked up a fuel can each, and Masood grabbed the heavy bag, slinging it over his shoulder.

'You know, Luke, technically it is illegal for you to even be carrying that can of fuel.'

'Well, if we get caught, I'll tell them it was all your idea.' Luke reached up and slammed the boot shut.

'Never fear the man carrying a can filled with fuel,' Masood said, his tone softened to a philosophical timbre. 'Fear the man carrying the empty can.'

'Why?'

'Because it means either he's broken down and is seriously pissed off trying to get fuel. Or you're too late, and the fire is already burning.'

They both broke into a half-crouched run down a side road lined with the fence to the property. It didn't take them long to find a position where a tree stood close enough on the other side to use as an aid to climbing over.

Luke looked up at the razor wire with a grimace. Masood winked back at him as he produced a folded heavy canvas sheet from the bag. He unfolded it twice and threw it over the top edge of the six-foot fence, its weight squashed the wire and slapped with a thud on the other side.

Masood dropped his voice to a conspiratorial whisper. 'I'll go first, up into the tree. You give me a shove.'

Luke stood behind him and gave just enough push to help him up. He was impressed at how nimble the man was for his age.

Forty. Or fifty.

Maybe.

Old.

Luke passed all their gear over and then pulled himself up, using the tree to help.

Once over the fence, they made their way through the wooded area until they could see the back of the house.

Masood leaned closer. 'I suppose we should have a plan.'

'Well, there's probably still other kids in there.'

'You handle the escaping, I'll do the burning.' Masood raised a pointed finger at Luke. 'Listen. Any point you see me running like hell from the place, catch up. When this place goes up, it will go quick.'

The sound of crunching leaves underfoot made them both freeze. It was followed by the distinctive metallic clink of a gun hammer being pulled back.

Turning as slow as they dared, Luke and Masood found themselves staring down the barrels of two guns.

.

Chapter 68

'If you knew, really knew who you were dealing with, you'd know when to back off.'

'And you should know me well enough that I won't.'

Carter's breathing deepened as they held the stand-off. 'I'm just a pawn. Kapllani is no more than a bishop.'

'Chess analogies?'

'He is part of a network that stretches far outside Birmingham, even the UK.'

Stone nodded. 'And you're in this network?'

She laughed without humour. 'I'm not a part of them.'

'But not a part of stopping them.'

She glared at him. 'All I do is make sure some things don't happen. Don't get said. Don't get noticed.'

'Even the murder of a fifteen-year-old girl?'

Carter rushed at Stone, her face tightened with anger. 'Fuck you, Mike. I tried everything I could to save her.'

'Bullshit.' He pushed back, barely in control. His neck tightened, chest puffed up. He roared at her in a way she'd never heard him. 'You stood by as she was abused. Let this network throw her off that bridge like a ragdoll.'

She pounded at his chest. 'That's not true. Damn you, it's not true.'

Stone grabbed her wrists. 'It took one boy to save her.'

'I couldn't stop Kapllani from bringing her here.'

'Do you know where he is now?'

'I couldn't do anything,' she began to sob. 'I was in too deep.'

'Listen to yourself. Do you really think you are the victim?'

She grappled with Stone but was no match for the grip he had on her wrists.

'You're a coward.'

Carter pushed him away and they separated by a few feet. 'My whole career has been spent protecting as many as I could. But I did what I could to save as many as possible.' The conviction in her voice trailed off.

He stared at her, clenching his fists. 'How many?'

She looked at him.

'Come on. If you care so much, tell me. How many victims can you name?'

Carter stood wearily and closed her eyes.

'Or have you forgotten more of those you left for the wolves than those you managed to save? Because you know what, Sue. I remember every victim.' Stone's mind flashed back across his cases. 'The ones we got justice for. The ones we failed. I failed. Because I still have a debt to pay them.'

He paused for a moment, noticing his breath in the cold air.

'What about your conscience? Is Amelja Halil one of your victims? Or are you happy leaving a great detective like Sandra Bolton carrying that one for you?'

Stone turned and began walking away from Carter, who stood leaning against the side of her car.

'I remember the first,' Carter shouted to him when he'd reached ten yards.

Stone stopped. His heart pounded in his chest. He knew the name she was about to say. He knew when she had first crossed that line. A dark fact he had discovered over a year ago whilst investigating a serial killer that nearly tore his world apart. A killer that had come from his past like a dark ghost, bringing darker ghosts with it.

'Malcolm Glenn.'

Stone turned, fists clenched, mind throbbing.

'You know how it started, don't you?' Carter didn't hide her bitterness.

Mike Stone grew up knowing only hatred for his father. For what he was told his father was.

'You never did know the truth about why he died.'

Don't you dare, you evil bitch.

'Sometimes voices must be silenced, especially when they are going to say too much. You understand that, Mike.'

'His reputation was murdered first.'

Arnold Stone had long been suspected of sexually abusing young boys. One of his alleged victims was Malcolm Glenn. Those lies forced Mike Stone to grow up convinced his father was a paedophile. The same lies dragged Malcolm Glenn through a life of real abuse at the hands of the same network.

Arnold Stone was the scapegoat.

And Sue Carter was the original arresting officer who knowingly let the lies take seed. Evidence was conjured up to the extent that the finger pointed at Arnold Stone, but not quite enough for a conviction. Just enough to take the heat off a growing network of abusers that spread as high and wide as could be imagined.

Arnold Stone was reduced to a sordid piece of misdirection.

'He took one for the network, Mike. Just think about it. And the only reason you aren't buried next to him is because of me.'

'Just one of the pawns, right?'

She rolled her eyes.

'So, who is Chambers? One of your pawns?'

Carter Shrugged. 'He was a damn good cop.'

'Undercover?'

'Deep cover. He was a ghost. Ex-Army. He became my

eyes and ears.'

'What did you have on him?'

'We all have secrets we'd rather people never discover.'

Stone took a slow step towards her. A voice mumbled over his shoulder.

But which side is he on now?

'You know the problem with ghosts, Sue?'

'They like saying boo.'

Stone smiled and shook his head. 'They never go away until they've seen to their unfinished business.'

'You know this will never be finished, don't you?'

Stone moved closer to Carter as he reached into his pocket for his phone.

Carter laughed. 'How the hell are you going to call this in? You're a good cop, but you're shit with politics.'

'Chief Superintendent, I have no idea what I can say, or who I should say it to. You were a part of creating a psychopath that nearly murdered my son.'

'Again with the melodrama.'

'Now, I am here with you, a body in your boot which you were, at the very least, part of a conspiracy to murder. At the very least, you'd deserve to see time for perverting the course of justice.'

'Sometimes, survival is all we have to hope for.'

Stone held up his phone to show Carter the voice recorder, which he stopped.

Carter's face dropped as Stone turned away, breaking into a jog back to his car.

He found the number he was looking for as he got back inside. Carter had not moved. Frozen in time. She would have to wait until later. His boiling rage was best spent somewhere else.

Chapter 69

The sight of the guns had Luke and Masood frozen to the spot.

'You made that too easy,' Steve Chambers said, looking each one in the eyes. He waited a moment before lowering the guns and crouching down to their level. 'If you intend to achieve anything here you need to be a bit more than rank amateur arsonists.'

Masood looked at Luke before glaring at Chambers. 'What the hell is going on?'

'You have no idea who I am, Masood, but I know exactly who you are.'

Luke nodded slowly, frowning as he pieced together shreds of ideas. 'But who are you? I thought you worked for them.'

'As far as they are concerned, I do.'

Masood nodded at the guns. 'You're raising the stakes.'

Chambers nodded at the petrol cans. 'Pot, kettle, black.' He looked at Luke. 'I should tell you there's no way I will let you back in there. But,' he sighed, 'I know well enough there is not much point telling you to walk away.'

Masood looked around impatiently. 'I still don't understand why you are here. You got some plan?'

'Stop you getting yourselves killed. And make sure the damage you do here is permanent. All you need to know is I've been deep undercover so long, so deep, there's no going back.'

Masood narrowed his eyes and jerked his chin at Chambers. 'Why should we trust you?

Chambers looked at the Glock in his hand, then back at Masood. 'In truth, you probably shouldn't.'

Luke shrugged his shoulders.

'So, let's just try not to get killed, okay?' Chambers looked over to the house. 'You two wait here. He took out a phone and threw it to Masood. 'Burner phone. It's on silent but will vibrate. I'll call you when,' he paused to find the word. 'Well, just wait.'

'Wait for you?' Masood verged on incredulous.

Luke looked at both of them.

'Yes, you wait. Look, Masood, these guys aren't running a fucking book club. Ask the kid.' He let a wry smile slip. He took a metal lighter from his pocket and threw it to Masood. 'Take this.'

Chambers started to move to the edge of the undergrowth and turned back. 'Oh, and Masood?'

'Yeh?'

'Don't get the kid killed.'

'What about me?'

'Not my problem.'

* * *

DS Bolton watched Khan and Reg Walters pull up close to the house. She waved them down, sent the marked car to get out of sight, and then got in the back of their car.

'What took you two so bloody long?'

'I thought we made good time,' Khan replied.

'Where's the guv?' she continued.

Khan waved his phone at her. 'On his way. He's put a call in for the ARU back-up.'

'All gun's blazing,' Reg added, a note of trepidation

lingering in his voice.

'He also says be on the lookout for Kapllani's car, but we have to hold back until the ARU and he gets here.'

Reg slumped back in the seat. 'Did anyone find Luke?'

Bolton looked away from him and tried to sound as nonchalant as she could. 'He left the city centre.'

'What? When?' Reg didn't hold back the snap in his tone until he got a steely glare from Bolton. 'Where the bloody hell is he?'

'I don't know. We think he got into a taxi.'

'Masood.' Reg slapped his head with his palm.

Khan tried to placate him. 'We have to wait for the guv.'

The atmosphere changed when they saw Kapllani's car pull up to the front gate of the property and pause as the driver waited for them to open.

'We can't just sit here, for Christ's sake. Harry? Sands? You know full well Luke is on his way here. And now Kapllani is back, do you not think if they see Luke, they won't just finish the job this time?'

* * *

Chambers kept himself low and close to the wall. He'd spent hours learning the blind spots of the CCTV the house had. Crouched low, he came to the French windows leading into the rear reception room. He tried the handle and felt a slight movement. Before opening it, he moved round to get a good view of the room. As he entered, he went straight to the fireplace, which was deep enough to give cover.

One of the regular guards was pacing in and out of the room, bored with his task, not paying all the attention he should have. Chambers waited for his back to be turned.

All the guard felt was a hand clasp his mouth and the blade slice his throat. His legs gave way within seconds, and Chambers dragged the dead weight out of sight.

Taking a moment to check his reflection for too many signs of blood, Chambers waited before glancing out the door into the hallway.

Another guard hovered near the front door, peering out the window. Chambers could hear the main living room was busy with drunken, jovial sickening plans for the evening.

He'd spent over a year on the case, and in the last six months, the undercover had got deeper and deeper. He knew the routines and all the movements.

The main staircase was to his right, central in the hall opposite the double front door. Moving with his eyes fixed on the man in front of him, just ten or so feet away, Chambers knew he was going to need to act fast. As soon as they were clear of the living room, Chambers tightened the grip on his knife again.

His elbow was up, ready to strike down through the neck with one blow to prevent the man from calling out. Just as he was about to strike, he saw movement coming from the living room.

A voice called out to him.

'Ah, Chambers,' an over-weight, red-faced man scoffed from the room.

The guard turned as Chambers slipped the knife out of sight behind his back. 'What the fuck are you doing there?' the guard snapped at Chambers, confusion and suspicion scrawled across his pock-marked face.

* * *

'What the hell is taking him so long?' Luke was getting jittery with waiting. The stillness had taken the edge off the adrenaline and the Fury.

Masood raised a hand but kept his eyes on the building. 'If we move too soon, we could blow the whole thing.'

Luke's patience wasn't allayed. He fidgeted, moving from knee to knee, poised ready to sprint. Every time he looked at the building, he felt the bile bubble, boiling at his memories of what had happened inside those walls.

He thought of Amelja. Her smile and beautiful eyes. The innocence he had broken. The guilt overwhelmed him.

He still couldn't understand the idea of a baby. Amelja would have known what to do. She had told him about her life in Albania. Everything her grandmother had taught her. She would have taught him everything.

Luke shook the thought away as his jaw tightened. The Fury was burning up inside him again.

'Screw this,' he said, standing.

Masood gripped his wrist to pull him back, but Luke snapped it away. He broke from the cover of the trees and headed towards the house. Masood kept him in sight as long as he could, wondering whether it was time to call the police. But he expected they would probably already on their way.

Luke got to the side of the house and crouched close against the wall. He moved round to the back, hunting the window he'd looked out from. He found the same area of flat roof and checked around for CCTV.

There was an old iron drainpipe running down the corner of the wall which he knew he could use to get a good foothold.

He picked up some stones from the dirt at the bottom of the wall in case he needed something to break windows. They'd also make good weapons, so he grabbed a couple with decidedly sharp edges.

Pounding filled his ears and chest, and Amelja's face filled his mind.

Before the red mist clouded her out and the Fury was back in control.

Chapter 70

DI Stone stepped out into the misty rain and ran over to the car in front. He was already unnerved by the lacklustre preparation for what could be a dangerous raid.

'You look like shit.' Bolton welcomed him.

'Thanks, Sands.' Stone looked at his team. 'Harry, do we have ARU and DCI Palmers on the way?'

'Yes. ETA, less than five minutes.'

'Is Kapllani here?'

Bolton confirmed the recent arrival.

Stone picked up a radio and put a call into the ARU team leader to make his way down to their car as soon as they arrived.

'Right, guys,' Stone began. 'Top brass have given authority to use lethal force under usual rules. Absolutely only as a last resort. This is based on immediate danger to life. The priority is the safety of potentially multiple innocents in that building.' He took a moment to carefully choose his words. 'There might be people in that house who are not innocent and have no good, legal reason to be there. I want them arrested, not dead.'

DC Khan nodded. 'Cuff them, duff them, try not to snuff them. Gotcha.'

Bolton looked at Stone with an expression that usually meant she had something dangerous to suggest. 'Guv, my firearms training is up-to-date.'

'We've got the ARU here, Sands.'

'And there's a chance they have a small arsenal in the house.' She could see him wavering. 'Look, I won't go in holding, but I might as well go in armed.'

'Okay, fine.' Stone didn't hide his reluctance, and he spotted a slight trepidation in Khan's eyes. 'You know full well that this,' he jabbed Khan's head with his forefinger, 'is a far more powerful weapon for me.'

'Come on, Harry,' Bolton smirked, 'I get to have a gun because I don't have a penis. Makes us proper equal, like.'

Stone tried to glare at her.

Fuck sake, don't make me laugh, Sands.

'Damn feminists,' Reg snorted from the back.

It was a moment of levity. They all needed it, just to breathe. Covering up the moral compass for a second eased the tension.

And the fear.

* * *

He had a split second to decide what to do.

'How d'you get in here?' the guard boomed, turning to face Chambers.

They'd never got on. Chambers always worried the guy doubted his loyalty. Waving the fat man away, he took the guard aside, giving him a conspiratorial gesture to be quiet, as if he was going to share something top-secret.

'Is the boss back yet?' Chambers asked in his best low, secretive tone.

'Nuh, why?' The guard's frown crumpled even more.

'Fuck me, I think we have a major fuckin problem, man.' Chambers hated hearing himself talk like a thirteen-year-old boy who'd watched too many Tarantino films and not read enough Tolkien. 'How well do you know his driver?'

'Mickey?'

Chambers snorted. 'Well, yeh, if that's his real name.'

The big man shrugged his shoulders. 'Only in work, like. Bit of a dick, really.'

'Well, I think that dick is here to fuck us all over.'

'Like what?'

'Don't know. But he stinks. Overheard him on the phone a couple of times, not to the Boss. Sounding like he was telling people the whens and wheres of our movements. What we're doing, and all that.'

'A cop?'

'Nah, he's too thick as shit. You woulda sniffed him out if he was a spook, I'm sure of it. But a mole, maybe. Informant? I am sure of it.'

The big man ran a hand over his bald head. 'Fuck me. You told the boss?'

Chambers knew he had the man hooked. Too easily.

'Not yet. Look, keep it quiet for now, right?' Chambers made a great effort to look around. 'I don't know who to trust. That's why I came in a back way.'

'Right, sure.'

'I need to get the boss on his own and warn him. But I need you to make sure no one else gets in the way, got it?'

'Sure.'

'And don't fucking let on to Mickey that we know.'

The big man stood a bit taller, appearing a little self-important to have been trusted with a secret mission.

Chambers couldn't quite believe how easy that had been. 'Now, go tell that fat fucker to go sit down. But do it nice, right.'

It seemed pathetic. The guy was such a stereotype of idiocy. Chambers' gut told him the man was probably unlikely to get through the rest of the evening.

He slipped the knife away, knowing he had to move fast. The Police on the way, and that lunatic kid on the loose with a deranged, rogue taxi driver, all sent shivers down his spine. Far too many cooks.

* * *

Luke clambered onto the flat roof, dragging himself up from the final foothold on the old black pipe. He kept himself flat against the roof as he looked up to the window to the room he'd stood at before.

There was a CCTV camera pointing right across it, but Luke knew there was nothing he could do about it other than to move fast and hope no one was watching too carefully. He also hoped the guy with the guns could cause enough of a distraction on the inside. If Chambers had already been caught, they were all screwed anyway.

He moved over to the window, careful to make as little noise as possible. Luke took a screwdriver he'd hidden in his pocket and jammed it into the gap in the bottom of the frame. With a fine wiggle and several stabs, he felt the tool slip under the old sash frame. He levered at the window until he felt it lift.

It was only then Luke realised the horrific risk. He had no idea who was in the room. He had to hope the room had been empty but cursed himself for not even thinking about it sooner.

He waited. Listened.

'Now or never,' he whispered to himself. There was no good reason to, but it felt reassuring. Perhaps it was the hero thing. Like Bruce Willis making a joke as he crawled through the air vents.

Luke wondered why the window hadn't been locked with some kind of bracket in the centre. And then he worked out why. Dumb, blind luck. No other reason.

The room was dark, and the only light cast a terrifying shadow on the wall and door opposite the window. He'd had to break in and out of many buildings by windows and he knew the worst thing to do was to dither on entry or exit. Sliding the rest of his body through, he dropped his foot down to feel the floor beneath.

There was a sound from somewhere in the darkness. Breathing. Shallow and fast. The bed was unmade, so Luke knew what that meant and knelt down.

'I'm not here to hurt you.' Luke knew the routine. The breathing suddenly stopped. 'It's okay. My name is Luke.'

No response.

'I know you're afraid, but I've come to get you out.'

He heard the movement of sliding across the carpet.

'Look, here's my hand,' Luke said, being sure to let his hand catch just enough light to be seen. 'I've been in this room before. A friend got me out. Now, it is my turn to get you out.'

A small hand appeared from under the bed, its fingers cautiously touching Luke's. He took the hand. 'Yeh, that's it. Stay quiet, though.'

The frame of a terrified boy appeared from beneath the bed and Luke guided him to sit on the edge. He looked around, listening for any other movement. There wasn't any shouting or reaction outside.

And that was when Luke's eyes met with the other boy's stare. A moment of recognition. The boy also sensed it. The realisation hit and the boy recoiled across the bed, terror ripping at his face. It was clear the boy had already wet himself by the stain on his pyjamas, but this terror was new.

Luke's eyes adjusted, and after having to search his mind he realised who the boy was.

The boy shook his head as silent sobs began trembling his body. He raised his hands to defend himself. 'Sorry, sorry, sorry.'

'No, no it's okay,' Luke tried to placate the boy if only to keep the room quiet.

But the boy snivelled the same words over and over.

'Listen to me,' Luke said, catching the boy's wrists,

leaning in to whisper. 'Listen. I recognise you, too. Okay. I know who you are.'

The boy looked up at him through tear-soaked eyes.

Luke smiled. The Fury calmed for a moment. He didn't even realise it. 'They made you do it. I know. But, look. I'm okay. Really, I'm okay.'

The boy struggled to get words from his shaking lips. 'You aren't a ghost?'

Luke couldn't help a small laugh slipping out. 'No, I'm not a ghost.'

'Not dead?'

'Come here.' He drew the boy into an embrace, knowing that is what he needed, even if he didn't realise himself. 'Now, what about you help me? Yeh?'

The boy nodded.

'We're gonna get you out of here.'

The boy looked worried.

'I'm not on my own. I have loads of friends helping me. Got a whole bloody army. Wanna join?'

The boy nodded enthusiastically.

The sound of a key in the lock cracked through the silence, and the small boy cowered back to the head of the bed.

An angry figure appeared in the doorway, barely lit by the murky half-light. He was a skeleton of a man in a suit, with a strange, sunken face.

'Who the fuck are you?' he growled, taking a step towards Luke.

And the Fury returned.

Luke barrelled into the man, pushing him back into the door frame. He used the advantage, kept his body low, and pummelled punches into the man's kidneys.

Two spiny hands gripped Luke's shoulders and shoved him back far enough for the man to land a punch on the side of Luke's head.

Luke managed to land another punch to the man's

chest but missed the vital sweet spot to wind him. The man shoved Luke back a step or two, sending him falling over the corner of the bed and onto the floor, landing painfully on the jagged contents of his pocket.

Luke reached just fast enough to grab one of the stones as he rolled over. He aimed at the man's face and whipped the stone like a baseball. It glanced off the man's forehead, the shock staggering him back, allowing Luke enough time to get back to his feet.

The skeleton-man rounded another attack and parried more punches as he took strides towards Luke, gripping him by the throat as they crashed back against the window.

Luke stomped on the man's feet and kicked at his shins, but he was losing strength as he tried to loosen the bony hands. They were too strong. Nothing seemed to stop the manic skeleton. The harder Luke fought, the weaker he got.

Blackness crept in from the sides of his vision. His hearing was thickening, and his fingers were going numb. He was feeling heavy and falling into a deep sleep.

The deepest.

His last.

A final thought crossed his mind.

Was this what Amelja felt?

* * *

Masood reached the back of the house with the bag and cans of fuel, his heart pounding through his chest. He was too old for that kind of exercise.

'What are you doing, Masood? Let the professionals do it. But how long will that take? You're a taxi driver, not an action hero. I am a human being, now shut up. What will your wife say? Shut up.'

He'd watched Chambers for as far as he could see and tried to retrace his steps. Night was drawing in and Luke was nowhere to be seen. The house was in relative quiet, besides occasional faint laughter coming from somewhere inside.

Masood came to a door that had been left slightly ajar and made an educated guess that was the best entry point.

He had to be careful not to clang the bag and cans on the frame and give himself away. He heard the voices get louder as he made his way inside.

That's when he noticed the heap of a man slumped in the corner of the room, motionless and already starting to look pale.

He hoped that was Chambers' work.

Setting the bags and cans down next to a large fireplace, Masood kept himself out of sight of the open door. He unzipped the bag and took out a crowbar. His ears were on high alert. How far had Chambers got? Where the hell was the boy?

He looked at the cans of fuel and began unscrewing one of the caps, recoiling at the vapour which stung his eyes. Crouched down on his knees, he wondered if pouring the fuel around would send the smell out into the hall.

'In for a penny…' he said, shrugging his shoulders.

Masood shuffled over to the body in the corner and started soaking it in petrol, repeatedly checking no one was approaching. He ran a trail of the fuel to the door he'd come in, making a larger puddle in a crude attempt to give himself some kind of flashpoint to light from a distance.

He headed back over to the bag and took out one of the glass bottles. He'd wrapped them in old rags to stop them clinking or breaking as he moved the bag around. It wasn't until he tried to pour fuel into the bottle that he noticed how much his hands were shaking.

Tearing off a piece of the material and pressing it into the bottle as a stopper, he finished off the first Molotov. He held it in his hand, staring at it, the weight of what he was about to do dropped on his shoulders.

He closed his eyes and thought of Amelja.

And he thought of his daughter.

It had been too long coming, his chance to finally avenge her. He had as much reason to burn this house to the ground as Luke felt he had.

Masood had to admit that he'd always lacked the courage to do anything after so-called justice had failed, and then covered it all up.

But now he found himself spurred on by the love of a boy for a girl. How innocent that love should have been. How much guilt there was within the walls of that house.

He put the bottle down and reached into the bag for another.

'If you're going to do this, Masood, do it right.'

Chapter 71

'You have got to be kidding me,' Stone shouted down the radio. 'Aren't you supposed to be covering the back?'

The radio crackled before the reply. 'For people coming out. Not for those going in, Guv.'

Everyone in the car shared a look of dread when the call had come in that a young person had been seen climbing up onto a rear roof and breaking into the house via a back window.

Bolton was the first to break the awkward silence. 'What do we do now?'

Stone scratched at his stubble-hidden scar. 'Right, we need to move. Surround the house, in position, and wait for a call to move.'

'DCI Palmers…'

'Get him on the phone, Sands. We need permission to go, and we need it now. We all need vests from the ARU.'

Stone got out of the car to meet the approaching armed officer rushing down the path, weapon held across his chest.

Harry watched Reg clenching his fists. He was staring across the road at the trees that hid the house from view.

'You alright, mate?' Khan said, knowing it was a futile question.

'We can't just sit here,' Reg snapped back.

'Rushing in uncoordinated would make it all worse.'

'Maybe someone should have told Luke that.'

Bolton was barking down her phone. 'We don't have five minutes. Get your ass here.' She held up her phone, looking for somewhere to slam it down without breaking it. The satisfaction of slamming a landline phone down was less effective if all it did was break the screen on your smartphone.

Again.

Stone came back to the car and handed out the vests as they rehearsed the plan for entrance. Khan started to explain a possible hotwiring approach to the front gate, but that was dismissed in favour of using the tank.

'What the hell is the tank?' Harry asked, unable to hide his excitement.

'Not what,' the team leader replied, 'it's a who.' He pointed to one of his team who saluted back to them.

The man was a giant. If he wasn't seven-foot-tall, he must have been close, and he was as wide as a small car. The automatic gun he was carrying looked more like a water pistol in his hands. He could probably have done more damage throwing it than firing it.

'Holy shit,' Khan gasped. 'He's hardly subtle.'

Stone interrupted. 'We need to be ready as soon as the DCI gets here. How long, Sands?'

She was about to pass the bad news onto Stone when Reg opened the door and got out of the car.

'Reg, what the hell?' Stone called after him.

Khan knew exactly what he was doing. 'Oh, shit.'

'Where's he going, Harry?' DC Khan's look answered the question with a slight wince telling them some of the shit hitting one of the fans would be landing on him.

Stone's faced reddened. 'Well, get your ass after him.'

'He's gonna get me killed,' Khan said, climbing out of the car, and taking a spare vest with him for Reg.

Stone turned to Bolton as she was fastening the gun holster to her utility belt. He gave her an imploring look and she nodded before following after Khan.

'Right, that's it,' Stone declared. 'No more waiting. We're going in.'

* * *

Reg scaled the fence in one go. His height and momentum, not to mention the grim determination, got him over.

He saw Khan and Bolton begin their pursuit and knew he should wait. But every second counted. As far as he was concerned, police officers were held back by procedures that he didn't have to follow. He might work with the police, but that didn't change the fact he was a civilian.

Reg could just about make out the border of the trees and shrubs. Keeping low and weaving through, he moved closer to the house. A car was parking, so he waited for the driver to get out and face the other way before running past a thinner area of the trees.

Making use of the shadows, he crouched down to make it without being seen. Reaching the wall, he paused to soften his nerves with a few deep breaths. He'd usually make a silent prayer. But for the first time, he didn't feel he could. He briefly cast a look up to the sky, but it struck him suddenly what an absurd gesture it was.

DC Khan and Bolton were out of sight, so he listened to the faint murmur emanating from the house. Too quiet for anything major to have kicked off. There was still time to stop Luke from doing anything stupid. Stop his Fury from getting him into more trouble.

Part of him admired the boy's courage.

The other part of him knew too well that true courage required a wilful act of self-sacrifice.

Chapter 72

The sound of a car door closing outside the front of the property was the signal Chambers needed. He gave the guard a nod before turning to scale the stairs, knowing there were two more he had to deal with.

On his right, leaned up against the wall fiddling with his cuff links in self-admiration, was a stocky man who liked his bling almost as much as Splint had.

The recognition between them came first, followed by confusion. 'Kapllani's back. Sent me up.' Chambers kept calm and began to walk over to the man.

Chamber's glanced to left to just catch the strange skeletal man entering a room in a hurry. Noise from the room drew their attention, and they headed down the landing. By the time they were just ten feet away the noise was far more clear.

A struggle.

Chambers knew it had to be Luke or Masood. Either way, the man in front of him was already drawing his gun and flipping off the safety, covering the distance in just a few paces. Chambers reached for the knife again and headed after him.

Mr T held his gun angled down, not wanting to let off a random shot. As far as he was concerned, his colleague was probably in a tussle with one of the merchandise.

It wasn't until he kicked the door open that the man's

eyes widened. He lifted his gun to take aim.

Chambers took just two steps to accelerate, drawing his knife up in his right hand and driving it down into the front of Mr T's neck, making sure to get through the gold chainmail.

The response was instant. He dropped the gun and shot his hands up to his throat as Chambers withdrew the blade. Blood sprayed the walls and gushed out between the gold chains and the man's fingers, drowning his shirt in crimson as he staggered back.

Chambers raised his left leg to kick the man further down the corridor and turned to his right to look inside the room.

Bones had his back to him, up against the window with his hands wrapped around Luke's neck. Chambers barged in and grabbed Bones by the back of the collar and pulled him away from Luke. He swung the man round and threw him into the wall to his right as Luke dropped to the floor.

Shaking off the shock, Bones clambered back and tried to swing a left hook at Chambers. But he found his arm tightly gripped and his body whiplash into the wall next to the door.

Chambers was between Luke and Skeletal man. He turned to look at the boy who was holding his throat, coughing and retching for breath.

A good sign he was still alive.

But the skeletal man gathered himself and reached for his coat to draw his gun. Chambers threw himself at the man, crashing his head into the bridge of his nose. Blood exploded between their faces as the gun crashed into the side of Chambers' head.

Burning pain wrapped Chambers' skull and his eyes felt as though they were about the explode. He staggered against the wall on his left shoulder, fighting the feeling to drop to the ground.

The skeletal man raised the gun and pointed it in Luke's

direction. But Chambers rugby tackled the skeletal man and they stumbled into the bed. Chambers dropped his whole weight onto the bony creature.

Bones jabbed his elbows into Chambers' ribs and rolled them both over. He dug his fingers into Chambers' face, planting all of his meagre body weight into one hand as he lifted the gun again.

Luke turned his head to see the gun appear in his sightline. His eyes locked on the black hole of the barrel.

* * *

Nesim Kapllani stepped out of the car onto the gravel driveway and pulled his collar up against the rain. His driver waited for him to step out of the way of the door before pushing it shut with a satisfying, expensive thud.

The two men caught each other's eye and shared a moment of confirmation that what had happened so far that evening never happened.

'I think it might be prudent to deliver a reminder of just how sincere I am,' Kapllani said.

The other man smiled with one side of his mouth.

'I want you to pay her family a visit,' Kapllani said. 'Her mother is still in the care home, is she not?' Kapllani nodded his answer to the question. 'It's been a while since her nephew paid a visit, don't you think?'

The driver nodded.

'Perhaps you could take some nice flowers. Chrysanthemums would be fitting.'

They smiled. He knew the meaning of the flowers, especially in Eastern European countries. He was also quite sure the clever cop would understand the reference, too.

'Make sure you take a nice photo, won't you?'

It was at that moment the unmistakable sound of a gunshot cracked the cold night air.

Kapllani reached into his coat and drew out his weapon in unison with his driver. They both crouched down and waited for another shot or any other sounds to help them locate exactly where in the building the shot had come from.

'You wait here,' Kapllani hissed to his driver. 'Something tells me we are about to get company. That crazy bitch has obviously made a call to someone.'

The driver nodded and took his place up against the car as Kapllani rushed up to the front door, peering in a side window to check it was clear to enter.

He couldn't help but wonder what kind of set-up Carter had going for anything to happen so quickly after their meeting. But he wasn't stupid enough to think it was merely a coincidence.

The problem was, he had clients waiting, and merchandise prepared. It was a bad time for anything to go wrong.

Chapter 73

Reg hid under the window at the side of the house. His heart was racing, and it was taking all his willpower not to chastise himself for racing off ahead.

He turned and raised his head just enough to see inside. It was a large kitchen with cupboards spanning the length of two long walls. An island stood in the middle of the space, topped with expensive jet-black marble and a large, flush electric hob. A chandelier of utensils hung from the high ceiling. The gleaming copper saucepans looked more for show than for use.

A door out onto the path was about six feet further down the wall towards the back of the house and he moved towards it, careful to keep his head low.

He pondered what his next move would be. Even if the door was unlocked, he couldn't just open it up and wander inside. It didn't matter how much determination he had, Reg knew he would be no match for the kinds of people in the house.

Raising his head again to see if there was anyone in sight, he caught a view of a man in a suit standing in the central hallway at least twenty feet away.

Before he could make any more decisions, Reg heard the dull crack of a gunshot from inside the building. Instinct kicked in and he shuddered at the sound, but his sudden movement caught the eye of the man inside.

Their eyes met and Reg froze. Time slowed and seconds passed as the two men were caught in a stand-off. Confusion and shock rippled the ugly man's face. The man had also heard the gunshot and cast a glance to somewhere upwards and out of Reg's view.

Reg was locked to the spot. The bulldog of a man dug into his jacket and pulled out a gun, turning to head his way, through the kitchen.

Fear took hold and Reg bolted down the side of the house towards the back. He glanced in the next window to see the man with a gun was making chase.

Reg launched himself around the corner just as he heard the kitchen door swing open.

He had no idea where he was heading, but sprinted down the next path, staying close to the house. He could have made his way out into the garden but there was no cover to hide behind for at least thirty feet or more.

A man appeared in front of him further down the path and Reg's heart leapt into his throat.

Masood looked as confused and terrified as Reg felt. He was standing outside an open rear door looking up at the back of the house, trying to make out where the gunshot had come from.

Reg saw the glass bottle Masood was holding and knew exactly what it was. His self-preservation called out.

'Masood, move.'

Masood dived back inside the building and Reg saw beyond him a mass expanse of open path and garden. His only possible cover would be to follow Masood inside.

As he swung himself into the room, Reg's foot vanished from beneath him. He crashed to the floor and took a lung full of fumes. His mind was firing on all cylinders. He knew he'd seen a Molotov cocktail.

Reg rolled over and struggled to his feet.

'What the fuck are you doing here?' Masood shouted.

Reg didn't have time to reply as they both saw the

bulldog catching up outside, opening the door, gun in hand.

The acrid smell of petrol hit the bulldog as quickly as it had caught Reg's attention, and he raised his gun instinctively confused about the whole situation.

'What the fuck is going on?' the gunman screamed.

Reg looked at Masood.

Masood looked at the bulldog.

The bulldog looked at the Molotov in Masood's hand, and then the petrol cans.

A moment of indecision held in the fume-filled air, none of the men knowing what move to make next.

Masood moved first, flicking open a metal lighter and holding it up.

'No one move. I swear to God I will blow this place to shit if you move.'

The bulldog looked back at him and pointed the gun at his head. He noticed the body lying in the corner and looked down at the puddles all around his feet.

'You gonna light it up mate? Or maybe I put a fucking bullet through your skull. You faster than a bullet?'

Masood looked at Reg with pleading eyes.

'Wait,' Reg barked at the Bulldog, 'do you really want to risk setting this lot off?' He could see a realisation in the bulldog's eyes. 'He's brought enough to blow up half the fucking city.'

Noises were coming from all over the house, filling the awkward silence as the man pointed the gun at Masood.

* * *

The ARU vehicle was sitting back by only a few feet as the Tank approach the centre of the front gates. DI Stone was in his car sitting right behind. Uniformed officers and marked cars had arrived and were being sent to positions around the perimeter of the house.

DCI Palmers was still a couple of minutes away.

The muted sound of a gunshot rattled through the air, and shouts of 'shots fired' came down the radio airwaves.

Stone made the snap decision. Knowing his neck was on the line, but also that he now had the 'imminent or immediate threat to life' authority he'd probably need to read up on before the inevitable inquiry.

Please don't go to shit.

'Go, go, go,' Stone shouted down the radio.

The call triggered the Tank to crash into the centre lock of the gate with a massive red battering ram that only he had the strength to swing like Thor's hammer.

Something metallic snapped and clinked on the ground and the magnetic lock seemed to fail. Tank ran to the side of the ARU van and hauled himself up onto a side-step just before it rolled forward to push the gates open.

Stone accelerated with them as soon as they'd cleared the gates. He could see in his mirror that at least two marked cars followed him in.

The ARU van swerved to the right on the driveway and skidded to a halt next to the black limo. Stone saw the front door of the house swinging open as two firearms officers stood over the driver outside the front of the house.

Stone got out of his car and joined behind two ARU officers heading up to the front door. One of them was Tank, and Stone felt a wave of relief at that.

They burst in through the front doorway just in time to see all hell breaking loose from every direction.

The door opened into a wide hallway. To the left, a group of well-dressed men burst out of a large room, chased out by the sound of breaking glass and cries of 'armed police.' Kapllani was already halfway up a central staircase.

A suited man was just inside the kitchen to the right.

His gun was raised, and he was siting a target.

Bolton and Khan reached the edge of the trees when the gunshot rang out. They saw Reg Walters sprint off to their right, heading around to the back of the house, hotly pursued by a bulldog of a man with a gun.

'Harry, get after them, now,' Bolton barked.

Khan didn't need to be told twice as he broke cover and made chase after the gunman pursuing Reg Walters.

Bolton made her way over to what she could see was the kitchen and stepped inside the door. As soon as she got inside, she heard the chaos erupting in the house.

Taking out her gun, clicking the safety off, she moved carefully towards the island in the centre of the kitchen. She could just see through to the hallway and heard the front door open.

At the same time, voices came from the room opposite.

That's when she saw Kapllani in the hallway.

'Armed police,' she shouted. Kapllani turned to her and his eyes lit up with anger. She could see he had a gun, but his focus moved away from her.

The movement sent an instant shiver down her spine. There was a defiance in him as if he knew she wouldn't fire the weapon.

'Take her,' Kapllani called to someone else in the hall before jolting out of sight, leaving Bolton in full view of another one of his staff moving in her direction.

The noise of men and crashing glass came from behind him as he raised his gun to point it directly at Bolton.

Bolton heard the words 'armed police' but couldn't tell where they had come from. She was locked in on the barrel pointing directly at her as time stood still.

Chapter 74

Chambers kicked his leg up into the skeletal man's arm, knocking the aim high as he pulled the trigger. The bullet crashed through the window a matter of inches above Luke's head.

Luke snapped out of his semi-consciousness and the Fury took back control. He launched forward and buried his right fist into the man's face. Bone and cartilage crunched as the man fell backwards, stumbling onto the floor. Luke went with him and landed two more blows.

The gun fell to the floor as Chambers clambered to his feet. He pushed Luke aside and dragged the battered man up. He wrapped his right arm around the man's throat, gripped his head with his left hand, and with one sudden jolt, whipped the man's head round to an unnatural angle.

Chambers dropped the dead weight to the floor.

Luke looked down at the body and then up at Chambers, and back down to the body. He'd seen the manoeuvre in films for years, but it was so much more horrific performed right in front of him.

Chambers held out a hand to Luke, a wry smile across his face. 'Bloody hell kid,' he said, pulling the boy up to his feet. 'I sure as hell don't wanna piss you off.' He turned to see the other boy cowered into the corner of the bed.

Noise from downstairs echoed up to the room. Chambers glanced out onto the landing and turned back to Luke.

'Let's get the others, send them in here, and you take them out that window.' He didn't wait for a reply as he turned to leave the room. No time for an Oscar-Winning deep and meaningful moment.

Chambers crossed the landing to the room opposite and drove his heel into the door just below the lock, splintering the frame and swinging the door open. Luke rushed into the room as Chambers moved to the next door down the landing.

Luke reappeared, dragging a terrified girl behind him. She was barely dressed, and at least a year or two younger than Luke. He all but threw her into the other room before following Chambers to get the next prisoner.

They were about to kick the third door open when a sound of crashing glass came from below, together with the call of armed police.

Amongst the noise, he just caught sight of someone coming up the stairs. He reached for his holster as another gunshot rattled up from the hallway.

By the time he'd drawn his gun, he was looking into the eyes of Nesim Kapllani standing at the top of the stairs.

* * *

Khan saw the stand-off between the bulldog and Masood before either of them had noticed his approach. Reg Walters was also in the room, hands up, trying to placate the men as if he was mediating a meeting that had gone terribly wrong.

When the sound of a second gunshot cracked, it hit him from two directions. From inside the room down the hallway, and from behind him, around the corner where Bolton had gone into the building.

Taking advantage of the distraction the shot had provided, Khan held up the spare Kevlar vest he was carrying and burst into the room. He tackled the bulldog with all the gusto he could deliver, and both men crashed to the floor.

The gun slid across the floorboards and Khan delivered a sharp jab to the man's jaw before grabbing his head and smacking it hard into the floorboards.

Masood had been squeezing the lighter so tight his fingers were going numb. But his bluff had worked.

'Bloody hell, Harry,' Reg shouted, dropping down to help detain the man on the floor.

'Alright, Reg?' Khan said, with a breathless, but slightly jovial tone. There was something about him that appeared to be excited by the adrenaline. He held up the Kevlar vest. 'You forgot this.'

'I'm glad to see you,' Reg said, taking the vest and fumbling his way into it. He turned to Masood. 'And you can put that fucking lighter away.'

Khan cuffed the man on the floor before looking over at the two men. 'Where's Luke?'

Masood felt their eyes on him. 'He went ahead. I couldn't stop him.'

Reg marched over and took the Molotov from his hand. 'And you can put this fucking thing down.'

'What do we do now?' Masood asked, half reaching for the bottle taken off him.

Khan held the semi-conscious man up. 'We need to put him somewhere.'

Reg walked back over to Khan, grabbed the man by the hair and drove his fist full force into the man's face, knocking him out cold.

Khan looked up. 'Reg, what the hell? You can't.'

'No, Harry. You can't. Arrest me for it later.' He stood and looked at Masood. 'Which way did Luke go?'

Masood told him the route Luke had taken and Reg left without a word. Khan sent Masood out after him before turning to look out into the hallway.

* * *

Stone burst in through the front door just in time to see one of the suited men drop to the floor like a brick. Kapllani was already most of the way up the staircase, gun in hand.

Bolton appeared from the kitchen on the right, gun in both hands and still training on the man on the floor. She was joined by two armed officers coming in from the front door, weapons pointing at the injured man.

Stone kept his focus on the man he wanted. He used the momentum and bounded up the stairs after Kapllani. The stairs split halfway up, heading in opposite directions, and Kapllani was almost at the top of the left side. There was no way he could let him out of his sight.

You're unarmed, Mike, stop now.

The voice over his shoulder was struggling to grab his attention, much like the ARU officer in pursuit from further down the stairs.

Stone saw Kapllani pause at the top before raising his gun.

'What the fuck are you doing?' Kapllani shouted at Chambers.

'It's over, Kapllani.' Chambers was drawing his gun when the shot came. It hit him high on the left of his chest, dropping him to the floor. The boy he'd just released from the room screamed and ran instinctively away from the falling man.

Chambers lost grip of the gun as he hit the floor, and it bounced over to lie at Luke's feet.

Luke reached down to pick up the gun.

Kapllani grabbed the boy making for an escape, wrapping his arm around his neck, and squeezing him tight to his body.

DI Stone was halfway up the second set of the stairs, his heart sinking at the worst possible outcome. The whole raid was about to go terrifyingly wrong. He knew where Bolton was but couldn't see down the landing. It was only when he got to the top of the stairs that the worst became clear.

Twenty feet away, Luke stood pointing a gun at Kapllani, and his eyes had the same dark look Stone had seen in the interview room.

The look of Fury.

Chapter 75

Reg Walters heard the struggling from the first floor and guessed from the trodden plants by the drainpipe that Luke must have made his way up to the flat roof from there.

As a relatively tall and agile man, it hadn't taken him much to scale the wall and roll onto the flat top roof. He saw the half-open window and ran straight over.

He almost fell into the room when he heard another gunshot coming from the landing.

Taking a moment to register the terrified child on the bed, and another hiding just inside the door, he saw a gun on the floor. Reg reached down and grabbed the gun as he flew towards the commotion. He'd fired guns before, mostly shotguns pointing at clay disks.

He reached the door and recoiled as he saw a vaguely familiar face crash to the floor. Stepping out onto the landing he saw Luke reaching down to pick up a gun just as a boy was gripped by Kapllani.

DI Stone was most of the way up the stairs, covered by an armed officer.

Reg held up the gun and pointed it directly at Kapllani.

'I got this, Luke,' he said.

The Fury didn't hear him.

Kapllani barked out a single, wry laugh as he pointed the gun at the head of the boy squeezed in his arm.

'You just won't go away, will you?' Kapllani said to Luke. 'Keep coming back for more. Like that whore you raped.'

Luke's hand began to shake, the gun feeling heavier in one hand than he'd expected it to feel. He gripped it with his second hand.

'Don't be stupid, boy. That's not a water pistol, you know.' Kapllani took a slow step towards him, pushing the boy in his arms with his stride.

Stone followed up a step. 'Kapllani, it's over. The whole place is surrounded with armed police.'

'You know what they say?' Kapllani shouted over his shoulder, keeping his eyes fixed on Luke. 'Never back your enemy into a corner unless you are prepared to face his final choice.' Kapllani focused on Luke again. 'You've never fired a real gun in your life. You wouldn't know how.'

Luke swung the barrel at the wall and pulled the trigger. The explosion deafened him, thc kick shocked him. But he kept hold of the weapon.

There was a moment of panic in the air until it was clear what he had done.

'Now I have,' Luke said to Kapllani.

Kapllani's steel expression faltered for a split second. Enough for Luke to see.

Reg spoke softly. 'Luke, please don't do this. Put the gun down.'

Stone was holding back the armed officer next to him, who was already training his red dot on Kapllani's head.

But the risk was too great. A sudden final jolt of life has been known to make the victim squeeze their hands and their trigger finger.

Kapllani shouted as if he wanted an audience. 'You might hit this boy, Luke. Then what? You'd have his death on your hands, too. Just like Amelja's.'

A moment of silence, real or imagined, filled the air as if the universe had paused for everyone to consider their options.

But then it broke.

Kapllani started speaking Albanian to the boy, whose face creased into sobs and his bladder gave way.

Then the Fury roared. 'Poshte.'

The boy's eyes widened for a split second.

As he slipped from Kapllani's grip and fell to the floor, the landing erupted into noise and muzzle flashes.

DI Stone hit the wall.

Reg flew forwards.

Kapllani pulled his trigger.

Luke's body dropped.

Chapter 76

Reg winced as the paramedic dabbed the wound on the top of his forehead with an antiseptic wipe. It wasn't a deep wound, but it was bleeding profusely. Unreasonably.

It was one of the reasons he trained as a pathologist rather than a trauma doctor. The whole human body was an absolute fascination of his.

When it was still.

Reg took the square swab from the paramedic and held it to his head. He could feel the throbbing and knew it would turn into a terrible headache later.

'Now I can say I've been shot in the head.'

Luke didn't reply. He was sitting next to Reg on the back step of the ambulance, looking down at the gravel drive.

Silent.

With the adrenaline gone and the Fury sleeping again, his face was heavy with sorrow.

Mike Stone walked over to them and leant against the vehicle next to Reg. Their eyes met and an unspoken conversation was shared.

How's the boy doing?

Not good.

Mike crouched down and placed a hand on Luke's shoulder.

'Alright?' He didn't expect a reply. 'What does 'poshte'

mean?'

It took a few moments for the question to register. Luke let out a deep sigh. 'Down. Like, get down.' He swallowed hard, and whispered, 'Amelja taught me.'

'You saved that boy's life, Luke.' He squeezed the boy's shoulder again as he stood and looked at Reg. 'And how are you, Mr Walters?'

'I suppose it would be proper British etiquette to say, I'm fine.' He glanced at the blood collecting on the swab. 'But in truth, my head really, really fucking hurts.'

One of the shots Kapllani had managed to fire caught him a glancing blow as he'd pushed Luke down, and fired a shot of his own. His shot hit Kapllani in the chest.

'It was a bloody stupid thing to do, Reg. You could have been killed.'

'And would you have missed me?'

'No. I would have been pissed that you couldn't do the PM.' Mike Smiled.

They gave each other a silent, appreciative nod.

Stone looked over to another ambulance which had two paramedics and a doctor rotating between CPR and a defibrillator on the guard that DS Bolton shot. A single bullet, centre mass. A perfect shot. By the book.

A nightmare for the inquiry.

The entire house was a mass of officers, detectives, and Scenes of Crime Smurfs, as Stone called them, bobbing around in their blue and white full bodysuits.

DC Khan came out the front door of the house and walked over to Stone.

'Palmers is looking for you, Guv.' Khan seemed impressively energetic, probably still running high on adrenaline. Or petrol fumes.

'Let him look, Harry.' Stone placed a hand on Kahn's shoulder and took him down the side of the Ambulance. 'Harry, I need you to do something for me.'

Khan welcomed a task to focus on. He knew he needed

to burn off excess energy.

'I want you to oversee the SOCOs.'

'Take charge?'

'Check every SOCO has their body camera on, and log their ID and their camera number. Make sure they are all switched on. Then, tomorrow, make sure none have gone missing, and work with Pete Barry back at the station to collate and log all the evidence.'

'Sure thing, boss.' The question was written all over his face.

'Because I know I can trust you.' Stone tapped his nose.

Khan gave a nod. 'One hundred per cent.' He paused before walking off to begin his order. 'Guv, how do I get the DCI to agree to this?'

'That's easy. Make him think it is his idea. Then tell him what a great idea it is.'

'Fair enough.' Khan smiled as he walked away with energy and purpose, and a slight spring in his step.

He's going to make a great sergeant.

Stone walked back round the ambulance to find Reg on his own. 'Where's Luke?'

Reg glanced up and winced again. 'He said he wanted to check Masood was okay, so I told him to make it quick.'

Stone shot him a disapproving look.

'He's okay for now, Mike. And I guess Molotov Masood's probably a nice guy, really,' Reg mocked.

'Molotov Masood?'

'Oh, nothing.'

Mike walked away from his pathologist friend to another of the ambulances gathered on the drive. Steve Chambers was lying on the gurney and Stone stepped up to sit in the seat opposite.

Chambers' Kevlar vest had stopped the bullet penetrating, but he'd taken a sledgehammer blow, and a broken collar bone was the likely outcome. He'd managed to reach for his second gun and put two of the shots into

Kapllani's chest just before the armed officer had added two more.

'I'll be honest,' Stone said, wiping the rain from his brow and then scratching at his stubble, 'I have no idea what to make of you.'

Chambers laughed, the small dose of morphine he'd been given was already softening his demeanour.

'I've met undercover officers before, but you are something else.'

'It's been a long one.'

'How long on this case?'

Chambers frowned and curled his lips slightly. 'Eighteen, nineteen months.'

'And before?'

'Civil servant. Before that, I was Army Special Forces.'

Stone nodded his realisation before his face dropped. More serious, slightly morose. 'You know what's going to happen, right?' Stone saw sadness in the man's eyes.

Chambers let out a long sigh as his gaze drifted out to nowhere. 'I only wish I could have been in two places on that night. Or that I'd killed that bastard sooner.'

Stone leaned forward on his knees and lowered his voice. 'I appreciate everything you did for Luke. But this evening is going to cause a massive inquiry and there are some details I can't hide.'

Chambers raised a hand and waved it off.

'I will put in a good word where it's due.'

'I can look after myself.'

'Maybe. But you have a lot of information I am going to need very soon. Help me and I'll help you.' He let the thought linger.

Stone got down from the ambulance and back onto the gravel drive. He scanned the surroundings. The chaos of vehicles and people.

It was the voice over his shoulder that made Stone pause and look around again. Something was missing. Walking back over to Reg sitting in the ambulance, Stone could feel his chest tighten.

'Where's Luke?'

'I told you, he said he wanted to check on Masood.'

'But where is Masood?'

The two men looked at each other as Bolton came out the front door and saw the look on their faces.

'That's not a good look, Guv.'

Stone didn't reply but turned and walked over to the officer by the marked car with open rear doors.

'Officer.' Stone pointed to the empty rear seats.

The officer's eyes popped out of his head almost comically before he whipped his head around. He swallowed hard.

'Um, where's he gone, sir?'

'That's my bloody question.'

Reg Walters appeared behind DI Stone. 'Oh, shit. Shit, shit, and bloody hell.'

'Where is he, Reg?'

'Give me your car keys, Mike.'

'Why? What did he say?'

'He didn't say anything. But I know where he's gone.'

Stone looked at him with his arms raised.

'Keys.'

Stone glared at him.

'Mike, just give me your fucking keys. This is on me.'

Stone held his keys out for Bolton. 'She drives.'

Reg stared at DI Stone, his defiance boiling.

A shout from the house for DS Bolton made her turn away just long enough for Reg to snatch the keys and run over to Stone's car. He was just fast enough to step on the gas and spit gravel up from the tyres as he pulled the door shut before Stone could get close enough to stop him.

Reg knew where Luke was going. He just hoped he wasn't too late.

Chapter 77

'Inspector Stone said it was okay,' Luke said.

The young officer had fallen for it.

And then it didn't take much to persuade Masood to help him one more time.

They waited for the hustle and bustle to allow them to slip away unnoticed through the bushes lining the driveway near the front of the house. The section of the surrounding fence was barely twenty feet from the drive and wasn't wrapped in razor wire. A quick lift over got them on the path only a short distance to Masood's cab.

A few moments later they were heading back towards the city centre. Masood swung the car off Bristol Road into a side street.

'Is this the right way?' Panic stirred into Luke's voice. He didn't know that part of the city.

Masood smiled. 'Trust me. I'm a taxi driver.'

Luke was reassured as they gained speed, weaving through the streets with expertise. Masood squeezed the steering wheel after each turn, willing the car to accelerate faster. The roads were wet, and he was keeping an eye out for traffic police.

Luke searched for a landmark to get his bearings.

'Not far now,' Masood said over his shoulder. 'Onto this main road, then it's just a minute or so straight down.'

Masood hit the brakes hard, looked to his right, and

then pulled out onto Tollhouse Way.

Luke felt his heart pound harder when Masood began cursing in another language at the traffic which roadworks had squeezed into a single lane.

The Fury was stirring, and Luke closed his eyes to picture her. Everything still seemed unreal. Love so young had been lost before it had the chance to grow into a life.

And a child. Months spent watching it grow, working so hard to keep them safe. He knew they were young. But some kids joined gangs. Some carried knives, or even guns. Some became killers.

All he'd wanted was to have his family and hold his baby. He closed his eyes and remembered the lullaby Amelja had taught him in Albanian and English. They had sung it together to soothe the restless babe as it waited to meet them. And join them.

To rule their world.

Grandma tells us of the time
there was once,
before us, a boy
who like myself had friends.
And listening,
I saw with my eyes,
a brave struggle
for the fate of freedom.

Chapter 78

Luke opened his eyes again, his vision blurred from the tears that had rolled down his cheeks. The rain was rattling the roof and windows as the cab crawled in the traffic.

Too slow.

He caught Masood's eyes in the mirror and noticed the same look in his eyes the first day they met.

The pain.

'It is not far now,' Masood's broken voice sighed.

Luke said nothing. Just held his eyes in the mirror.

'You see the roundabout up there? It's just past that.'

The car rolled to a stop again, and the automatic door lock clicked. Luke made the snap decision and opened the door on the right. He got out into the rain as Masood wound down his window.

'Luke, what are you doing? Get back in.'

'It's taking too long.'

'It's not safe.'

'I have to go. Thanks for everything.'

Luke stepped up onto the central reservation and began walking faster than the traffic was rolling. The rain was picking up and the wind was turning the air to ice.

His heart pounded as he felt the Fury coming back.

And he started to run.

Pushing harder and harder, squinting to keep his vision through the rain, Luke's feet slapped at the film of water on the ground. The freezing air crushed his chest as his clothes soaked through.

But he kept running, faster and faster.

He could just make out the roundabout through the wall of rain a hundred yards ahead.

The Fury was fighting back against his choking body.

Cars jostled for space on the roundabout, but Luke felt the momentum carry him forward as he darted into the road, narrowly missing cars coming from his right, and ran over the traffic island.

He barely slowed before crossing the other side. Blind luck alone saved him from being crushed by a large van, which braked and slid violently into the curb. Angry gestures and words faded into the background.

Running up Oldbury Road, Luke closed his eyes for a moment.

Her beautiful face filled his mind. Her soft, self-conscious smile, her long hair glistening.

But pain rolled itself into a cannonball and started to work its way up from his stomach. He tried to breathe it away, but all it did was contort his face and shudder him into a sobbing wreck as he reached the crossing by the bridge.

Luke came to a stop, drenched by the rain, unable to breathe from exertion and freezing air. He ran a hand down his face, wiping away more than just the rain. He doubled over as his stomach heaved bile onto the soaked ground. His throat, mouth and nose burned from the acid.

The Fury stood him up, turning to look down the darkened bridge. He could just make out the few battered bunches of flowers drowning at the foot of the lamppost.

He only needed one more burst of energy.

Luke sprinted onto the bridge, driven by love and anger, memories and loss, power and pain.

He collapsed to his knees at the foot of the lamppost and wept.

* * *

Reg had no idea what speed he was travelling, and he didn't care. He'd swerved through traffic and cut a route through the city to finally get onto Tollhouse Way.

He had no plan. Just a hunch. Something churned in his stomach, a feeling that he had to hurry.

That's when he saw the traffic ahead. His heart skipped a beat. There was no way he could get around as the dual carriageway was reduced to the single right lane.

Nowhere to turn off and find another route.

A thought crossed his mind. Ridiculous. Dangerous. Probably get him locked up.

'Fuck it,' he said to himself as he snapped the steering wheel to the right, bouncing DI Stone's car up onto the central reservation. He was lucky it wasn't littered with lampposts for most of the way, as he stepped on the gas and built up speed.

Cars on the other side of the road were swerving as they saw the maniac coming head-on towards them.

It didn't take him long to reach the roundabout, blaring his horn in warning, gritting his teeth at what he was about to do.

Without stopping, he swung the car to the right, around a lamppost, and back left, throwing the rear end out into the skidding traffic. The tyres fought for grip as he forced it round and onto Oldbury Road.

He knew Galton bridge was barely a few hundred yards away, and he had to get there before it was too late.

Reg screeched the car to a halt just past the crossing. He looked out the driver side window down across Galton Bridge and could just make out a figure kneeling by the lamppost.

It had to be Luke.

He clambered out of the car and sprinted across the first half of the road, barely missing the traffic to his right. Swerving around the railings of the crossing, he launched himself out into the next two lanes, eyes fixed on the shadowy figure.

The screech of tyres sliding gave him a split-second warning to jump up in defence as he glanced at the bright light approaching. His body clattered into the bonnet and cracked against the car windscreen before sliding off and hurling down onto the road.

Reg tried to lift his head, but the ringing in his ears screamed and his world vanished into spinning darkness.

* * *

Luke looked down at the flowers and small gifts left for Amelja. Tealights had long since burnt out and filled with rain. Some had floated away.

A picture of Amelja that someone had cut from a newspaper and covered in sticky tape flapped in the wind. He picked it up and stroked her face, then held her to his cheek, trying to feel her warmth again. His other hand reached up to touch both halves of their necklaces.

The screech and cracking sound in the distance barely registered as he dragged himself to his feet with a roar. He kicked at the flowers and tributes from strangers.

He punched the lamppost and pummelled his fists on top of the railing. Gripping it with both hands, he pushed and tugged as if trying to wrench it from the side of the bridge.

Luke wailed her name into the night sky and pouring rain so loud he could feel his breaking voice tear through his throat.

Blood poured from his fists, but they were too numb to feel anything. He gasped for a breath and then grabbed at the post and wedged one foot into the side of the railings.

He pulled himself up with his final act of strength, drawing his other foot on top of the railings.

* * *

Reg's eyes blurred around the messy shape of a figure. His mouth and nose were clammy with a metallic taste of blood. He rubbed his eyes, trying to make sense of images flashing in his mind.

Until one fixed.

He jolted up, rolling onto his side, spitting blood out into the river of rainwater on the pavement.

'Luke,' he gasped.

'You gotta stay still, bab,' a voice squeaked back.

But Reg ignored the voice and pushed himself up, swerving like a drunk until his right arm clattered into a bollard. He grabbed at it as the adrenaline kicked in again.

Reg's memory snapped back into place. He pulled himself up as he felt the blood down the side of his head.

His shoulder burnt, his chest tightened, and he almost fell back to the ground. He could feel hands holding him up, but voices telling him to sit down.

Sirens wailed in the distance and noise surrounded him.

A woman screamed.

'Oh my god. Look. On the bridge.'

Reg looked up to see Luke clamber his second foot up onto the railing, a hand gripping the lamppost.

He tried to shout, but his chest fought back. His throat was filled with gravel and blood. He staggered a couple of steps, before falling back to one knee.

* * *

Luke drew his second foot up onto the railing and gripped the lamppost. He swayed in the wind as his heart pounded.

461

The Fury had faded. There was no fear left to feel.

He looked out into the distance and the world faded into the dark, spotted with tiny lights dying out in the distance.

Closing his eyes, searching for her image, he kissed the necklaces in his hand.

All the pain dissolved. His breath held. He smelt only her hair, her cheek, and felt her soft warm skin.

Releasing his grip on the lamppost, he rocked onto the balls of his feet.

* * *

Adrenaline kicked in. Reg pushed his burning thighs as hard as he could. He was twenty feet away when he saw Luke release his grip from the lamppost.

He closed his eyes and was driven by pure fear and anger, finally truly understanding the Fury.

The boy appeared to float upwards for a second, taking a final breath before flight.

Reg caught the lamppost with his left hand and swung himself round with all his strength, grabbing Luke around the waist.

The boy buckled with the force that tore him from the air and launched him backwards, crashing back onto the bridge.

Reg collapsed next to him.

Luke sat up and looked over at the mess of a man before him. Blood covered his face, and his eyes were barely open. He crawled over and lifted Reg by the shoulders, resting his head in his lap as they sat against the railing.

His eyes were bloodshot and dark and Luke pulled him up, holding him closer. He felt Reg's arms reach up, a hand clasping the back of his neck.

Reg whispered. 'Twenty-Three. Thirty-Four.'

Chapter 79

The massive screen exploded with garish colours and the walls screamed with jabbering nonsense voices and bizarre sound effects. But Mike Stone didn't care. He had a giant tub of popcorn balanced on his lap, which Jack was emptying at an alarming rate.

He's like a vacuum cleaner for junk food.

Mike was beginning an extended period of leave from work after the debriefing from the Bristol Road incident over two weeks before.

Various inquiries had been launched and would take substantial time to complete. But as it stood, none of his team were going to be facing disciplinary or legal backlashes.

Steve Chambers was recovering from his injuries and faced an uncertain future. Questions needed answers, including those surrounding the hospitalisation of Martin 'Gnome' Sketchford.

Mike Stone had his own theories about that.

Masood's part in the events leading up to the incident had been documented in detail by DI Stone, who had put him forward for a formal commendation for bravery. It had been recorded how he discovered members of the Organised Crime Group appeared to be trying to destroy evidence by burning down the property, endangering lives in doing so. Two witnesses had corroborated that account.

The biggest shockwave was the part Chief Superintendent Carter played in actions connected to the OCG, led locally by the late Nesim Kapllani. She'd been suspended from all duties and promptly arrested for a range of criminal charges.

Further arrests were planned of a wide variety of public and private business people connected with the same OCG.

Mike had already been told to expect an invitation to promote to Detective Chief Inspector, filling the space left by Palmers climbing the ladder himself. Nothing had been finalised, but Stone demanded to choose his core team. He needed a new DI, and an extra DS, and knew just the right people. He also had an eye on a certain uniform constable that he wanted to train for CID.

But time had to pass, and dust had to settle.

In the meantime, Luke was classed as a witness in ensuing cases against a variety of dangerous, influential people. His solicitors and barrister also ensured that there were no legal grounds to keep his child away from him. The long-term plan was still uncertain, but Luke and his daughter, Lucy Amelja, were residing with experienced foster carers under police protection.

After showing good signs of recovery, Reg Walters was seeking to formalise his part in supporting Luke and Lucy.

Mike looked down at Jack and his thoughts turned to how he was entering completely new territory. It was at that age when his father had been transformed into a monster and ceased to be a part of his life. Mike had no reference point for the years to come with his son.

It scared and excited him in equal measure.

Before long, Jack would turn into one of those hormonal teenager things. That was even more scary. But Mike thought, as examples went, Luke had proven to be a bloody good one.

He also thought about the bigger questions of truth

and justice, and how to make sure Jack's moral compass was strong. But realistic.

Jack's hand dived into the popcorn again and he looked up to his dad with a wide smile, pinching a piece between his finger and thumb. Mike opened his mouth and felt the popcorn bounce off his nose. Jack's mischievous giggle could have melted him on the spot. Mike winked at him and slid further down in his chair, pulling his son a little closer as his mind momentarily slipped back to Amelja.

'This is the funniest film ever, isn't it?'

He placed his hand on Jack's cheek, gently leant down to kiss the boy on the forehead.

'Definitely,' he whispered, matching Jack's smile.

Please, let it finish soon.

Mike Stone knew he would gladly hear a thousand innocent lies to end a single terrible guilty truth.

Epilogue

She hadn't been back to the bridge since that fateful night. When Sandra Bolton finally plucked up the courage, Reg Walters offered to go with her as he had some unfinished business, too.

They'd met at the Gunmaker's Arms for a couple of drinks before making the short walk over to Snow Hill station. It was a short hop on the train to Smethwick Galton Bridge.

When they arrived at the edge of the bridge, Sandra reached down and took Reg's hand. He was a little taken aback a first until he realised that he needed it as much as she did.

They walked to the centre of the bridge and stood next to the lamppost without saying a word. Reg put an arm around Sandra's shoulders and felt the gentle shudder as a couple of tears filled her eyes, and a lump filled his throat.

Circular ripples glistened in the black water as the moon cast its chilling light across the canal. The effect seemed to echo the ephemeral nature of life. In any other place, with any other context, it would have been beautiful.

But tragedy tainted its elegance.

Reg reached up to feel the metal dog tag hanging from a simple leather necklace. Sandra turned to look at it and holding it in her fingers, read the lettering crudely hammered out. On the front, "RW" marked his initials.

The reverse had "LA" once in large, and again in smaller letters.

Their eyes met and she gave Reg a small nod, understanding the importance of it.

She let it drop back around his neck and placed the palm of her hand on his chest but drew back when she noticed him wince.

Reg dropped his arm from her shoulders and took her hand again, squeezing it harder than before, just for a moment. Sandra looked at him and saw the pain in his eyes. When tears ran down his cheeks, and his jaw tightened, she almost spoke. But she could find no words.

Reg reached up to his neck again and felt the crucifix hanging on its gold chain. He gripped the chain, and with one sharp tug, snapped it away from his neck. He looked at it in his hand before squeezing it tight in his fist.

His head dropped and he had to lean on the railing to steady himself. Sandra saw his shoulders shake from gentle, silent sobs, and placed her hand lightly on his back.

They stood in silence for a moment.

Reg raised his head again, showing eyes darkened with anger Sandra had never seen in him before. He swung his arm back and with all the strength of his being, threw the crucifix out into the night sky. It glimmered in the moonlight as it flew until hitting the water and vanishing into the blackness.

He turned to meet Sandra's wide eyes and gave a single, sharp nod of resolution, before turning and walking away.

Sandra kissed her fingers.

'A message from Luke.'

Touched the lamppost.

'He said he forgives you.'

She let her hand linger for a moment to say a final goodbye.

Acknowledgements

It's taken four long years to finally get this book finished. And what a journey it has been. It would be impossible to remember everyone who has helped in that time. Nevertheless, thanks to each and every one of you for the support, badgering, and enthusiasm to read the second instalment of the Detective Mike Stone trilogy.

I would like to mention the most recent important people pushing me over the finish line. Nick Howl and A.A. Abbott both gave essential critical feedback of earlier drafts and helped to steer the book towards its best version. They asked the right questions at the right time.

Diane McCarty provided the essential editing and proofreading that every novel needs, no matter who is writing it.

Other Books by the Author

Novels
To Die For

Short Stories
Stench of Death

Poetry
Ripples
Silhouette in the Sunset

Plays
No Smoke

Printed in Great Britain
by Amazon